A COSY COUNTRYSIDE CHRISTMAS

ELIZA J SCOTT

Storm
PUBLISHING

Ebook ISBN: 978-1-83700-353-2
Paperback ISBN: 978-1-83700-354-9

Cover design: Rose Cooper
Cover images: Shutterstock

Published by Storm Publishing.
For further information, visit:
www.stormpublishing.co

ALSO BY ELIZA J SCOTT

Welcome to Micklewick Bay Series

The Little Bookshop by the Sea

Summer Days at Clifftop Cottage

Finding Love in Micklewick Bay

Christmas at the Little Bookshop by the Sea

Cupcakes and Kisses in Micklewick Bay

Life on the Moors Series

The Letter – Kitty's Story

The Talisman – Molly's Story

The Secret – Violet's Story

A Christmas Kiss

A Christmas Wedding at the Castle

Sunny Skies and Summer Kisses

A Cosy Christmas with the Village Vet

Heartshaped Series

Tell That to My Heart

To my family, for their unwavering love and support.

ONE

Ella

Snow had been falling steadily all afternoon. The severe weather warnings issued to the north of England earlier that week had proved right, and a band of Arctic conditions had landed with an angry roar just as dawn was breaking. Charging over the North Yorkshire Moors, the wind had snarled savagely, bringing with it dark, brooding clouds laden with icy hailstones that pummelled everything in their path.

Winter was baring its teeth, its bite every bit as bad as its bark. Heaven forbid that anyone was fool enough to challenge it.

But to the quaint vernacular longhouses of Lytell Stangdale that had withstood five or six centuries of Mother Nature's histrionics, it was just another test of their endurance. They'd do what they did every time she challenged them: with their three-feet-deep walls, they'd hunker down under their heavily thatched roofs and ride it out with the very same stoicism ingrained in their inhabitants. It was as if they were saying, "Here we go again, she's off on one! Hold tight!"

Wind was whistling through the cracks in the window frames, making them rattle in their Victorian casements at the small village primary school where Ella Welford worked as a teaching assistant. She flicked her dark ponytail over her shoulder and rubbed a circle in the condensation, the glass chilly against her fingertips. She peered out to see huge, feather-like snowflakes tumbling from the sky in mesmerising swirls. 'Oh!' She placed her hand on her chest, taking in the scene reminiscent of a recently-shaken snowglobe. She hadn't been expecting such a dramatic change since she'd last checked on the weather an hour-and-a-half earlier. Here, from the school's vantage point, perched on the brow of Bramble Hill, she could see that the broad expanse of Great Stangdale had been transformed into a sea of white, the rooftops of the cottages down in the village already covered in a thick blanket of snow. "Christmas-card-pretty" is how her mum would describe it.

Further along, Ella's chocolate-brown eyes alighted on her dad, Pete's, tractor. It was pulling out of Thistle Field where a huddle of sheep were crowding around a bale of newly-delivered hay, bleating woefully. She watched as the vehicle began making its way steadily along the Danskelfe road back to Tinkel Bottom Farm, leaving a broad trail of tyre tracks in its wake, the hum of its engine muted by the snow.

Poor old Bill. Ella's thoughts segued to Bill Campion – the owner of the flock and the field, and her dad's oldest friend. The widower had taken a bad turn a couple of days earlier and was under observation in hospital, with no idea of what was wrong with him, or when he would be discharged. Thanks to a serious falling out with his eldest son, Rich, it meant there was no one to run the farm in his absence, so her dad had jumped in to help, along with her older brother, Greg. It was what folk did around here, but it was far from ideal, especially this close to Christmas. But Bill really didn't help himself sometimes.

A small sigh escaped Ella's lips as her mind slipped back to events of eighteen years earlier when she was just sixteen and the devastating consequences they'd had on the Campion family. It was hard to believe the after-effects had lasted this long. *As if they hadn't already suffered enough.* She closed her eyes, her stomach squeezing at the memory. It hadn't needed to end that way... If Bill and his youngest son, Joss, hadn't been so hot-headed...

'Is it looking any better out there?' asked Mrs Prudom.

'Uhh!' Ella started, and her memories went scurrying back to the dark corners from whence they'd sneaked. She turned to see the headteacher smiling at her, her cheeks flushed from the stuffiness of the Key Stage 1 classroom, her Christmas jumper hugging the curves of her generous bosom. Jean Prudom also doubled-up as the infant teacher, which was a necessity in rural schools where student numbers were small and budgets tight. Ella understood the subtext of her colleague's question: *Any sign of Santa Claus making his way up the drive?* 'Umm... well, erm... it's looking very... festive.' Ella chose her words carefully; she didn't want the children to pick up on her doubts about Santa – whose arrival was imminent – being able to reach them in the snow; there was no point in dampening their spirits unnecessarily. The said Father Christmas was local aristocrat, Lord Danskelfe – who was also known locally as Lord Hammondely. And judging by the amount of snow that had been dumped over the last few hours, he'd have his work cut out tackling the roads from the family seat at Danskelfe Castle; they were notoriously dangerous, especially the exposed stretch high on Great Stangdale Rigg.

'When you say *festive*...' With a hint of concern in her eyes, Mrs Prudom made her way over to the window, her smile fading.

It was the last day of term. Eight days before Christmas Day. Everyone, including the staff, were wearing colourful Christmas jumpers and the classroom was buzzing with excitement. The shrill voices of the sixteen young pupils – aged from Reception to Year 2 – were bouncing off the walls, their peals of laughter reaching right up to the vaulted ceiling of the old building. The week had been jam-packed with festive activities, ranging from a trip to the pantomime, the school's Nativity play (Ella's favourite event of the year – apart from the Year 3 recorder recital at the end, which had been ear-splittingly awful – not that she would ever tell them that!), to a whole host of Christmas-craft-making – after which Ella had ended up so covered in glitter, she'd left a sparkly trail of the stuff wherever she went.

The celebrations had culminated in a Christmas party which had finished a quarter-of-an-hour earlier. The children's excitement had reached such dizzying heights, anyone would be forgiven for thinking they'd been force-fed concentrated e-numbers. In a bid to calm them down, the Infants and Juniors had been separated and sent back to their respective classrooms in readiness for the much-anticipated visit from Santa Claus.

Ella glanced out of the window once more, fiddling with the silver infinity pendant of the necklace she always wore, a flutter of anxiety in her chest. She could kick herself for not having a "Plan B". Why hadn't she thought of organising an understudy Santa? She'd known the weather was set to turn; it was all folk in the village had been talking about, well, that and the subject of Bill Campion and how he was going to manage the farm when he came out of hospital. The children would be gutted if Santa didn't get here; she didn't even want to think about the level of guilt that would trigger. *Uhh, jeez. My brains must've been in my backside this week!* She drew in a deep breath, thinking how best to answer Mrs Prudom without alerting the children. 'Erm... well, it looks like... a winter wonderland.' She wrinkled her nose, hoping to convey with her eyes that there was no sign of "Father Christmas" and at the rate the snow was falling, there was a risk there wasn't likely to be.

'Yay! A winter wonderland!' Little Alistair Balmer beamed and punched the air. His band of cheeky-faced friends followed suit, cheering happily, oblivious to their teacher's concerns.

'Yeah, but how's Santa supposed to get here in the snow? My dad says he can only use his sleigh on Christmas Eve. What if his car gets stuck in a snow drift like my Uncle Kev's did last year?' Six-year-old Christopher Tiptree was close to tears as his classmates looked on, their smiles gradually slipping as they processed the prospect of a no-show from Santa.

'Santa doesn't drive a *car*!' said five-year-old Seamus Smithson, his pale blue eyes glittering with outrage.

'He'll ride here on Rudolph!' said golden-haired Jenny Godwin, beaming angelically, and looking pleased with her idea. 'Just like my mummy rides her horse.'

Ella felt a giggle brewing as an image of septuagenarian Lord Danskelfe dressed up in his Father Christmas suit bloomed in her mind, his ruddy face hidden beneath a huge white beard, and a sack slung over his shoulder, battling the elements as he raced across the moors on a sturdy reindeer with a bright red nose. His snooty wife, Lady Davinia, wouldn't be too pleased about that! Before she could block it, a snort of laughter escaped and she clamped her hand across her mouth. 'Oh, excuse me!' she said, disguising it as a sneeze, and dashing the image of Lord Danskelfe away before it generated any more giggles.

'Bless you,' said Mrs Prudom, looking amused.

Ella's mind began scrambling for ideas just in case the worst did actually come to the worst; she couldn't have the children disappointed on the last day of term. That would be too awful. But where could she get her hands on a spare Santa suit? She drummed her fingers on her chin as she thought. *Gerald! That's who!* She was sure the local artist would have something in his stash of colourful clothes they could cobble together to make a Santa suit; she was happy to improvise if they were desperate; needs must, and all that. Though she had to admit, the octogenarian wouldn't be the most ideal Santa, his lilting Wearside Geordie accent and larger-than-life personality would be too much of a giveaway, not to mention his own long beard was dyed a festive shade of green to match his hair. The wily older kids would have him rumbled in no time.

'Santa can borrow my dad's motorbike.' Tommy Dukes cut through Ella's musings. 'It's *massive*! It's as big as a *dinosaur*!' He threw his hands wide to demonstrate. 'It'll crush the snow to pieces.'

Ella felt another giggle brewing at the prospect of Lord Danskelfe hunched over a motorbike.

'Well, my cousin's bike's a *mazillion* times bigger than that! Santa can borrow *his*,' said little Arnie Fishlock with a heart-melting lisp.

'Ughh! Boys are so silly!' Carla Bainbridge shook her head despairingly. She was seven going on forty-five. With her hair in a neat plait that snaked down her poker-straight back, she had the poise of a prima ballerina. Carla had a lot of sway with the younger students in the class, and she knew it. She folded her arms, adopting a patient expression. 'Arnie, there's no such number as a *mazillion* and Santa does *not* ride on Rudolph, he's *too* big. And he *especially* does *not* ride on motorbikes. Santa will get here using his magic. Simple as that.'

'He does too ride motorbikes; I've *seen* him! And there *is* a number called mazillion, my big cousin Patrick told me. He's eleven-and-three-quarters and he should know,' said Arnie, sticking out his tongue.

'Don't tell fibs, Arnie. And don't you know it's rude to stick out your tongue?' Carla pinned him with one of her authoritative stares and his bottom lip quivered.

'Well, my step-sister said she saw Santa in the queue for the toilets at a burger bar in York,' Lizzy Buckle said matter-of-factly. 'And he was holding a carrier bag full of cans of beer as well. Then she saw him smoking outside; he had one of those vape thingies. Said it smelt like a bonfire.'

Arnie turned to Lizzy, his mouth hanging open in disbelief, his tears forgotten.

'Goodness!' Mrs Prudom said quickly, doing her best to hide her shock at the revelation. 'I'm sure that can't have been the real San—'

'That's a big, fat, fib, Lizzy! My daddy says Santa's like the Queen and doesn't go to the toilet, and my mummy says my daddy knows everything, so there!' said Milly Templeton, pressing her lips together in an angry pout.

Ella and Mrs Prudom exchanged a knowing glance; Mr Templeton had established his reputation as a superior, irritating know-all at Milly's first parents' evening; it was reassuring to know Mrs Templeton shared their views.

Carla tutted and rolled her eyes. 'And Santa doesn't drink *mucky beer* either. Everyone knows he drinks milk. That's what we leave out for him every Christmas Eve. And a mince pie too.'

'Don't be daft, he doesn't drink milk! He drinks *whisky*,' said Tommy, wrinkling his nose. 'That's what my daddy says. We always have to pour a *ginormous* glass of it, full to the top for him. One as big as *that*.' He pointed towards a two litre jug. Ella and Miss Prudom's eyes widened. 'And we leave him a massive pork pie the same size as Arnie's head. It's Rudolph who drinks milk, *smarty-pants!*'

Arnie shot Tommy a look, his brow furrowed, unsure if the comparison with his head was a good thing.

Mrs Prudom leaned into Ella, and lowered her voice. 'I'll bet Mr Dukes doesn't see much of Christmas Day if Tommy's right about the two litres of whisky.'

Ella pressed her lips together and forced down a snort. 'Or Boxing Day for that matter.' The family secrets were coming out now. It was amazing what insights into the home life of their students such conversations could generate. Smiling, she gazed around at the eager faces; the children were adorable and the very reason she loved her job here. They, and the close bond she had with the staff, were why she'd worked at the school for so long. But recently, she'd found herself feeling restless.

'Miss Welford.' Ella felt someone tugging at the sleeve of her Christmas jumper, and she turned to see little Emmie Pennock looking up at her with big brown eyes.

'Yes, Emmie.' Ella smiled and got down on her haunches to the little girl's level.

'Miss Welford, Santa will still be able to get here, won't he?' Emmie's chocolate-brown curls had escaped their festive hair bobble and sat in a mass around her face. With a chubby hand, she brushed them away. She was the image of her mum, Molly, who was a cousin of Ella's – she wasn't sure exactly how many times removed they were, but they were linked by blood on her dad's side, just as she was with many of the other residents of the village and the others surrounding it.

Before Ella could answer, Carla wrapped her arm around the younger girl. 'Of course he will, Em. Like I said, Santa's *magic*.'

Carla's words had just left her mouth when the scraping sound of the snow plough could be heard pushing its way up the hill towards school. Emmie's eyes grew wide. Her stepdad, Camm, had the contract to keep the local roads clear in winter, and she knew it would be him.

'It's the snow plough! Emmie's daddy's come to the rescue!' said six-year-old Davey Wilkinson.

'The plough!' Emmie's eyes twinkled as she smiled with shy pride for the man she now called Daddy.

A rousing cheer went up, adding to the fizzing atmosphere of the room. Ella pushed her fingers in her ears and caught Mrs Prudom's eye, the pair of them laughing. 'Phew!'

TWO

THE PREVIOUS EVENING

Joss

'Right then, that's us done for the night, Sid. Time to get a warm by the fire,' said Joss Campion as he fastened the door to the cow byre, his words suspended in cloud of mist. The air was crisp and the ground sparkled with a thick hoar frost as winter tightened its grip. He clicked his tongue for the black Labrador/Wolfhound cross, and strode across the farmyard, his loyal pal trotting beside him, bushy tail swishing happily. It was just gone nine o'clock as Joss finished his nightly rounds, checking on the livestock at Skeller Rigg Farm in the village of Helderthorpe, the place he'd called home since he was sixteen, the familiar scent of Holstein Friesians and hay mingling with woodsmoke. Up above, millions of twinkling stars were splashed across an inky-blue sky, a luminescent moon shining down, silently casting its ethereal glow over the surrounding fields. Being out in the sticks meant there was no light pollution to diminish such natural beauty. Joss cast his green-blue eyes around him and gave a contented sigh.

A screech from a nearby barn owl spliced through the stillness. Sid came to an abrupt halt, cocking his ear, one paw off the ground, his bushy whiskers twitching as he sniffed the air. Joss laughed and shook his head. 'Come on, fella, never mind the gun dog pose.' Sid wagged his tail in response.

Joss was halfway across the yard when his mobile started ringing. He paused, fumbling about for it in the pocket of his padded work jacket, frowning as he saw his older brother's name lighting up the screen. Their phone calls were sporadic at the best of times, and they'd only just spoken the previous week. An uneasy feeling swirled in his gut; something was amiss. Sid looked up at him and whined, sensing his dad's concern. 'Yeah, that's what I was thinking. Funny time to ring, isn't it, lad?' Joss took a fortifying breath and tapped the "answer" icon. 'Hey, Rich.'

'Joss!' The urgent tone in Rich's voice sent a spike of adrenalin shooting through him.

'Yeah, what's up?' A rash of goosebumps prickled over his skin.

'Look, mate, I'm sorry, but there's really no easy way to say this: it's Dad...'

'What d'you mean it's Dad? What's the matter with him?' Joss's pulse whooshed loudly in his ears.

There was a pause before Rich answered. 'He took poorly a few days ago. Debbie Welford found him slumped on the kitchen floor. By all accounts, he'd been there a good few hours. She went round 'cos he wasn't answering his phone, said she'd thought he'd looked a bit off when she'd seen him last week, and what with me not working at the farm anymore... well, she knew something was amiss. Turned out she was right. Anyway, I'm afraid he's in Middleton Hospital for the foreseeable future.'

Joss took a moment to process Rich's words, his body bombarded by myriad emotions coming at him from all angles, concern, irritation and confusion amongst them. 'Hospital?' he said, his frown deepening as he walked slowly across the farmyard, Sid close beside him.

'Yeah, not that he's too chuffed about it. As bad as he was, he didn't want her to ring for an ambulance, insisted there was nowt wrong with him. Debbie said she had a right old battle, ended up having to go out into the yard so he couldn't hear her make the call. You know what a stubborn old so-and-so he is.'

Joss knew exactly what a stubborn old so-and-so their father was; eighteen years of hostility and estrangement was proof enough of that. 'Aye, I do.' His chest was rising quickly, his breath catching at the back of his throat. 'So, do they know what's wrong with him?' He stopped, putting his finger in his ear to block out an impromptu bout of baying from the cows in the barn.

'He's saying nothing, and he won't let the medical team tell me anything at the moment. He doesn't look too grand at all, but they're doing tests, he's had loads of blood taken – complained like heck about it. He's been there a couple of days now. I didn't ring you straight away... didn't know what to do... you know, what with how things are between the two of you. I was in two minds about getting in touch at all, but Dawn said I should, said you'd want to know; Uncle Joe and Aunty Hannah too.'

A blast of icy air rushed around the farm buildings, kicking up bits of hay that had sneaked out of the feeders in the barn, and making the loose gate to the top field rattle. Joss shivered, as much from the cold as shock. 'Right... yeah... course I want to know... and, erm, do they know when the test results should come back?'

'Within the next few days; we should have a clearer picture of what's up with him by then.'

'Okay.' *They're taking it seriously then.* Joss nodded as he headed over to the small, converted barn that was his home, his wellies trudging over the age-worn flagstones. Sid trotted over to the door, waiting, his soft brown eyes trained intently on his dad. Joss had always known this day would come; it had lurked at the back of his mind like an unwelcome guest, occasionally showing up and reminding him of its presence. There had been times when he'd thought about biting the bullet and getting in touch with his father; he'd even considered just turning up at his childhood home. But he'd always talked himself out of it, telling himself it would just end up in another argument, another round of hurtful recriminations, their sting lingering for years afterwards. He'd had a life-time's-worth of that.

He glanced across at the farmhouse where his aunt and uncle lived with their seventeen-year-old son, Lawrence. It was where Joss himself had lived when he'd first arrived here aged sixteen, his spirit broken, feeling an utter failure. Its straight walls and tall chimneys loomed silently against the night sky, a warm glow framing the curtains of the Georgian windows where cracks of light sneaked out. Smoke curled out of the high chimney pots, the scent of woodsmoke being blown down by the wind. No doubt the family would be nestled in front of the television, the usual pot of tea on the go, Skip, the sheepdog curled up on the clippy mat by the Aga, oblivious to what was happening over in Lytell Stangdale.

'See, the thing is, Joss,' Rich's voice pulled him out of his musings, 'I'm not going to be able to help out on the farm. I've got too much work on myself, what with this new job... I can't just jack it in. And Dawn, well, she's not keen for me to go back there after everything that's happened... things are just getting settled between us.' Rich released a weary sigh. 'I know I sound like a right selfish git, but it'd be like taking a massive step back, undoing everything I fought for with my marriage; it wasn't easy... you of all people know how things can be with Dad. I just can't risk losing Dawn and Amy. And I agree with Dawn; she says I've done my share...'

Done my share... His brother's words struck Joss with the force of a steam train. He winced. 'I totally understand, Rich, and I don't blame either of you for not wanting to go back to the farm. But dare I ask, what's happening with it at the moment? Who's seeing to the livestock? Who's doing the milking?' He reached the back door to his cottage and pushed it open, his phone pressed to his cheek. Sid shot past him and ran straight over to his food bowl where he set about giving it a thorough checking-over, his nose nudging it across the floor while Joss heeled off his wellies. The warmth of the kitchen was a welcome change to the biting cold of the farmyard; it set his skin tingling.

After leaving school, Rich had joined their father working on the farm full-time. It was a job he loved, working outdoors, being in touch with nature. But Bill Campion wasn't an easy man to get along with since he'd lost his wife to breast cancer when Rich was just thirteen and Joss was twelve. Her loss had made him angry with the world, and, in particular, angry with his sons.

'Pete Welford and his son, Greg, are helping out as best they can, but they can't do it forever; they've got their own farm to run. And, what with the weather set to turn, it's going to make things even more difficult.'

Mention of the Welford name again triggered a whole different host of emotions. Joss felt his cheeks burn at the memory of his last day in Lytell Stangdale. *Ughh! Jeez.* It had been an unmitigated disaster. He rubbed his fingers back and forth over his forehead; he hadn't been back for eighteen years, and the last thing he needed right now was to come face-to-face with his past.

'So what d'you want me to do?' he asked, though he knew full well and his gut clenched as he awaited his brother's words.

'Flaming 'eck, Joss! Isn't it flaming obvious?' said Rich, his voice sharp with irritation.

Joss closed his eyes and blew out a shaky sigh. 'Rich, you know how hard it is for me. Just like you can't leave your job, I can't leave mine. Uncle Joe needs me here, I can't just shoot off; it wouldn't be fair. Can't you get someone in to run the farm until Dad gets better?'

'Have you any idea how selfish you sound? I'm sure Uncle Joe and Aunty Hannah will understand. I mean, it's not as if you'd be going off gallivanting or dumping them to go on holiday; Dad's Uncle Joe's brother for Chrissake. And I appreciate it'll be hard for you to come back here after all these years, but I honestly thought you were a bigger man than that, Joss. Thought you'd be able to put the past behind you, if not for Dad's sake, then for Mum's.'

And there it was. Rich had played his trump card. He knew Joss wouldn't be able to refuse anything for the memory of their beloved mother. The sting of tears caught him off guard and he quickly blinked them back. 'That's a low blow, Richard,' he said, his voice tight with emotion. Sid paused snuffling around the floor and ran over to him. He rested a paw on Joss's leg and whimpered.

'Well, what else was I supposed to do? I had to say something to make you see sense,' Rich said. Joss detected a trace of guilt in his brother's words.

Joss sniffed, regaining his composure. 'Right, I'll speak to Uncle Joe and call you back first thing tomorrow.' With that he ended the call, dropping his phone onto the granite worktop with a clatter. He leaned back against the kitchen unit and dragged his hand down his face. 'Uhh! Why does life have to be so bloomin' complicated, eh, Sid?'

Sid replied with a blink of his bushy eyebrows.

The following morning, Joss joined his Uncle Joe in the milking parlour. At five o'clock it was still dark and the birds were still roosting in the trees. Joss had spent most of the night tossing and turning, his mind in torment as he tried to fathom out what was best to do. Whatever his decision, there would be problems to contend with. It would be so much easier to just stay here, where he'd become settled. Well, as settled as he could be since his divorce from Manda last year. But that was another story; one he'd moved on from and closed the door firmly behind. Deep down, Joss knew he had no choice in the matter; he was duty-bound to go and take the helm at the farm in Lytell Stangdale – "step up to the plate" as Rich had implied – but his sense of obligation did little to ease his dread of seeing his old home again. He really should visit his father in hospital too, whether or not he went back. That thought bothered him more than anything else. Would his dad be civil to him, or was the hostility he felt towards his son too entrenched? Joss suspected he knew the answer to that.

He decided to wait until the whole family were together before he shared his news. And it was with a heavy heart that he headed over to the Skeller Rigg farmhouse for breakfast as was their usual routine after milking, walking shoulder-to-shoulder with his Uncle Joe, Sid trotting along happily, stopping when he encountered an intriguing scent.

'You all right, lad? You've been quiet all morning, anyone'd think you'd lost a tenner and found a quid.' Uncle Joe glanced across at Joss as he paused to open the gate to the house, his pale green-blue eyes full of concern. Uncle Joe was Joss's namesake, both bearing the name Joseph, a family name that had travelled down the Campion family tree for several centuries.

'Sorry, Uncle Joe, my mind's all over the place at the minute.'

'Oh? I hope it's nowt to do with Manda; I thought that was all sorted ages ago. Surely she can't be after owt else?'

Joss followed his uncle into the hallway of the house, both kicking of their wellies. 'No, it's nothing to do with Manda.' *It'd be a heck of a lot easier if it was.* 'I, erm... I had a phone call from Rich last night.' The ache in the pit of his stomach grew more intense.

'Rich?' Uncle Joe frowned. 'Why do I get the feeling this isn't good?'

'Well...' Joss braced himself as the pair made their way into the kitchen, wary that his news could open up a whole new can of worms. It wasn't only Joss who hadn't spoken to his father in eighteen years. Uncle Joe, Bill's older brother by two years, had been stonewalled for apparently "taking Joss's side". Animosity ran deep in the Campion family; at least it did with his father.

'Morning, lads. By, that's good timing.' Aunty Hannah was standing next to the old black Aga where she was filling a clutch of mugs with tea so strong you could stand a spoon in it. She looked up, a broad smile lighting up her gentle face. 'Get your hands washed, you two, then sit yourselves down.' She nodded towards the scrubbed pine table that dominated the room. It was set with cutlery, and there was a decorative jug of holly with vivid red berries in the centre. 'Breakfast's just about ready, I expect you'll both be famished; cold weather always makes for a hearty appetite.'

'Morning,' said Joss. Sid dashed in, brushing by his legs, and settled down beside Skip who was curled up near the old pine dresser, the pair observing Aunty Hannah closely.

'Ey up, Joss,' said his cousin, Lawrence, pulling his gaze away from his mobile phone. He was sitting in a well-loved squishy chair by the window, his gangly legs slung over the arm. He and Joss shared the same slightly messy dark-blond hair, green-blue eyes and strong jawline of the Campion men. Though there was seventeen years between them, they were regularly mistaken for brothers, which was exactly the relationship they'd developed, Lawrence arriving the year after Joss had landed on the doorstep, suitcase in hand, all those years ago.

'Now then, Lawry.' Joss mustered up a smile as he padded across the floor in his sock feet. The familiar mouth-watering aroma of Aunty Hannah's cooked breakfast, which normally set his tastebuds dancing, was having little effect this morning. The way he was feeling, he'd have all on to manage a slice of toast.

'You okay, lovey?' A frown crumpled his aunt's brow as she watched Joss take his seat at the table, the wooden chair scraping noisily over the flagstones.

'He had a call from our Rich last night,' Uncle Joe answered for him.

'Last night?' Her eyes grew wide as she set the teapot in the centre of the table and stretched a snug cosy over it. 'It's not like him to call late.'

'I know.' Joss nodded. 'And I'm afraid it wasn't good news.' His heart was heavy as he shared the contents of the phone call.

'Well, there's nowt else for it, lad, you've got to go back to Lytell Stangdale,' Uncle Joe said when Joss had finished. 'The farm needs you, no two ways about it.'

'Joe's right, lovey. We can manage here; we've got Lawry and I'm happy to muck in a bit more.' Aunty Hannah smiled kindly, covering his hand with hers. 'It's only right you go. And I think it's best you get yourself there today.'

'Aye, me too. And you never know, this situation might end up knocking some sense into that stubborn old fool of a brother of mine. Lord knows, it's long overdue.' Joe shook his head wearily. 'Mind, I reckon it'll take some bloomin' doing.'

'What a shame he's had to end up in hospital if it does,' said Aunty Hannah.

Joss sat back in his seat and glanced around at this branch of his family who'd offered him a sanctuary when he had nowhere else to turn. They'd shown him love and affection and cared for him as if he was their own son at a time he was *persona non grata* to his own father – and even Rich to a lesser extent. They hadn't judged him when he'd shared the details of the heinous actions that had sent him fleeing from his home as a reckless sixteen-year-old, instead they'd listened to him, talked to him in kind voices.

Their reaction to his news that morning had felt like a weight being lifted from his shoulders. He shouldn't have been surprised; they were decent people. And it meant more to him than they could ever know that they didn't feel he was turning his back on them, or make him feel guilty for going to help his father out. How was it, even after all these years, that any conversation concerning his father always managed to set Joss on edge, make him feel like he'd done something wrong? Probably because Bill Campion's standard response to anything that didn't suit him was to guilt-trip people, particularly Joss. How could two brothers be so different? Joss wondered. But then he compared himself to Rich; maybe he could understand a little.

'Well, if you're sure you can manage, at least let me get through the jobs I'd be doing this morning, then I'll leave for Lytell Stangdale later on this afternoon,' Joss said.

'Mind, don't leave it too late, son, you know what the weather forecasters are saying, and you know how bad it can get over there, particularly on that moortop,' said Uncle Joe, nursing his mug of tea on his chest. 'I assume you'll be taking His Lordship.' He nodded to where Sid was stretched out alongside Skip, the pair of them snoring blissfully, their stomachs full of leftover sausages.

'Aye, he'll be coming with me.' Joss gave a small smile; he couldn't imagine going anywhere without his pal.

THREE

Ella

Ella was making her way cautiously down Bramble Hill, her feet crunching over the snow. Evening was settling over the village and the Victorian-style streetlamps cast pools of golden light across the ground. Her arms, laden with brightly-wrapped gifts from the children, were already beginning to ache under the weight and she carefully hitched up her shoulder in an attempt to balance out the load, conscious of a parcel that was perched precariously on top. She was beginning to regret not travelling to work in her little four-wheel drive that morning. Living just over a quarter of a mile away from school, she always walked, but today it would've made the journey to her rented home at Rose Cottage a heck of a lot easier, rather than slipping and sliding all over the place, struggling to see over the teetering pile of parcels. 'Hindsight is a wonderful thing,' she muttered to herself.

She had been late leaving school thanks to Davey Wilkinson's mother who hadn't turned up to collect him until gone four o'clock. Wearing an air of impatience, and offering no apology, she arrived issuing brusque instructions to Davey to get his coat and to "flippin' well hurry up about it". It had made Ella's blood boil and she'd struggled to bite her tongue. Her body was still bristling with a lingering background hum of annoyance. Since Ella was the only member of staff who lived in the village, she'd offered to stay behind with him, urging everyone else to make their way home before the roads became impassable, which was something that could happen with surprising speed on the moors. Hanging back hadn't been a hardship; Davey was a sweet kid with a ready smile that lit up his freckle-strewn face; a conversation with him always left her feeling happy. She couldn't understand how his mother could treat him like some kind of afterthought, a nuisance, even. And, if Davey felt this, he never showed it; he was always upbeat and quick to help others. Ella's heart squeezed for him as an image of his little face, beaming when "Santa" had pulled a present from his sack and called out Davey's name, popped into her mind.

'Well, young Davey, I know you've been a very good boy all year. You've treated everyone kindly, helped your teachers, worked hard at your lessons, and been a thoughtful and considerate friend. All of those are excellent qualities in one so young. I see a wonderful future ahead of you, young man.'

'Thank you, Santa.' Davey had taken his parcel, his face flushed, his eyes shining happily. Ella had felt herself welling up and had had to swallow down a lump of emotion, avoiding eye contact with any of the other staff for fear of unleashing her tears.

Unbeknown to the children, she and Mrs Marr, the school secretary, had sat together one lunchtime in the small upstairs staffroom and written a few words for "Santa" to say about each child as he handed out the gifts. Finding something good to say about Davey was easy, but that wasn't the case for nine-year-old Ruby Milford. She was a sly, spiteful piece of work who took pleasure in doling out cruel pinches to the younger pupils or damaging their work when the grown-ups weren't looking. There'd been numerous complaints about her from both pupils and parents alike, but when Mr and Mrs Milford were tackled about it, the response was one of disbelief and denial; their daughter was well-behaved, she wouldn't do such a thing. So Ruby's reign of terror continued.

'What can we put about Ruby?' Mrs Marr had asked, scratching her head. 'I know she's a little madam, but surely she's got some redeeming feature. I mean, after all, she's only a child.'

'Hmm! If she has, she's doing a bloomin' good job of hiding it, child or not. I've never encountered a pupil like her,' Ella had said. Mrs Marr had pressed a hand over her mouth to stifle a laugh. 'I was hoping you'd be able to conjure up something; you can always find something nice to say about folk, even the mean and nasty ones. If it was down to me, I'd put something like, "Ruby's a rude-mannered little bra—'

'How're you getting on?' Mrs Prudom had peered around the doorway.

'We're just on with finding something for Santa to say about Ruby Milford.'

'Ah. Good luck with that.' She'd raised her eyebrows. 'Oh, and don't forget to give some thought to what I said about teacher train-ing, Ella, you're more than capable,' she'd said, before slipping back out into the corridor, closing the door firmly behind her.

Apart from her snappy encounter with Davey's mum, it had been a wonderful day, the excitement of the children, heart-warming and infectious. That said, there was no denying the last half-term had been a slog. And though she loved her job, Ella was looking forward to the fortnight's break from school, which she was going to kick off by opening the tub of sweets she'd been saving for tonight and playing some festive music. It would hopefully pep her up in readiness for her shift at the Sunne where she worked part-time behind the bar.

Ella was grateful the wind had dropped, but it was still bitingly cold. The frosty air was making her eyes water and nipping at any exposed area of skin. Her nose was tingling, and she dipped her chin into her scarf, glad to have her thick pom-pom hat pulled down well over her ears. At least she'd had the foresight to bring her wellies – the ankle boots she'd been wearing earlier were stowed away in the carrier bag that was now swinging from her wrist and digging into her skin alongside a bulging bag of gifts. She'd slid an equally heavy one on her other arm in a bid to balance herself out and now she felt like a packhorse!

As she reached the bottom of the hill, Ella stopped to redistribute the pile of parcels which had shifted when she'd almost lost her footing on a lethal patch of compressed snow. 'Ouch!' She winced as the heaviest of the carrier bags pinched the skin of her wrist. Adding to her woes, the cold was beginning to seep through the soles of her wellies and her toes were starting to feel numb.

She was about to make her way across the road when a familiar mud-spattered Land Rover drew up alongside her.

'Ey up, Ells, looks like Santa's come early.'

She peered over the parcels to see Jimby Fairfax leaning out of the window. He was another of her relations, and was wearing his trademark broad smile, a thick woolly hat covering his short crop of dark curls. His upbeat demeanour was always infectious, and she couldn't help but grin back.

'Hiya, Jimby, something like that. I'm kicking myself for not bringing my car.'

'In that case, why don't you let me give you a lift?' His words hung in a plume of condensation in the chilly air.

'Oh, you've no idea how good that sounds – as long as it's no trouble. It's way slippier than I thought and there's a real risk I'll go A-over-T. I've just had a near miss and a freezing, wet bum is the last thing I need.'

He gave a hearty chuckle. 'I can imagine, and it's no bother at all. We can shove that lot in the back, quick as a flash.' He nodded to her parcels. 'Here, let me give you a hand.' With that, he jumped out of the vehicle and headed round to the back where the broad rear door opened with a groan.

'Thanks, Jimby, you're a star,' Ella said gratefully as she eyed the trod; the ancient, worn flags were now several inches deep in snow; it would have been a hard slog trudging back in that.

'There we go, that didn't take long,' said Jimby, slamming the door shut and dusting off his hands just as a smart-looking Land

Rover with an unfamiliar registration plate approached them, a thick wodge of snow covering its roof.

The vehicle slowed to a crawl as it passed them, the road being made narrow by the snow banked up at the sides; a combination of drifting and what had been pushed back by the plough. Though the light was fading, it was still easy to make out that the passenger seat was occupied by a large black dog of Labrador proportions and an impressive set of whiskers. It regarded Ella and Jimby with haughty interest. Ella couldn't help but smile; the dog had such a characterful face. With a gloved hand, she swiped away a wayward straggle of hair that was tickling her nose, her gaze shifting to the driver. He had mussed-up dark-blond hair and looked to be in his early thirties. Their eyes locked and Ella gasped as a bolt of attraction and a flicker of recognition assaulted her senses simultaneously. She watched, her lips parted, as the vehicle slowly pulled away, her mind rifling through her memories in a bid to pin down where she'd seen the handsome stranger before. And judging by the expression that had flitted across his face, she got the feeling he'd recognised her too.

Jimby gave a low whistle. 'Wow! Smart Landie.' He too watched the four-wheel drive disappear down the lane. 'I haven't seen it round here before and I don't recall clapping eyes on the fella behind the wheel either. Don't suppose you've any idea who he is?'

'Nope, none.' Ella shook her head, her dark, unruly brows drawn together. 'Though I have to say, there was something vaguely familiar about him.'

It was more than familiar; it tugged at something deep inside her, and it would niggle her until she could remember where she knew him from.

'Aye, I know what you mean.' Jimby frowned too, smoothing his hand across his chin. 'Mind, knowing how quickly news spreads round these parts, I dare say we'll know his name, age, height and shoe size by the end of the night.' He chuckled.

'I reckon you're right.' Ella laughed distractedly.

After a moment's pause, Jimby rubbed his hands together briskly and said, 'Right then, Ells, it's bloomin' freezing; let's get cracking.'

'You're not wrong there, my feet are turning to lead.'

'Arghh!' Ella was making her way round to the passenger door when a yell stopped her in her tracks. She turned to see Jimby frantically battling to stay upright, his feet sliding every which-way over a compacted patch of snow, his arms flying around like the sails of a windmill. 'Woah! Arghh... no... oh, bugger!'

'Jimby!' Ella watched, her hand clamped over her mouth, as he fell flat on his back, his head landing in a pile of snow. She was laughing so hard, she was rendered speechless, tears of mirth running down her cold cheeks.

'You've got to be kidding me!' Jimby said, with a groan. He lay still for a few seconds. 'Why does it always have to happen to me?'

'Are you okay, Jimby?' Ella finally managed to speak, though her voice was choked by her giggles.

'I'd be a whole lot better if I didn't have an avalanche of snow down my neck and a soaking wet backside,' he said, pushing himself up onto his elbows and shaking snow from his head.

Ella made her way gingerly over to him, being careful to avoid the patch he'd slipped on. 'Here, let me help you.' She held out her hand.

'Thanks, but I reckon it's best if you don't; you know what I'm like, you'll end up in a heap down here; it's pointless both of us being drenched.'

Still struggling to contain her giggles, she said, 'Oh, Jimby, I'm sorry. If you hadn't stopped to help me, this wouldn't have happened.'

'No worries, Ells.' He beamed at her good-naturedly as he brushed clumps of snow from his jeans. 'No harm done; well, there might be a couple of bruises for the missus to laugh at, but other than that, it's fine.'

In no time, they were parked-up outside Rose Cottage, with

Jimby helping his cousin to unload the parcels, depositing them in the small hallway.

'Right, that's the last of 'em,' he said, handing her a couple of carrier bags.

'Thanks, Jimby.'

'Pleasure.' He grinned. 'You working at the Sunne tonight?'

'Yep, my shift starts at six.'

'I'll see you later then. Ollie and me are popping in for a beer sometime, we feel we need to put the world to rights,' he said, a mischievous twinkle in his eyes.

'Ah, is that the reason? It's got nothing to do with the fact that Jonty serves a decent pint?' She grinned back at him.

'Well, I suppose that might have something to do with it.'

Ella laughed. 'Well, thanks for helping, Jimby, and sorry again about your soggy backside.'

'No worries. And good luck with fitting all those parcels under your Christmas tree.'

Ella eyed the pile. 'Thanks, I think I'm going to need it.'

FOUR

Joss

Light was fading quickly and the sky had taken on an unusual purple hue as Joss took the junction off the main road and onto the twisty-turning one that led to the moors. It wasn't long before the scenery around him started to change, the road narrowing to a single-track lane lined with dry stone walls and hawthorn hedges, punctuated by pull-in places. The landscape was altogether more rugged than that around Skeller Rigg Farm and Helderthorpe, with its sweeping verdant green dales and rounded hills. Here, the valleys were deeper, broader, with vertiginous ridges – or "riggs" as they were known locally – the occasional craggy outcrop of sand-stone standing proud. The North Yorkshire Moors had a savage beauty and he'd forgotten just how quickly snow could make an impact on them, their situation being higher and more exposed than back home. They had a bleakness he found indescribably appealing. They harboured clusters of dense woodland that gave shelter to an array of wildlife, including roe deer – two of which had dashed across the road and leapt effortlessly over the dry stone wall. Sid had watched with interest as the graceful creatures raced across the field, their white bottoms bobbing up and down.

As Joss drove on, he felt his pulse quicken, and the grip of anxiety in his chest squeeze tighter as his old home drew nearer. From the drifts already banked up against the dry stone walls, he could see it had been snowing hard and he was thankful that the plough had been through to clear the route, that the local farmers had been out scattering grit in a bid to keep them snow and frost-free. Nevertheless, he decided to take it steady; at the end of the day, if you hit an icy patch going downhill, it didn't matter what vehicle you were in or how fancy the tyres were, you were going to skid like everybody else. He didn't relish coming a cropper before he'd even had a chance to show his face at the farm. Rich wouldn't be too chuffed about that.

Joss pushed on, flicking on the wipers when the snow started tumbling gently and settling on the windscreen. 'Uh-oh! Here it comes, Sid,' he said under his breath, concentrating hard. He passed a sign for Danskelfe, catching a glimpse of the battlements of its ancient castle peering out of the snow-dusted trees, a flag fluttering limply from one of the turrets

Sid glanced around him, taking it all in, and Joss couldn't help but smile at the interest he showed.

'What d'you make of this, eh, lad?' Joss reached across and ruffled the dog's fluffy head, making his tail beat against the seat. 'At least we're nice and warm in here.' He suddenly wondered as to the temperature in the farmhouse at Camplin Farm. He gave an involuntary shiver, struck by a memory of the freezing cold winters they'd endured there after his mum had passed away. At times it had been too cold to sleep and he'd find ice on the inside of his bedroom windows. He'd resorted to piling his dressing-gown and coats on top of his duvet in a bid to keep warm. His father had refused to "waste" oil – as he'd put it – to fuel the central heating, stating Rich and Joss needed to "toughen up", and how there'd been no radiators in the place when he was a lad and he'd been fine. It was a far cry from the winters when his mum had been alive and the old farmhouse had been so toasty Joss used to imagine it glowed, particularly the kitchen where the huge old cream

Rayburn radiated an ambient warmth as well as producing vast pots of mouth-watering stews and his mum's famous crumbles she'd serve with jugs of thick home-made custard.

His heart squeezed at the memory.

Camplin Hall Farm – or as it was known locally, Camplin Farm – had been in the Campion family since the mid-sixteen-hundreds, "Camplin" being a corruption of the Campion name. The farmstead had been passed down through generations of Campions, and as a younger man, Bill Campion had been enormously proud of his home's heritage and the respect the Campion name had afforded him. He'd occasionally pull out ancient deeds from an old metal tin stored in the same old oak coffer that had been in the house since the early Campions and show his sons, his chest filling with pride at the family's loyalty to the place. 'We're just custodians, lads, we have to treat this place with love and care, ready to pass down to the next line of the family. What you do with your time here will bear directly on its future; events and happenings are stored in its walls like memories. Don't ever forget that.' Joss and Rich had listened in silence, feeling not a little daunted by their father's words, and the weight of responsibility that would one day be theirs.

Before he knew it, Joss was heading along the road to Lytell Stangdale, his heart hammering in his chest. It may have been eighteen years since his last visit, but the place looked exactly as he remembered – except for The Sunne Inne, that appeared to have undergone a complete revamp he noticed, slowing down to get a better look. His eyes lingered on the potted Christmas trees placed either side of the door, their fairy lights already twinkling in the half-light. The last time he'd seen the place, it was owned by Hacky Harold and the thatch had been slumping badly, the paint-work peeling; it had looked almost derelict. But now, it looked stylish in a genteel, country pursuits kind of way, the sort of place whose dishes would feature regularly on the social media posts of foodie influencers. Dare he call in while he stayed at the farm? he wondered. Would anyone recognise him if he did? The questions his sudden appearance would instigate made a visit less than tempting, and he didn't fancy partaking in the conversations it would stir up. He sighed; it was probably best if he just slipped by unobserved, do what needed to be done at the farm and slope off before anyone realised he was there. Well, that was the plan at least; he still hadn't given up on the idea of employing someone to run it until his father was well enough to take the helm again.

Up ahead, at the foot of the drive to his old primary school, he spotted a vintage series Land Rover. A couple were standing beside it, laughing and chatting. He felt his pulse quicken once more, unsure of how he'd feel if they recognised him. Thanks to the snow, the road was narrow, and he was forced to slow right down to pass. He did his best not to make eye contact, but the temptation was too hard to resist. Recognition fired in his mind; the man was without a doubt Jimby Fairfax – he'd know that face-splitting smile anywhere, plus the fact the man had barely changed. Joss's eyes rested on the young woman beside Jimby, a spike of attraction taking him by surprise as it shot through him; he thought he'd become immune, that his senses had been dulled since the drama with Manda. He'd sworn off women for the foreseeable future, but this woman's striking dark eyes had caught his attention. And as he drove away, it dawned on him just who the striking eyes belonged to. Talk about a blast from the past.

'Ella,' he said softly, his heart lifting. It felt surprisingly good to say her name. Despite what had happened in the past. Despite the fact she'd broken his heart.

He sucked in a deep breath and Sid eyed him with interest.

Joss knew it was inevitable he'd see her – though he'd vowed to do his best to avoid her – but what he hadn't anticipated was the strength of his reaction when he laid eyes on her. Hadn't expected it to feel like he'd had the wind knocked right out of his sails. 'Oh, jeez,' he said, pushing his hand through his hair. It had totally blindsided him.

As he drove on, he felt old memories dust themselves down, his face flaming as one of Ella – owner of the most beautiful chocolate-brown eyes, flecked with gold he'd ever seen, and the first girl to capture his heart – took up centre stage. He winced as he remembered their last conversation when they were both sixteen. He scrunched up his eyes and shook his head. 'Ughh! Don't go there, you loser! You've moved on, no point going over it and torturing yourself.'

Sid whimpered, sensing a change in his dad. Joss reached across and gave him a quick pat on the back. 'Honestly, fella, if you want my advice, just keep away from women, you only end up making a fool of yourself. Well, at least that's what I do; you only need to take a look at my pathetic track-record to see.' His shoulders sagged. 'Actually, it's probably best if you don't, it's miserable, depressing stuff. My advice to you, is to just stick with me, buddy, and we'll be fine. We'll keep women safely at arm's length. Deal?' He stole a look at Sid who blinked his bushy eyebrows and gave a quick wag of his tail.

FIVE

Ella

Ella placed the last of the parcels under the Christmas tree that sat in the window at Rose Cottage, its pine aroma scenting the room and its warm-white fairy lights twinkling against the dark sky beyond. Her favourite playlist of Christmas songs was murmuring softly in the background – a far cry from the ones belted out with unbridled enthusiasm by the kids at school that afternoon. She sat back on her haunches and gave a contented sigh as Tabby-Cat, the tortoiseshell stray who'd invited herself to stay, brushed by, mewing loudly, her tail curling under Ella's nose. 'Is that a hint for some attention, young lady?' she asked, laughing as she tickled the cat under her chin. Tabby-Cat mewed some more. 'Righto, I'll just put another log on the fire then we can have a cuddle. How's that?'

The living room was small but achingly cosy, with its low beamed ceiling, wall lights sending out a soft glow and squat wood-burner radiating warmth from the little inglenook fireplace. The bulk of the furniture had come with the old weavers' cottage she rented from local joiner, Ollie Cartwright. He'd previously lived there with his daughter, Anoushka, until his marriage to Ella's cousin, Kitty Fairfax, (who was also Jimby's younger sister), after which he'd moved into Oak Tree Farm. His carpentry skills were evident throughout the house, from the sturdy oak front door to the built-in wardrobes in the bedrooms, and the fitted kitchen that managed to utilise every inch of the tiny room without it feeling cluttered. She was glad it had come up for rent when it did.

Ella had made the place her own with the addition of cushions and throws, hanging pictures and dotting her own ornaments around. Ollie had kindly let her paint the walls in her choice of colours. And she'd enjoyed decorating it for Christmas, fixing a wreath to the door, winding a fake pine swag around the bannister and looping extra fairy lights here and there. It had been her haven since her split with Owen almost a year ago, and she liked nothing better than to get home from school, kick off her shoes and sit in the kitchen with a cup of tea, the radio burbling away in the background while she gazed out of the window at the view that ran across the garden and out over the dale. And, even though she and Owen had only lived a few miles away in Danskelfe, it still felt good to be back home in Lytell Stangdale. It had been the perfect balm to soothe her sore heart. Her *sore* but not *broken* heart she regularly had to remind her mum, who looked at her with concern every time she saw her, and was the reason Ella could never have accepted her parents' invitation and gone back home to live after she'd left Owen.

'I just wish you could find a nice young man, that's all, lovey,' Debbie Welford said regularly.

'I'm only thirty-four, Mum, there's plenty of time for that.'

Ella knew her mum meant well, but a "young man", even if he was the nicest bloke on the planet, was the last thing she needed right now. It would be a while before she'd be tempted to go down the relationship route again – she might consider it when hell froze over she regularly told her friends. And besides, she'd been somewhat surprised to find she quite liked her own company, the perks of being able to choose what to eat, what to wear and what to watch on TV had been a welcome revelation. Three years of living with Owen, who liked everything done his way with little room for flexibility, had seen to that. And the thought of having to listen to her mum tut or make sympathetic noises every time her errant ex's name was mentioned made her stomach curdle. Ella just wanted to forget him. *Loser!*

Before she'd set the parcels under the tree, she'd had a quick tidy round, as she did every evening after school. She wasn't exactly what you'd call house-proud, but she liked her home to be neat and tidy, and kept on top of the housework, ensuring her weekends weren't taken over by huge amounts of it. Those two precious days were reserved for spending time on her parents' farm, where she helped out and tended her rescue animals: Clive the donkey and two goats, mother and daughter, Clover and Dandy.

She'd already been out to the little shed in the garden and fed her guinea pigs, Dave and Nigel. The pair had squeaked excitedly as soon as she'd opened the door. 'Now then boys, have you had a good day?' She'd scooped them up and snuggled them close, their plump bodies warm and solid.

She'd inherited the pair a few months earlier from Ali, an old school friend from Middleton-le-Moors who was emigrating to Australia with her husband and two young daughters. 'Please, Ells, no one else wants them, and I know you love piggies, you had loads when we were kids, so you already know they're no bother. And these boys are *so* cute. Look,' Ali had said persuasively, holding up Dave who was nibbling on a piece of straw that was disappearing into his mouth at an impressive rate. He had a glossy chocolate-brown coat, while his brother, Nigel, was brown and white. Nigel had a cheeky rosette of fur on the crown of his head, which resembled a badly-cut fringe. Ella's heart had melted instantly; Ali was right, they were very cute. How could she resist?

'Oh, go on then,' she'd said, the words rushing out before she could stop herself. She'd reached for Nigel, smoothing her hand along his back. 'Hello, little fella. I'd forgotten how sweet they are,' she'd said, looking over at Ali who was smiling at her victoriously.

'You won't regret it, Ells, I promise.'

'Hmm.'

But Ali was right, Ella hadn't regretted it.

She got to her feet, Tabby-Cat curling around her legs. 'Come on then, miss, let's have that cuddle.' She scooped the cat up and flopped onto the sofa, Tabby-Cat curling up on her lap and purring luxuriously. 'We haven't got long, I'm afraid, I've promised myself a quick shower before I have to get ready for the pub, so we'd best make the most of it, Tabs. But I promise I'll make it up to you over the weekend.'

Ella rested her head back on the sofa, letting the festive music wash over her, her thoughts wandering to the mystery Land Rover that had driven through the village earlier. Her mind roved over the driver's features, searching for anything to latch onto in the hope it would trigger some distant memory, or turn up a name, but to no avail. She reached for her necklace, her fingers moving over the smooth curves of the infinity pendant; it soon became warm to her touch. She tried telling herself he was probably just someone she'd served in the pub, that he'd only stuck in her mind because he was attractive. But something in her gut told her otherwise. She sighed softly, remembering Jimby's words about how quickly news spread round the village; she'd be sure to make enquiries in the pub tonight.

Her mind shifted to Mrs Prudom's comments about considering teacher training. The head had been dropping hints for a few months now. It had given Ella food for thought and she'd set herself a deadline of the Christmas break to make her decision. Though, if she was honest with herself, she already knew what it would be.

Much as she loved her job at school, she'd been feeling restless since she'd returned after the summer break. The role of teaching assistant was one she'd somehow fallen into. Her parents, not wanting her to feel she had to stay on the farm and work for them – which would have been oh-so-easy since working on the farm was what she loved to do – had encouraged her to go to college and study something totally unrelated. Since Ella had always got on well with young children, and being a much-in-demand babysitter, it was obvious to her that she should enrol on a teaching assistant course – its appeal was heightened since most of her group of friends were doing the same; they'd be able to have a laugh while they learnt. Perfect!

Almost as soon as she'd qualified, Ella was lucky enough to find employment at Lytell Stangdale Primary School, her predecessor very conveniently choosing that term to retire. That had been sixteen years ago now and boy how those years had whizzed by. During her time there, and with much encouragement from the Head who could see the amiable young woman's potential, Ella had challenged herself and kept her interest by studying, working her way up to the position of Higher Level Teaching Assistant. To train as a teacher was a natural progression, she supposed. In truth, falling into the gentle rhythm of the school had been too easy, it being such a happy place to work. So much so, the staff had remained pretty much the same since her first day there.

And the years had somehow drifted by without her noticing.

But the pull of working outdoors was growing ever stronger and Mrs Prudom's suggestion had only served to shine a light on Ella's yearning.

SIX

Joss

It wasn't long before the Land Rover was climbing steadily up the steep hill to Camplin Hall Farm and heading along the narrow track which was more riven with potholes than Joss remembered. As the vehicle nosed into the farmyard, he spotted a shiny four-wheel drive. From the personalised numberplate, it could only belong to Rich. Working for his father-in-law clearly had its perks.

Joss climbed out of the car, emotions rushing at him, rendering him oblivious to the biting cold. He felt a tightness in his chest as his eyes swept over the old farmhouse constructed of buttery sandstone. It looked just as he remembered it, though an air of neglect seemed to hang over the place now, the piles of junk dotted about the yard doing little to dispel his first impression. Camplin Hall Farm was a mish-mash of different building phases, each one so typical of the North Yorkshire Moors. From its origins as a long-house with stone mullions and thick walls – the thatch long-since removed and replaced by red pantiles – to the Georgian symmetry of the main house with its central door, the huge dressed-herring-bone bricks punctuated by large windows with their wobbly crown glass, finishing with the Victorian extension with its cat-slide roof. His old home appeared to be looking down at him with mistrust, hostility almost, its walls looming up, creating an impenetrable barrier to him. It appeared to be saying, 'What are you doing here? Why have you turned up after all these years? After what you did? Come to gloat, have you?'

The door flew open, startling Joss, and his brother stepped out, his face like thunder. 'I thought you'd be here long before now.' Rich strode purposefully towards him. 'I've been texting you and trying to call you, wondering where the bloody heck you'd got to. It doesn't take that long to get here from flaming Helderthorpe. Don't you ever pick up that damn phone of yours?' He threw his arms up, exasperated.

Hello, Rich, it's nice to see you too! Thanks for coming. Joss hadn't been expecting a welcoming committee, but he thought his brother would at least be pleased to see him, especially since they hadn't clapped eyes on one another for well over a year. He bit down on a sharp retort and suppressed a sigh. 'Sorry, Rich, I texted you when I set off. I didn't think you'd be expecting me to arrive any earlier than this.'

'Well, if you did send a text, it hasn't flaming-well arrived. I've been stuck up here for hours, waiting. Thought you'd be setting off this morning. Dawn's been giving me earache, wondering where I've got to.'

Rich's pinched, angry expression triggered a memory of their father. It sent a ripple of unease running up Joss's spine. He fought with the urge to get back in the Land Rover and turn right around. He didn't need this grief; he hadn't been welcome here for the best part of twenty years and he wasn't obliged to be here now. He didn't owe his dad or Rich anything. He pressed his lips together in a bid to calm his rising annoyance.

'Look, I'm sorry, Rich, I thought you understood I'd be finishing my jobs this morning and heading over after lunch. That's what I said in my text. And I had to take it steady 'cos the roads have been a bit dicey in places, what with the snow, then there was a diversion I wasn't expecting, thanks to roadworks.' He mustered up a smile, hoping to appeal to his brother's good-natured side – if he still had one.

Rich's face softened and he pushed his fingers through his dark-blond hair, a shade darker than his brother's. Hostility was weakening its grip and his body language appeared to yield. 'Listen, I'm sorry. It's just been a difficult time, and now I'm working for Dawn's dad... well, I don't like to rock the boat. Rod's been good enough to give me this opportunity and I don't want to look like I'm not taking it seriously. Things have been going really well, I'm earning decent money for a change, we're going to be able to afford to send our Amy to that private school in Middleton-le-Moors, you know the one, Middleton Hall. Dawn went there, it's got a good reputation. I'm not going to do anything that risks stuffing things up.'

Joss nodded, he was familiar with the school in question. It did have a good reputation, and a hefty price-tag to go with it. He regarded his brother; the designer clothes he was wearing looked out of place in a mucky old farmyard. Rich had always been money orientated but it would seem things had been cranked up a notch or two recently. It must have rubbed off from Dawn's dad, Rod Walker, who'd had a reputation for being flash when they were kids.

Rod was a successful businessman who owned a chain of popular garden centres and a fleet of swanky cars. The Walker family lived in a large new build on the outskirts of the quaint market town of Middleton-le-Moors. It stuck out like a sore thumb with its pale-blond bricks and oversized portico, the fleet of flash cars that gleamed on the gravel drive, the incongruous stone lions standing guard either side of the huge electric gates. Dawn was known for being "daddy's little princess" and her father had been none-too-keen when his daughter started dating someone he referred to as a "lowly farm-yakker"; he'd had bigger plans for her. But she was undeterred. She'd set her sights on Rich, who hadn't been able to believe his luck when she'd struck up a conversation with him at Middleton's annual country show. And what Dawn wanted, Dawn got. Unable to refuse his daughter anything, Rod had found himself easing up with his objections, much as it had stuck in his craw.

At the time, Rod had tried to persuade Rich to give up his job at the farm and work for him instead, taking the younger man to one side on numerous occasions, hoping to tempt him with an extensive list of the perks he'd get if he joined the Walker empire – generous salary, company car, sizeable house with a pepper-corn rent, ten weeks holiday each year, decent pension – the list grew longer with each attempt. But Rich had always refused. Campion family loyalty tethered him to the farm and he felt obliged to stay. Until six months ago when he'd finally caved. Joss knew it had something to do with Rich wanting to get his marriage back on track, which his brother had confided had been on increasingly shaky ground. It had obviously helped; from what Joss understood in their phone conversations, the couple were in a better place now – in every sense of the word. The family had upped-sticks from their little cottage in Danskelfe and been transplanted into a large, showy new build on a sprawling estate on the fringes of Middleton-le-Moors. Naturally, it was owned by Rod. Nevertheless, Joss was glad things had improved for his brother.

Rich's voice pulled him back into the conversation. 'I'm supposed to be joining Rod for a meeting back at Middleton soon.' He checked the expensive-looking watch on his wrist then cast his eyes up to the sky where thick, foreboding clouds were gathering. 'I should get there in time if I leave now, provided the weather behaves itself, that is.' He paused for a moment before patting Joss on the arm and offering a weak smile. 'Anyroad, I apologise for being grouchy; it's good to see you, mate.'

'It's all right, I get it. And I'm here now, so why don't we go inside and you can bring me up-to-speed?'

'Sounds like a plan, but it'll have to be quick, mind.'

'No problem. Just give me a minute while I go and get Sid.'

'Sid?' Rich turned to the Land Rover, his frown reappearing. 'I thought you'd come on your own.'

'Sid's my dog. I've told you about him before.' From their infrequent phone conversations, Joss regularly got the impression his brother wasn't listening to him, it was as if his mind was on other things. He'd tried not to let it niggle him but it was hard. *If you can't be bothered to listen to me, why call?* he often found himself thinking.

Rich grunted and made his way to the house.

As soon as Joss opened the door, Sid shot out of the vehicle and headed straight to the farmhouse. Inside, he ran up to Rich, his tail wagging enthusiastically. Joss walked in to see his brother inching back, looking less than happy again. 'Ey, mutt, you can keep those massive wet paws to yourself; I've got to go to a meeting and I don't want these trousers getting mucky.'

'Sid, here!' Joss said, clicking his tongue. Sid obliged, running over to him and sitting beside him obediently; he knew a non-doggy person when he saw one.

Joss gazed around the large kitchen, a sea of emotions swirling inside him. The room was bitterly cold, a whiff of dampness lingering in the air as if there'd been no heating on for months. The huge oak table was still in residence in the middle of the room, just as he remembered. It was covered in crumbs and ring-marks, a solitary mug of half-drunk tea set on it. From the skin on the surface, it had been there a while. A worn-looking cardigan hung forlornly on the back of one of the chairs. The old Rayburn, sporting a variety of baked-on spillages, sat in the inglenook on the far wall. Judging by the temperature, it hadn't been on for a long time – a far cry from when his mum had been here and it had belted out heat. A memory of her lifting a tray of Yorkshire puddings out of one of the ovens loomed in his mind, making his chest tighten. She'd prided herself on her Yorkshire puds; they were like huge, buttery clouds with their crisp exterior and slightly soft middle, their edges ever-so-slightly caught; just the way Joss liked them. He blinked, pushing the image away, resuming his survey of the room. He noted the thick layer of dust that covered the surfaces, the cobwebs that hung from the dark oak beams. It had been a cold, uninviting place when he was last here, but things had taken a nosedive since then. Something had clearly been amiss for a while. A wave of sadness washed over him. Had he been as stubborn as his dad for staying away for so long? For not trying harder to build bridges? At the age of sixty-two, Bill Campion was by no means old, but he wasn't getting any younger either. Anything could be waiting around the corner; you never knew. As the current situation proved.

'Until a couple of months ago, Aunty Babs was still popping over from Arkleby a couple of times a week, like she did when we were kids... after Mum... you know... she'd do a bit of cleaning round, try to make the place look homely, take some washing home with her and bring it all back washed and ironed, putting meals in the freezer – not that Dad ever appreciated any of it mind.' Rich rolled his eyes. 'He was getting so cantankerous, always barking at her, it was embarrassing. To be honest, I was amazed she carried on coming over for as long as she did.'

'Right,' said Joss, rubbing his hand over the two-day-old stubble of his chin. Concern prickled over him at hearing of the treatment his father had doled out to their kind-hearted aunt. 'She didn't deserve that.'

'No, she didn't.'

Aunty Babs was their mother's older sister and the two women had not only shared the same thick, dark hair but also the same warm and happy nature; it was hard to think anyone could find reason to "bark" at her. 'That woman has a heart of gold,' Uncle Joe said regularly. 'She deserves a medal the size of a dustbin lid, putting up with that brother of mine. A lesser person would've given up years ago; told him to stick his obnoxious attitude where the sun don't shine.'

Joss had quietly agreed. Aunty Babs and her husband, Uncle Maff, had kept in touch with him since he'd left the area, regularly reminding him there was always room with them and his cousins, Matt and Daisy, at Staineythorpe Farm if ever he needed it. They'd never once bad-mouthed his father, explaining away his bleak moods and bad temper as grief. Even so, it didn't excuse treating someone with such blatant contempt. 'Don't worry, Joss, lovey, he'll come round and you'll be back at Camplin Farm before you know it,' Aunty Babs had said six months after Joss's departure. But he had no wish to return to the bad atmospheres, the yelling and the confidence-quashing put downs he'd endured for the last four years; he'd had a taste of living in an environment filled with the love and kindness that had been missing from his life since his mother had gone, and he wasn't prepared to give it up. Having Aunty Babs popping in twice a week couldn't compensate for that, as kind and caring as she was.

His eyebrows drew together; he wondered why she'd made no mention of his father's behaviour in their phone conversation a fortnight earlier. But then again, knowing her, she wouldn't want to worry him, or for him to think she was criticising his father.

'You said she was coming over 'til a couple of months ago, so have you any idea what stopped her?' Joss asked.

'Er, yeah. Dad really lost his rag with her the last time she was here. Told her to clear off. Said he'd put up with her interfering for years and he'd had enough of her sticking her nose in his life. That she just came here to gloat and be smug about her *perfect life* with Uncle Maff on their *perfect farm* with their *perfect family*.'

'What? No!'

Rich rolled his eyes. 'I know, daft bloke doesn't help himself. And I felt awful; she left in a hurry, looking pretty tearful.'

'I'm not surprised.' Joss paused, his brother's words running through his mind. 'I know he's been difficult since Mum died, but this behaviour seems extreme even by his standards. I wonder what's at the core of it? Surely there must be more to it than that?' Joss couldn't shake the feeling that there was something his brother wasn't telling him. It was hard to put the pieces of a puzzle together when some of the important ones were missing, but something told Joss he'd need to tread carefully. 'Do you think it's got anything to do with why he collapsed?'

Rich shrugged, averting his eyes, shuffling his feet. 'Dunno.'

'Was he like that when you were still working here? I mean, did he seem okay? It just seems really sudden, him taking ill like this.'

'Look, he seemed fine, okay? There was nothing about him that gave me cause for concern. He was bad-tempered, moody, but he's always been a flaming bad-tempered, moody sod!' Rich's eyes flashed angrily.

Joss raised his palms, he'd clearly hit a nerve and he didn't know why. 'Hey, I'm not having a go at you, I'm only trying to fathom out what's been happening with him, that's all. You have to understand, up until last night, I didn't know any of this.'

'Well, maybe if you'd been here instead of avoiding your responsibilities for all these years, then you'd have seen what's been happening with him, instead of leaving it to me. That way, you wouldn't be able to accuse me of not taking more interest in *our* father and his health.'

My responsibilities? 'Rich... that's not what I meant.'

Rich set his mouth into a hard line, his face livid as he fished inside his pocket. 'There's the keys.' He threw them and they skittered across the table. 'The cows need milking; make sure you clean the parlour down properly when you've done. It might be a dump in here, but Dad's still meticulous about milking.'

His brother's comment about cleaning the parlour properly sent a prickle of annoyance running up Joss's spine, just as was intended. He shook his head, pushing down the urge to bite back. Rich knew full-well Joss was involved in milking at Skeller Rigg Farm and had been since his arrival there; it went without saying he was fully aware of the high standards of hygiene that had to be complied with in a milking parlour. 'Rich, I—'

But Rich was in no mood to listen. 'I've made a list of things, stuff you need to know.' He pointed to a crumpled piece of paper next to where the keys had landed. 'I've got to go.' With that, he strode past Joss and out into the farmyard. Seconds later, the muffled sound of his four-wheel drive could be heard swooshing across the snowy yard and out of the gate.

Joss looked down at Sid whose eyes were still trained on the open door. 'Was it something I said? I reckon I made a pig's backside of that, what do you think, fella?' he said, his shoulders heaving with a sigh.

SEVEN

Ella

At ten-to-six, Ella pushed open the heavy oak door of The Sunne Inne, her eyes lingering on the sumptuous festive wreath fixed to it. She was greeted by a wall of warmth and the aroma of landlady Bea's delicious food rushing at her all at once. Rose Cottage wasn't far from the pub, but the walk there hadn't stopped the cold from nipping at her nose and cheeks, which had started to tingle almost immediately thanks to the change of temperature.

Unbuttoning her thick jacket, she made her way across the low-beamed room to the oak bar, the brass beer pumps shining in the soft lights. A fire blazed merrily in the wide inglenook fireplace, while the Christmas tree twinkled away quietly in the corner. Festive music crooned softly in the background. Bea's former incarnation as an interior designer was evident in the artfully arranged Christmas decorations in rich, winter tones.

'Ella!' A plummy voice from the direction of the kitchen made her turn to see Portia Latimer, Bea's daughter, beaming at her round the door.

'Portia! It's so good to see you, I didn't think you were getting here 'til Monday.' Ella smiled broadly, genuinely pleased to see her friend, who rushed at her and pulled her into an enthusiastic hug, squeezing her so tight she struggled to catch her breath. 'Warghh!' she said, giggling.

Twenty-nine-year-old Portia had inherited her poker-straight blonde hair and vibrant blue eyes from her mother, but she had her dad to thank for her aquiline nose, her statuesque height and coltish limbs. The attributes made for a striking combination. Ella regularly thought her friend could make it as a model if she was ever tempted to give up Wisteria House Interiors, the interior design company she'd taken over from Bea.

Portia released Ella and tucked her long hair behind her ears, her eyes shining happily. 'I wasn't, but Mum gave me the heads-up about the weather turning ghastly, so I decided to chuck my things into the car and head here pronto. It's ages since I was last in Lytell Stangdale, and I didn't want to risk missing Christmas dinner with the folks, or not being able to make my appointment with Caro Hammondely over at Danskelfe Castle.'

'Ooh, yes, congratulations, I'd heard you'd got the commission to design the interiors of the new lodges. You must be really excited about that!'

'I so am! I can't wait to get my teeth into it, my mind's been brimming with ideas.' She grinned, bouncing up and down on her heels. 'Anyway, enough about work, it's so good to see you, darling, we've got loads of catching up to do. I see you're looking as gorgeous as ever.' She appraised Ella, who didn't feel particularly gorgeous in her usual work garb of black skinny jeans and fitted white blouse which showed off her curves a little more than she was comfortable with. Her freshly-washed hair was hanging in loose, dark waves over her shoulders, the lighting picking out warm, glossy highlights, and though she wasn't usually one for much make-up, she'd given her lashes a flick of mascara, completing the look with a slick of raspberry-tinted gloss to her plump lips. Anyone would think she was hoping the handsome stranger she'd seen earlier that day might pop into the pub. Though, if anyone suggested it, Ella would argue fiercely that was definitely *not* the case; she was simply "making an effort for Christmas". Nothing more.

'Hmphh! I'm not so sure about that, and you certainly wouldn't have thought it if you'd seen me an hour ago when I still had half a ton of stuff from the school art cupboard in my hair. Don't let anyone ever tell you that glitter, glue and red paint is a good look. It's so not. And it's a flaming nightmare to get out,' Ella said, laughing as she slipped off her coat. 'Anyway, check you out, you're looking hot to trot yourself, lady. I'm loving those boots.'

'What, these old things?' Portia lifted an expensive-looking brogue ankle-boot in tan leather and gave it a wiggle. Just like her mother, she was effortlessly stylish. Ella always felt both women could wear a potato sack and make it look amazing. But, whereas Bea favoured a more classic look, her daughter's wardrobe had a younger, edgier, more urban vibe. Ella, who'd been described as a tomboy as far back as she could remember, favoured jeans and jumpers or t-shirts, and usually felt like a scruff alongside the two women, not that it bothered her. 'Anyway, honey, let me grab us both a cuppa and I'll join you behind the bar, then you can get me up-to-speed with all the goss before the place starts to fill up.'

Ella went to hang her coat up in the little store cupboard by the kitchen. 'I hate to disappoint you, but I'm not so sure there's much goss to tell. Don't forget this is a quiet little village in the middle of the North Yorkshire Moors; it's not exactly a buzzing metropolis.'

'Pfft! Who are you trying to kid? *Loads* happens here!' Portia said, her eyes widening as they always did when she was trying to emphasise a point. 'And you lot see *way* more action round here than I do in my little corner of Leeds. What about that predatory little wrinkly woman, for instance?' She waved her hand around, trying to remember the woman's name. 'You know, the one who looks like an over-cooked chicken, slaps her makeup on with a trowel and wears the most inappropriate clothing – too short, too tight, too revealing, too... hideous. Chases all the men in the village. Ughh!' Portia gave a mock shudder. 'Now, *she* provides loads of fodder for a juicy gossip and a good old laugh.'

'From that description, you can only mean Anita Matheson, or Maneater as everyone round here calls her.' Ella winced slightly at Portia's harsh critique of the village vamp.

'Yes, Maneater, that's the one. And I know I sound like a moo for talking about her like that, but I've no time for women who don't support other women, or go after married men.'

'You don't sound like a moo, Porsh, she's definitely not a woman's woman, that one. She'd happily trample over any of us to get to a man she wanted to get her claws into; I've seen her in action.'

'Hmm. Anyway, last time I was here, she was trying to convince poor old Dad of the benefits of tantric sex, even said she was prepared to give him a quick demo at her place if he fancied. Honestly, I've never seen those gangly legs of his move so fast; he shot out of the bar like a racehorse out of the starting gate. Mum found him cowering in the cellar, asking if it was safe to come out,' said Portia and the two friends hooted with laughter. 'He's never been the same since.'

'Oh, I remember that, it was hilarious.' Ella put her hand to her mouth to stifle her giggles. 'Poor old Jonty. He used to come out in a cold sweat and hide whenever she came into the bar for months afterwards. He'd practically do a commando-style crawl out of the place so he didn't risk her seeing him. Can't say I blame him; she has no shame, that one, and she's hard to shake off; just ask our Jimby.'

'Well,' said Portia, dragging the word out and lifting an eyebrow at Ella. 'I can kind of get where she's coming from with Jimby, he is rather cute. I'd go after him myself if he was single, that hot doctor from Danskelfe Surgery, Zander Gillespie too, but since – unlike Maneater – I don't chase married men, they're both safe from my amorous attentions.'

Ella laughed. 'Speaking of amour, how's your love life going? Did you end up going on a second date with that bloke... what was his name?'

'In answer to your first question: no, and in answer to your second: Dickhead,' Portia said matter-of-factly.

Ella made an "O" with her mouth. 'Can't say I've heard that name before. So what happened? I thought things sounded promising with him.'

'I thought so too,' Portia said, pressing her lips together. 'Actually, don't move, I'll just grab us that tea, then I'll bring you up-to-speed with "Dickhead-Gate" as I'm calling it.' She flashed a cheeky grin as she headed towards the kitchen. 'Two ticks.'

Ella smiled back, relieved to see her friend didn't seem too upset about it.

The two women had hit it off straight away on Portia's first visit to Lytell Stangdale almost six years ago. They'd become firm friends, sharing a dirty laugh, a mischievous sense of humour and a love of animals. Whenever Portia was over, the friends would meet for a coffee at the local teashop or take long walks over the moors with Bea and Jonty's rescue dogs, Nomad and Scruff, chatting away like they'd been friends forever. Portia was the first person Ella had confided in of her doubts about Owen, appreciating her friend's honesty. 'Sounds to me like the slimeball's screwing around. Time to kick him to the kerb and move on; he's not good enough for you, darling. I've never liked him, he has a shifty look to him.' Portia didn't sugarcoat things, which is how Ella liked it.

And Ella had been the first person with whom Portia had shared that she was attracted to girls as well as boys. They'd been walking the dogs up on Lytell Stangdale Rigg one summer's afternoon, it had been warm and the pair had dropped down on a wooden bench overlooking the dale, Nomad and Scruff flopping down on the ground beside them, tongues lolling, panting heavily. Ella had listened quietly, a barely discernible breeze skimming over her skin and lifting her hair, as Portia dropped into the conversation that she'd fallen for one of the girls who'd recently joined her friendship group back in Leeds.

'She's called Saffron, Saffy – even her name's pretty – and at first, I wasn't sure if it was just a "girl-crush",' Portia had said in her cut-glass accent, putting finger quotes around the phrase. 'I've had a couple of those, where I've sort of appreciated another girl's beauty, her cool sense of style... her mannerisms, you know, just kind of the way she *is*... without actually fancying her.' Portia had paused, rolling a piece of grass between her fingers. 'Then it gradually dawned on me that my feelings for Saffy ran a little deeper, that I actually properly fancied her.'

'And does Saffy know how you feel?' Ella had asked, squinting in the sunshine, wafting a bee away from her face.

'I think she does, and I'm kind of getting vibes back that she likes me too.' Portia had turned to Ella, her face breaking into a smile.

'Well, what are you waiting for? Ask her out on a date,' Ella had said, smiling back at her friend and nudging her with her elbow.

'You really think I should?' Portia had asked, her expression hopeful.

'Yes! Go for it!'

'You know what? I think I will, just as soon as I get back to Leeds.' Portia's smile had grown wider, her eyes twinkling. 'Thanks, Ella, I don't know what I'd do without your words of wisdom.'

Portia's time with Saffy had burnt hot but brief, with Saffy declaring she wasn't ready to settle into a steady relationship. Though Portia's heart had been badly bruised, she'd told Ella it hadn't stopped her being glad she'd taken her advice and that she was happy to have pinned her sexuality to the mast and had the confidence to be herself.

EIGHT

Joss

With Rich gone, Joss headed over to the table and picked up the crumpled sheet of paper covered in his brother's messy scrawl. He scanned it, taking in the list of jobs that needed doing, any quirks he'd need to know about. Apparently the diesel tank for the farm vehicles needed topping up, as did the oil tank for central heating, and there was only enough coal and logs in the shed for one more day. 'Handy,' Joss said aloud, wondering why Rich couldn't have organised this. *Surely he's still got access to the farm bank cards?*

He set the sheet of paper down and cast his eyes around the room. How long was it since the walls had been treated to a lick of paint or even a wipe down with a bucket of soapy water? he wondered. His gaze settled on the old butler's sink which was piled high with crockery. As for the worn flagstone floor, it looked like it hadn't seen a vacuum for months, never mind a mop. Joss couldn't shake the feeling there was more to his father's situation than Rich had shared with him.

He made his way through to the living room which looked equally pitiful, dust tickling his nostrils. Sid trotted around in his element, his nose never leaving the floor as he sniffed and snorted his way over every inch. Already from the little he'd seen of the old farmhouse, Joss could tell the set up was far removed from how it was when his mum was still alive. And there was nothing to suggest Christmas was just around the corner. She'd be mortified if she saw it now: cold, unkempt and unloved. His heart squeezed at the thought.

In the dog grate of the old inglenook fireplace he noted the ashy remains of a fire, long-since gone out. A handful of logs were stacked on the hearth beside it. His gaze was drawn to the photo on the mantlepiece. It was of his parents on their wedding day, occupying the same spot it had for as long as Joss could remember. He went over to it, lifting it down, his thumbs smoothing over the dust on the glass. A smile flickered over his face. His parents were looking out at him, their faces plump with youth, happiness dancing in their eyes; his mum, with confetti in her long dark hair, was laughing as she always was in his memories. Both were oblivious to the fact that their time together would be cut short so cruelly.

Joss felt his throat tighten and the sting of tears at the back of his eyes. He quickly set the photo down and headed out of the room, blinking quickly as he went. 'C'mon, Sid, let's see what else we can find,' he said, clicking his tongue.

Upstairs, the bathroom was cold and uninviting, a grubby towel thrown over the side of the old cast-iron bath, the lino on the floor cracked in places, while patches of mould speckled the walls. Joss sucked in a deep breath and ventured down the long landing towards his bedroom, the old floorboards creaking with every step, his eyes lifting to the bare light bulb hanging from the ceiling. He passed Rich's old room, stopping when he reached the one that used to be his. He paused with his hand on the Bakelite doorknob, his heart suddenly racing as he pushed at the Victorian pine door. It opened reluctantly, the hinges groaning loudly in complaint, like arthritic joints that hadn't moved for years. Tentatively, Joss peered in, holding in his mind's eye an image of how the room used to look. He stood in silence as his memories came crashing to the floor, swept away in an instant as he took in the sight before him. Gone was the blue and white striped duvet cover and matching curtains, the notice board with pictures of him and his friends, of Young Farmers' parties. Of Ella. Lots of Ella. His desk and chair, posters on the walls, all gone. Every piece of evidence of his existence had been removed.

Eradicated.

Sadness washed over him. *Why was I even thinking it would still look the same after all these years? After what had happened between us, Dad would hardly keep it as a shrine.*

He swallowed, composing himself as he took a step inside.

Like the other four bedrooms, this room was large and square, with age-darkened beams and a cast-iron fireplace – from which an icy draught was currently rushing down the chimney, the dusty cobwebs suspended within it fluttering tremulously. A layer of soot was scattered across the hearth. The walls had been painted a nondescript shade of cream, and the curtains had been replaced with an old floral pair that were a touch too short. The overall effect was characterless and tired.

Joss walked over to the large window, his eyes falling to the black mould that now darkened the edges of the frames; it too was festooned with grubby cobwebs. He peered out at the view over to Tinkel Bottom Farm, further down the valley. Ella's childhood home. His heart lifted. Even in the half-light and under a thick covering of snow, he could see it hadn't changed much from how he remembered it. Maybe a few of the rowan trees had grown a little taller, filled out a bit, but other than that, it seemed to be just the same as when he'd last looked out as a teenager. He was pleasantly surprised to find it a comforting sight. The vast fields that had been his playground spread out before him. His and Ella's playground, there wasn't an inch of them they didn't know when they were kids. Lights were on in the windows of the old farmhouse, and the cosy view made his heart ache with longing, taking him back to how he and Ella used to send signals with their torches when everyone else had gone to bed, meeting up for midnight feasts, hiding in the hedges, watching as the nocturnal creatures came to life. Ella used to love gazing up at the night sky, fascinated by the billions of stars that twinkled down at them, untarnished by light pollution. 'I wonder where the sky leads to,' she'd said one night as she sat beside him, her knees drawn up to her chest, her dark hair hanging in a curtain down her back. 'I mean, it's got to lead somewhere, hasn't it?'

'It just goes on to infinity,' he'd said softly.

'Infinity?' She'd turned to him, her eyes shining, and he'd nodded.

'Aye, infinity. Forever.'

'Wow! That's so awesome. Infinity,' she'd said again, as if trying it out for size. 'I love that word.' Since that night, Ella had become obsessed with the infinity symbol, doodling it everywhere: her school books, pencil cases, the desk in her bedroom. Sometimes, if they'd done their homework together, Joss would find one scribbled on his notes.

His memories triggered a hint of a smile; he wondered if Ella still held her fondness for the concept, and if her love of animals still ran as deep.

Ella had been a part of his life as far back as he could remember, taking up a huge chunk of his memories. A classic tomboy; she hated dresses with a passion, favouring jeans and t-shirts or rugby shirts. Added to that, she was fearless and bold; she had more guts than any of the boys in school, even Phillip Green, who was a right hard-knock. Joss remembered thinking it was cool that she wasn't like the other girls he knew who were terrified of spiders and worms and would run off shrieking if one came within four feet of them. And she didn't bat an eyelid at the frogs who ventured from the pond at the bottom of the field at her parents' farm, or the snakes they would happen upon while they were roaming the moors; she'd learnt at an early age to treat them with respect.

The pair had been inseparable, their August birthdays just two days apart. With Ella being the older of the two, she'd declared it had given her the right to boss him around and have the final decision on their games. Joss had learnt quickly she was a force to be reckoned with; it was best not to argue. Not that he minded. They'd been through playgroup and school together, attended the Young Farmers' rallies and dances together, shared a love of animals and the outdoors. They'd been best friends right up until the day he left.

It felt like a lifetime ago.

He pictured her face the last time he'd seen her; her expression of utter horror still haunted him. How she'd raced off. He clamped his hand to his forehead, the feelings of that day rushing back. *Ughh! What a mess I made of everything.* What he'd give to turn the clock back.

With sorrow and regret filling his heart, he turned and headed back downstairs. He had no time to indulge in self-pity when there was a herd of dairy cows in need of milking.

Once Joss had recovered from the shock of seeing how depleted his father's dairy herd had become – at twenty-six Holstein Friesians, it was a quarter of the size it used to be – he'd cracked on with the milking. The set-up in the milking parlour was the same as when he used to live here, and one he was still familiar with; the herring-bone system was also installed at Skeller Rigg Farm, albeit with slightly more up-to-date machinery. It meant milking hadn't taken as long as he'd expected.

With the cows safely ensconced back in their stalls in the barn, Joss set to, cleaning the parlour down, Rich's words ringing in his ears, anger pushing him on. '"Make sure you clean the milking parlour down properly",' he said, mocking his brother. 'As if I flaming-well wouldn't, Rich!'

That done, Joss headed across to the farmhouse, his breath hanging in the cold air as his feet crunched over the snow. The only other sound was the occasional baying from the herd echoing around the yard. He glanced up at the clear navy-blue sky, the Milky Way splashed across it in all its sparkling glory, a wisp of a cloud scudding over the pale moon. The wind, with its spiteful nip, was now sneaking around the buildings; it had picked up since he'd first gone into the milking parlour, though there'd been no more snow, much to his relief.

As soon as he opened the door to the kitchen, Sid flew out, his tail wagging so hard it was making his whole body wiggle, little whimpers of happiness escaping him. Once he'd finished dancing about and leaping up into the air, he nudged his head into his dad's hand and Joss obliged by rubbing his ears.

'Now then, fella. You been all right in here?' Joss laughed, pleased to see Sid hadn't been distressed by being left on his own in a strange house. Since complying with hygiene standards meant that milking parlours were out of bounds for dogs, Joss felt he had no alternative but to leave Sid in the farmhouse, but not before he'd made his canine pal comfortable. He'd pulled out a rug from the boot of his Land Rover and lay it out on the old clippy mat on the kitchen floor for Sid to curl up on, hoping the comforting, familiar smells retained by the rug would help him settle. Joss had also set up the electric heater Aunty Hannah had suggested he take – something he was thankful for since it had taken the edge off the chill in the room. It wasn't ideal, but it was the best he could do in the circumstances. 'If I'm not mistaken, Sid, there's a tiny hint of warmth in here,' he said.

Sid looked up at him and blinked, his tail thudding against the old pine dresser.

Joss's gaze swept the room, he was relieved to see no evidence of chewing. He felt a wave of affection for his furry companion, who'd clearly just curled up and patiently awaited his dad's return. 'I think someone deserves a treat, don't you? I'll grab you a couple of dog biscuits for now, but I'll see what I can find for you at the village shop tomorrow. You never know, there might be a tasty-looking chew with your name on it, Sid.'

Sid's tail wagging was cranked up several notches, his ears pricking up with interest. "Biscuit" was one of his favourite words

– alongside, "dinner", "treat" and "walk". He was also quite partial to "gravy" and "milk".

As Joss smoothed Sid's fluffy head, his eyes alighted on the old solid fuel Rayburn; it would no doubt need servicing, and the chimney sweeping. He stood, thoughtful for a moment. He'd be better off waiting to speak to his Aunty Babs before attempting to light it, the same went for the fire in the sitting room; she might have an idea of how long it had been since they'd been done. The last thing he needed was to be responsible for causing a chimney fire if either of the flues were playing host to a birds' nest. He winced at the thought of what his father would have to say about that. There was no doubting he'd have to get onto it quickly. A bone-numbing cold had taken a firm grip of the place – a sure sign it had been without heating for quite some time. It had crept into every corner of the building's bricks and mortar. Joss knew from experience, it would take a couple of days for the house to heat through properly, for the warmth to soak into the walls; old properties like this were notorious for it.

Since Rich had left in such haste, Joss wasn't sure if his brother had let Aunty Babs and Uncle Maff know of his presence at the farm; it was one of the many things his brother had neglected to share with him. Joss decided he'd call them in the morning rather than interrupt their evening. In any event, things weren't completely desperate; he'd already made up his mind that he and Sid would bed-down on the sofa in the sitting room for the night. He'd move the electric heater into the room and that, along with the warmth generated by Sid's solid, furry body, should hopefully mean he'd have a passable night's sleep. The option of spending the night in his old bedroom held little appeal; it would be cold and damp and he dreaded to think the last time the bed had been aired. Probably never. He shivered at the thought.

Joss hadn't felt hungry all day; his stomach hadn't stopped churning from the moment he'd opened his eyes, taking the edge off his appetite. But the familiar routine of milking had helped take his mind off his worries and his empty stomach was now grumbling at him.

With the Rayburn being off, he'd have to rustle-up something on the old electric oven his mum used to put into action when the stove was unlit, awaiting its annual service.

He checked the pantry and was shocked to see how sparsely-stocked the shelves were. He found himself wishing he'd had the foresight to stop off en route to gather some essentials. Amongst the few tins – soup, beans and tomatoes – were a handful of teabags in an old caddy he remembered from his days living there, an opened box of breakfast cereal, half a bag of dried pasta, a loaf of mouldy brown bread and a pack of crackers that had gone soft.

His heart sank and a wave of sympathy for his father rushed through him. If this was how he'd been living, then it was nothing short of pitiful. It was followed by the nagging feeling that kept rearing its head: there was more to the situation than Rich was letting on. It fuelled his need to get to the bottom of it.

Joss puffed out his cheeks and sighed. 'At least I had the fore-sight to bring a bagful of grub for you, fella,' he said, looking at Sid, who had a gluttonous appetite. 'Bet you're glad about that.'

Sid's tail swished across the floor.

Joss closed the door of the pantry on its less-than-tempting contents. His stomach was continuing its noisy complaint as a thought crept into his mind despite his initial promise to himself of not venturing into the village. Could he risk going to the Sunne for a meal? From the way it had looked when he drove by earlier, he reckoned the food there would be delicious. His stomach grumbled even louder as he visualised a plate piled high with piping-hot chicken and mushroom pie – his favourite – mashed potato, brightly-coloured vegetables and lashings of gravy. *Mmm. Heaven!* It stood in stark contrast to what he'd no doubt concoct for himself here: pasta mixed with one of the tins of tomatoes, or chicken soup. *Definitely not heaven! And definitely no contest!* He pushed his hands into the back pocket of his jeans, chewing on his bottom lip. 'Hmm.' Since there'd been no more snow, the roads should still be passable. And, from his memory, the pub was full of dimly-lit corners; he could slip into one of those and enjoy his meal anonymously and undisturbed. Plus, it was the Friday before Christmas, the pub was bound to be deadly quiet. He pictured a plateful of soggy pasta in tomato sauce and glanced down at Sid who was looking up at him expectantly. 'How do you fancy a trip into the village, lad?'

Sid's ears shot up.

Before he could change his mind, Joss strode over to the row of coat hooks by the kitchen door, Sid trotting beside him excitedly. He shrugged on his waxed jacket and reached for Sid's lead. 'Right, let's see what The Sunne Inne has to tempt our tastebuds, young man.'

Joss pulled up on the road opposite the pub and stilled the engine, his nerve suddenly deserting him. *What do you think you're doing? Don't you know you're tempting fate showing your face in there? Are you really so daft as to think no one will recognise you?* He sucked in a deep breath. Would he be better off just throwing together a bowl of pasta? It would definitely be the easier option. But it was hardly appetising and he was absolutely ravenous now. There was a lot of manual work to be done at the farm and he needed to keep his strength up. And he had to admit, The Sunne Inne did look inviting, with warm, golden light pouring from its stout mullioned windows, the fairy lights on the potted Christmas trees either side of the door twinkling away in the frosty air and its thick thatch covered with a blanket of snow. It looked every inch like a scene from a Christmas card.

'Hmm. What shall we do, Sid? Are we brave enough to risk it?'

But Sid was too busy watching a couple make their way along the trod before turning into the pub. The man pushed open the door and the heart-warming sound of laughter and chatter spilled out into the night. It looked so inviting, its appeal suddenly too great for Joss to resist.

'Right, come on, fella, let's go and find ourselves a nice quiet corner and see what The Sunne Inne has to offer,' said Joss, hunger and more than a little curiosity nudging his earlier resolution to keep well away from the village to one side.

As he pushed open the heavy oak door to the pub, his heart rate increasing, he was enveloped by a wall of warmth and the scrumptious aroma of roast dinner. His stomach growled in appreciation.

Joss took a couple of tentative steps into the bar area, and glanced around approvingly. The place had undergone a massive transformation and was barely recognisable from the notoriously scruffy dump it had been before he left.

A round of laughter drew his eyes to a table in the far corner by the fire where Jimby Fairfax was beaming broadly. He was sitting with a man who he'd swear was Ollie Cartwright. It probably was, he told himself, remembering that the two men had been best friends since forever and were rarely seen apart. The pair were sitting with a couple of men Joss definitely didn't recognise.

A young waiter hurried by, two well-filled plates of food in his hands. From the fleeting glance Joss was able to get, he clocked generous portions of roast beef and Yorkshire puddings with a mound of creamy mashed potato and jewel-coloured vegetables. *Mmm.* His stomach rumbled some more; he could polish that off quite nicely. Sid, who was pulling on the lead, his nose sniffing the air intently, clearly liked what he smelt too. In that moment, Joss was pleased he'd talked himself into venturing out.

He turned his gaze back to the bar where a tall, attractive blonde woman he could swear he'd never seen before was blatantly staring at him, her mouth hanging open. Next to her was Ella Welford. He stopped in his tracks, his face falling as myriad thoughts started crashing round his head. What should he say to Ella? How should he be with her? Would she remember him? *Of course she would, you bloomin' idiot!* And why was the blonde woman looking at him like that? Had Ella said something about him to her? Had Rich told people about him being back at the farm? Were people gossiping about him already? He suddenly felt swamped by anxiety and his pulse started whooshing in his ears. *Coming here was a mistake.* He needed to leave, and quick. He turned and beat a hasty retreat to the door.

Back in the Land Rover, Joss leant back into the headrest, anxiety squeezing tightly in his chest as he gripped onto the steering wheel. Seeing Ella had knocked the wind out of his sails. She'd grown even more beautiful than he remembered. Those huge, dark eyes of hers had triggered a somersault in his stomach. Evidently, his feelings for her hadn't disappeared, they'd just tucked themselves out of the way until now. It had been a mistake coming to the pub, and it could well have been a mistake coming back to the village.

He released a drawn-out sigh, Sid observing him closely.

'Sorry, buddy, I'm afraid it's back home for a plate of soggy pasta and a mug of tea.' He started the engine up and flicked the indicator on. 'Don't say we don't know how to live.'

NINE

Ella

'Oh, my days! Someone pinch me, quickly!'

'Pinch you?' Ella pulled her eyes away from the slice of lemon she was adding to a gin and tonic to see Portia's mouth hanging open, a bottle of wine stilled in her hand.

'Yes, my heart's *stampeding*, not to mention my libido.' Portia placed her hand on her chest. 'The man of my dreams has just walked in and he's heading this way. I need to be sure I'm not dreaming, that he's not a mirage. Oh, gosh.' She picked up a beer mat and fanned her face with it.

'The man of your dreams?' Ella said, grinning as she followed her friend's gaze but the door was closing; the gentleman in question had apparently already left.

'No! Don't go! Come back!' said Portia, looking crestfallen. 'Why's he leaving?'

'Maybe he thought the place looked too busy.'

'Or maybe I scared him off. Maybe he could read my wantonly wicked thoughts and was worried I was going to pounce on him.' She turned to Ella. 'Do you think I might've looked like some sort of predatory vixen and frightened the life out of him as soon as he clapped eyes on me?'

'Don't be daft, Porsh.' Ella couldn't help but chuckle. 'He could only have been in the place for about five seconds, how on earth do you think he could've come to that conclusion in such a short space of time?'

'Good point. Anyway, I still wouldn't mind giving him a good ravishing,' she said with a dirty laugh. 'He looked so tall and muscular and delicious. And those eyes... Mmm-mm.'

'You got all that from the few short seconds he was in here?'

'All that, and *more*.' Portia hitched an eyebrow, giving it a suggestive wiggle.

'I daren't ask.' Ella laughed, her mind drifting off to the hand-some stranger she'd seen earlier, the feeling that their paths had crossed before still niggling at her. What a shame she hadn't had a chance to get a better look at him.

Ella's shift at the pub had flown by, the waiting staff had been rushed off their feet, serving plates full of Bea's delicious food. Before she knew it, numbers had thinned and Jonty was calling time.

She pulled on her coat. 'Right, I'm off.' She flicked her hair out of the collar. 'I'll catch up with you tomorrow, Porsh.'

'Definitely.' Portia looked up from stacking dirty glasses on a tray. 'I'm meeting up with Lady Carolyn at some point, and I'm expecting to be up at the castle for a good few hours – weather permitting, of course – so we'll have to work it around that. If the snow's not too bad, maybe we could go for a walk sometime in the afternoon, if you'd like?'

'Yep, I like the sound of that, though we'll have to be careful where we go, I reckon the drifts could be quite deep in some places. I've promised to help my parents on the farm, what with Dad and Greg taking on some of the jobs up at the Campion's place while Bill's still in hospital.'

'Oh, yes, I'd heard he was poorly. I hope he's okay.'

'Me too. Hopefully, we'll be able to meet up when I get finished, if it's not too dark, that is. I think we'd better play it by ear.'

'Agreed. Why don't we just leave it that you'll text me when you're free? And if it doesn't pan out, I'll see you here in the evening – don't forget to warm-up your vocal chords for the sing-song,' Portia said, grinning.

The monthly "Songs at the Sunne" event, which was usually held on a Thursday, had been moved to the Saturday, with partici-pants requested to sing festive songs with a traditional, Yorkshire theme.

'Lalalalalaaaaaaa! That do you?' Ella chuckled at her attempt at fake opera.

Portia pulled a horrified face. 'I think it'll be kinder for everyone if you mime, darling.'

Ella feigned a sad expression. 'That's hurtful.'

'When you say "hurtful", I assume you're referring to your warbling?'

'Cheek!' said Ella, and the pair of them giggled. 'See you later.'

TEN

Joss

Joss woke to find Sid's whiskery face next to his and a crick in his neck. His canine companion was snoring, little puffs of doggy-breath sneaking out through his bushy beard. Joss pulled a face. 'Ughh, someone should have a serious word with you about oral hygiene, Sid,' he said, trying to ease himself up, wincing as he did so.

Sid blinked his eyes open and rewarded his dad with a lick across his cheek.

'Thanks – I think. I take it you slept better than me.' The sofa had proved to be lumpy and uncomfortable. Added to that, Sid had been a wriggly bed-fellow whose slumber had been punctuated by a series of lively dreams. Throughout the night, he'd treated Joss to a mixture of little yelps and rumbling growls, his paws twitching restlessly.

Sid wagged his tail. Joss rubbed the sore muscle in his neck and couldn't help but smile; the hound was nothing if not upbeat. 'If the cupboard wasn't so bare I'd offer you a share of a fry-up, but I'm afraid the best I can do until I get to the shops is a bowl of mangy cereal.'

Sid wagged his tail some more.

'You like the sound of that?' Joss lifted an eyebrow at him. 'Well, I wish I could say you had a discerning palate, young man, but that would be a big fat lie; we both know you'd eat a dead frog with as much enthusiasm as a medium-rare steak. And on the subject of dead frogs, if your breath's anything to go by, I wonder if you devoured one of those on the sly last night.'

Sid's tail wagging increased in vigour and he swiped his tongue across Joss's face once more.

'Ughh! I suppose I asked for that,' Joss said, ruffling his companion's head.

The uncomfortable sofa and Sid's fidgeting hadn't been the only reasons Joss had struggled to get to sleep. The minute he'd closed his eyes, all he could see was Ella's face, those big brown eyes of hers gazing back at him. It had made his heart race with a mixture of anxiety and longing. From the brief glimpses he'd snatched of her the previous day, he'd been surprised by the intensity of the reaction they'd triggered inside him, and now he knew it was going to be impossible to come into proper contact with her, or worse, run the risk of having a conversation with her; he'd only make a fool of himself. A bigger one than she already, no doubt, thought he was. He wouldn't know what to say anyway. And there was always the chance she wouldn't want to speak to him after all these years. After what he'd done, he couldn't blame her for that.

No, he decided, as he threw the blankets back and sat up, the best course of action would be to keep well out of her way. In fact, he thought it would probably be best if he kept out of the way of all Lytell Stangdale residents rather than run the risk of their questioning, or the risk of them mentioning that last fateful day before he left the village. Yes, the misdemeanour that had caused his hasty departure had been an accident, but it still hadn't lessened the shame of it to Joss. It was still excruciating, still had the power to make his insides twist whenever his mind decided to drag it out and parade it in front of his conscience, thinking of all the gossip it would have generated. Of that, there would have been plenty.

'Ughh!' He shuddered, trying to shake the thought away. And then there was his behaviour towards Ella. The memory of that made his stomach churn. Yes, he'd do what he needed to do here – contacting an agency and organising someone to step in and run the farm was by far the best option. A sudden thought struck him: had Rich told the Welfords he was here? Had he told them their help was no longer needed? Jeez, he hoped so. Either way, the sooner he could head back to Skeller Rigg Farm, the better. Coming face-to-face with any member of the Welford family didn't bear thinking about.

With milking out of the way, Joss had checked around the farm once daylight graced the moors. It was still bitingly cold, but there'd been no more snow as far as he could see. He'd tried ringing his Aunty Babs but there'd been no reply, and her mobile phone had gone straight to voicemail. He'd try again, once he'd got back from the little supermarket he'd spotted as he drove through Middleton-le-Moors the previous day. He decided going there to stock up on a few basics to tide him over was preferable to heading into the village, risking bumping into someone he knew. Someone like Ella.

Frustratingly, he'd had as much success getting hold of Rich as he'd had with Aunty Babs. He had a few questions relating to the farm, a pressing one being whether his brother had ordered a delivery of feed for the dairy herd which Joss had noticed was running worryingly low. Another was fuel, for both the central heating and the farm vehicles. Though Rich had mentioned there wasn't much of either left, he hadn't said if he'd ordered any to replenish it. And despite the fact they weren't sure how long their father was likely to remain in hospital, he'd still need to be warm when he was discharged. Joss needed to be sure both fuel tanks were topped up. More so than ever. It would help if he knew which companies the farm had accounts with, then he could check for himself and, if necessary, place an order. But since Rich hadn't shared these details, he was helpless. Joss had tried booting up the old farm computer, discovering he needed a password to gain access to it, but Rich hadn't left details for that either. Joss exhaled noisily. 'Talk about frustrating,' he said quietly to himself.

Frowning, he glanced around the kitchen, his eyes alighting on the drawers of the old pine dresser, so bulging with letters and envelopes they evidently wouldn't close properly. He toyed with the idea of having a rootle through them, hoping they'd throw up some answers, but quickly talked himself out of it; he'd feel he was being intrusive, overstepping the mark. What his father would have to say started ringing in his ears, causing his pulse rate to gather speed. No, it would be best to speak to Rich first.

He placed his mobile phone on the kitchen table and scratched his head. His wander around the farm had thrown up a few concerns. He'd noticed several places where the fences needed repairing, make-shift solutions blocking the gaps that had obviously been there for some time. Parts of the dry stone walls needed rebuilding too and he'd spotted a couple of barn doors hanging off their hinges. All things his father would have been onto straight away. A general air of shabbiness and neglect hung over the place – though he was pleased to see the dairy herd and sheep were well cared for and in tip-top condition. It was clear that his father had been ill for a while, but had he been having financial troubles too? If so, had they contributed to the decline in his health and subsequent collapse? A prickle of unease ran over Joss's skin. Though he and his dad were estranged, that thought didn't sit well with Joss.

Rich had been working on the farm until recently. What had *he* been doing in all of this? The responsibility and blame wasn't all down to their father; Rich could have fixed the fences and the barn doors, contacted someone to fix the dry stone walls. There was no excuse for the farm to be in such a sorry state.

Again, the feeling that there was something Rich wasn't telling him washed over him.

Joss sighed and reached for his keys. 'Right, Sid, there's nowt much we can do 'til we find out what's what. We might as well go and get some grub in before the weather changes. Let's brave it, let's go and see what Middleton-le-Moors has to offer.'

ELEVEN

Ella

Ella's little four-wheel drive bumped and bounced its way up the snow-covered track to Camplin Farm. How long since it had been resurfaced? she wondered. It had been years since she'd been along it. When she was younger and Joss still lived here, she used to take a shortcut across the fields to meet him.

As she rumbled over the cattle grid, a memory of rushing along the edge of the field that linked her parents' farm to the Campion's sprang into her mind. The sweet-smelling meadow grass, ripe and ready for silaging, swaying idly in the breeze, the sun warm on her skin, shining down from a bright blue sky. She found herself smiling, her heart filling with happiness, taking her by surprise. It was a far cry from today's weather, with the fields a sea of white as far as the eye could see, the hedges and dry stone walls dusted with snow.

Before she'd found herself heading to Camplin Farm, she'd called in on her parents at Tinkel Bottom Farm with a view to tackling a few jobs to help out, as well as the usual mucking out of Clive and the goats.

They'd shared a pot of tea at the kitchen table as they'd

discussed their plans for the day. Her mum had already mentioned her intention to head over to Arkleby to check on Grandma Cecily who was recovering from a hip replacement. 'I'd planned on heading up to Camplin Farm to give it a bit of a once over before Bill gets discharged from hospital, but I'll have to do that when I get back from your grandma's,' Debbie had said with a sigh. 'I bumped into Babs yesterday and she said she hadn't been there for a while. Seemed a bit concerned about the state of the house, though she didn't say it in so many words. I dare say it'll need a good warming through as well.'

'Worst thing Bill did was to push her away,' her dad had said.

'Aye, you're right there, Pete,' Debbie had said, shaking her head.

From the expression in her mum's eyes it had been clear to Ella she felt she was being pulled in all sorts of directions, trying to share herself around. Not what you needed on the run up to Christmas. 'I don't mind going over to help Grandma Cecily if that would help?'

'That's very kind of you, lovey, but she said something about some forms she wants me to sign, so I'd better go myself. And there's no point saying you could bring them back here; you know how set in her ways she is and likes things done just how she wants them.'

Ella nodded. Lovely as her grandmother was, her stubbornness was legendary in the Welford household; once she'd made up her mind about something there was no way of budging her. Even if a suggestion was made that would make things easier for herself or others, she'd refuse outright to entertain it and simply dig her heels in even harder. Her attitude had frustrated Ella's parents on more than one occasion.

'How about I go up to Camplin Farm then? I could make a start on getting it tidied up, get the fires lit.' She'd ignored the swirling in her gut her words had triggered, tried not to think about how odd it would feel going back there.

'I couldn't ask you to do that on your day off, Ella.'

'Why not? You'll be run ragged if you have to see to Grandma Cecily, then go up to Camplin Farm on top of everything else you've got going on.'

'Well, if you're sure?' Relief had lit up Debbie's eyes.

'Course she's sure, aren't you, flower?' her dad had said.

'I am, I don't want you wearing yourself out, Mum.'

'I suppose I could join you there straight from your grandma's.' Debbie had rubbed her hand over her chin as she'd thought it through. 'Would you mind taking a few tubs of casserole and putting them in Bill's freezer? Save me having to take it back and forth with me. I made extra for him and your grandma.'

'No probs at all, and there's no rush. Have a cup of tea with Dad before you join me.'

'Thanks, lovey.' Debbie had smiled gratefully at her daughter.

'Aye, I reckon Bill's going to need a fair bit of help when he gets out, much as he won't like it,' her dad had said. 'Mind, with the lights being on last night, I reckon Rich probably stayed over in case the weather got worse. Can't imagine Dawn liking that much.'

'Me neither.' Her had mum shot him a knowing look.

'I wonder if Joss knows? He might come and help out if he knew his dad was in hospital,' Ella had said, feeling a ripple in her stomach when she'd uttered his name.

'I doubt that, much as I think the lad has a right to know. But knowing how Bill still thinks of him, the last thing the stubborn old goat'll want is Joss turning up. It's a bloomin' shame that feud's lasted all these years,' Pete had said, shaking his head before taking a last gulp of his tea. 'Right, that's me done, lasses. Thanks for the breakfast, love, but I'd best get back to work.' He'd delivered a noisy kiss to his wife's cheek before heading to the door.

'You're very welcome.' Debbie had beamed up at him. 'I'll see you once I'm back from Grandma Cecily's, then I'll bob up to the Campion's to give our Ella a hand.'

'Aye, righto.' Pete had smiled, pushing his feet into his wellies.

'And I'd best go and see to Clive and the goats, then I'll head off; I need to pop in to the village shop, grab some cleaning bits and bobs,' Ella had said.

'Take some from here, lovey, there's plenty in the cupboard under the sink,' her mum had said.

'Thanks, but I need to stock up anyway,' Ella had said, rinsing her mug and placing it in the dishwasher.

The bell jangled noisily as Ella pushed the door of the village shop open, a wall of warmth greeting her. 'Hi, Lucy,' she said, smiling.

'Hiya, Ella, bet you're glad you've broken up for the Christmas holidays.' Lucy beamed at her.

'Too right, I was getting perilously close to glitter-overload.' Ella chuckled as she reached for a basket, dropping a large bottle of multi-purpose cleaner and a packet of cloths into it.

'And I'm getting perilously close to popping,' said a voice behind her.

Ella turned to see a heavily-pregnant Livvie Gillespie rubbing the small of her back, her lustrous auburn hair framing her face.

'Oh, Livvie, poor you. I'm surprised to see you tackling the icy roads from your little cottage on the moors.' Ella grabbed a bottle of anti-bacterial spray.

'They're not too bad actually, Camm's been up and down them with the plough a couple of times – just in case baby Gillespie decides to make an early appearance and we have to rush off to hospital – not that I think it will; I've had none of the warning signs I keep getting told about. Anyway, I was in desperate need of Lucy's homemade ginger chutney; my supplies are running dangerously low, so the journey was absolutely necessary.' She waved a jar of the pickle at Ella. 'I would've asked Zander to grab some for me but I just needed to pop into the studio, make sure I've got all my loose-ends tied up before I go on maternity leave, so I thought I'd risk it. It's interesting fitting behind the steering wheel, I can tell you,' she said, making the three of them laugh.

Livvie worked with Ella's cousin, Kitty Cartwright, and

Jimby's wife, Violet, designing and making wedding dresses and vintage-inspired underwear. Their studio was situated in the back garden of Sunshine Cottage; Vi's old home and where her parents now lived since they'd retired from farming. Livvie had been married to local GP Zander Gillespie for a year and, despite their plans to wait before they started a family, things hadn't gone quite as expected and four months after their wedding, she'd found herself pregnant.

'When did you say the baby's due, Liv?' asked Ella.

'Not for another three weeks – eighth of January – but Lord knows how I'm going to last that long. Surely I can't get any bigger; if I didn't know better, I'd think I was expecting quadruplets!' She smoothed a hand over her enormous bump, puffing out her cheeks.

They were distracted by the door opening and closing quickly as Violet Fairfax slipped into the shop looking hassled. Her arrival had just given them time to catch the sound of a cockerel squawking angrily outside

'You okay, Vi?' asked Lucy.

Vi smoothed her hand over the aubergine waves of her fifties-style bob. As ever, she was dressed immaculately, her make-up flawless. Today, she was wearing a fitted emerald-green woollen overcoat and amethyst leather boots, her handbag and leather gloves in complementary shades of purple. 'Honestly, Jimby needs to do something about that stupid bird of his. It's terrorising Hugh Heifer as we speak.'

'Ahh, by that I assume you mean Reg?'

'What else? The bloomin' thing's becoming a bigger nuisance than ever. I expect you'll have heard what he did to Rev Nev as he was cycling to the church earlier in the week?'

'Ooh, I did.' Lucy giggled. 'It was the first I knew he wore a toupee.'

'Same here,' said Vi, her green eyes sparkling.

'Well, he doesn't anymore,' said Ella and the three of them hooted with laughter.

'What was even more hilarious was seeing Rev Nev hurtling

down the road after Reg who'd run off with it between his beak. He was waving his fist and shouting, "Come back, you scoundrel".' Vi could barely speak for laughing. 'Jimby found it on the roadside a couple of days later, looking somewhat bedraggled.'

'Did he give it back to Rev Nev?' asked Ella, covering her mouth with her hand, her giggles spluttering between her fingers.

Vi's shoulders were shaking with mirth. 'No.' Her voice came out in a squeak. 'But I'll be sure to suggest it to him.'

A series of bellows from outside caught their attention. Lucy and Ella rushed to the door with Livvie waddling behind them as quickly as she was able. There they saw Hugh Heifer wearing his usual garb of grubby tweed overcoat, fastened around the middle with a length of twine, his threadbare flat cap covering the wispy hairs of his pate. His face was red with anger as he hurled a series of expletives at Reg who was perched on the back of Hugh's prize cow, Daisy – since his retirement from farming, Hugh had always kept a heifer from the treasured line he'd bred, always naming it Daisy.

'Oh no, poor Hugh,' said Lucy. 'Reg seems to have got it in for him too.'

They watched, fascinated, as Hugh untied the rope around Daisy's neck and fiddled about with it for a minute or two. All the while, Reg remained perched on the heifer's back, crowing boastfully and flapping his wings.

'Right, you little nuisance, let's see what you make of this,' said Hugh as he started whirling his make-shift lasso in the air. He aimed it at Reg, but the bird was too quick for him and shot off down the street in a flap of feathers, Hugh in hot pursuit – as much as his awkward gait would allow – leaving Daisy to complain woefully in the street. 'Get back here, you obnoxious little pest!' Hugh said. He didn't have a hope in hell of catching his quarry.

'Anyone who says life in the countryside is dull hasn't got a clue what they're talking about,' said Livvie. 'Trust me, in all my years of living in a town, I never saw anything half as entertaining as the stuff that happens here.'

'Yeah, much as I'm tempted to nag Jimby into getting rid of that bird, he's the source of so much entertainment, I haven't the heart,' said Vi.

'On that happy note, I'd better get the rest of what I need, then settle up.' Ella checked the contents of her basket and selected more cloths and another bottle of cleaning fluid.

'Looks like you're going to be busy this weekend,' said Lucy as she rang the items through the till.

'Yeah, I'm doing a spot of pre-Christmas cleaning.' Ella smiled. She didn't feel comfortable saying it was for Bill Campion's place, deciding to keep that detail to herself.

When Ella reached the farmyard at Camplin Farm, she was surprised to see no sign of Rich's vehicle. Instead, there were just a series of churned up by tyre marks and paw prints in the snow. Rich must have been and gone as quickly as possible. She gave a derisory snort; why didn't that surprise her?

She made her way carefully over the yard, making a mental note to text her dad and ask him to bring a load of grit with him. It wouldn't take much for the flagstones to become lethal if it thawed then froze; it was the last thing Bill would need to face fresh out of hospital.

The old farmhouse door opened with a creak and she cautiously stepped inside, a feeling of awkwardness gripping her. 'Hello,' she said, feeling almost like an intruder. No reply came. Her nose twitched at the unfamiliar musty smell. It had been eighteen years since she'd last set foot inside the house. Everything was exactly as she remembered it, though now an air of melancholy sat over the place, the cosy aroma of home cooking or clean washing that used to pervade the farmhouse long since gone. It didn't help that it was cold, though not as much as she'd been expecting. Her eyes alighted on the small electric heater; Rich must have brought that with him when he stayed over the previous night.

She placed the keys on the dresser and set her bag of cleaning supplies on the old oak table, the quietness of the house crowding round her. Shrugging the feeling away, she pulled her gloves off and stuffed them into her coat pockets before slipping that off and hanging it on the row of coat pegs by the door, just as she used to when she'd visited all those years ago. Cold as the house was, it would be easier to work without the confines of such a bulky garment, and she had a long-sleeved t-shirt under her navy V-neck jumper to keep her warm. Her hand went instinctively to her necklace, her fingers smoothing over the pendant as she surveyed the large room.

Ignoring the wave of sadness that washed over her at how unloved the old house felt, she pushed up her sleeves, determined to get things looking how they used to. 'Right, first things first, let's get this Rayburn on,' she said, rubbing her hands together. She knew the chimneys here had been recently swept since the sweep had said the farm was next on the list after hers at Rose Cottage just a couple of weeks earlier.

It took a few attempts at lighting both the Rayburn and the living room fire since the flues were so cold, impeding the draw, but it wasn't long before flames were dancing merrily in both appliances. Ella knew from memory that the Rayburn would have a tankful of hot water and be ready to cook on within a few hours, which was something Sue Campion had always said she'd loved about it. And Ella noted the low level of fuel and added logs to the list of things for her dad to drop off. She'd rung Paul Harker, the coalman from Danskelfe, explaining how low Bill's supply had got and he'd promised to drop off a load later that afternoon.

Next, working quickly in a bid to keep warm, and pushing aside the feeling she was intruding, Ella stripped Bill's bed, grabbed the pitiful towels from the bathroom and kitchen and bunged them into the washing machine on as hot a wash as she'd dare. With that humming into action, she gave the bathroom suite a thorough dousing with cleaning solution, did the same to the butler's sink in the kitchen and left the cleaner to work its magic. Then she fetched the vacuum from the utility room, popped her earbuds in, setting away her favourite playlist before launching into giving the floor a much-needed vacuuming.

All the while she was busying herself, thoughts of Joss filled her mind, memories of his tall, skinny frame, that had earnt him the nickname "Joss Stick" at secondary school in Middleton-le-Moors, in these very rooms. Her mum always used to describe him as having an "open face" which Ella had initially found strange until she understood what it meant. And, thinking back now, his open face had got him out of a host of scrapes, particularly when he was a teenager, relishing in his growing reputation as a joker when his pranks had backfired. It had made it easy for people to believe he was telling the truth when he said he hadn't meant to cause any harm. Until that last day. Nothing had been able help him then.

With all of the downstairs rooms vacuumed, Ella filled a bucket with hot water from the kettle – though the Rayburn had already started to warm the water in the tank, it still wasn't hot enough to cut through the grime of the paintwork. She set too, scrubbing at the door frames, the window sills, the deep skirting boards, a zingy, lemony scent filling the air. With a fresh bucket of soapy water, she grabbed a mop and tackled the age-smoothed flagstone floor with great gusto, her efforts warming her through until her cheeks were glowing pink and wisps of hair had escaped her ponytail.

Cleaning a neighbour's house wasn't how she'd expected to spend her Saturday – particularly the one before Christmas when there was still loads she needed to do for herself – but Ella relished getting stuck into a challenge. Hopefully, she'd get finished in plenty of time to meet up with Portia, though she was keen to get through as much here as possible, reluctant to leave her mum to do it. It had crossed her mind several times that Rich could have organised someone to come in to clean on a regular basis, especially since he knew his dad was struggling. But helping neighbours out was what you did round here and Ella wasn't going to argue with that. Her thoughts wandered over to Babs and Maff. Something had obviously happened to bring their involvement here to such an abrupt halt. No doubt Bill's temper had got the better of him and he'd said something unpleasant. What a shame he'd become so angry with life. He'd never been like that when Sue was alive.

Ella was pulled out of her thoughts when one of her favourite tracks came on. She turned up the sound and launched into song, dancing and shaking her hips as she pushed the mop around.

She was singing away at the top of her voice, wiggling her bottom in time to the music as she focussed the mop on a stubborn bit of dirt when she got the unnerving feeling she wasn't alone.

TWELVE

Joss

The roads to Middleton-le-Moors had been mostly clear but for a few patches on the more exposed areas where the dry, Alpine-like snow was still being blown across from the moortop.

Joss had quickly nipped into the supermarket on the outskirts of town. He'd cracked open the front passenger window of the Land Rover and left Sid in the vehicle while he stocked up, promising him a walk on the way back. The jolly festive music had been at odds with his sombre mood and he'd been thankful to find the shop was relatively quiet, and even more thankful he hadn't spotted any faces from the past, which was always a possibility even though Middleton-le-Moors was ten miles away. And, much as he was tempted to take a look around the old Georgian square edged with tasteful shops in the town, he'd thought better of it. His mind cast back to the old-fashioned toyshop he and Rich had loved to visit as small boys, the sense of excitement as they'd caught sight of the huge Christmas tree that dominated the square, it's lights twinkling merrily. The shop windows were always beautifully decorated at the best of times, but at Christmas the store owners really pushed the boat out, their stunning festive creations becoming more elaborate with each passing year.

The bell of the old lichen-covered church rang out loud and clear, announcing the hour of eleven. The morning was whizzing by and Joss still hadn't made any of the phone calls on his list. He needed to get a wriggle on.

'I see you've been a good lad,' he said to Sid, opening the rear door and depositing the bags of shopping. 'And, if you're thinking there might be something with your name on in one of these bags, then you'd be right.'

Sid gave a little bark, his tail sweeping happily over the seat. Joss couldn't help but grin at his upbeat companion.

As promised, on the way back, he parked up near a lane end and let Sid have a run around, laughing as the Labrador took great leaps into the deep snow before rolling in it, kicking his legs about frantically. A pheasant perched on a gate post looked on in disapproval before taking flight in an angry cackle, the rich tones of its feathers a contrast to the stark white of the land. Sid ceased rolling and leapt to his feet, watching as the bird skimmed over the field before disappearing into the small cluster of trees.

'Don't think he was very impressed, do you, fella?' Joss asked, feeling the cold nip at his exposed face.

Sid turned to look at Joss before snorting and charging over to his dad, shaking the clumps of snow from his body.

'Arghh! Thanks for that,' said Joss, laughing. 'And I suspect you're going to smell rather charming on the way home; I clearly didn't think this through or I'd have brought a towel for you.' He opened the passenger door and Sid leapt in, oblivious to his dad's concerns.

Back at the farm, Joss was puzzled to see a small four-wheel drive in the yard. His heart sank; he knew it didn't belong to Rich nor Aunty Babs and Uncle Maff. Groaning inwardly, he climbed out of the Land Rover; he really wasn't in the mood to face anyone local, or to have to explain himself, or answer a million questions. 'You stay here a minute, Sid.' He glanced around the buildings but there was no sign of anyone. As he headed to the house he could hear the strains of a woman's voice, it sounded like she was singing – badly, at that. Tentatively, he pushed the door open and stepped inside.

His heart stilled and his breath caught in his throat as he took in a woman dancing around the kitchen, her singing every bit as enthusiastic as the way she was attacking the floor with a mop. He couldn't stop the corners of his mouth quirking into a smile.

As if sensing someone watching her, the woman turned. 'Omigod!' She let go of the mop as if it was on fire, sending it clattering to the floor, her face turning puce as she clasped her hands to her chest. 'You scared the bloomin' life out of me!'

His heart started racing. It was her! It was Ella. He blinked back at her, his smile wavering, no words forthcoming.

'Oh, er... um... sorry, I didn't hear you come in. I, erm... I had these in,' she said, giving an embarrassed smile as she removed her earbuds. 'If you're after Rich, I'm afraid he's not here.'

Joss stood rooted to the spot for several seconds. 'Ella,' was all he could manage when he finally spoke. His gaze ran over her face, the dark-brown eyes that were still a regular feature of his thoughts, her brows – every bit as wild and unruly as he remembered – the full lips he'd... *Best not go there*, he told himself, swallowing. It hadn't escaped his notice that her figure had filled out into gentle curves. It sent a pulse of lust shooting through him. The thought of feeling her in his arms, those curves pressed against his body, burst into his mind. He quickly blinked his wayward thoughts away.

She looked at him, blankly at first, her expression changing as realisation slowly dawned. She gasped, her eyes growing wide. 'Joss?'

He nodded. 'Yeah, it's me.' His eyes went to her necklace, settling on the infinity symbol. She still wore it. After all these years? His mind started racing, as he tried to make sense of the scene before him.

Ella gulped, absently fingering the pendant of her necklace. 'When? I mean... how? No way! When did you get here?'

'Yesterday evening.' He wished his heart would stop thudding so loudly; it was distracting. 'I got a call from Rich...' He felt his emotions rising, knocking him off guard; he didn't know what else to say without making a fool of himself.

'Right.' She nodded, smoothing her hand over her hair. 'I was just having a bit of a tidy round before your dad comes home. I've lit the Rayburn and the fire in the living room, though it'll be tomorrow before the place warms through properly.'

Joss nodded, clearing his throat, glancing around. Things certainly looked neater and cleaner than when he'd left. 'Oh, okay. Thanks.'

'Would you prefer it if I left?' she asked, biting her bottom lip, her eyes uncertain.

'No. Not at all.' He stepped towards her, forgetting himself for a moment.

A loaded silence stretched out between them as their eyes locked. Ella was the first to speak. 'So, I'm guessing you've heard about your dad then?'

Joss nodded. Her voice was just as he remembered, though the lightness of youth had been erased by maturity just a smidgeon. Still, he'd know it anywhere, of that he had no doubt. 'Yeah, Rich brought me up to speed the night before last.' He was struggling to tear his eyes away from her. She was every bit as beautiful as he remembered. More so. Memories of his clumsy gesture the last time he saw her, of what she'd said to him, were pushed out of his mind. For now, he was utterly mesmerised. No other woman had ever aroused these feelings in him.

'How long are you staying for?' She softened the question with a smile, her dark eyes looking at him intently.

'Erm, I'm not sure.' He cleared his throat again. 'I don't know how long my dad's going to be in hospital for; I'm not really sure what's wrong with him at the moment, and I've noticed there are a few things that need fixing on the farm.'

'Hmm.' She nodded.

For a brief moment, Joss felt she was going to say something else, but a hint in her eyes told him she was holding back. Was she about to lay into him about staying away, or did she know something more about the situation than he did? Did she have the answers to the questions that had been puzzling him since he arrived? He had a nagging suspicion she probably did.

'Don't suppose you fancy a cuppa, do you?' he asked, a hopeful expression replacing his frown.

Her face brightened. 'Are you sure? I mean, I don't expect one.'

'Seems to me you've earnt one after doing all this work. I've got some chocolate biscuits too.'

'Chocolate biscuits? Now you're talking, there's no way I could refuse one of those,' said Ella, grinning.

The tension suddenly lifted. Joss found himself returning her smile. 'I'll just go and bring the shopping in from the Landie,' he said, his heart feeling lighter.

THIRTEEN

Ella

Ella watched Joss head towards the door, her stomach doing somersaults. He was the mystery man she'd seen driving by in the Land Rover yesterday. And the last person she'd expected to see in this house today. Any day, come to think of it. A flurry of thoughts began bombarding her mind: did Bill know his son was here? How much of what had happened had Rich told him? Not the whole story, of that she was sure. What had he been doing with his life since he left? She'd caught snippets of information from her parents, but the details were always scant, since Bill pretty much refused to speak about his son. Most information came via Babs and Maff. And, oh, he'd grown so tall and handsome. She felt a buzz of attraction run through her.

Snapping out of her thoughts, she picked up the mop and bucket, standing them out of the way against the wall, then went to fill the electric kettle.

She'd just set it down and clicked it on when the sound of claws on the flagstone filled her ears. She turned to see a black ball of fur hurtling towards her, its pink tongue lolling from the side of its mouth.

'Sid! Stop!' Joss was standing in the doorway, a concerned expression on his face.

But Sid was apparently hard of hearing and lunged at Ella, his fluffy tail wagging hard.

Ella roared with laughter as she fussed her new friend. 'Well, hello there. Aren't you just gorgeous, eh?'

Joss clapped his hand to his forehead. 'I'm so sorry. He's too friendly for his own good and thinks everyone's the same as him. And I'm afraid he's wet; he's been rolling in the snow.' He made his way over to Ella and his wayward hound, taking hold of Sid's collar. 'Come on, trouble, that's enough. Ella doesn't want you slobbering all over her.'

'Honestly, it's fine, I really don't mind. Trust me, I've had worse slobber.'

Joss's eyebrows shot up and he caught her eye. 'I'm talking about dogs!' she said with a giggle.

'Oh, right. I'm glad you clarified that.' A grin pulled at the corners of his mouth.

She shot him an amused look. 'Someone brought a St Bernard into the pub once. It took a real shine to me. Trust me, they drool buckets.'

Joss pulled a face at the thought.

'But this boy, Sid did you say his name is?'

Joss nodded. 'Yes, Sidney, to give him his full title, but he mostly gets Sid, well, that and other select names depending upon his behaviour – a few of which are running through my mind right now.'

Ella chuckled. 'Well, Sid is just gorgeous.' She bent and ruffled his ears and Sid looked up at her adoringly.

'From the way he's looking at you, I reckon the feeling's mutual.'

At the kitchen table, Ella poured tea into two mugs and passed one to Joss. 'There you go,' she said with a small smile. It felt strange to be playing hostess in his former home; she wondered if he thought so too.

'Thanks. Biscuit?' He pushed the plate towards her.

'Mm.' She took one, nibbling on it, acutely aware of the awkwardness that hovered around them. She rested her gaze on Sid who was sitting by the Rayburn, his eyes glued to the plate of biscuits.

'So,' Joss said slowly. 'How've you been keeping?'

Ella felt her stomach squeeze. How could such a simple question ask so much? She drew in a deep breath. 'I've been fine. I've been working at the school as a teaching assistant since I left college, and I do a couple of shifts a week at the pub.' She paused, taking a sip of her tea, peering over the rim of her mug. 'How about you?' She'd noticed his eyes dropping to the infinity pendant around her neck.

'I've been okay.' He gave a small shrug. 'Been working at Skeller Rigg for my aunt and uncle, as you probably know. I live in a barn conversion on the farm there. Have done for a couple of years now. Still pop over to the main house for one of Aunty Hannah's breakfasts and the odd meal.'

Ella nodded, she'd heard about him living in the barn conversion. 'Sounds good.'

'Aye, it's not a bad life. How about you? Are you still rescuing all sorts of abandoned or injured animals?'

Ella grinned. 'So it would seem. I've been adopted by a cat, found myself owner of two guinea pigs—'

'Guinea pigs?' He nodded, smiling. 'I remember you always had a couple of guinea pigs when we were kids; they used to squeak like mad when you went near them rustling a bag of carrots.'

'They did.' She smiled back, touched that he'd remembered. 'And I have a donkey – Clive – who I adopted from the sanctuary yon side of Middleton-le-Moors and two goats – Clover and Dandy – who I got through the local vet, Chris Crabtree, but those three are at my parents' farm since there's not enough room in the back garden of the cottage I rent –Rose Cottage, from Ollie Cartwright, remember him?'

'Course; he's a few years older than us. He was Jimby Fairfax's best friend.'

'Still is, and he's Jimby's brother-in-law now too.'

'Ah, yes, I'd forgotten he'd married Kitty.' A flicker of a smile crossed his lips. 'I think those two were destined to be together.'

'You're not the first person to have said that.' Ella looked across at him, her eyes meeting his. 'And how about you? Is there a significant other in your life?'

Joss sat back and blew out his breath. 'I'm resolutely single since my marriage came to a very messy end last year.'

Ella had heard a whisper he'd been married and that it had fallen apart in less than a year. 'I'm sorry to hear that.'

'Don't be. Unlike Kitty and Ollie who were destined to be together, Manda and me weren't. We were polar opposites; we should never have got married. I don't know what I was thinking. But, hey...'

Ella didn't know how to respond and just gave a sympathetic smile. 'More tea?'

'Please.' Joss nodded, pushing his mug towards her. 'And how about you? Word hasn't filtered through to Helderthorpe that you've tied the knot.'

Ella shook her head and gave a laugh. 'Nope, there's no chance of that for the foreseeable, thank goodness. I was with someone for three years but it didn't work out, and now I'm enjoying the single life. I've promised myself not to get involved with anyone for a good while yet.'

'Ahh.'

Silence stretched out between them again. Ella stole a look at him, his strong jaw peppered with dark-golden stubble, his green-blue eyes, edged with thick, dark lashes, thick, straight brows sitting above. His lips were full, just how she remembered them, making her heart flip. And judging by the layer of muscle that was evident despite his winter layers, he definitely couldn't be described as skinny now. As for those broad shoulders... *Oh, my days, he's grown so handsome.*

Joss sighed, dragging his hand down his face, pulling her out of her daydreams. 'Do you ever think about that last day?' His eyes searched hers.

Ella bowed her head and gave a barely discernible nod. 'Of course; it's impossible to forget.' In truth, she thought about it almost every day; she'd never forgiven herself. Her actions had been the catalyst to Joss being banished from his home.

She looked at him, regret filling her chest and squeezing tight. 'I'm so sorry, Joss. If I hadn't reacted the way I did, you would never have had to leave.'

His brow crumpled and he looked at her askance. 'Why are you sorry? You had nothing to do with it; the blame rests fully with me. If I hadn't behaved like a knob twice that day, none of it would've happened.'

FOURTEEN

EIGHTEEN YEARS EARLIER

Joss

Joss watched Ella saunter along the track towards him from Tinkel Bottom Farm, her thumbs hooked into the handles of a backpack, her long, dark ponytail swinging from side-to-side. She was wearing a pair of frayed cut-off jeans and a white t-shirt with thin straps. He liked her in that top. Dust kicked up from her white plimsolls with every step. It was the third week in August and the weather had been dry and hot. She caught sight of him and waved enthusiastically, her face lighting up. 'Hiya,' she called, her voice echoing around the dale. He felt his heart lilt with happiness.

'Now then. Got some stuff for the picnic?' Joss asked, beaming, his eyes scrunched against the bright sunshine as he walked towards her. He felt a shimmer of happiness rush over him to see she was wearing the silver necklace he'd given her for her sixteenth birthday a week earlier.

'Yep.' She squinted up at him, gesturing with her thumb to her backpack.

'Cool.' He tried not stare but it was proving difficult. She looked so beautiful; her cheeks pink like a rosy apple.

They set off along the bridle path, heading towards their

favourite spot, Arncliffe Crag – so called because it was where eagles were regularly seen circling in years gone by. But the eagles had long-since left the area and Ella and Joss had claimed the rocky shelf for themselves. Not being visible from the track, hidden by the statuesque fronds of bracken over the summer months, meant its location wasn't known to many.

The pair made their way along the track, the sky above a vast expanse of cloudless cornflower blue, the sun a golden ball, beating down relentlessly. The moors were resplendent in their summer finery and swathes of rich, purple heather hugged the ground, punctuated by odd patches of charcoaled land where the local gamekeepers had carried out their annual burning sessions. Lower down the valley side, the fields were set out in luscious shades of green, the odd one filled with golden stubble where the grass had been cut for winter silage. All were neatly edged by centuries old dry stone walls or hawthorn hedges. The sound of crickets chirping rang in their ears, while in the distance a curlew's distinctive cries reverberated around the dale, mingling with the plaintive bleating of the sheep that roamed the moors. Ella was chatting away about the duck she'd rescued from the clutches of one of the farm cats. 'I know I can't blame the cat, she was only following her instincts, but I really wish she wouldn't chase other creatures. Anyway, the vet put a splint on Desmond's leg, said he'll be right as rain in no time.'

Joss chuckled. 'Only you would call a duck Desmond.'

'Well, it's no different to Donald, and no one complains about that, do they?'

'S'pose not,' he said, giving a small shrug.

Soon, they'd reached the crag, their agile, young legs scrambling down to where the land formed a small sandstone plateau. Joss pulled the picnic rug from his backpack and spread it out while Ella smoothed the corners. In no time, they'd had their lunch set out, a delicious mixture of home-cured ham sandwiches, slices of Ella's mum's famous quiche, Scotch eggs, a selection of crisps, and chicken drumsticks. There was chocolate brownie and a punnet of juicy strawberries for afterwards. To wash it all down, they had a bottle of homemade lemonade courtesy of Aunty Babs.

'Man, I'm *starving*,' said Joss as he admired their feast. He'd had a relentless growing spurt over the last six months which had stretched him long and skinny. Already, at the age of just sixteen, he was over six feet tall and towered above his friends, particularly Ella.

'Just as well there's loads to get stuck into then,' she said with a giggle. 'Here, try this Scotch egg; I made it yesterday.'

Joss sank his teeth into it, rolling his eyes in ecstasy, the yolk still semi-runny, just the way he liked them. 'Mmm. S'good,' he said through his mouthful. Ella beamed.

'Still like your necklace?' he asked.

'I love it,' she said, her hand reaching for the pendant, sliding it back and forth on the chain. She'd seen it in the window of the little jewellers in Middleton-le-Moors one afternoon when the school bus was late.

'Look! That's the infinity symbol,' she'd said, pointing to it, her voice shrill with excitement. 'You know, like the sky and the stars. It's my absolute favourite thing.'

'Where?'

'There. It's on that silver chain, the one to the right of the one with the stars. Third row down, fifth across.'

'Oh, aye, so it is,' said Joss, an idea germinating in his mind as the bus rumbled into the square. 'Come on, if we're not quick, we'll miss it,' he'd said, grabbing hold of the arm of her blazer and pulling her along to the stop.

'All right, keep your hair on!' She'd laughed, struggling to keep up with his long strides.

Once his stomach was full and what little was left of the food had been packed away – except for the strawberries Ella was still nibbling on – Joss lay back on the rug, resting his arm across his face as he watched a buzzard circling overhead, aware of a bumblebee buzzing nearby. Ella sat beside him, leaning back on her hands, her knees drawn up. Joss felt his eyes go to the lacy strap of her vest top that had slipped off her shoulder, taking in the freckles that led to the nape of her neck where fine hairs were curly and damp with perspiration. His gaze dropped to her breast, the fabric of the t-shirt hugging the curve revealing she wasn't wearing a bra.

'Phwahh!' He tore his eyes away, the pent-up feelings for her that had been brewing inside him for months now were in serious danger of breaking free. They'd been best friends since forever and he wasn't sure how she'd welcome finding out his feelings had changed. That they'd blossomed into something very different to friendship.

'You okay?' Ella turned to him, her lips stained red from the strawberries, sending a wayward pulse through his body.

'Yeah, just a bit hot.' He struggled to make eye contact with her, the silent battle raging inside him ready to surface at any moment.

'I know what you mean,' she said. 'And this ponytail's giving me a right flippin' headache.' She dragged the bobble off, pushing it onto her wrist, letting her hair fall free before laying down beside him.

Having her in such close proximity, her familiar scent gently wafting his way, was too much for Joss to bear. He pushed himself up on his elbows and tried to focus on something else, anything that didn't make him think of Ella. He pinned his gaze on a tractor making its way slowly across one of the fields at Oak Tree Farm. Jimby or his dad, John, would be driving it.

Ella released a contented sigh and the urge to look at her was too strong to resist. Turning, he saw she had her eyes shut, one arm stretched above her head. His eyes drank in her glossy, dark hair splayed out around her, the long, dark lashes resting on her cheeks, her dewy, sun-kissed skin, the handful of freckles that peppered her nose, his gaze finally coming to rest on her plump, red-stained lips.

Before he knew what he was doing, Joss was bent over her. Resting a hand against her cheek, he tenderly pressed his lips to hers. *Oh, man!* The feeling was incredible. He felt her hand reach up and grip the back of his head, his kisses becoming more urgent, his tongue seeking hers, emotions washing over him in an almighty wave. He groaned, he had no idea how he was going to stop this, not that he wanted to.

'What the heck are you doing?' Her voice was sharp in his ear.

Before he had a chance to marshal his thoughts, Joss felt himself being pushed backwards, their moment evaporating into the air around them. Ella leapt to her feet, her eyes flashing with a fury he'd never seen before. 'What did you have to go and do that for, you turkey?' He pulled himself up and she shoved his shoulder angrily. 'Don't you realise you've ruined everything now? Everything!' With that, she pushed the last of her things into her back pack and shrugged it angrily onto her shoulders. As she turned to leave she looked back at him, her face like thunder. 'Keep away from me. I never want to see you again.'

No! 'Ella! Don't say that! I'm sorry! I got it wrong. Please come back!' He scurried off the crag and clambered up onto the track, watching as she stomped away, a trickle of sweat running down his back. 'Please, can't we just forget it ever happened?' He threw his arms up despairingly.

But his pleas fell on stony ground and she continued without looking back, ignoring him. He swung back down onto the crag, flopping onto the blanket, his head in his hands. 'What have I done?' He gave his face a slap. 'You absolute dickhead!' *How could I get it so wrong? I was sure she was kissing me back. Arghh!* 'Ella's right, I am a turkey,' Joss said to a grouse that had flown down and landed on a rock not far from him.

FIFTEEN

Ella

Ella stomped her way along the bridle path, her heart pumping, sweat prickling her brow. Why did he have to go and do that? 'Stupid, stupid boy!' she said loudly, sending a couple of sheep scurrying over the heather. Didn't he realise they were best friends? *Friends* being the operative word. But now he'd gone and ruined that friendship. There wasn't a hope in hell they could go back to how they were before. Before that kiss.

That kiss. If she was being completely honest with herself she might be tempted to admit she'd found herself quite liking it, might be tempted to admit she might possibly have kissed him back... actually, scrap that. He'd overstepped the mark, crossed the boundaries of their friendship and tried to turn it into something it wasn't; something it could never be. And now everything was ruined. All because he'd been a stupid, weak boy.

'Ughh!' Ella stomped even faster. 'Lads are a nothing but a pain in the bum!'

'You all right, Ella?'

'Uhh?' She turned to see local gamekeeper, Pip Pennock,

looking at her, an amused smile hovering over his lips. 'Yes, I'm fine, thanks. I'm just on my way home.'

His smile widened. 'Our Moll's at home if you fancy popping in on her. The twins are driving her bonkers, I reckon she'd welcome a visit. I can bob you over there in the off-roader if you fancy?' He nodded towards the vehicle in question.

Ella thought about it for a moment. If she went back home now, the way she was feeling, her mum would rumble there was something wrong between her and Joss; the last thing she wanted was to tell her they'd actually locked lips. That would be way too embarrassing. 'Aye, I like the idea of that. Thanks, Pip.'

'Ooh, Ells, you're a sight for sore eyes.' Molly greeted her with a smile. 'Mind, you look all hot and bothered with yourself. The twins are asleep – thank heavens. They've been little monsters all morning – we can take a cold drink through to the living room; it's nice and cool in there.'

Ella followed her cousin down to the living room, the cooler air skimming over her skin like a sigh of relief.

'Park your pants wherever you fancy,' said Molly, pushing her dark curls off her forehead and perching on the end of a squishy armchair, scrutinising Ella all the while. 'So what's made you have a face like a slapped backside?'

'Boy trouble.' Ella rolled her eyes and took a sip of her drink, setting the ice cubes rattling. A welcome wave of cold flooded her chest.

'Ahh.' Molly nodded slowly. 'And when you say *boy* trouble, am I right in assuming you mean a certain boy by the name of Joss Campion?'

Ella felt her cheeks burn. 'Mm-hm.' She hardly dared look Molly in the eye.

'Well, as far as I can see, Joss is a nice enough lad.'

'He is. He was. I mean, he's my best friend but...'

'But he wants to be more than friends?' Molly said, taking a sip from her glass.

'Yeah.' Ella nodded, feeling her face burn hotter than ever.

'And why would that be so bad? You get on really well, some would argue that's a pretty good starting point.'

Ella heaved a sigh. 'I just don't think about him in that way,' she said, flicking her hand dismissively.

'Right.' Annoyingly, Molly didn't sound convinced.

'And, say, if we did date, and it didn't work out, we could never go back to being best mates again, could we? I'd hate that, Joss has been my best friend since forever; I never want to lose that.'

'And would it be nosy of me to ask what's brought all this about? Feel free to tell me to keep my beak out, I won't be offended.' Molly laughed, sitting back in her chair.

Ella puffed out her cheeks, summoning the courage to say the words. She took a gulp of her drink, swallowing noisily. 'He kissed me.' She felt her face prickle with embarrassment. 'Just now. On the moor at Arncliffe Crag. I ran into Pip just after.'

'Oh, flippin' 'eck. He's got it bad then.' Molly's chuckle made Ella laugh too.

'Don't say that!'

'Can you imagine how much courage that'll have taken the lad? Bless him. And I'm guessing you didn't respond how he'd hoped.'

You kissed him back, said a little voice as the feeling of his lips on hers, warm and tender and delicious, slipped into her mind, releasing butterflies in her stomach. Ella coughed. 'I, erm, I pushed him away. Told him he was a turkey and walked off.' Ella winced as she recalled the look of pure mortification on his face.

'Ouch.'

'I know.' Guilt flooded Ella's veins. 'I feel bad for shouting at him, but... well... it was just so unexpected. A total shocker. I mean, it's not as if we'd discussed anything like that. Ever! Oh, God,' she said, clamping her hand to her brow. 'What can I do to put it right?

To make him realise I'm not still mad at him? This is such a mess.' She looked at Molly, her eyes full of remorse.

'You need to talk to him. Give him a few days; his pride'll be hurt and he'll be feeling embarrassed, I should imagine. But given time, I reckon things'll be right as rain between the two of you. You haven't been best mates for this long for it not to be.'

Ella sucked in a deep breath, feeling suddenly brighter. 'Thanks, Moll. I'm glad I could talk to you. I'll let him have a bit of space like you say, then I'll text him, see if he wants to meet up.' She smiled at her cousin, feeling a weight lift from her shoulders and float away.

SIXTEEN

Joss

Joss watched Ella climb into Pip's off-roader and drive off, his heart aching, his mind whirling. What he'd give to turn the clock back; he'd have kept his stupid wayward lips to himself.

He'd been trying to catch up with her, but she was stomping at such a determined rate even his lanky legs were finding it a struggle. It was unbearably hot too and it didn't help that there was no shade up here on the exposed moortop, the sun's burning rays stretching far and wide. With his eyes fixed to the ground, Joss strode on, only stopping when a snake shimmied across the path in front of him, bearing the distinctive black zig-zag pattern of an adder. Growing up in the countryside meant Joss had a healthy respect for wildlife. The reptile hadn't scared him; he knew it would be more fearful of him, and he stood in silence until it disappeared amongst the heather. Anyway, he thought, as he continued on his way, a venomous snake was the least of his worries today. Losing his lifelong best buddy because of his own stupidity was far worse than that.

His mind kept replaying the look in Ella's eyes when she was shouting at him. It was like a punch in the gut. 'Oh, jeez,' he said, pushing his hand through his damp hair. 'Ella's right, I'm a turkey and I've ruined everything.'

When he reached home, he burst through the door and stormed to his bedroom, speaking to no one.

'Whose pinched your teddy?' Rich shouted after him, followed by an elongated, 'Ooh,' when Joss slammed his bedroom door.

Joss threw himself down on his bed, covering his face with his arms, feeling the threat of tears burning. He sniffed and leapt up, swiping his fingers beneath his eyes and started pacing around his room, his heart hammering in his chest. 'Why did I have to go and do it?' He tapped his knuckles against his head which was already pounding. He felt hot and clammy. His t-shirt was clinging to him so he headed for a shower, turning the dial to cold, letting the water run over his face, hoping it would wash this horrible feeling away.

Afterwards, he felt no better so he headed downstairs.

'What's up with you, knobhead?' asked Rich, who was washing his hands at the sink.

'Nowt.' Joss grabbed the tractor keys off the worktop and headed for the door.

'Where are you going with them?'

'Where d'you think?'

'Duh! I wouldn't ask if I knew.'

'I'm going to check on the sheep in the bottom field.'

'Does Dad know?'

Joss stopped in the doorway. 'He doesn't need to; I'm helping out. Saving him a job, which is more than you're doing, sitting around on your lazy backside all day. So you can back off.'

Rich went to retaliate but Joss was out of the door and across the yard before he had the chance.

He climbed up into the cab of the tractor and started it up, rumbling his way out to the track that led away from the farmhouse. He hadn't really intended to check on the sheep, that had been a lie to get Rich off his back. He just needed to get away from the house before Aunty Babs arrived with their dinner, and started asking questions. Joss knew she meant well, but he really wasn't in the mood for it. He felt a sudden pang of loss for his mum, squeezing in his chest, gripping ever tighter. How he wished she was here to talk to; she'd understand how he felt, why he'd done what he did. She'd know the right words. She'd know how to stop him feeling like the biggest loser in North Yorkshire. But he'd lost her and now he'd lost Ella. A tear trickled down his cheek.

With the sheep checked, Joss trundled along the twisting country lanes to Arkleby and Danskelfe. He knew he was taking a risk being out on public roads without passing his test, but he'd been driving the tractor since he was twelve and he'd got his provisional licence; he knew how to handle it; he'd take it steady. But one thing was for sure, he wasn't ready to head home just yet. He passed the sign at the lane end of Tinkel Bottom Farm, wondering what Ella was doing, wondering if she'd told her family about his stupid behaviour. He cringed at that thought.

Back at Camplin Farm, Rich met him before Joss had had chance to stop the tractor. 'Where the hell've you been?' he asked, swatting a fly away from his face impatiently.

'You know where I've been.'

'You've been gone a long bloomin' while. You'd better get your backside in there.' He nodded towards the house. 'Dad's that mad he's bouncing off the walls. Says he's going to give you a right bollocking for taking the tractor without telling him. Reckons he didn't know where it'd gone, thought it'd been nicked.' There was a gleam of pleasure in Rich's eyes.

Could this day get any worse? Joss jumped down from the cab and shut the door, his brows knitting together. Best get this over and done with, he thought. He'd park the tractor in its usual place once his dad had finished with him. 'But you knew I'd got it. You could've told him I was checking the flock.'

'Not my problem, mate,' Rich said with a smirk.

Rich's warning proved right; their dad went ballistic with Joss, yelling at him for being irresponsible for leaving farm land in the tractor, refusing to listen to Joss's argument of thinking he was helping out. Rich had looked on, sniggering, until their father sent him out.

The sooner I can leave this place, the better, Joss thought when his dad had finished wiping the floor with him, promising himself that's exactly what he'd do just as soon as he was old enough.

After today, there was nothing to keep him here.

Remembering where he'd left the tractor, and knowing it would further infuriate his father even more so – if that was possible! – he thought he'd best go and move it to its usual place in the stone outbuilding. 'Am I okay to put the tractor away, Dad? It's just parked at the end of the house.'

Bill rolled his eyes, his temper lowered to a simmer. 'Aye, you'd better had.'

Joss scooped up the keys and headed into the yard. Dusk was just beginning to settle and midges hovered in the cooler air. He drew in a deep breath; much as he was relieved to have got the rollocking over and done with, his heart still felt heavy. He trudged his way to the side of the building, stopping in his tracks, his mouth agape.

The tractor had gone.

Had Rich put it away? Joss doubted it. His eyes fell to the ground, following a set of tracks that led to the fence where a gaping hole looked back at him accusingly. A barn owl hooted from the large oak tree just by, sending a shiver up his spine. Joss's gaze travelled all the way down to the bottom of the field to see the fence there had been ripped through and what appeared to be a tractor lying at an angle in the pond.

'Oh, no!'

SEVENTEEN

Ella

'I can't believe it,' said Ella's mum. 'I just can't believe Bill's done that to his lad.' She was standing in the kitchen at Tinkel Bottom Farm, her hand pressed to her mouth, her face drained of colour.

'Can't believe he's done what?' asked Ella, padding into the room in her pyjamas, her hair all over the place, the crease of her pillow imprinted on her cheek. She stopped and her stomach twisted; she knew instinctively it was something to do with Joss and not Rich.

She'd struggled to get to sleep the previous night, what had happened between her and Joss playing over and over in her mind. She couldn't wait for the couple of days' breathing space to be up, then she could text him. She'd finally drifted off to sleep just as the first strains of the dawn chorus started up, and had slept right through to just gone eleven o'clock.

'Oh, lovey, you're not going to like this.' Debbie rushed over and pulled Ella into a hug, squeezing her tight and smoothing her hair. Ella could hardly breathe.

'Mum! Just tell me, will you?'

'Sorry, sweetheart.' She released her daughter, the look of disbelief still troubling her features.

'What's happened?' Panic was creeping up Ella's spine. 'What's Bill done? Is it Joss?'

'Oh, lovey, he's sent Joss away.'

'What?' Ella's pulse started whooshing in her ears. She pulled out a chair and collapsed onto it. 'He's sent Joss away? Where?' *Please, God, make it not be because of me.* Her breath was coming in short bursts. She felt suddenly stifled.

'I'm afraid you missed all the drama while you were in bed – I did check on you to make sure you were okay, but you were absolutely flat out, so I didn't like to disturb you; you obviously had some sleep to catch up on.'

'Drama? What drama?' Ella tried to keep the impatience out of her voice, not wanting to take her frustration out on her mum. 'And where's he sent Joss? And why?'

It transpired that Joss hadn't put the tractor into gear properly and the vehicle had slowly inched forward on the incline, gradually gathering speed until it tore through the fence, hurtled down the field, all the while, gaining momentum, before it ripped through the boundary fence to Tinkel Bottom Farm, ending up in the pond.

Ella clapped her hand to her mouth. 'Oh, my god! How did that happen? And why's Joss getting the blame?'

'Joss was the last one to use the tractor. And that's not all; before it landed in the pond, it hit our off-roader; took it with it.'

Ella couldn't believe what she was hearing. Poor Joss, his day had gone from bad to worse. 'Can either of the vehicles be saved?'

Her mum shook her head. ''Fraid not, lovey. Regardless of the effects of the water, the Campion's tractor rolled part way down; it's in a bit of a state. The off-roader's not come off too good either.'

An icy hand gripped Ella's heart. 'Why was the off-roader down there? Are Dad and Greg okay?' she asked, her words coming out in a gabble.

Debbie nodded. 'Yes, thankfully. Your dad was here when it

happened but Greg had been seeing to a sheep that had got its head fast in the wire of the fence. Said he couldn't' believe his eyes. Doesn't bear thinking about if it had happened a minute or two later.' She gave a shudder.

Ella felt her stomach churning as she processed the turn of events.

'But what about Joss? He wasn't in the tractor, was he?'

'No, by all accounts he'd parked it up and gone in the house.' Her mum went over to her, wrapping her arm around her shoulder. 'He came and apologised first thing. In a right state he was. Later on, Bill showed up, told us he'd sent him packing to his brother, Joe's, over in Helderthorpe. Says he never wants to set eyes on him again. Poor lad, said he's been nothing but trouble. Can you believe he'd say something like that about his own son?' Tears shone in Debbie's eyes. She was fond of Joss who'd been a regular visitor to the farm over the years, treating their home as his own, just as Ella had his.

Ella jumped up, startling her mum. The urge to see Joss was suddenly overwhelming. 'Are you sure he's gone? How was he getting there? I need to talk to him before he goes.' Tears were swimming in her eyes.

'Ella, lovey, it's too late; he's been gone hours. Babs and Maff took him first thing apparently. If he hasn't been in touch yet, I'm sure he will be as soon as he's settled there.'

Ella ran to her bedroom, tears streaming down her cheeks, a feeling of utter helplessness enveloping her. If it hadn't been for how she'd spoken to Joss, he wouldn't have been distracted; he would've remembered to put the tractor in gear, and none of this would have happened.

She was the one to blame, not Joss.

EIGHTEEN

PRESENT DAY

Joss

'How long are you planning on staying for?' Ella asked.

Joss blew out his cheeks and scratched his head. 'I'm not sure. Not long probably. I'm needed back at Skeller Rigg Farm. I was actually hoping to hire someone from an agency to help. With Rich no longer working here, Dad can't manage the farm on his own, and he can't rely on your family's kindness forever; we need to get something sorted and fast.' He felt a pang of guilt that was at odds with his loyalties to his aunt and uncle.

'Does your dad know you're back?'

Joss gave a sardonic laugh. 'I don't know. Probably not, or he'd have leapt out of the hospital bed and charged over here in a rage telling me to clear off in no uncertain terms.'

Ella gave him a sympathetic smile. She paused for a moment as if mulling something over. 'Have you got any plans for tonight? Only the Sunne are having their monthly music night and it's always brilliant fun.'

'Will you be there?'

'Yes, but not in a work capacity; it's my night off. Honestly, you wouldn't recognise the place since you were last here. The new owners, Bea and Jonty, have spent a fortune doing it up and there's a brilliant atmosphere, especially on the run up to Christmas. The food's pretty amazing too, and Bea puts a buffet on when it's music night.'

'You sell it well,' he said with a grin. He didn't like to mention his brief visit the previous evening; he felt suddenly foolish for turning tail the way he had. It melded with relief she hadn't spotted him.

'Well, if you fancy popping in, you'd be very welcome.'

'I'm not sure... it's been a while...' The thought of facing a host of locals still didn't feel too tempting.

'That's all the more reason to join us.' She gave him a smile that made his heart lift. 'You don't have to stay long; but it's got to be better than being stuck up here on your own while the place is warming up. And Bea makes the best chicken and mushroom pie ever; you could order one of those if the sound of the buffet doesn't tempt you.'

She remembered! Ella remembered his favourite dinner, after all these years.

'And everyone would be chuffed to bits to see you.'

'Really?'

'Of course they would, Joss. People missed you when you'd gone,' she said softly, sending a ripple of mixed emotions through him.

Had she missed him? He'd missed her, more than he could ever articulate. He'd spent years trying to put her out of his mind and thought he'd done a good job. Until now, and all those feelings had come rushing back. He cleared his throat. 'Well, our Rich wouldn't be pleased to see me there, that's for sure,' he said with a laugh.

'Rich?' Ella's smile dropped. 'He hasn't been in the pub for donkey's years.'

The way she said his brother's name, with a thinly veiled snarl, would suggest she wasn't keen on him. He couldn't recall picking up on that when they were younger.

Just then, the sound of a vehicle arriving in the yard caught their attention and they both turned to the window. Sid's ears pricked up in interest.

'It's my mum.' Ella headed towards the door. 'She's been at Grandma Cecily's this morning – she's recovering from a hip replacement. Mum said she'd pop up here and give me a hand with the cleaning when she got back.'

'Oh.' Joss didn't know what else to add to that. Nerves started churning in his stomach. He hadn't seen Debbie Welford, nor her husband, since the morning after the accident when he'd gone to apologise for his actions. Feeling suddenly awkward, he got to his feet as Ella's mum appeared in the doorway. Sid rushed over, sniffing at the carrier bags she was holding, his tail wagging as vigorously as ever.

'Hello there, lovey,' she said to Ella. 'Smells lemony fresh in here, you've obviously been a busy bee.' With her arms laden, she bustled through the door her daughter was holding open. 'And who's this fluffy boy?' She nodded to Sid. 'Oh, hello there.' She stopped in her tracks, looking at Joss, puzzled.

'Mum, it's Joss,' said Ella, a smile in her voice. 'And this is his dog, Sid.'

Though Debbie had never been anything but kind to him when he was a boy, Joss braced himself for a barrage of angry words or sounds of disapproval. He looked at her, anxiety flickering in his eyes.

'Joss? Joss Campion?' Debbie said in disbelief.

'Hi, Debbie.' He rubbed the back of his neck, giving her a hesitant smile.

'Well I never. And there's no need to look so terrified, lad. Come here.' She went over to the table, dumped her shopping on it and wrapped her arms around him. 'It's good to see you, Joss. You've been away too long.' She released him, wiping a tear from her eye.

'It's good to see you too, Debbie.' A wave of relief washed over him. She'd always had a generous heart and he was glad to see that kindness still extended to him.

'Blimey, you're even taller than I remember but not so skinny – no one'll be able to call you Joss Stick anymore and get away with it.' She chuckled and patted his arm. 'And Pete's going to be thrilled to bits when he hears you're here, lovey.'

'How's Pete doing?' Joss asked. He was doubtful he'd get such a warm welcome from her husband, him still being such a good friend of his dad's.

'He's grand, thanks. Keeping busy, as always. You know how it is.' She beamed at Ella. 'Any more tea in that pot, chick? I'm parched. I didn't have time to stop off at home; Grandma Cecily kept me busy.'

'Course. How's she doing?'

'Fighting fit, as ever. Grumbling about the old fella over the road from her, something about him leaving his rubbish bin out longer than necessary; it's very annoying apparently.' She shook her head and chuckled.

'Ah, well, as long as she's on the mend.' Ella smiled fondly and went to fetch another mug from the cupboard.

The three of them sat round the table, sipping tea, Ella's mum asking how things had been for Joss at his aunt and uncle's farm, listening to his replies with interest. She and Ella filled him in on the changes that had taken place in Lytell Stangdale and the villages nearby. Whenever Rich was touched upon, Joss noticed both women seemed uncomfortable, disapproving almost. It piqued his interest further.

Out of the blue, he found himself sucking in a fortifying breath. It was time to broach the elephant in the room. *Here goes.* He let a couple of beats pass. 'I want you to know, Debbie, that I'm truly sorry for my careless actions that night. I was foolish and irresponsible and I'd give anything to turn time back to that day. I'd change so many things if I could.' He sensed Ella shuffle in her seat opposite but resisted the urge to look at her. 'There's not a day goes by when I don't regret it.'

Debbie put her hand over his, concern etched on her face. 'There's really no need to apologise any more. You gave your apologies at the time and it saddens me to think you've been beating yourself up all of these years. Mind, the way you were punished for it beggars belief...' Her voice tailed off.

'You and Pete took it so well, I felt so ashamed.' He felt his throat tightening and swallowed down a lump.

'Pete and me could see that you were torturing yourself enough, never mind what your dad doled out; we didn't think it necessary to add to that. We couldn't make head nor tail of his actions. As far as we were concerned, you'd been through enough already, what with losing your mum so young. And the situation with the tractor, well, that was a plain and simple accident.'

Joss took her hand, giving it a squeeze. 'Thank you, Debbie, you've always been lovely.' He glanced across at Ella to see her eyes shining with tears. She returned his watery smile.

'Anyway, that's all in the past now.' Debbie sat up straight in her chair, clapping her hands together. 'I don't think we need to waste any more time talking about it. As far as Pete and me are concerned, it's all forgotten and we moved on years ago, which is exactly what you should do, Joss. Life's too short. Anyway, how long are you planning on staying? And when are you going to join us for a meal?'

Joss laughed. 'To be honest, I don't expect I'll be staying long.' He went on to explain his plans, watching her expression change when he mentioned getting someone in to help.

'Hmm. Your dad'll hate that.'

'The thing is, he needs help here – thank you for all you and your family have done, by the way, it's much appreciated – but I think we've put on you too long.'

'It's what friends do. But I take your point, Bill definitely needs another pair of hands now Rich has moved on.'

There was that disapproving tone of voice again.

It struck Joss that Ella had been quiet for a while. He looked across to see her hand on the infinity pendant, moving it back and forth on the silver chain. He caught her gaze which seemed to prompt her to speak. 'Are you going to visit your dad in hospital while you're here?' she asked.

The question caught him off guard. 'Oh, erm... I don't know... I'm not so sure he'd want to see me.' He released a sigh. 'It's been a long time...'

'Hmm.' Debbie pushed her lips together, looking thoughtful. 'How about you join us for lunch tomorrow? Ella will be there as well. Pete and me had planned on going to see Bill afterwards, provided the weather behaves itself that is. You're very welcome to come with us, if you feel up to it.'

He knew Debbie meant well, but this was exactly why he hadn't wanted to run into anyone; he hadn't wanted to fend off situations like this, hadn't wanted to look bad by saying he had no intentions of seeing his father. His eyes flicked to Ella, unsure of how to reply without sounding rude or uncaring.

He was relieved when she came to his rescue. 'Mum! Joss hasn't been here five minutes, give him time to catch his breath. When I asked if he planned on visiting his dad, I didn't mean to pin him down to a date and time.' She turned to Joss. 'Please excuse my mother, her heart's in the right place.' She rolled her eyes good-naturedly.

Debbie's hand flew to her mouth, her face glowing a vivid beet-root red. 'Oh, no! I didn't mean to sound pushy, I was just letting you know what we were doing, that's all. I'll shut up and go and put this stuff away.' She got to her feet and scooped up the carrier bags of essentials she'd picked up at the village shop. 'But you're still very welcome to join us for lunch tomorrow if you fancy. We usually have it about twelve but there's really no pressure.'

Debbie's suggestion had served as a catalyst to the three of them ploughing on with their jobs, despite Joss's protestations that they'd already done more than enough. Satisfied that he didn't feel they were interfering, Ella headed upstairs with the vacuum cleaner while Debbie set to making Bill's bed and putting fresh bedding on the one in Joss's old bedroom.

. . .

Ella came downstairs to see Joss at the old farm computer in the small room off the living room. He had papers strewn around the desk, a puzzled expression crumpling his brow. There was just the two of them and Sid at the house. Her mum had left half an hour earlier, reminding Joss of the lunch invitation as she went.

'Everything okay?' Ella asked from the hallway.

'Not really, no. I don't suppose you know which company the farm has an account with for animal feed, do you? Or where we get oil from? Or diesel come to that? Rich said they're all running low so I thought I'd better get stocked up, only thing is, he hasn't left me with any details.'

'Hm. I'm not sure.' Ella tucked the vacuum cleaner away in the cupboard under the stairs and headed over, stopping in the doorway. Sid trotted over to her, nudging her hand with his fluffy head. She obliged by ruffling his ears. 'I expect it's the same ones we use. I could check with my dad, he'll probably know.' Her eyes landed on the computer. 'Can't you find out from the records on there?'

'I dare say I could if only I was able to get into the flippin' thing. Rich didn't leave the password either and he's not answering my calls or texts.' Joss ran his hand across his chin.

'Really? I wonder why?' she said.

He definitely hadn't imagined the note of scorn in her voice or the barely-discernible hitch of her eyebrows, not to mention the look of disapproval that fleeted across her face. He didn't recall Ella disliking his brother so intensely. Something had clearly happened to bring it about. He made a mental note to ask her about it later; it didn't feel right to put her on the spot at the moment.

Joss flopped back in the chair and puffed out his cheeks. He'd made little progress since their earlier cup of tea. After spending an age trying to log on to the computer, he'd had a root around the masses of mixed up bits of paper he'd found in the drawers of the desk, albeit reluctantly. He'd hoped to come across some correspondence revealing the contact details of the farm's suppliers, or even something with the password scribbled on it. But his search had proved futile. Fed up with that, he'd used his phone to Google farm contract workers, but none of the companies he'd spoken to had anyone available on their books. 'Blast!' he'd said as he ended the call with the last one on his list. All he'd managed to achieve was wasting a huge chunk of time. Joss hated wasting time. He reminded himself that at least he'd managed to get a timber delivery for Monday, that was something positive. On his trip to Middleton-le-Moors, he'd spotted the sign for a builder's merchants a mile out of the town and followed them to a small industrial estate. There, he'd picked up a few supplies, as well as placing an order for wood to fix the damaged fences he'd spotted on the farm. They'd need seeing to as soon as possible. He'd also grabbed half-a-dozen bags of logs from the unit two doors down while he was there.

'I'm heading off now, but I'll see what I can find out from my dad if you like?' Ella said.

Joss exhaled noisily. 'Yeah, I'd appreciate that.'

Though they'd spent several hours under the same roof, there was still a hint of awkwardness between them. Hardly surprising in such a bizarre set of circumstances, he thought.

'Don't forget what I said about the Sunne tonight. It's usually a laugh, and you look like you could do with one. Sid would be welcome too.'

'Thanks. And thanks for all you've done today. It means a lot.' Joss mustered up a smile.

'Hey, no probs. Like my mum said, it's what friends do.'

He got to his feet and followed her down the hall to the kitchen where she took her coat from the peg.

'Take it steady on the roads,' he said as he saw her to the door.

She smiled up at him, her brown eyes soft. 'I will.'

With his hands in his jeans pockets, he stepped out into the yard, watching as she let her car warm up for a few minutes, allowing the windows to demist. Sid sat beside him, looking on with interest. The cold air snapped sharp in contrast to the newly warm indoors. She rubbed a circle in the condensation of the passenger window and waved before pulling away, leaving his heart racing.

'Well, Sid, what d'you make of that?'

Sid replied with a whimper and a swish of his tail.

NINETEEN

Ella

The car was freezing cold; Ella had turned the air vents on full blast in a bid to demist the windscreen and it was taking ages for the air to warm up. She drove carefully down the track from Camplin Farm. The temperature had dropped since she'd first arrived and already she could see frost glinting on the snow. Though it was only two-thirty in the afternoon, dusk was already creeping in. The crisp, winter-blue sky of earlier that day had taken on a more sombre hue and clouds were gathering in the distance, huddling together as if conspiring to make mischief. Ella shivered as she drove on. Lights were flickering in the windows of the farmhouses in the dale, making them look achingly cosy. She imagined the fires roaring away in the old fireplaces, the rooms decorated for the festive season with Christmas trees, their fairy lights twinkling, pine scent filling the air.

After week-long forecasts and multiple severe weather warnings, Ella had been expecting the village to be hit with another load of snow that day. Yes, it was bone-numbingly cold but an uncanny quietness had settled over the moors. It meant she'd kept an eye on the sky from the windows during her time at Camplin Farm. Years of moorland winters had told her to be wary; this was merely the calm before the storm.

As she drove on, she was relieved to see the road to the village was clear and had been well-gritted. *What would we do without Camm?* Hopefully it would stay that way until after the big day.

Her thoughts turned to Joss. Joss Campion! Who'd have thought he'd turn up out of the blue like that? Looking all handsome and rugged too. He was the last person she'd expected to see when she got up that morning. She felt a ripple in her stomach. Though he'd changed physically, he still had the same smile that had regularly crept into her mind over the last eighteen years. She felt a bite of regret. What if she hadn't reacted the way she had when he'd kissed her? Would they have grown closer or would it have eventually pushed them apart?

That, she thought as she pulled up outside Rose Cottage, was something they'd never know. *And you might as well get him right out of your mind. You had your chance eighteen years ago and you blew it. And he isn't going to be hanging around anyway. He's made that perfectly clear. His life isn't here anymore. It's miles away.*

The pub was already packed when Ella arrived just after seven. She made her way over to the bar where Portia was pulling a pint for local cycling enthusiast Len – who'd swapped his usual cycling gear for navy chinos and a smart shirt – while chatting away to his lady friend, Rhoda.

'Hello, darling.' Portia's face lit up when she saw Ella. 'Such a shame we didn't get a chance to meet up today but I just got so engrossed talking to Lady Caro, I completely lost track of time.'

'Hi, Porsh. No worries, we can make up for it tonight.' Ella fished her purse out of her bag. 'Hi, Len, hi, Rhoda.' She smiled at the pair.

'Now then,' said Len, taking his pint from Portia, creamy froth running down the sides. 'By, that looks good.'

'Hello, lovey. Bet you're glad you've broken up for a few weeks.

When I used to teach, we were on our last legs by the end of term.'
Rhoda beamed at her. She was Livvie's step-mum and had moved
to the village earlier in the year when her fledgling romance with
Len had blossomed.

'I love the kids to bits, but I can't lie, the thought of a couple of
weeks away from school is bliss.'

'Hiya, Ella.' Ella turned to see her cousin Kitty smiling at her,
her pretty elfin face glowing in the soft light. 'I know it's absolutely
chocca but there's a spare couple of seats at our table if you fancy
having one. Rosie and Robbie can't make it apparently.'

'Ooh, I might take you up on that, thanks, Kitts.' She turned
back to Portia who'd already poured her a glass of Pinot Grigio. 'I'll
be over at the table by the fire when you get a free moment. Take
for a drink for yourself out of that,' she said, handing her friend a
ten pound note.

'Thank you muchly, think I'll join you in a wine. Brogan
should be here any moment, so she'll be able to take over.'

Ella wove her way across the bar to the fireplace where a sea of
smiling faces and a chorus of cheery hellos greeted her.

'Ella, chick, it's good to see you,' said Molly. 'Come and park
your bum.'

'Now then, lass.' Jimby beamed at her, pint in hand. 'Did you
get all them parcels under the tree?'

'I did, thanks, Jimby. And dare I ask, how are the bruises?'

'Vibrant,' said Vi, chuckling into her gin and tonic. 'He's got a
right beauty on his left butt cheek. I took a photo if you fancy a
look?'

Molly mimed a gagging gesture, shaking her head. 'Please,
spare us.'

'Woah, calm your jets there, Vi,' said Ollie holding his hands
up. 'We're here to have a good time tonight and seeing Jimby's
backside is the last thing we need.'

'Hear, hear,' said Camm, his dark eyes twinkling as he
chuckled heartily.

'I'll have you know I have a rather fine pair of pert buttocks, even if I do say so myself, as my lady wife can testify,' Jimby said with fake pride.

'Dare I ask why we're talking about Jimby's bottom?' Kitty returned to the table, sliding onto the banquette alongside husband Ollie.

'It's covered in an array of bruises after he landed on it yesterday,' said Vi, arching a perfectly-sculpted aubergine eyebrow. 'Not a pretty sight.'

Kitty pulled a face, making the others laugh. 'Much as I hope you're all right, Jimby, I'd rather not hear any more about your bum.'

'Sounds like a good time to change the subject,' said Ella, taking a sip of her wine. 'I've solved the mystery of that smart Landie that caught your eye yesterday, Jimby.'

'Oh, aye.' He looked at her with interest.

'What Landie's this?' asked Ollie.

'Uh-oh. Here we go. Diving straight into talking Landies, tractors and tups before we've finished our first drinks. Doesn't bode well for us, lasses. I reckon you're going to regret starting this conversation, Ella; you'll be bored rigid in half an hour.' Molly winked at her.

Ella giggled. 'Well, I reckon it won't end up where you're expecting.'

'Ooh, the plot thickens.' Jimby grinned. 'Come on then, put me out of my misery.'

'It belongs to Joss Campion.' She looked around the group, watching a variety of confused expressions.

'Don't think I know a Joss Campion,' said Camm.

'Joss Campion as in Pete's lad you mean?' asked Ollie.

'Never!' said Molly, blunt as ever. She turned to Camm. 'You won't know him; he was before your time. He hasn't been seen round here for years.'

Jimby nodded slowly, scratching his chin. 'Come to think of it, I know we only got a short glimpse of the driver, but he did strike me as familiar.'

'So, how do you know it's Joss Campion?' asked Ollie.

Ella swirled the wine around her glass; for a brief moment, she regretted saying anything. She didn't want to come across as a gossip; she'd only thought Jimby would be interested because of the Landie. 'I've spoken to him. He's come to help at the farm while his dad's in hospital.'

'Well, I never thought I'd see the day Joss Campion would be back at Camplin Farm. Does his dad know he's there?' asked Vi.

Ella was grateful she didn't get the chance to answer since Jonty announced the first participants of the evening's singing session. Everyone looked on as local artist Gerald and his wife Big Mary took the microphones. Gerald rummaged around the pocket of his colourful patchwork trousers and pulled out his set of false teeth. After giving them a quick wipe on his wife's cardigan, he popped them into his mouth and gave a toothy grin. 'Ready, pet?' he asked her.

'As I'll ever be, lover boy.' She grinned back and a moment later they launched into a lively rendition of Slade's "Merry Christmas Everybody", customising it with their Wearside twang. They belted the words out, encouraging the audience to sing along with them, which they did with great gusto. Gerald and Big Mary were a well-loved couple who'd thrown themselves wholeheartedly into village life since their move from County Durham. They couldn't be described as the most accomplished singers but their enthusiastic efforts left the audience applauding uproariously.

Next up was Brogan who had the local dog-walking business – Pond Farm Pooches – and had recently started working behind the bar at the Sunne. It was her first time taking part in the pub's music night and everyone looked on with bated breath.

Looking nervous, she pushed a wayward strand of red hair off her face and cleared her throat. A moment later, her light, clear voice glided angelically over the words of "O, Holy Night", leaving the audience spellbound and a tear in more than one person's eye. Once finished, she made her way back behind the bar to riotous applause, smiling bashfully as she went.

'That was awesome,' said Ella, clapping heartily. Something caught her eye and she looked up to see Portia making her way over to them, her face bright with excitement. Joss was right behind her, his hand in hers.

'Look who I found,' Portia said, her eyes dancing. 'It's the handsome stranger who popped in briefly last night.'

Ella felt her heart plummet unexpectedly. It would seem the handsome stranger was Joss.

TWENTY

Joss

After milking, Joss had talked himself in and out of taking Ella up on her invitation to join her and her friends at the pub. He'd settled on not going as the easiest option; that would save him having to explain himself; he didn't fancy offering himself up as an easy target for gossip, or having attention focused on him for the bulk of the evening.

He was sitting at the kitchen table, a mug of tea in his hand. Sid was curled up in his new favourite spot on the clippy mat by the Rayburn. The cold edge had been taken off the old farmhouse, but it still wasn't what you'd call cosy. Joss was disappointed not to have been able to order any oil for the central heating. It would be so much easier for his dad just to flick a switch, rather than have to clean out two stoves every day in a bid to keep the place warm. But Joss still hadn't heard back from Rich and when he'd tried to place an order at Thompson's, the nearest fuel suppliers, he was told in no uncertain terms, albeit politely, it wouldn't be possible.

Joss scratched his head. An uneasy thought creeping into his mind. Was the farm having financial troubles? If so, why hadn't Rich mentioned it?

The farmhouse suddenly felt large and empty and lonely. He was struck by an unexpected wave of sympathy for his father who must have felt this way on so many occasions; sitting here, on his own with only the television for company. His mum had urged his dad to remarry when he felt ready, but he'd refused to entertain the idea. Joss could imagine his dad's dour moods would send out very clear signals to any woman who took a shine to him to keep away.

Feeling his own mood dip, Joss pushed his chair back, its feet scraping across the flagstones. He was going to seize the moment before he changed his mind. He refused to sit here and stew, feel sorry for himself and feed the avoidance tactics that he'd developed since his return to the area. That wasn't his style. It was time to man up and face folk in the village. After all, what was the worst that could happen?

'Right, Sid, time to dust of your dancing shoes, buddy. How d'you fancy a night out with your dad?'

Sid shot to his feet and raced over to him. 'I'll take that as a yes, shall I?' Joss said, chuckling as he scratched his companion under the chin.

Stepping out into the yard, Joss gasped as a nithering wind rushed at him. 'Brrr! By 'eck it's bloomin' nippy.' He hurried over to his Land Rover, glancing up at the sky as he went. He was rewarded with a clear midnight-blue backdrop scattered with twinkling stars. His mind leapt to Ella – as it had frequently done since his return – and the times they'd spent gazing up at such a sky. *Infinity.* Her words filled his head, loud and clear. Without warning, a spike of doubt pierced his thoughts. With his hand poised on the passenger door handle he paused for a moment, misgivings racing through his mind. He wanted to go... and yet... He looked down at Sid who was looking up at him expectantly. 'Ah, stuff it!' In the next moment he'd opened the door and Sid had jumped onto the seat. 'Come on, lad, let's go and see what the village has in store for us, eh?'

Before he knew it, he was pushing open the door of the pub

with a feeling of déjà vu and not a little trepidation. In an instant, warmth wrapped itself around him, drawing him in, the atmosphere cosy and inviting. Just as it had the previous evening, a scrumptious aroma filled the air, though unlike last time, the babble of chatter had been replaced by the sweet tones of a woman's voice singing a Christmas song that tugged at his memory. It took a few moments for him to remember it had been a favourite of his mum's. His mind raced back to her singing it as they decorated the house for Christmas. Happy times.

He cast his gaze around the low-beamed room. Even though it was heaving with people it was evident the place had been treated to a massive refurbishment. The formerly shabby curtains had been replaced with heavy ones made of wool in sumptuous moor-land shades. The thick, wonky walls, once grimy and mottled with tobacco stains, were now limewashed a rich ochre. Gone was the nineteen-seventies carpet with its mind-boggling swirls of browns and orange. Not only had your feet been in danger of sticking to it, but it had the reputation of being the unpalatable harbourer of fleas and heaven-knows what else. Hand-forged iron wall lights cast a warm glow over the room, reflecting in the polished brass beer pumps, while a tastefully-decorated Christmas tree twinkled quietly in the corner.

Sid pulled on the lead, eager to investigate his new surround-ings. 'Bide your passion, fella.' Joss gently tugged him back as he made his way over to the bar to see the blonde woman from last night beaming at him.

'Hi,' she said quietly, tossing her sleek, glossy hair back, her smile growing wider, revealing straight, white teeth.

'Hi,' he said, keeping his voice low so as not to detract from the singing. He licked his lips, feeling suddenly nervous.

'What can I get you?' Her blue eyes twinkled at him. She was inordinately pretty, he thought, and from her cut-glass accent, she definitely wasn't a local. 'I can recommend the Old Micklewick Magic; it's a Yorkshire beer from Micklewick Bay, not a million miles from here, and it's going down a storm at the moment,' she said.

'Sounds good, but I'd best stick to shandy since I'm driving.'

'Ah.' She nodded and got busy fixing his drink. 'You're not from round here, are you?'

He really didn't want to get into the ins and outs of how he had been a local at one time but now... *Ughh! No, best keep it simple.* 'Erm, I'm just here for a few days.' He gave her a quick smile.

'I'm Portia, by the way. Portia Latimer.' She leaned across the bar, extending her hand to him – her short nails perfectly mani-cured – her eyes catching his flirtatiously. 'But my friends call me Porsh.'

He took her hand. It was cool and soft in his that was calloused and rough with work. 'Hi, I'm Joss.'

'Well, Joss, it's very nice to meet you.' She beamed another smile at him. 'So is Joss short for anything?'

'Joseph. I'm named after my uncle, but everyone calls him Joe.' He took in the flimsy fabric of her dark, floral blouse, the flounces plunging to a deep "v" at the front, the thin ties at her neck. The lace of her bra was visible beneath. She gave off an air of confi-dence that was attractive and a little dangerous at the same time.

'Well, Joss, I'll be free as soon as our little songbird, Brogan, has finished her gorgeous song, then I can join you on that side of the bar, introduce you to a few locals, if you like? My friend's saving me a place over by the fire, we can join her there.'

Joss felt his heart sink. This was exactly what he'd dreaded. What demon of madness had convinced him it was a good idea to come here tonight? He didn't want to be introduced to anyone, locals especially. Then he remembered how lonely and isolated he'd felt in his few short hours alone at the farmhouse and it smoothed the edges off his feeling of doom. *You're only going to be here for a few days. You'll be old news before you've gone. And if he was reading the vibes right, Portia could help pass that time quite nicely.*

Before he knew it, Portia had taken his hand and was leading him across the room, a glass of wine in her free hand, her exotic perfume wafting seductively under his nose. His eyes were drawn to the curves of her trim bottom, clad in a figure-hugging pair of black skinny jeans, swaying from side-to-side. He puffed out his cheeks and released a discreet breath, his hormones suddenly coming to life. It had been a while since he'd lost himself in the arms of a beautiful women, safe in the knowledge there'd be no strings attached. After Manda, he was steering well clear of commitment, make no mistake. But a little light-hearted dalliance was a different matter and would make his time here that little bit sweeter.

Portia came to a halt at a large table beside the vast inglenook fireplace he remembered from his days here. A huge fire was crackling in the hearth, kicking out the sweet scent of woodsmoke, sparks shooting up the chimney. The group of friends glanced up at him, smiling warmly. Amongst them he spotted Jimby Fairfax sitting next to a woman who was undoubtedly Violet – how could he forget her distinctive fifties movie-star style and striking deep-purple hair? Were they an item now? he wondered. His mind played catch-up as he took in the other faces: Kitty, Ollie and Molly, though he didn't recognise the dark-haired man sitting near her. Then his eyes fell to Ella, briefly dropping to the necklace, the infinity pendant catching the light, then back to her face again. That she looked beautiful flashed through his mind, chasing away his musings about Portia. He noticed her smile had faltered as his new friend introduced him. Was Ella having second thoughts about inviting him?

'Everyone, this is Joss Campion, he's going to be staying in the area for a while. I've invited him to join us in the fun tonight so he's not lonely.' Portia pouted prettily on the last word.

'Ey up, Joss, mate, it's good to see you. Sit yourself down.' Jimby got to his feet and pulled another chair out. 'You're in luck, we've got a few spare seats tonight. Robbie and Rosie can't make it, and I can't see Zander and Livvie joining us now; I saw Zan earlier and he was doubtful, said Livvie's feeling knackered. Apparently she's been overdoing it a bit recently. Left her feeling shattered. But I told him we'd keep a couple of seats tucked away just in case.'

'Ooh, that sounds ominous,' said Ella.

'Aye, that's what I thought.' Jimby nodded before turning to Sid. 'And who's this fine-looking fella, then?' He went to fuss Sid, who welcomed the ear-ruffling with great enthusiasm.

'Thanks, Jimby. And the hairy mutt's Sid; he's a Labrador crossed with an Irish Wolfhound, which is where he gets his crazy whiskers and bushy tail.'

Jimby chuckled. 'Well, he's grand, aren't you, lad?' He continued with his attentions to Sid who was enjoying every minute.

'Joss! How lovely to see you back here again.' Kitty beamed at him. Her appearance had changed most out of everyone. The last time he'd seen her she'd had long, poker-straight blonde hair and was as skinny as a rake. She suited the dark, wavy elfin crop; it emphasised her big brown eyes. And she looked better for having some meat on her bones too.

'Kitty.' He smiled and nodded at her.

'Now then, trouble,' said Molly, grinning at him warmly. 'How's life been keeping you?'

'Not too bad, thanks.' Though he wasn't overly keen on the moniker – he didn't want the name to stick – he couldn't help but return her smile.

'This is Camm, he's my partner.' Her smile fell briefly. 'I'm not sure if you know about Pip?' Her voice tailed off, sadness fleeting across her face.

Joss's heart squeezed for Molly; he'd heard from Aunty Babs and Uncle Maff that Pip had passed away a few years ago. 'Aye, I was very sorry to hear about it, Molly.'

Molly nodded and gave a tight smile; her response reminding him she was a tough cookie who didn't like to show emotion. He extended his hand to Camm, whose face had immediately struck him as kind. 'Pleased to meet you, Camm.'

'Aye, you too, lad.' Camm took Joss's hand, patting the back of it in a friendly gesture.

Portia looked nonplussed. She put her hands on her hips. 'So, hang on a minute; you know everyone?'

'Course he does, Porsh, the lad's Lytell Stangdale born and bred,' said Jimby, clapping Joss on the back and chuckling. 'He's Bill Campion's lad; Rich's kid brother.'

Joss spotted Molly exchange a look with Vi, the pair of them rolling their eyes at the mention of Rich's name, followed by a discreet warning look directed at the pair from Kitty.

He was going to have to get to the bottom of whatever it was that triggered these negative reactions. He felt sure it was linked to why his brother had gone AWOL.

'You're a local? Why didn't you tell me?' Portia asked, slipping her slender frame onto the banquette opposite him and next to Ella, who'd shuffled up and made room for her.

'I didn't say anything 'cos I'm not really local anymore, haven't been for quite a stretch.' He clicked his tongue for Sid to come and sit beside him, which he did immediately, curling up on the floor with a noisy 'harumph'. 'Good lad,' he said, bending to stroke Sid's head.

'Well, in the grand scheme of things, that really doesn't matter. But it seems I've got some catching up to do, so why don't you tell me all about yourself?' She placed her elbow on the table and rested her head on her hand, leaning forward so Joss got the full effect of her cleavage and the lacy trim of her push-up bra.

He was distracted from heading down the route he most dreaded of bringing up his past, wondering where to start, when he felt the gentle caress of her foot running up and down his leg. The only giveaway to the rest of the table was a fleeting hitch of his eyebrows, a slight lifting of the corners of his mouth. *Hello, I wasn't expecting this!* His eyes went to hers to find them dark and smouldering, leaving him in no doubt as to her intentions. From the way Ella was glancing between them, it was clear she sensed there was something going on.

Jimby and Vi had just finished a spectacular version of a crooner's carol, their voices rich and smoky, blending seamlessly together, when Bea declared the buffet open to all who had a ticket. It couldn't have been better timed for Joss, whose eyes had been glued to Portia's full mouth as she ran her tongue across her top lip. It sent a shiver of longing through him.

'Don't worry, I'll sort you out with a ticket,' she said.

'Oh, right. Thanks.'

As they were making their way across the bar, he saw Portia lean into Ella, heard her whisper excitedly, 'I can hardly believe it! Joss is the gorgeous man who popped into the pub last night, albeit briefly. You know, the one who set my insides on fire? How fortuitous is that? My future husband has returned.'

'Erm, yeah, it's really fortuitous.'

He gave a lopsided smile, amused.

'We'll have the wedding at Danskelfe Castle, and I've already got you marked as my chief bridesmaid, darling,' Portia said, gabbling light-heartedly. 'And don't worry, I promise I won't make you wear a hideous meringue-of-a-dress in a vile colour – I love you *far* too much for that – I prefer a more understated style; I'm thinking sleek and elegant.'

'Phew! That's good to know.' Though she didn't vocalize it, Ella very much doubted whether she could carry off sleek and elegant.

'Yes, I see you looking divine in an ethereal blue sheath dress, shimmering away like the dark-haired beauty you are. Anyway,' Portia waved her hand, 'just as soon as we get a chance, I want you to give me all the deets on Mr Gorgeous over there.'

In the dining room, Joss brushed away the conversation he'd just overheard, dismissing it as light-hearted and jokey; he didn't think for one minute Portia was serious; she didn't give off vibes that she was husband-hunting. Thank goodness!

His attention turned to the buffet. He couldn't remember the last time he'd seen a table so laden with such delicious-looking food. He'd heard Bea was a fantastic cook, and even though this was buffet food, it was on another scale. The mini game pies with their rustic, golden crusts caught his eye, they looked particularly mouth-watering, as did the accompanying homemade bramble chutney. And he'd have to have a slice of the impressive joint of roast ham; it looked magnificent, studded with cloves and smothered in Bea's secret recipe golden glaze.

Sid was patiently waiting where Joss had left him, obeying his orders to stay. He watched the door, blinking as the group headed back to their seats. The tempting aroma of food wafted his way and he sniffed the air appreciatively. There was no sign of his dad.

Joss had been following Jimby when he heard a whisper in his ear, soft breath caressing the skin of his neck. 'There's no need to rush back.' He turned to see Portia sloping off to a dimly lit corner of the dining room.

'It's so noisy in there, I can hardly hear myself think. Why don't we have our food in here? You can tell me all about yourself.' She gave him a flirtatious smile. 'We won't be missed.'

'There's Sid; he'll be wondering where I am.' Talking about himself would inevitably lead to questions about why he'd left, and the idea held little appeal. But there was something intriguing about Portia. 'Well, I suppose we could sit in here for a bit then head back through to the bar; I don't want the others to think I'm being rude by not eating with them.'

'Well, that's fine by me.'

The pair had been chatting for a good ten minutes, each enjoying an increasingly flirtatious rally of words, when Joss found his lips pressed against hers, their kiss becoming increasingly hot and urgent. He released a pent-up groan as his pulse rate skyrocketed, a wave of testosterone surging through his veins. *Woah!*

'Portia, darling, are you there?' Hearing Bea's voice, the pair jumped apart like scalded cats. Portia's mother headed towards them, her tortoiseshell glasses perched on her head, her glossy, blonde bob, swinging. 'Ah, there you are.' Her eyes shifted to Joss. 'Hello, I'm terribly sorry to interrupt, I just wondered if you'd found time to have something to eat, darling, but I see you have. I'll leave you to it.'

'Yes, it's all good in here, thanks, Mum.' Portia flashed her eyes at Joss, massaging her lips together, as if savouring their kiss. 'What I've just had was delicious.'

'Hello.' Joss, smiled, his face burning with embarrassment. Was Bea referring to *him* when she said Portia had found something to eat? Jeez, he hoped not, but her daughter certainly seemed to insinuate as much.

When she'd gone, Portia turned back to him, twirling a strand of hair around her finger. 'Fancy getting together some other time so we can pick up where we left off?' She kissed him again, tugging his bottom lip between her teeth.

Joss gulped. He had to concede, Portia was beautiful, and it was a very tempting offer. 'Yeah, that would be good.'

'Ey up, I wondered where the sparks were coming from.' Jimby strode into the room, empty plate in hand, a cheeky grin on his face. 'I'll just grab another one of Bea's very tasty game pies, then I'll be out of your way.' He winked at Joss.

Joss rolled his eyes, his libido plummeting down to his boots.

TWENTY-ONE

Ella

Back in the bar, the playlist of festive music had resumed. Ella sat at their table, watching as everyone but Joss and Portia returned. As she lifted a forkful of couscous to her mouth, she felt her mood dip, her appetite suddenly draining away. The chatter of her friends going on around her suddenly muted as thoughts of Joss and Portia swamped her mind.

She was halfway through her plateful of food when a shadow fell over the table. She looked up to see the pair, her friend's lips looking plump and almost bruised, a tell-tale gleam in her eyes. An unexpected spike of jealousy shot through her. Ella pushed it down, annoyed at herself. *Why on earth should I be jealous? It's ridiculous! Portia's a good friend; if she's happy, then I should be happy for her. It's not as if me and Joss had ever been an item, and he's a free agent now he's divorced and single. And I haven't had anything to do with him for eighteen years!*

'Just got a smidge waylaid.' Portia gave a loaded smile as she slipped in beside Ella.

Again, Ella mustered up a smile, noting Joss seemed reluctant to make eye contact with her. There were suddenly a lot of weird non-verbals flying around.

'Is that what they're calling it these days?' Jimby said, waggling his eyebrows at Joss, whose cheeks flushed in response.

Portia leaned into her, a hint of Joss's woody cologne wafting tormentingly under her nose. 'I can confirm that Mr Gorgeous over there is a seriously good kisser. *Seriously good,*' she said in a whisper.

'Yikes! TMI, Porsh.' Ella hoped her laughter reached her eyes, though she was doubtful. Where was this green-eyed monster coming from?

A soft groan escaped Portia's lips. 'Not sure I can wait much longer; I think I'm going to have to take myself off for a cold shower before I reach over there and rip his clothes off.' She turned to Ella, flicking her eyebrows up.

Ella coughed, quickly swallowing down a mouthful of beetroot and roasted pear salad. She glanced across at Joss; he did look ridiculously handsome, the natural highlights in his hair golden in the soft lights of the room.

Before she could respond, Portia jumped in. 'And are you honestly telling me there really wasn't ever a time when you two didn't get close? Didn't even try an experimental kiss? I mean, look at him, he's a magnificent specimen of a man; tall, broad-shouldered, muscular, face of Adonis,' she glanced under the table, 'big feet – and we all know what *that* means.' She gave a dirty chuckle. 'Or is Joss a classic case of the ugly duckling who bloomed into a handsome swan while he was away?'

Oh, jeez. If only you knew. 'We were just friends; best friends, nothing more; I never looked at him in that way. I was too much of a tomboy, never showed any interest in lads,' said Ella, conscious of injecting a neutral tone into her voice.

Over the next few hours, Ella endured an uncomfortable mix of watching Portia flirt shamelessly with Joss and, when he was involved in conversation with the others, having to answer her friend's whispered, probing questions about him. Who had he dated from the village? What was his ex-wife like? Did Ella know if he still had feelings for her? Did she think he was ready for commitment? Did she think he could be tempted to stay here? It was beginning to feel like an interrogation. Ella was aware that Portia had been in search of love since her relationship with Saffy ended. But why did her friend have to fall for Joss? *But why do you mind that she has?* said a little voice in her head. *Ughh!* How she wished she could shake off this unfamiliar, unwelcome feeling.

'You okay, Ella?'

She was pulled out of her thoughts to see Kitty looking at her, a kind smile on her face, her cheeks flushed from the warmth of the fire.

She mustered up a smile. 'Yeah, fine thanks, Kitts. Just feeling a bit tired, that's all. Been a busy couple of days.' She suddenly felt the intensity of everyone's eyes on her. Time to shift attention away, she thought. 'I meant to ask how Granny Aggie's doing, Molly? Has she recovered from her cold?'

Molly pulled a face. 'Ughh! Don't ask,' she said, before taking a generous slug of white wine.

'That good, Moll?' asked Ollie, chuckling.

'Hmphh. The wicked old minx has made a full recovery, and has only been torturing Rev Nev with her texts again. I tell you, if she carries on, I'm seriously going to have to confiscate that flaming phone of hers.'

'Ahh, don't do that, Moll, we get loads of laughs out of it,' said Vi, giggling.

'Come on, share what delights she's treated him to,' said Jimby.

Molly was struggling to keep from laughing as she shared Granny Aggie's latest misdemeanour. 'She's apparently invited him to what she called a "Crack Your Knackers Night" on Christmas Eve. Just him, her and Little Mary.'

'Cosy,' said Vi drily, arching an eyebrow.

Jimby spluttered on his beer, almost spraying it all over Ollie. 'Flippin' 'eck! Crack your knackers? That sounds nasty.'

'Ey up, go steady, mate,' Ollie said, grinning and wiping imaginary droplets from his navy Aran jumper.

'Sorry, Oll, but that's one seriously scary mental image I've just conjured up.' Jimby set his beer down on the table and wiped his chin with his hand.

Sid looked up from his spot in front of the fire where he'd curled up with Nomad and Scruff, who'd given him their approval after an initial thorough sniffing.

'Yep, that's one party I'm not sorry I didn't get an invitation to,' said Camm.

'I'd heard about Granny Aggie and her texts,' said Joss, amusement dancing in his eyes. 'So she's still sending them?'

Molly nodded, a matter-of-fact expression on her face. 'With alarming regularity. And they've been getting worse.'

'Oh dear.'

'Yes, oh dear,' Molly said.

'And dare we ask what she really meant?' asked Vi.

'Pleaded ignorance, as usual. When I confronted her about it, she reckoned she'd invited him to join her and little Mary for tea on Christmas Eve, told them she'd bought Christmas crackers specially. Honest to goodness, the predictive text, arthritic fingers excuse is wearing so thin, it's bloomin' threadbare. I'm just amazed Rev Nev's still here and hasn't asked for a transfer.'

'Or a restraining order,' said Camm, chuckling into his pint.

'I can see the reasons he'd include in his transfer application now: "Being hounded by old lady with filthy mouth and severe sexting habit". That would raise a few questions.' Jimby's ensuing hearty laughter was infectious, and the others couldn't help but join in. Though it had to be said, Ella's heart lacked its usual enthusiasm.

'And that's exactly why I love this village,' said Portia, her plummy tones a contrast to the North Yorkshire moorland accents around the table. 'There's always something happening; it's full of amazing characters like Granny Aggie and Hugh Heifer, Gerald and Big Mary to name but a few.'

'Not sure Rev Nev'd agree with you about Granny flaming Aggie,' said Molly.

'Yes, but something's keeping him here,' said Portia, flicking her hair over her shoulder. 'If he really found Granny Aggie's texts so unbearable I dare say he'd have made a run for it by now. I'm seriously considering moving here full time. Are you tempted, Joss?'

'Oh, I, er, I doubt that very much.' Ella noted an expression of discomfort had wiped his smile away. 'My life's over in Helderthorpe now; I'm settled there, doing a job I love.'

Portia was undeterred. She sat upright, her back ramrod straight. 'But you could do that job here, surely? What's stopping you from staying on at Camplin Farm and running it? As far as I can see, that would be the perfect solution.' She flashed a wide smile at him before sweeping her gaze around the others at the table, oblivious to the air of awkwardness that had descended.

Joss cleared his throat, briefly catching Ella's eye. Her heart squeezed for him. 'Well, I think my dad might have other plans, and I can't just up sticks and leave my aunt and uncle, that wouldn't be fair.'

'Yes, but you could give them notice; like everyone does when they switch jobs, give them time to find a replacement.' Portia shrugged, her eyes on him as she awaited his answer.

Joss shifted uncomfortably in his seat and drew in a deep breath.

'Anyway, I don't know about the rest of you, but I reckon it's time to go and grab some of those delicious-looking puddings Bea made, before they're all gone.' Ella grabbed the first diversionary tactic that sprang to mind. She knew Portia wouldn't back down once she'd started, and her friend's forceful questioning – albeit well-intended – appeared to be making Joss a little uncomfortable. With everything he'd had to face over the last few days, she felt he deserved a break. Especially since he didn't know the half of what had been going on. Rich, she thought, had a lot to answer for.

Joss's eyes met hers again, an unmistakable glimmer of gratitude in his gaze.

'Aye, good plan.' Jimby pushed his chair back; he'd obviously detected Joss's discomfort too. 'How about us menfolk bring back a selection of those mini puddings for us all?' he asked, giving his wife's shoulder a squeeze.

'Ooh, sounds good. Thanks.' Vi beamed up at him as various sounds of approval from her friends followed.

An hour after they'd demolished their food, Jonty called for a break in the singing to allow everyone to replenish their glasses. Anita Matheson had just finished a ropey rendition of a Christmas number nobody recognised and was making her way over to the friends' table.

'Uh-oh. Watch yourselves, fellas, Maneater's heading this way and it looks like she means business,' Molly said, picking up her wine glass.

'Oh, flippin' 'eck,' said Jimby as all the men but Joss visibly braced themselves.

'Judging by the way she's walking, I reckon she's had a few,' said Ollie.

'A few what? Beers or fellas?' asked Molly, hooting with laughter.

'Both, knowing her!' said Jimby.

'Dad'll be relieved she's leaving him alone tonight,' said Portia, eyeing the ageing vamp with distaste. 'And why doesn't she wear anything that fits? Her dress is obscenely tiny.'

'She prefers to flash what she's had for breakfast to the world, that's why,' said Molly.

'Molly! That's awful,' said Kitty.

'Moll has a point though,' said Vi.

Before Joss knew what had hit him, Anita pounced in a waft of overpowering, cheap perfume. She snaked her arm around his neck and slipped onto his lap. Ella couldn't help but laugh as his expression morphed from confusion to horror.

'And who's this handsome hunk of raw man?' Slurring her

words, Anita looked at Joss lasciviously, inching her bosom closer to his face. She ran a vivid red talon down his cheek, almost poking him in the eye. He leaned back, blinking.

Jimby, Camm and Ollie all bit back laughter; the three of them were no strangers to fighting off Anita's blatant advances and knew exactly the mortification Joss was experiencing.

'The handsome hunk of "raw man" as you so very aptly describe him is Joss,' said Jimby.

'Joss, eh? Well, let me tell you something, Joss. I think you're *very* good-looking.' She wriggled on his knee, her narrowed, heavily made-up eyes looking right into his. 'Mmm. And you're just my type.'

Joss swallowed nervously.

'Her type: male with a pulse,' said Molly sotto voce, causing a variety of stifled snorts to run around the table.

Ella felt a giggle rising up inside her and pressed her lips together in a bid to hold it in. Vi, who had a hand covering her mouth, wasn't so successful and her laugh spluttered through her fingers.

'And is Joss taken?' Anita looked around at everyone, bleary-eyed and apparently oblivious.

'Help!' Joss said, mouthing the word silently to Ella, his eyes pleading.

Anita's gaze landed on Ella, her eyes boring into hers, wiping the younger woman's smile away. If she wasn't so comical, she'd be scary. Did she think Ella and Joss were an item? 'Yes, he's taken.' Ella blurted out the first thing that came into her mind.

'Indeed he is,' said Portia. 'The handsome hunk's mine.' She gave Anita a victorious look.

'Ah, but for how long?' asked Anita, throwing down the gauntlet. She turned to Joss. 'When you've tired of little Miss Posh Knickers over there and you fancy a taste of real woman, I'll be waiting.' Joss blinked rapidly as she breathed alcoholic fumes over him. 'There's nothing like a woman with experience, and I have plenty of that. Let me tell you, I've got a few techniques that'll keep you begging for more.'

Joss gulped. 'I'll keep that in mind,' he said as she pushed herself up.

Swaying precariously, Anita blew him a kiss, pushed her fingers into her over-processed bird's nest of blonde hair and turned to leave. She didn't see Sid who'd overheated and left his place by the fire with his new pals, stretching out behind Joss's chair.

'Arghh!' Her voice came out in an ear-splitting screech. Sid yelped and shot under the table.

'What the...' Molly's head shot round.

Before the friends could process what was happening, Anita had lurched forwards and landed flat on her face, flashing a skimpy pair of red nylon knickers that barely covered her pale bottom. It gleamed up at them starkly in the soft light.

'Tempted, Joss?' asked Molly, sniggering as Len and Rhoda rushed to Anita's aid.

'What was that you were saying about her flashing her breakfast, Moll?' asked Jimby, making Molly gag.

'Who put that stupid, effing mutt there?' Anita shook off Len and Rhoda's help, tugging her dress down as she wobbled her way back to the bar.

It wasn't long before order was restored. Ella tried to not to watch as Joss and Portia fell into conversation. Judging by the look on his face, he seemed to have recovered from his ordeal at the hands of Anita and was enjoying every minute.

'Right, I think I'll head off.' Ella reached for her coat. It was only nine-thirty, but something had whipped away her enthusiasm for the evening she usually enjoyed. Tonight, she felt decidedly flat.

'What? But it's still early,' said Portia, surprise in her voice.

'I know, but I'm tired. Think I'll treat myself to an early night.' She reached for her coat, pushing her arms into it, shrugging it on.

'Won't you stay for just one more?' Portia rested her hand on Ella's arm, her eyes hopeful.

'Yeah, come on, Ells, have another. Surely if I'm staying for another shandy, you can stay for a bit longer too.' Joss smiled at her, his green-blue eyes annoyingly making her stomach flip, not to mention his casual use of her nickname. It was almost as if he'd never been away.

Ella glanced between the two of them, noting how Portia was looking at Joss. Why did it make her heart sink? She hooked her bag over her shoulder and gave a flat smile. 'No. You enjoy. Maybe catch you tomorrow for that walk?' she said to Portia.

'Okay.' Portia nodded. 'I'll text you.'

After bidding everyone goodbye, Ella headed for the door, her mind in turmoil. She wasn't interested in Joss romantically; he was a friend, or at least, he had been years ago. And Portia was one of her dearest girlfriends. She and Joss were both single. Surely, if they fancied getting better acquainted it shouldn't bother her. On the contrary, it should make her happy, maybe even assuage the guilt she felt from when Joss was so hastily dispatched from the village.

But if that was the case, how did she explain the feelings of jealousy that were currently swirling in her stomach?

TWENTY-TWO

Joss

With milking out of the way, Joss was wrestling with the barn door, attempting to fix the hinges and thinking how much easier the job would be with an extra pair of hands. He brushed the cobwebs away, taking with it patches of dark-green paint where it was peeling. His mind was drifting from Rich – and the looks of distaste the mere mention of his name seemed to generate – to Ella, then to Portia. It was a combination that had been keeping his mind busy all morning.

The cold was biting, the north wind scurrying across the moors, numbing his fingers and making them clumsy. He dropped the screwdriver for the fourth, or was it the fifth time? 'Blast!' His breath tumbled out in a cloud before being whipped away. Sid, fed up with the freezing temperature, had sought warmth by the Rayburn half an hour since. Joss couldn't blame him.

The distinctive rumble of a Land Rover engine made him look up. He watched as the vehicle nosed its way into the yard before coming to a stop. A vaguely familiar man jumped out, his face ruddy with the cold. He pulled his woolly hat further down on his head. 'By, bloomin' cold spot, this,' he said, giving an exaggerated shiver.

It took a couple of seconds for Joss to recognise the man was Pete Welford. 'So my fingers are telling me,' he said, smiling as he crunched over the snow to him, a wave of fondness filling his chest. 'It's good to see you, Pete.' He offered his hand, and the older man took it, shaking it vigorously.

'And it's grand to see you too, lad.' Pete's smile carved deep lines into his weather-beaten face.

'I have to thank you for all your help while my dad's been in hospital. You're a good friend to him; I'm very grateful for all you and your family have done.'

'Aye, well, it's nowt he wouldn't do for us if the tables were turned.' Pete sniffed and wiped his hand under his nose. 'Need a hand?' He nodded towards the barn door.

'Aye, I wouldn't mind; if you've got time that is.'

'Course, I have. You can make me a brew after as payment.'

With Pete's help, the barn doors were fixed in no time, and the pair headed into the farmhouse, the kitchen now warm and toasty. Joss set to making a pot of tea while Pete made a fuss of Sid. 'By, you're a grand-looking fella, aren't you?'

Joss chuckled, throwing teabags into the pot. 'Sid'll take all the compliments and belly rubs you're prepared to give.'

'So I'm learning.' Pete laughed as Sid rolled onto his back, offering up his belly, his gangly legs splayed.

Joss handed Pete a steaming mug of tea, then set a plate of biscuits down on the table. Pete took one and dunked it into his drink. While he'd waited for the kettle to boil, Joss had been toying with the idea of asking his father's friend about Rich and the reactions mere mention of his name seemed to generate. If anyone would know about it, he was sure it would be Pete.

'Place's warmed through nicely now,' Pete said, wiping biscuit crumbs from his mouth with the back of his hand.

'Aye, thanks to Ella and you; you must let me know how much I owe you both for the coal and the logs.'

'Ah, there's no rush for that, lad. I'm just glad the place isn't like a fridge anymore. Just thought I'd pop in see if there was owt else you needed. I can still feed the sheep down in Thistle Field if you like?'

'Thanks, Pete, that's very kind of you, but I reckon you'll have enough of your own stuff to keep you busy. I might as well do that while I'm here.'

'Aye, fair enough.'

Joss sat quiet for a moment, building the courage, gathering the right words. He sucked in a deep breath and blew it out slowly, aware of Pete's eyes on him.

'Since I've been back, I've noticed a few things; felt something wasn't quite right.' He paused. 'I can't put my finger on it, but I'm definitely not imagining it. Since I first met Rich up here and he handed the keys over, I haven't been able to get hold of him; he hasn't replied to any of my texts or calls. And I've noticed when-ever I mention his name, people seem to react in what I can only describe as a disapproving manner; rolling their eyes, exchanging loaded looks, that kind of thing.'

He glanced over at Pete who was wearing a troubled expression.

'And when I tried to place an order at Thompson's for some oil, I was told very firmly it wouldn't be possible. It was as if they had a problem with us.' He took a gulp of his tea, his eyes still on Pete. 'I hate to ask, but I wondered if you could shed any light on things? Wondered if Dad had mentioned anything to you?'

Pete puffed out his cheeks and scratched his head. 'I was expecting you to ask me; I'd spoken to our Debbie about what I should do if you did, and we both agree you deserve the truth. It's best if you know where you're splodging.'

Joss felt his heart pick up speed. 'Oh, heck, is it that bad? Maybe I'm better off being in the dark.'

'T'ain't good, I'm afraid, lad. And it's not as if I'm spreading gossip, you're family and there's plenty of folk who aren't who know what that brother of yours has been up to. As far as I'm concerned, he's lucky Dawn had him back, never mind her father giving him a job. He doesn't deserve either as far as me and mine are concerned.'

Joss listened quietly as Pete went on to say how for a year-and-a-half, Rich had been having an affair with a woman called Julie who'd moved to Arkleby from Middleton-le-Moors. It had been a risky business, moving to the village right next to Danskelfe, which was where Rich lived with his wife and child, but he'd considered it safer than living in the same town as his in-laws. Plus, Rich had liked the idea of having her on the doorstep, popping in for a quick tumble between the sheets whenever he fancied, sneaking in through the back gate of her little detached property on the edge of the village. He'd been wining and dining her, buying her expensive gifts, having weekends away, telling Dawn he was away on courses. He'd been caught red-handed when his father-in-law, Rod, had spotted him at a hotel he'd been staying at. Rich had been having dinner with Julie, reaching across the table for her hand, pressing it to his lips. Rod, who'd been attending a conference there, had calmly walked up to him and asked him if he was enjoying his evening. 'I'll look forward to catching up with you when we get back home,' he'd said with a sinister smile and a warning look mean enough to turn a man to stone.

It had been the catalyst to all hell breaking out in Rich's world. Not only did his affair expose his lies and deceit to his wife, but the fallout revealed that he'd been dipping his hand into the farm's coffers and had left a considerable hole in them by all accounts.

The upshot was that, though Dawn was heartbroken, she was so blindly in love with Rich, she was prepared to forgive him. Prepared – read desperate – to give her marriage another chance. Her father had stepped in, formidably declaring his hand. If this was what his daughter wanted, then that was what she'd have – no matter how much the "waste of space", as he now referred to Rich, made his insides churn with a boiling rage. But there were conditions, as Rich found out when his father-in-law got him on his own. He'd go back to Dawn, grovelling on his belly, do everything she asked and more. The final demand was that Rich would take a job with Rod's firm. No quibbling. That way, Rod would be able to keep his errant son-in-law under close scrutiny – and it would be so close, Rich would be able to feel Rod breathing down his neck with every move he made. 'There'll be no sneaking away on fake training courses on my watch, you little worm. You won't even be able to fart without me knowing about it,' he'd said, standing nose-to-nose with Rich, his eyes dark and menacing. 'And if I hear so much as a whisper you've stepped out of line, you'll wish you hadn't been born. You don't need me to tell you your life won't be worth living around here. You'll be persona non grata. Got it?'

Rich hadn't had to think too hard about his options; he liked the perks that came with being married to Dawn, the little luxuries, the expensive holidays abroad. Making his decision, he dumped his paramour somewhat unceremoniously by text before blocking her number, swearing to Dawn and her father he'd never stray again. As for leaving his job on the farm? When Rich had mulled over Rod's ultimatum, the prospect hadn't been as unpalatable as he'd anticipated; he'd been getting pretty fed up of working in all weathers, with not a word of gratitude from his father, of putting up with his cantankerous moods. But Rich had been oblivious to the fact that things had been brewing at Camplin Farm and were about to come to a head, culminating in an ugly, acrimonious eruption. Pacification of his father-in-law hadn't been a pleasant experience, but it had been easier than he'd expected. What Rich hadn't banked on was his own father's reaction when he uncovered Rich's misdemeanours at the farm.

Joss shook his head in disbelief. 'I knew Rich had been having marriage troubles, but he never went into detail, and I didn't like to ask. I had no idea any of this was going on.' He rubbed his hand across his face. 'Was his affair common knowledge locally?'

'There'd been the odd whisper, but no one had anything concrete; they'd been very sneaky by all accounts.'

'So how did my dad take Rich leaving?' asked Joss. He took a gulp of tea, grimacing when he realised it had gone cold.

'Well, you honestly wouldn't believe the timing of it; you couldn't make it up. After Rich had been confronted by Rod Walker, he'd gone to the farm to tell your dad he was leaving. By all accounts he hadn't prepared himself for your dad's reaction.'

'What do you mean?'

Pete heaved a sigh, pressing his lips together as he went on to explain.

It transpired that Bill had heard a whisper that Rich was having a dalliance with a woman. A staunch believer in the sanctity of marriage, it hadn't gone down well with him and he'd been biding his time before he confronted his son about it, priming his anger to gain maximum impact.

That time came when Bill had found a letter from the bank informing him the farm's overdraft wasn't going to be extended. It had been the first Bill had known of such an overdraft. Rich had taken care of the financial side of things for years, it was something he'd said he was happy to do. It took a brief meeting at the bank for Bill to discover that Rich had been plundering the farm's bank account, not only to fund his affair with Julie; it would seem it had been going on for years before that had started.

Joss pinched the bridge of his nose between his thumb and forefinger, absorbing what Pete had told him. 'That explains a lot of things, it's probably the reason Rich is avoiding me, and not leaving me with the password to the computer.' A plethora of thoughts were jostling for his attention and a throb had started up in his temples.

'Aye, me and Deb wondered how he'd handled things with you.'

'Hmm. I'd have to say not great.'

'Anyroad, the upshot was that when Rich told your dad he was handing his notice in, Bill told him he knew what had been getting up to, knew about his affair, helping himself to the farm's money like it was his own. He told Rich to leave there and then. Said he didn't want him back.'

'Shit.'

'That's exactly what I said when I heard.' Pete glanced out of the window, nodding towards it. 'Ey up, looks like it's starting up again.'

Joss followed his gaze to see the sky had turned an ominous dark grey, snowflakes tumbling gently down and settling on the sill.

'Anyroad, I'm sorry to have to dump all that on you, but hopefully it's helped shed some light on what's been going on round here. Deb and me reckon it's a good thing you've come home.'

Home? It's been eighteen years since I called this place home.

'Bill'd been looking off colour for a while, hadn't been looking after himself properly. Deb and me tried to help, and I know your Aunty Babs and Uncle Maff did too, but you know what a stubborn old so-and-so your dad is. Anyroad, he's in the best place at the moment. Let's hope the doctors can find out what's up with him.' Pete drained his mug and placed it on the table. 'Right, I'd best be off. Thanks for the tea and biscuits, much appreciated.'

'Thanks for the help with the barn doors; saved me a lot of juggling.' Joss gave a small laugh, hesitating before he spoke again. 'Before you go, Bill, I just want to apologise for my behaviour before I left. I'm so sorry for the damage I cau—'

Pete held up his hand, silencing Joss. 'Listen, lad, I know you're sorry. It was an accident, plain and simple. But you've served your penance – and some. In my family, we don't go in for bearing grudges. It doesn't do anyone any good to hold onto bitterness.'

Joss felt a wave of relief wash over him. He smiled gratefully at his dad's oldest friend. He was surprised to find his eyes stinging with tears, the emotion of what he'd just learnt swimming to the surface. Before he knew it, Pete was slapping him heartily on the back.

'Ey, young 'un, everything'll be all right.' His smile crinkled the corners of his eyes. 'And our Debs asked me to remind you you're welcome to join us for lunch. I reckon the snow isn't going to get that bad you won't be able to bob down to us today.'

'Thanks, Bill. I might just take you up on that offer. And thanks again for being such a good friend to my dad.'

He walked the farmer to the door, watching as he swung his Land Rover round, the sturdy tyres making new tracks in the snow.

Mention of a meal at Tinkel Bottom Farm brought Ella to mind, making him frown. She'd been quiet the previous evening, the flashes of her old sparkle he'd seen earlier in the day appeared to have deserted her. Had she regretted inviting him to join her friends? Would she be okay if he turned up at her parents' house today? For a split-second he thought about not going, but decided it would look rude if he didn't. They were good people and he didn't want to offend them.

He was rinsing the mugs under the tap when there was a knock at the door. Sid barked and jumped up, racing towards it, his claws clicking over the flagstones. Joss set the tea towel down on the worktop, his heart beating quickly.

Icy air rushed in as he opened the door to see Portia on the doorstep, her blue eyes striking against the white fur trim of her fitted padded jacket. 'Oh!' was all he could think to say. In truth, he'd been half-expecting to see Ella.

'Aren't you going to invite me in?' She flashed him a flirtatious smile.

TWENTY-THREE

Ella

The large, low-beamed kitchen at Tinkel Bottom Farm was toasty warm and filled with the delicious aroma of chicken casserole and herby dumplings. Christmas songs belted out from the speaker on the vintage pine dresser that was choc-a-bloc with the blue and white china Debbie collected, interspersed with festive decorations and Christmas cards.

'You all right, lovey? S'just you seem a bit quiet.' Debbie was standing at the Aga that occupied a vast sandstone inglenook, checking on a pan of sprouts. She gave a couple a quick prod with a fork to test they were still al dente, glancing over at her daughter who was busy setting the table.

Ella forced a smile, swiping a stray strand of hair off her face. 'I'm fine thanks, Mum. I'm just mulling over a suggestion Jean Prudom made about me taking the plunge and looking into the options for teacher training; there are a few different ways to go about it apparently.' She wasn't being completely honest, but the Head's suggestion had crossed her mind a few times over the weekend. Well, more than a few times actually. But what had been occupying most of her thoughts was Joss. And Portia. And the thought of them being together. *And* the thought of why that was bothering her as much as it did. But she didn't want to admit that to her mum. Nor did she want to admit to the feelings that Joss's arrival had stirred inside her.

'You don't sound too keen.'

'Hm?'

'I'm getting the impression you're not blown away by Mrs Prudom's idea.' Debbie drained the sprouts over the sink, tipping them into a bowl and adding a generous dollop of butter, and a quick grating of lemon zest, before swirling them around. She flicked her eyes over to Ella.

Ella leaned against the table and sighed. 'I'm torn, well, kind of. Don't get me wrong, I really enjoy working up at the school; the kids and the staff are fantastic. It's just I love being outdoors, working with animals. That's my passion.' She nibbled on the side of her mouth, looking thoughtful. 'I should've trained to be a vet nurse; I don't know why I didn't think of that years ago.'

'Well it's not too late, chick.' Her dad appeared through the utility room door where he'd removed his wellies and outdoor clothing and washed his hands. Frosty air and the scent of woodsmoke lingered on him. 'By, it smells bloomin' lovely in here. I'm that hungry I could eat a scabby hoss between two mattresses.' He rubbed his nose which was a vivid red from the cold.

'Won't be long now, love.' Debbie smiled affectionately over at her husband. She turned to Ella. 'But being a vet nurse still wouldn't mean you'd be working outside.'

'Mm. You're right. I'll keep racking my brains; I'm bound to think of something.' She hesitated for a moment, her eyes fixed to the cutlery in her hands. 'I've actually got an idea brewing; it's just in its early stages – *very* early stages – but I was going to run it by you both, see what you thought.'

'Oh aye, and what's that then?' asked her dad, sneaking a sprout from the bowl Debbie was just about to put in the warming oven. He chomped on it enthusiastically, grinning at his wife.

Over the meal, Ella explained how during a shift at the Sunne a couple of weeks earlier, she'd been talking to Brogan who had the dog-walking business at nearby Pond Farm Pooches. She'd explained to her friend how she felt ready for a career change, which had resulted in Brogan offering her a job.

Brogan had a kind manner about her that both dogs and their owners were drawn to, and word quickly spread of her canine enterprise – the fact she allowed the better behaved of her charges stay at her house for the day only added to her already glowing reputation. Before she knew it, her small business had mush-roomed thanks to the tranche of dog owners who lived in the surrounding villages and commuted to work – some as far as York. She'd been so inundated with bookings, she'd found herself having to turn folk away, which went against the grain. 'I've been giving serious thought about taking someone on. I can only walk so many dogs at a time and I like to give them all a decent run around. But it's got that I spend my whole day traipsing across the moors; as soon as I take one group of dogs back, I have to set off with another one. I dread to think how many miles I do. And it kills me to turn down a booking,' Brogan had said, chuckling as she filled the fridge behind the bar with mixers. Though dog walking wasn't really what Ella had planned, Brogan's offer had planted a little seed in her mind; one that had now started to germinate and push out tentative little shoots.

The nearest boarding kennels was a good ten miles away at Middleton-le-Moors, and from what she'd heard it was fairly basic. She figured there was a definite gap in the market for a more homely boarding kennels, but not just for dogs; Ella's idea ran to a variety of pets: cats, guinea pigs, hamsters. Pretty much anything – within reason. She'd even toyed with the idea of offering to care for animals who didn't need too much attention at their owners' home – fish had crossed her mind – dropping in to tend to them, giving their owners peace of mind. Though she wasn't quite sure how that would work. She needed to sit down and think things through properly.

'And the emphasis would be on home-from-home as far as

possible, with lots of cuddles thrown in. I'd want the kennels to be comfortable and homely; they'd have to be heated. I'd encourage owners to let their pets have their own blankets, or to leave something with their scent on as a comfort,' Ella said, looking at her parents earnestly.

'Well, if you ask me, that sounds right up your street, lovey,' said Debbie, smiling.

'I agree,' said her dad, swallowing his mouthful. 'There's only one problem, and I'm afraid it's a big 'un, flower: where you're going to have these kennels? I mean, Rose Cottage is hardly big enough, is it? And I doubt Ollie'd be too happy about you having a load of animals running riot around his property.'

Ella giggled. 'No, I wasn't planning on using Rose Cottage.' She set her knife and fork down. 'I was wondering if I could construct something here?' She glanced between her parents, a tentative look of hope in her eyes.

Debbie snatched a look at the clock on the wall. 'Tell you what,' she said, pushing herself up. 'Time's cracking on, and we'll have to be setting off to the hospital to see Bill soon. So why don't you tell us what you've got in mind while we get the table cleared and the dishwasher filled?'

'Aye, good plan.' Pete sat back in his seat. 'I'm interested to hear what you've got to say, and you know your mum and me will support you as much as we're able.' He picked up his plate and glass, and was heading over to the sink. 'Ey up, I've just realised, Joss didn't show up.'

'So he didn't,' said Debbie.

Pete's brow crumpled. 'He seemed keen enough when I talked to him this morning; must've been waylaid.'

'More than likely; there's a fair bit for the lad to do up at Camplin Farm, he's got his work cut out for him while he's there,' said Debbie, shaking her head. 'Mind, it could be the thought of going to see his dad that put him off, not that I blame him after all these years.'

'Aye, and there was always the risk Bill wouldn't see him.'

'That'd crossed my mind too.' Debbie gave her husband a knowing look.

Mention of Joss was like a wet blanket over Ella's excitement for her proposed new business venture, though she tried not to let her parents see, but she really didn't feel like talking about it now. 'I'll give you a hand, then I'll head back to the cottage. We can continue our chat later.'

'All right, lovey. I'm intrigued to hear more.' Debbie smiled as she placed the left-over dumplings in a tub for the fridge.

Portia had texted Ella earlier saying she was tied up all morning but said she could drop by Rose Cottage around two, suggesting they could maybe head out for a walk if the weather wasn't too dreadful. After her friend's flirtatious performance with Joss the previous evening, Ella couldn't decide if she was looking forward to seeing her or not.

The sky's half-hearted attempt at dumping a fresh load of snow had fizzled out to nothing and the spiteful wind had eased off. Ella and Portia walked along the track to the small wood at the edge of the village, snow crunching underfoot. A thick wodge of grey sky hung above, muffling the familiar moorland sounds. Nomad and Scruff raced ahead, tumbling about in pure joy, sending snow flying everywhere and making the two friends laugh.

'So, how's your day been?' Portia turned to Ella, her face a healthy pink with the cold, her eyes shining. Her tall, slender frame looked effortlessly elegant in her fitted white puffa coat, blue skinny jeans and designer wellies. Ella felt decidedly dowdy next to her in her faithful navy padded jacket, bargain supermarket jeans and the wellies she'd had for years. A wardrobe full of trendy clothes wasn't Ella's thing; she regularly said she'd rather stick pins in her eyes than go clothes shopping. But today, for the first time, she felt conscious of her lack of style. Her mood suddenly mirrored the sky.

'Yeah, it's been okay. Had lunch with my parents, haven't done much else really. How about you?' She forced a smile, hoping her friend wouldn't pick up on her lack of enthusiasm. *What is the matter with you? Get a grip! Portia's your friend and you're always saying you don't get to see her as much as you'd like. Don't spoil this time with her.*

Portia stopped and placed her hand on Ella's arm. Ella looked up to see her friend's face animated, her eyes dancing.

'I've had the most *amazing* morning!' Portia was practically bouncing on the spot, her smile couldn't have been any wider if she'd tried.

It was infectious, and Ella found herself smiling back. 'Now I'm intrigued. Have you been up at Danskelfe Castle again? How's the project going by the way? I bet Lady Caro loves your designs.'

Portia waved her hand dismissively. 'Oh, gosh, no! It's nothing to do with Danskelfe Castle or the Hammondelys.' She gripped onto Ella's arms and squealed. 'I only spent a rather delicious couple of hours having the best sex of my life.'

Ella felt the ground crumble beneath her feet. 'You did?' Despite her best efforts, her smile faltered. She tried her hardest to fix it back in place before her friend noticed.

Portia released her and strode along, throwing her head back. 'Oh, boy, did I? I mean, Joss Campion seriously knows how to make a girl feel good. Anyone would think he hadn't been near a woman for months; he was... phew!... mind-blowing.'

If Ella could have stuck her fingers in her ears she would have. She so wasn't prepared to hear that. Her mind was frantically scrabbling over the implications of Portia's revelation. Envy, anger – at herself for feeling jealous, and at Portia and Joss for making her feel this way, for having to go and have sex – and confusion churned inside her. It was a destructive mix and not one Ella was used to. *Arghh!* But why did what they'd done make her feel this way? She had no right to be jealous, no right to be angry. She had no claim on Joss; they hadn't been close for years and he hadn't been back five minutes. On top of all that, he was a free agent, as was Portia.

Ella glanced up to see Portia looking at her, her face animated and happy. 'So, what do you think?' she asked, giving a dazzling smile.

'Sorry, I missed what you just said.' Ella forced a light tone into her voice.

'You're away with the fairies today, Ells.' Oblivious to Ella's turmoil, Portia giggled, giving her a friendly nudge with her shoulder. 'I said, do you think we have a future together? I mean, I know you haven't seen him for a while, but do you get a good vibe about us?'

Much as she was tempted to tell her friend not to hold her breath, that he'd told her he'd sworn off relationships for a while, the hopeful expression on Portia's face meant Ella didn't have the heart to pour cold water on her happiness. But her friend's track record meant her initial over-the-top enthusiasm for new relationships usually burned out after a few short months, weeks even. She found herself traitorously hoping that would be the case with Joss. 'Oh, erm, well, it's early days for me to be able to say just yet.' Jeez, this was awful.

'I've never met a man as hot and just, well, "phwoar" as Joss Campion.' Portia giggled, pushing her hands into the pockets of her jacket. 'Honestly, Ells, he's magnificent naked; seriously ripped, he just oozes strength and... Warghh! He's got me all unnecessary. Anyway, I'm going to have to go back up to the farm tonight; I need some more of him; I simply can't get enough.' She turned to her friend. 'I'm just so pleased you don't think the same way about him.'

Ella's breath caught in her throat. 'Don't worry, there's no fear of that.' She forced a laugh. She wouldn't stand a chance against stunningly beautiful, exciting and self-assured Portia.

TWENTY-FOUR

Joss

Seeing Portia on the doorstep was the last thing Joss had expected that morning. As was ending up in bed with her. She'd been enthusiastic and passionate and had definitely helped take his mind of his worries. There was no getting away from the fact she was a beautiful woman with a mischievous sense of humour, and from the little he knew of her, she seemed to have a kind heart too. She was also a good friend of Ella's.

Ella. Thought of her triggered a pang of regret in his chest. It shifted quickly to her parents and their lunch invitation. He suddenly felt awash with guilt. He'd been so consumed in losing himself in Portia, he hadn't even had the decency to contact them to say he couldn't make it. He groaned. Why had he been so weak? So shallow? Was he leading Portia on? He'd hate himself if he thought he'd been giving out the wrong signals. The last thing he was interested in was starting a new relationship; it was the furthest thing from his mind. He hadn't wanted to go into detail with her about his failed marriage; that would have felt like picking at a scab, and his brain was dealing with enough without having to take the lid off that little box of horrors. Nor had he felt it necessary. He didn't know Portia well enough – or actually at all, apart from in the physical sense – but he felt sure she was just out to have some no-strings fun. And he was sure he wasn't mistaken that she'd done all the running. She was the one who'd instigated the kissing in the pub last night. She was the one who'd turned up on the doorstep and laughed at his offer of a cup of tea. Instead she'd wrapped herself around him, delivering tantalising kisses that had stirred up months' worth of pent-up desire. He hadn't taken much persuading to head upstairs to his bedroom. Poor old Sid hadn't known where to look.

So why did he feel like crap?

Because, though he'd sworn to himself that he'd keep everyone in the village at arm's length, he'd been unable to resist Portia.

'Ughh! Man!' He rubbed his brow with his fingertips. Sid's ears twitched from his spot curled up in front of the Rayburn. 'I've been here two days, and already I'm making a balls-up of things.' He heaved a sigh. First things first, he'd ring the Welfords and apologise, tell them he had to deal with something unexpected. Which was true; he just wouldn't say what the "unexpected" something was. Next, he'd...? His father sprang to mind; the Welfords had mentioned the possibility of going with them to visit him, though nothing had been set in stone. That felt like a bad idea for so many reasons.

He felt a wave of relief once he'd tried to call the Welfords, hearing their landline go straight to answerphone. It offered a brief reprieve, though he'd have to call them later.

While he had his phone in his hand, he tried Rich's number. Though it rang, Joss wasn't surprised that his brother didn't pick up. This time, he left a message saying he'd spoken to Pete who'd brought him up to speed with what had been going on; the affair, the bank account, everything. Gazing out of the kitchen window, he wondered how long it would take his brother to call back after that bombshell. Or if he would call at all.

Joss was still clutching his phone when Rich's number illuminated the screen. He pressed it to his ear. 'Hi, Rich. Thanks for calli—'

'I just want to get something straight; I don't appreciate messages like that. I don't know who you think you are, accusing me of stuff you know nowt about. Swanning back here, fixing things up like you own the place. Let me remind you, I'm not the one who was sent packing for his irresponsible behaviour. I'm the one who was left behind to work his backside off to keep the farm running.'

'Rich, I—' Joss started pacing the floor, his hackles bristling.

'I haven't finished.' Rich muttered something indecipherable under his breath. 'Just so you know, the wages Dad paid didn't come anywhere near to reflecting the hours and graft I put in up there; I deserved that money, I didn't take anything I wasn't entitled to. And he flaming-well knows it.'

Joss held back a moment before speaking, making sure his brother's diatribe had come to an end. He could hear him breathing heavily down the phone, barely able to contain his rage. Joss used all his strength to keep a lid on his own anger. 'Look, I appreciate where you're coming from about the wages, but Dad didn't deserve you putting the farm into financial difficulties because of what you thought you were entitled to. And you didn't have the right to take it without checking with him first. I'm sorry, Rich, but you left him with a mess to sort out.'

'Now just you hang on a minute, I didn't leave! He told me to go! I was willing to work a month's notice but he wouldn't hear of it.'

Rich was practically yelling now. Joss held the phone away from his ear, wincing. He waited for a pause before he attempted to speak again. 'I understa—'

'You, of all people, should know what that feels like. You shouldn't be defending the stupid old fool. Where's your empathy? Where's your brotherly loyalty? I'm the one who's kept in touch with you while you've been away, not him. You should be standing up for me, instead of wading in, acting all sanctimonious, like you're the farm's bloody saviour. No one thinks that of you, Joss; everyone knows you for the waste of space you actually are. If you're hoping to change folks' opinion of you round here, you're wasting your time. It's never going to happen.'

Before Joss had time to reply, the call was cut.

'Wow!' He stared at the screen, momentarily punch-drunk, his heart thumping in his chest. 'Don't mince your words, Rich.' He slid his phone onto the kitchen table, flopping down into a chair. This wasn't great. In Joss's mind, his brother's angry, defensive response only served to confirm his guilt – and remind him he was a hot-head like their father – but tackling him about it had put the pair of them at loggerheads, which wasn't ideal in the current circumstances.

He pushed his fingers into his hair, and puffed out his cheeks, attempting to work through the thoughts that were crowding his mind and clamouring for attention. As he did so, one question kept cropping up: how was his father going to get out of this mess? An image of his mum's smiling face pushed through, sending a wave of sorrow over him. He swallowed the lump of emotion that suddenly clogged his throat; it would break her heart to see what had become of the three of them.

Joss sat back in his seat. 'This has to stop,' he said aloud. 'It has to stop now.'

He needed to speak to his father, whether his father wanted to speak to him or not. The situation couldn't go on ignored.

With milking out of the way, Joss peered out of the kitchen window to see more lights shining at Tinkel Bottom Farm; the Welfords must have returned from the hospital. He fished out the number of their landline and dialled, anticipation squeezing in his stomach.

'Hi, Debbie, it's me, Joss.'

'Oh, hello there, lovey.' He was relieved to hear her tone was friendly. 'Pete and me were just talking about you.'

His heart sank. 'Oh, right. Well, I, erm, I just wanted to apologise for not getting to you for lunch but, like I said, something came up and I lost track of time.'

'No need to apologise, you've got a lot on your plate at the moment; we completely understand.'

Guilt prodded at him, and he cringed at his white lie. 'Thanks for being so understanding. And, er, the second thing is, I was just wondering how things are with my dad.'

'I'm pleased to say he was looking much brighter when we saw him, had a bit more colour to his cheeks.'

'That's good to hear. And do you know if he's had a diagnosis yet?'

'Well, we did ask, but the staff couldn't tell us and he was tight as a clam about it.'

Sounded like his dad. 'Right.' He pressed his lips together. 'And do you know if they've given him any indication of when he's likely to be discharged?'

'It's looking like it's going to be early next week, they said it would definitely be before Christmas. You've actually saved Pete a trip, he was going to pop up to see you, tell you all this.' A beat passed. 'Don't suppose you know how long you're planning to hang around?'

Joss heard the hesitation in her voice. 'I'm not sure. But I can't just leave things as they are. I suppose it depends on whether he'll be happy to let me continue staying here.'

Before he'd called the Welfords, Joss had already made up his mind he wasn't going to leave the farm until he had a firm grip on the situation, until he could rest easy that the farm wasn't going to go under and drag his father with it. He owed that to his mum, if no one else. He'd already spoken about it to his Uncle Joe and Aunty Hannah. Just as he'd expected, they'd wholeheartedly supported his decision. 'It's not the same without your smiling face round here, lad, but you have to do what's necessary. We completely understand. And young Lawry is stepping up to the plate rather nicely,' his Uncle Joe had said before passing the phone to Aunty Hannah who'd repeated her husband's words, adding that they all sent their love.

Although he hadn't expected anything less from them, Joss had heaved a sigh of relief that they were so understanding. Not for the first time he wished his dad had a splash of Uncle Joe's good nature.

TWENTY-FIVE

Ella

The moors had been keeping the snow at bay for the last couple of days. But, come Tuesday morning, the sky had taken on a threatening hue, glowering down, ready to let rip with its anger at any moment. The residents of Lytell Stangdale braced themselves.

Ella made her way carefully along the icy trod from Rose Cottage, her face tingling in the frosty air. The sub-zero temperatures of the last few days meant snow still hung around. It was piled high at the edges of the roads and pavements, while frost sparkled on the ground where it had been cleared. John Danks rumbled by in his tractor, giving her a friendly wave. Once he'd passed, she crossed the road to the village shop. The bell rang cheerfully as she opened the door, the ensuing wall of warm air a welcome respite. She spotted Freddie, the owner, who was busy on the phone behind the counter, writing down an order by the look of things.

'Hello there, lovey.' Molly's mum, Annie, gave her a warm smile, her large brown eyes so like her daughter's. She slipped a bag of flour into the basket on her arm. 'I feel like I haven't seen you for ages, how are you diddling?'

'Hiya, Annie. I'm fine thanks; just popped in to grab a bottle of milk.' She beamed back at her. 'You and Jack keeping okay up at Withrin Hill?'

'Aye, that we are, thanks, chick. Glad that Camm's keeping the roads clear so we can get into the village. Don't know what we'd do without him.'

'You're not the only one,' said Livvie, who appeared around the row of shelves. 'I've run out of cleaning stuff so I've had to come back to stock up.'

'Didn't you buy a load just the other day?' Ella felt sure she'd seen Livvie's basket heaving with bottles of household cleaner, cloths and the like when she was in the shop only a few days earlier.

Livvie giggled. 'I did, but I've got through loads of it trying to make sure the cottage is ready for when this little person arrives.' As she patted her bump, the bell jangled and Joss bowled in, his eyes bright with the cold. 'Hi,' he said, smiling, glancing round at the three women.

Ella felt her heart lift at the sight of him, plummeting a second later as what Portia had shared of their Sunday antics jumped into her mind. 'Hi.' She pushed her mouth into a smile as Annie and Livvie chorused their hellos, eyeing him with curiosity.

'Oh, erm, Annie, you remember Joss Campion, don't you?' Ella suddenly realised Annie probably didn't recognise him and Livvie definitely wouldn't know who he was. She turned to Livvie. 'Joss is from Camplin Farm; he's Bill's youngest son.'

'Oh, hi, Joss, it's good to meet you.' Livvie beamed a smile at him.

Ella glanced over at Joss. 'Livvie moved here from Rickelthorpe a couple of years ago. She's married to Zander Gillespie who's a GP at Danskelfe Surgery, they live over at Dale View Cottage just on the moor out of the village,' said Ella.

Joss nodded. 'Ahh, yes, I know it; nice location.'

'It's gorgeous,' said Livvie dreamily.

'Joss? Well, I never! Our Molly said you were back. It's so good to see you, lovey. Our Jack'll be over the moon when I tell him I've seen you.' Annie reached across and patted him gently on the arm. 'You're very welcome to pop up for a cuppa if you've got time.'

'Thanks, Annie. And I have to say, you haven't changed a bit.'

Annie giggled, reaching a hand up to touch her hair, two dots of colour appearing on her cheeks. 'Get away with you. Mind, our Molly taking over the farm has definitely made life easier; I dread to think how many wrinkles I'd have if we were still struggling on there, what with Jack's Parkinson's. He's happy as Larry now, just pottering about with the little flock of sheep he keeps for showing.'

Ella noticed Joss's smile falter; she wondered if he hadn't known about Jack's diagnosis.

'It's good to hear you're both doing well,' he said, his smile lifting again.

'Aye, we are that.' Smiling, Annie reached for a bag of currants. 'Right, well, I'd best get these paid for and head off; I've got Emmie coming for a visit this afternoon and she's keen to do a spot of baking.'

Ella and Livvie exchanged a knowing look as Annie made her way over to Freddie at the counter; Molly made no secret of the fact that her mother's cookery skills were absolutely diabolical.

'And I need to crack on with my cleaning. Good to meet you, Joss. Let's hope we see you around a bit more.' Livvie smiled up at him. 'Make way, woman the size of a hippo coming through,' she said as she squeezed past before following Annie to the counter.

Ella found her gaze drawn to Joss. She knew from her parents his dad was getting discharged from hospital later today, Joss was no doubt heading to Middleton-le-Moors to pick him up. He was bound to be feeling apprehensive.

Though Debbie and Pete had told Joss they were unable to collect his father owing to other commitments, it hadn't been strictly true. They thought Bill not having a choice but to travel back with Joss would give the pair a chance to talk; give Bill a chance to see his son wasn't the black sheep he'd convinced himself he was these last eighteen years. That it would, hopefully, make him start to realise Joss had grown into a responsible and decent man to be proud of. They'd heard enough over the years from Babs and Maff to know that to be true.

'You off to get your dad?' Ella asked.

'Yeah.' He drew in a long breath. 'Not sure he's going to take it too well when I rock up for him. But,' he said, splaying his palms, 'it's me or nothing.'

'You might be surprised; he might be chuffed to see you.'

Joss gave a throaty laugh. 'I think we both know that's not going to be the case.'

'Hey, you never know. My parents won't mind me telling you they've been having a bit of a chat with him. From what I can gather, I think he's aware he needs your help. Could be a good starting point for you both.' She looked up at him to see his expression had become serious. She bit down on her bottom lip, hoping she hadn't overstepped the mark.

'Aye, I suppose it could.' Despite his words, he didn't sound convinced.

An uncomfortable silence hovered and Ella was glad when Livvie passed them on her way out. 'See you guys later. Hope to see you again, Joss.'

At the door, Livvie met Little Mary, they exchanged a quick hello, each commenting on the state of the weather. The chilly air seized its opportunity and sneaked in.

'Well, I never! If it isn't young Joss Campion! I'd know those bonny greeny-blue eyes anywhere!' Little Mary hurried over to him. Her petite frame was wrapped up well against the bitterly cold temperatures thanks to her thick overcoat and fleece-lined boots, while a cheerful red felt hat was pulled low over her lily-white rows of curls. She looked up at Joss, a happy smile lighting up her face. 'It's grand to see you, lad. And, by, haven't you grown ever so tall?'

'Hi, Mary, it's grand to see you too. You're looking well.' Joss smiled down at her.

'Hi, Little Mary,' said Ella, thinking Joss was right; Little Mary was looking well. She seemed to have made a full recovery from the heavy cold that had gripped her for a couple of weeks.

'And can I say, how lovely it is to see you back here.' She reached up and patted his cheek, her face turning suddenly serious. 'Your dad needs you, son, though he might not show it at first. Just do your best to see past his moods and try not to give up on him.'

'I will, Mary.'

Ella noticed Joss's smile falter. It couldn't be easy for him, feeling that everyone knew what had been going on better than he.

Just then, his mobile phone rang. 'S'cuse me,' he said, reaching into the back pocket of his jeans. Little Mary bid him goodbye and disappeared down the shop in search of hair grips and teabags.

Ella caught a glimpse of the screen as Joss tapped his phone, quickly averting her eyes in case he caught her. The caller was Portia. Her face fell and she felt a surge of jealousy, hating herself for it. She hoped Joss hadn't noticed the change in her demeanour.

'I thought it might be something to do with my dad, but it's not. I can call back,' he said, closing the screen and putting his phone away.

'Don't on my account, I was just leaving.' Ella felt the overwhelming urge to get away from him, ignoring the fact she hadn't bought the bottle of milk she'd come in for. She made for the door, struggling to manage the cocktail of emotions swirling around inside her. Amongst them: jealousy, hurt, confusion, and something else she wasn't ready to put a name to.

'I'll follow you out; I was hoping to have a quick word.'

Ella felt her spirits sink. She didn't have anything to say to him, nothing that would make any kind of sense at least. Outside, she turned to him, hoping her face wouldn't reflect her feelings. 'I'm in a bit of a hurry actually. I'm heading over to my parents; I've got a few things to discuss with them.' Her voice came out sharper than she intended.

'Oh.' His smile dropped, making her feel suddenly guilty. 'I just wanted to check you're okay. It's just you seemed pretty quiet in the pub the other night; after you'd gone, everyone said so, and how it wasn't like you to leave early. And I haven't seen you since.'

Ughh! Ella was regretting coming to the shop. Somehow Joss Campion had managed to turn her perfectly peaceful existence upside down. How she hated feeling churned up like this. She mustered up a smile. 'I'm fine. I was just tired on Friday night, that's all. It had been a crazy busy last day at school after a frantic half-term. And I've been caught up doing other things too.' She shrugged and pulled her eyes away from his, feeling a tug in her heart. She resisted the temptation to say if he'd bothered to accept her parents' invitation for Sunday dinner, he'd have seen her then.

She could feel the weight of his gaze on her, her skin prickling at the atmosphere between them. It was the sort that circled round people who knew – or had known – each other well, when the words they'd left unsaid hung in the air like uninvited guests.

'Well, as long as you're okay.'

'I am,' she said resolutely, their breath merging together in the air.

Joss arched a questioning eyebrow at her, and she couldn't help but laugh.

'Honestly, I really am.'

His phone went again, the shrill sound ringing out into the peace and quiet of the village.

Ella took that as her cue to leave. 'See you later.' She gave a small smile before making her escape, heading towards the post office, sensing his eyes on her all the while. She'd pop back to the shop for her bottle of milk when he'd gone.

As she walked away, her mind was filled with thoughts of him and Portia, an image of them laughing together at the pub. The flirtatious vibes that had danced between the pair of them that night had been impossible to ignore. And it clearly hadn't taken long for the flirtation to become physical. That thought wrenched at her heart. *Ughh!* Why did it have to be Portia who took a fancy to him, of all people? Ella cursed herself; she was going to have to get rid of this pathetic school-girl jealously and get used to them being an item. She walked on, a tiny part of her hoping the relationship would be over as quickly as it started. Was it unkind of her to think that way? Yes! she told herself, but it still didn't stop her. She hoped the chat with her parents about her plans for the kennels would help take her mind off the pair of them before she got herself in a right old stew.

TWENTY-SIX

Joss

It was with great trepidation Joss made his way along to his father's ward, the strip-lighting bright overhead, the heavy scent of disinfectant in the air. The temperature in the hospital stood in stark contrast to that outside, and he felt stiflingly hot in his padded jacket and woollen scarf. After making enquiries at the desk, he followed the nurse's directions, his heart hammering. He hoped his dad's temper wasn't going to get the better of him. Joss was here to help; the last thing he wanted was a scene.

He scanned the half-dozen beds, all but one occupied by pyjama-clad men with matching wan expressions. His eyes stopped at the one empty bed, a holdall set on top of the crumpled sheets. The man sitting in the chair beside it looked up, his face clouding over. It took several moments before Joss realised the hollow-cheeked man with thinning hair and tired eyes was his father. He looked a good decade older than his sixty-two years. Joss's breath caught in his throat, pity washing over him. This felt surreal. Where was the muscular, broad-shouldered farmer of his memories?

'Dad,' he said, hesitantly stepping into the room and heading over to him, taking in the clothes that hung loose on his frame. He fought to hide his shock, hoping his father hadn't detected it.

'Aye.' His father gave him a curt nod, refusing to make eye contact with him.

Anxiety burnt in his stomach, Joss feeling every minute of the eighteen years it had been since they'd been in the same room as one another. 'Are you ready to go, or are you still waiting to be discharged?'

'Been done. I've been sat here waiting over an hour,' Bill said dourly.

Joss groaned inside. Not a great start. He resisted the urge to say he'd left a message explaining it would be early afternoon before he got to him. 'Right, well, I'll just tell one of the nurses we're heading off.' He leaned across and picked up his father's holdall. 'You ready?'

'Aye.' Bill retrieved his coat from the back of the chair, pushing his arms into it. He pulled a woolly hat from the pocket and put it on, then picked up a couple of pieces of paper and a leaflet from the over-bed table. Joss assumed it was what the hospital had given him to take away with him.

The pair made their way along the labyrinthine corridors and out into the carpark. Joss's attempts at conversation were met with nothing more than a perfunctory "aye" or a "no". His heart sank deeper with every step. It was going to be a long journey back to Lytell Stangdale.

Once in the Land Rover, Bill sat looking out of the passenger window, exuding hostility, his face set firm. Joss stole a sideways look at him as he went to pull out of the carpark, his mind searching for something – anything – to say to start up a conversation. Which wasn't easy since so much of their common ground was tainted by controversy: Rich, the farm, the fact they hadn't seen one another for nearly two decades, and the reason behind it.

'Pete and Debbie Welford have been a good help. They're really decent folk.' It was all Joss could think to say.

'Aye.'

'Debbie's made some meals for the freezer; casseroles mostly, which is kind of her. They sound tasty.'

Bill continued to look out of the window, making no reply, as if fascinated by the miles of snow-covered fields that stretched out either side of the road.

Joss headed out of Middleton-le-Moors, changing gear as he negotiated a sharp bend, the tyres of the Land Rover splashing through the slush that had melted thanks to a recent distribution of salt. 'I hope it's okay with you, but I brought my dog, Sid. He's a mix of Labrador and Irish Wolfhound and a bit of a character, but he's well-behaved.' Joss waited for his father to reply. He was to be disappointed.

He ploughed on. 'I've left him at the farm, in the kitchen; I didn't know how long we'd have to wait at hospital and I didn't think it was fair he had to wait in the Land Rover.'

Nothing.

The atmosphere thickened and he drew in a weary breath. 'Look, Dad, I know this isn't easy – for either of us – and I know you don't want me here.' Joss thought better of saying he didn't want to be there either. 'But don't you think it would be a good idea if we tried speaking to one another? Tried to be civil? I mean, I'm here to help because I was told you needed it. And despite the... despite what's gone on between us, you're my dad and I couldn't ignore that.' He glanced across at his father, disappointed to see his face still expressionless. He gave a small eye roll.

Undeterred, Joss continued. 'I'm sorry you haven't been well, Dad. And I know it must've been a massive shock to you. It shocked the life out of me to hear you'd collapsed; I came as soon as I could. Uncle Joe and Aunty Hannah were great about it. And I'm here to help with the farm 'til you're well enough for me to go.'

Bill remained impassive.

Joss still had no idea what had put his father in hospital. 'So, what did the doctors have to say? Did they give you a diagnosis? Do you need more tests?'

Silence. Bloomin' 'eck, this was like pulling teeth.

Time to try a different tack. 'I gather Pete and Debbie told you I know about the situation with Rich and the farm finances.'

No reply, though he did sense his father tense beside him.

'I'm not here to judge, but if you like, I can have a look at the accounts, Try and make sense of everything, see if we can get things back on track.'

Still nothing. Joss could feel irritation inching up his spine.

He squeezed on the steering wheel, his knuckles blanching white. Frustration bubbled up, filling his chest until it came out in an angry torrent. 'Look, Dad, like I said, I know you don't want me here, and truth be told, I'd rather not be here either. But I'm afraid neither of us has a choice in the matter unless you want the farm to go completely pear-shaped. And there's absolutely no point in you giving me the silent treatment, stonewalling me like I'm not here. That's not going to get us anywhere.' He shook his head in disbelief. 'Don't you think I've been punished enough? Don't you think I've paid my dues, being banished from home for all these years without a word from you? I know I did wrong. I know I was careless, foolish, stupid, thoughtless, any other name you care to throw at me. But at the end of the day, I was a kid, and I didn't do it on purpose, there was no malice involved. I made a mistake. It was an accident. No one got hurt. And, Lord knows, I've bloomin' well paid for it.' His breathing was shallow, his face hot and red. 'And if you must know, I haven't come back for you. I've come back for Mum; for her memory, because she'd hate to see you like this. Gah!' He hit his hand against the steering wheel, making his father jump.

From the corner of his eye Joss saw Bill wipe a tear from his eye. 'Diabetes,' the older man said in a wavery voice.

'Diabetes?'

'Aye, that's what they say I've got, what made me collapse. Type 2 diabetes. If Debbie hadn't turned up when she had I could've fallen into a coma.'

Joss drove on, his brows drawn down as he processed his father's revelation, the fear in his voice. His chest squeezed with concern. He briefly took his eyes away from the road. 'Bloody hell, Dad. You must've been feeling ill for a while. Diabetes isn't the sort of thing you just suddenly come down with; you must've had warning signs.'

'Aye, well, maybe I did but I don't like to trouble the doctors. Them at the hospital told me I had a bit of arthritis too, but I'd already guessed at that one. Joints have been giving me gyp for a while.' Bill sniffed, wiping his nose with the back of his gloved hand.

'Right.' Joss nodded. Progress! 'I assume they've given you some medication?'

'Aye, I've got a week's worth in my bag, but I need to drop a prescription in at the surgery in Danskelfe, and there's a letter from the hospital I have to give them too.'

'That's okay, we can swing by there on our way back.'

Bill nodded.

As they drew closer to the moors the sky darkened and fluffy snowflakes started dancing in front of the windscreen. Joss set the wipers away and flicked the vehicle's lights on. Dusk was already descending, smothering the daylight and bringing with it a sense of foreboding.

The remainder of the journey passed in relative silence but the relief Joss felt that his father had actually conversed with him was immeasurable. What he'd told him about coming back to help out for the memory of his mum was true. It hadn't been easy putting so many years' worth of bitterness and hurt behind him, but after talking things through with his Uncle Joe and Aunty Hannah, the prospect had seemed a little less daunting. The three of them had agreed that his mother would be devastated if she could see the predicament his father was in. Joss had needed no further motivation. 'And she'd be heartbroken if she knew you hadn't been home for all these years, lad,' Uncle Joe had said. 'It's time to get things sorted. Time you and he put your past differences behind you.'

.   .   .

'By, you're a grand lad, aren't you?' Bill bent to scratch Sid's head, who'd shot over to him after treating Joss to a warm greeting. Bill might not always get on with humans but he loved animals and they loved him.

'Meet Sid,' said Joss, smiling and hanging up his coat, watching as Sid's tail wagged vigorously. 'He's a friendly lad with a big heart.' Though his dad speaking to him had been a major break-through, making conversation still felt decidedly uncomfortable. But Joss was determined to plough on, trying his hardest to sound casual. Normal. As if the chasm of eighteen years didn't exist, and he'd only seen his dad yesterday. It didn't stop it from feeling weird though. He set Bill's bag down on the floor by the dresser. Sid didn't waste a moment, and ran over to give it a serious sniffing.

Joss rubbed his hands together, searching for something to say. 'Can I get you a cuppa?' The British answer to everything. Though he had to admit, it felt odd offering his father a cup of tea when he himself had been a stranger in this kitchen for so long. Joss pushed the discomfort away, reasoning that he'd have to face countless situations like this before he headed home.

'Aye, thanks.'

Bill was sitting in the rocking chair and Joss at the table when the hum of an engine cut through the air of awkwardness that had descended. It was quickly followed by the sound of a car door clos-ing. Joss made his way to the window at the sink and peered out to see Ella heading cautiously over the ice towards the house, a large dish in her hand. Boy, was he glad to see her.

'Hi.' He opened the door, his heart leaping as she looked up and smiled, a feather-like snowflake landing on the tip of her nose. The way she giggled sent an unexpected ripple of longing through him, taking him all the way back to when they were sixteen. It had driven him crazy then, and it appeared to have the same effect on him now.

'Hiya, sorry to intrude. I wasn't expecting you to be here; thought you'd be ages at the hospital. My mum asked if I'd put this in the Rayburn so it'd be ready for when you got back.'

'Oh, right, that's very good of you both.' Joss stood back, holding the door wide.

'Thanks.' She stamped the snow off her feet on the outside doormat and stepped inside.

Sid left Bill's side and raced over to her, his tail wagging hard. 'Hello, Sid. Is this enthusiastic greeting for me or for the sausage casserole I'm holding, eh?' Ella said, chuckling. 'Hello there, Bill. It's good to see you looking better.' She beamed at him as she headed over to the worktop by the stove. Joss was pleased to note she seemed brighter than she had this morning.

'Now then, lass. It's good to be feeling better, I can tell you.' Bill smiled back at her. 'And will you thank your mum and dad for all they've been doing while I was in hospital – Greg too. It's much appreciated. And thank you too for what you've done in here; you've got the place cosy again.'

Joss looked on, surprised at the transformation in his father as he spoke to Ella, how his face had brightened.

'No problem, Bill; you know what it's like round here, folk pull together when needs be. We were just happy we could help.'

'Don't suppose you've got time for a cup of tea?' Joss pushed his hands into the front pockets of his jeans, a warm feeling spreading in his chest as his eyes lingered on her.

'Erm...'

He glanced up at the clock on the wall. 'It's the least I can do after all you've done for us.'

'Don't you have things you should be doing? I mean, I don't want to take up your time.'

'Well, I don't need to tell you of all people there's always stuff needs doing on a farm, but I can make an exception for today; I'd expected things to take longer at the hospital, and I'm not due to start milking for another hour.'

'Well, if you're sure, I'll take you up on that. Come to think of it, I haven't had a drink for hours.'

While Joss made a fresh pot of tea, Ella divested herself of her coat and hung it on the back of a dining chair before plonking herself down.

Bill yawned, pushing himself up out of the rocking chair. 'Well, if you two'll excuse me, I think I'll go and have a bit of a lie down. Didn't get much sleep in hospital, bloomin' noisy place, the fella in the next bed to me snored like a pig. I'll get back to work tomorrow.' He put his mug on the draining board and trudged his way out of the kitchen. 'Nice to see you, lass.' He patted her shoulder as he passed.

'Nice to see you too, Bill.' She looked up at him and smiled.

'Have a good kip, Dad.' Joss set two mugs down on the table, taking the seat opposite Ella. He watched his father leave, waited until he heard the creaks of the stairs as Bill made his way up them. 'Pftt!' He sat back in his seat, raking his fingers through his hair, making it stick up on end.

'How's it going?' asked Ella, resting her elbows on the table and looking across at him.

Joss was caught off guard, struck by how beautiful she was. Her make-up-free face was dewy and fresh, her cheeks still pink from the cold. He drank her in, savouring her large brown eyes with the amber flecks, edged with long, dark lashes, her unruly, thick dark brows and her plump, raspberry-red lips. She was a true natural beauty. He felt a sudden yearning inside him. His attraction to her went way deeper than the one he had for Portia. He liked Portia in a superficial, no-strings kind of way – a feeling he felt sure she reciprocated. She was attractive and fun. But what he felt for Ella touched him in a way his feelings for no other woman had; they shared a connection that meant no one else could ever come close. He knew that now. What a shame it was too late.

'Joss?'

Ella's voice dragged him from his thoughts. 'Oh, er, sorry. I was miles away.'

'I asked how things are? With you and your dad? They don't seem too bad.' An amused smile danced over her lips.

He took a deep breath, turning his attention away from

wondering what those lips would feel like on his right now; that had got him into trouble once before and he wasn't prepared to risk it again. 'Well, after a bit of a bumpy start when he refused to look at me, never mind speak to me, things seem to be okay. I'm not going to kid myself everything in the garden's rosy. There's still an uncomfortable air between us, still a lot of talking to be done, but today's not the day. He needs to rest before we tackle that.'

'Yeah, you're right; he looks pretty frail.'

'Hmm. Looks like I'm going to be here a good while longer.' How did she feel about that? he wondered. 'Anyway, how about you? Are you working at the Sunne tonight?'

She shook her head. 'No, I'm heading to my parents'. There's a few things I need to have a chat with them about. How about you? Meeting up with Portia?'

His eyes flicked up to hers and he felt his face flush. 'Portia?' It suddenly hit him; Ella knew about his dalliance with her friend. *Why wouldn't she, you turkey? They're buddies.*

'Yeah, Portia's told me you've been seeing quite a bit of each other recently.'

Joss knew what that meant: She knew they'd slept together. 'Ah, right.' If he wasn't mistaken, he felt sure her smile faltered. 'Yeah, it's nothing serious for either of us. Just a bit of fun. It's not going anywhere. Portia knows I'm not looking for anything long term, that I need a break after Manda.' Why did he suddenly feel like a rat?

'Oh, right. Are you sure Portia knows that?' Ella sat back, cradling her mug in her hands.

Her question surprised him. 'I'm pretty sure she does. I mean, she gives the impression she does.' He scratched his head, wondering if Ella knew more than she was letting on. Since her call this morning, Portia had rung him a couple more times, leaving a message about them meeting up again. He'd been so tied up, what with the farm and collecting his father, he hadn't had a chance to get back to her. Maybe they needed a chat to clarify their respective positions. If what Ella was alluding to was right, he didn't want

Portia to feel he was leading her on. 'I kind of got the feeling she knew I wasn't looking for a relationship. It's why I was okay to hook up with her.'

Ella nodded slowly. What he'd give to know what she was thinking.

He wondered which of them was guilty of sending out the wrong signals: him or Portia? Either way, embarking on a serious relationship had been the furthest thing from his mind when he'd been tempted by her kisses. And, with everything else that was going on, he could really do without the hassle of having to explain it to her again.

He released a quick sigh, raising his mug to his mouth. 'Anyway, what have you been doing with yourself today?' Time to change the conversation.

'Well, you've got to promise to keep this to yourself...' Ella launched into an enthusiastic sharing of her ideas for a boarding kennels, telling him how she'd been discussing it with her parents with a view to setting the business up at Tinkel Bottom Farm. She swore him to secrecy since she didn't want word getting out before she'd had the chance to work out if it was viable; she wanted to be the first to tell the staff at school; the last thing she wanted was for them to find out through gossip. He mimed pulling a zip across his mouth, making her giggle.

The animated way she'd spoken about her plans almost felt like old times, their awkwardness falling away. He sat back in his seat, arms folded across his chest, watching her. It felt good, sitting here in this room, the two of them together. He was savouring every moment.

'So, what do you think?' she asked when she'd finished, looking at him, her eyes shining hopefully.

Joss leaned forward, resting his arms on the table, flashing a wide smile. 'I think it's a brilliant idea, especially if the closest boarding kennels is at Middleton-le-Moors. And just looking at how your face lit up when you were talking about it, you've got to do it.'

'You really think so?'

'I do.' He nodded. 'It sounds like the perfect business for you; you've always been animal crazy. You'll put your all into it and make it a roaring success.'

'Thanks.' Ella beamed, her face blushing an attractive shade of pink that made his heart beat that little bit faster.

Her eyes met his, setting electricity crackling in the air around them. Joss felt longing surge through his veins, making his pupils darken. He swallowed as he struggled with the urge not to reach across the table and pull her into a kiss.

The moment was shattered when a yelp came from Sid who was flat out by the Rayburn. His eyes were tight shut and his paws were twitching frantically as he raced over fields after who-knew-what in his dream. A long, low growl rumbled from him making Joss and Ella laugh. The spell was broken.

TWENTY-SEVEN

Ella

'Will you be around tonight, darling?' From the way Portia was shouting and the accompanying background noise, Ella guessed her friend was driving and had her mobile on speakerphone.

'You mean at Rose Cottage?' Ella had left Joss and headed straight to her parents' farm where they'd had a wander around the place, working out where would be best to site the boarding kennels. She'd been disappointed that nowhere obvious had leapt out as being the ideal spot. That done, she'd migrated to Clive the donkey's stable and had just finished grooming him, the air sweet with the scent of the fresh hay he was now munching on. Ella scratched between his ears. 'Yeah, I should be back by about half five. Why? Are you planning on popping in?'

'If that's okay?'

'Course. It'll be good to see you.' Ella felt a twinge of discomfort. She wondered if Joss had spoken to her friend, set her straight as far as his feelings were concerned.

'You're welcome to grab a bite to eat with me, if you fancy? Just spag bol and garlic bread; I can get an extra portion out of the freezer. Won't be quite up to your mum's standard, but it'll be edible, especially if it's washed down with a glass of vino.'

Portia gave a throaty chuckle. 'Sounds fabulous. I'm just on my way back from a meeting with Caro at Danskelfe Castle. I'll be with you around six, if that's all right?'

'Looking forward to it, chick. And mind how you go; that road from the castle is notorious in this weather, what with black ice and snow drifts. It might look okay, especially now it's putting in dark, but don't be fooled; it's best to keep in a low gear.'

'Will do. Ciao, darling.'

'See you.' Ella slotted her phone into the back pocket of her jeans, chewing on the corner of her mouth as she did so. Much as she was looking forward to spending the evening with Portia, the situation with Joss had ever-so-slightly taken the shine off her friend's visit. She heaved a sigh. There was no way she was going to let Portia's "romance" – for want of a better word – with him affect their friendship. And there was no way she was going to mention that Joss had brought it up with her; that was up to him, if he hadn't done so already. That set the cogs of her mind cranking up a gear. Was Portia wanting to call round because Joss had set her straight and she was upset? Ella hoped not; she didn't like the thought of her friend being sad, especially this close to Christmas.

But there was a tiny part of her that had been relieved when Joss had told her Portia and he weren't serious. Actually, that was a big fat lie. An enormous part of her had been relieved. And, much as she wasn't proud of herself for feeling that way, it didn't stop the little nugget of happiness from growing inside her.

Spending time with Joss earlier that afternoon, the way they'd laughed and chatted together, it had felt like the years had fallen away, leaving two best friends sitting together. The awkwardness of earlier had disappeared. Just like old times. Only it wasn't quite. Ella had found herself looking at Joss in a new light, observing his handsome features as he'd spoken, as he'd listened. The way he'd looked at her with those striking eyes, the smile that hovered over his full – and very tempting – mouth, the golden highlights in his hair where the light caught it. And don't get her started on those muscular shoulders. She felt a shiver of desire ripple through her. The air had buzzed with electricity between them, and she knew he'd felt it too.

But he'd made it perfectly clear he wasn't interested in getting involved with anyone. And after her stifling relationship with Owen, Ella wasn't ready to give up her freedom just yet. Though it didn't stop her from wondering what would have happened if things had been different. Would they have succumbed to the feelings that were so clearly blooming and gaining pace between them? Would they have found themselves unable to resist the magnetic pull that had been drawing them together, her ending up in his arms? If the attraction had been that strong, nothing would've stopped it, said a little voice in her head. 'Best not get carried away with yourself, Ella,' she said to herself. She sighed and gave Clive an affectionate pat.

'Are you sure I can't help?' Portia asked, watching Ella plate up the spaghetti Bolognese in the tiny kitchen of Rose Cottage. Tabby-Cat was weaving through her legs, mewing noisily for attention. 'Hello there, Tabs, it's good to see you too.'

'You can top up the wine.' Ella added a garnish of parsley to the plates.

'Ah, yes. I think I can manage that, as long as Tabs here doesn't trip me up. Mmm. That looks seriously good; I'm starving.' Portia glanced across at Ella's handiwork as she headed towards the fridge, reaching in for the bottle. Tabby-Cat shot off into the living room where she stretched out in front of the wood-burner.

'Help yourself to Parmesan.' Ella set the plates down and pulled out a chair at the little pine dining table.

'Will do. Chin-chin,' said Portia, holding her glass aloft and grinning.

'Cheers, chick.' Ella clinked her glass against it, pleased to see her friend was in good spirits. 'So, tell me about your day; how's it going up at the castle?'

'Oh, I totally *adore* working with Caro. She's an absolute hoot; not at all what I expected. And she's got some fabulous ideas for the future of the place once she's finished working on the lodge project.'

Ella listened, grinding black pepper over her pasta.

'We're going for a slightly different theme with each of the lodges, with an overall style linking them; think contemporary country chic and you're along the right lines. I'm talking thick carpets, underfloor heating, sumptuous fabrics, luxurious bath-rooms. It'll be cosy yet stylish at the same time.' She gave a theatrical sigh. 'I'm so totally in my element.'

Ella smiled. 'Sounds amazing.' She twirled pasta around her fork and popped it into her mouth, chewing as Portia continued.

'It is, and I love how Caro has put all her trust in me; not all clients are like that, I can tell you. Oh! Oh! Oh! Golly, how could I have forgotten?' Portia's eyes grew wide as she flapped her hand around. 'You'll never guess who I saw up at the castle. Oh, my goodness! I got such a surprise when I saw him, and he's even more drop-dead gorgeous in the flesh.'

Ella couldn't help but giggle. 'Gabe Dublin, by any chance?'

'How did you know?' Portia paused mid-flap.

'I heard a whisper he'd been spotted in the village again.'

'Oh, I do like whispers like that, and he's really quite delicious.'

Ella couldn't help but chuckle at Portia's reaction to the popular Irish singer. Gabe Dublin had been a good friend of Lady Carolyn's sound engineer husband, Sim, for years, and he regu-larly sought refuge behind the battle-scarred walls of Danskelfe Castle when press interest in him became too intense. She was tempted to say there was another whisper that he'd been pursuing Kitty's step-daughter, Anoushka, for the last year – though she appeared to be immune to his charms – but thought better of it. Much as she loved Portia, her friend had a habit of occasionally letting confidential matters slip quite by accident. She was always utterly mortified afterwards, and full of apologies, making it hard to be cross with her, but all the same, it had made Ella cautious about what she shared. She'd keep quiet about Noushka and Gabe.

'Anyway, how about you, darling? Best not talk any more about gorgeous Gabe or I'll end up all hot and bothered.' She made a show of fanning herself with her festive paper napkin, making Ella giggle. 'So, tell me what mischief you've been up to today,' Portia asked, moving on from the singer rather more hastily than Ella expected.

She swallowed her mouthful. 'I helped out on the farm like I usually do on my days off, popped up to Camplin Farm to drop off a sausage casserole my mum had made for Bill coming out of hospital.' Ella's pulse upped its speed as she noted the flicker in Portia's eyes. She braced herself, anticipating her friend's pending interrogation.

'Oh, okay. He was at the hospital,' Portia said, more to herself than Ella. 'So, was there any sign of Mr Hot-To-Trot while you were there?'

'Mr Hot-To-Trot?' Ella feigned ignorance. *You know full well who Portia means!*

'Well, I don't mean crusty old Bill!' Portia hooted with laughter, taking a sip of her wine. 'I'm talking about Joss! Just because you don't find him attractive, doesn't mean the rest of us don't. Did you clap eyes on him at all?'

Ella found she couldn't meet her friend's gaze. 'Um, yeah, Joss was there too. I actually wasn't expecting them back that early. I just intended to sneak in, put the casserole in the Rayburn, leave a note telling them, then beat a hasty retreat.' Ella gave what she hoped was a casual shrug. 'After I left there, I headed back down to my parents', had a bit of a chat with them. Saw to the goats, groomed Clive, which was what I was doing when you rang. Oh, while I remember, are you going to Vi and Jimby's party tomorrow night?' She hoped mention of a party would steer Portia nicely away from the subject of Joss.

'Since when have I ever missed a party I've been invited to?' Portia gave an exaggerated arch of her eyebrows.

'Umm, that would be never.' The pair of them giggled. Ella breathed an inward sigh of relief; Portia appeared to have been distracted.

'Too right. And this is absolutely divine by the way.' Portia circled her fork above her plate of food.

'Thanks, glad you think so, it's my mum's recipe. I made a huge batch and put a load of individual portions in the freezer.'

'Mmm. It's yum. You're super-organised. Anyway, getting back to Joss.' Portia set her fork down and ran her tongue across her teeth.

Ella groaned inwardly. *Uh-oh.*

'I popped up to the farm this afternoon – you and I must've just missed each other.'

'Oh, right.' Ella could feel her spirits slowly sinking. She reached for her glass and took a glug.

'I'd been trying to get hold of him with no success, so I thought I'd take the proverbial bull by the horns; I'd got the feeling he was avoiding me, and you know what I'm like, I just had to get to the bottom of it.'

Ella knew exactly what Portia was like. Direct, but with a kind heart, was how someone had once described her, throwing in "could do with a bit of a filter" as an afterthought. Ella thought it a pretty apt description. But she admired how her friend preferred to face things head on, no matter how unpalatable; she could take it on the chin and dust herself down afterwards. It was a good trait, but also a bit of a failing as it meant she had the tendency to put people on the spot. Which was what Ella suspected she'd done to Joss today.

'Right, and did the trip to the farm help?' Her mind began whirling, she couldn't begin to imagine how the conversation had gone. Though Portia did appear to be in good spirits, so she can't have heard anything too upsetting.

Portia chewed, looking thoughtful. 'Um, yes, I think it did.'

'Oh?'

'When Joss explained how busy he'd been, I totally understood. To be honest, I felt a bit silly for not even considering how much he'd have to do, facing the chaos up there, never mind having to collect his father from hospital. Can't have been easy for him to land in the middle of all that.'

'Yeah, he's got a lot on.' Ella felt a pang of sympathy for him. But it didn't stop her from being eager to find out what, if anything, Joss had said to Portia about their romance.

Portia chewed on her mouthful earnestly. 'He has. Anyway, he went on to say how much he found me attractive, thought I was great fun, the usual blah-di-blah-di-blah.' She waved her hand around. 'Then went on to say how he wasn't ready for a deep and meaningful relationship. And how, after the breakdown of his marriage, he wasn't likely to be for quite a while. Apologised if he'd been giving out the wrong signals.'

Ella nodded, absorbing Portia's words. The thought that she could be potentially included in that umbrella statement triggered an ache in her heart. She blinked, trying to ignore it, turning her focus instead to twirling spaghetti onto her fork. 'Okay. And how did you leave it with him?'

'Well, I listened, of course, but what I didn't tell him was that I can bide my passion, for want of a better word.' Portia grinned, her eyes glinting. 'Especially when something's worth waiting for. I mean, let's not forget, I've sampled what's on offer, and delectable Joss Campion is most definitely worth waiting for. I'm not about to let him get away any time soon, I think we'd be so good together.' She pinned Ella with her ice-blue eyes. 'Do you think there's a chance he'll change his mind?'

Ella's heart hit her feet with an almighty thwump, Portia's words sending a tidal wave of emotions washing over her. What kind of messed-up situation had she found herself in, for crying out loud? A pathetic one, that's what. Confusion swirled around her mind. Why did she feel this way? She loved her friend dearly and if Portia had been talking about waiting for any other man, Ella knew she'd be making lots of encouraging sounds right now, but how the heck did she answer Portia's question? This was so awkward. Joss had told her himself he wasn't looking for a relationship, that he regarded what he had with Portia as just a fling. *Arghh!* Ella felt torn for so many reasons. Porsh didn't seem to have taken on board what Joss had said, which was making Ella wonder if he'd actually said it like he'd meant it, or worded it in such a way he'd inadvertently given her friend false hope. But, then again, Portia did sometimes have a habit of hearing what she wanted, deliberately ignoring the bits she found unpalatable. Ughh! This was difficult.

'Ells!'

'Uhh!' Ella was startled to see Portia's long, elegant fingers clicking in front of her face.

'Seems your mind's been off on a little wander again.' Her friend chuckled.

'Sorry, Porsh.' She shook her head, ridding it of the muddled thoughts, and smiled across at her friend.

'No worries, darling. I was just wondering if you thought my feminine wiles stood a chance of making Joss change his mind about a long-term relationship?'

'Erm,' her brows drew together as she contemplated the question, 'I honestly don't know.' And, in truth, she didn't.

Later that evening, after Portia had returned to the pub, Ella curled up on the sofa, Tabby-Cat snuggling into her, purring noisily as she was treated to a tummy rub. The room was cosy, courtesy of the wood-burner that had been on all day, the soft glow from the table lamps adding to the effect. A Christmas movie played gently in the background as Ella contemplated her conversation with Portia. She'd arrived at the decision that she was going to put Joss firmly out of her mind, arguing that his sudden arrival had merely resurrected feelings she'd had as a teenager; ones she'd denied at the time. They were nothing more than a school-girl crush. They didn't fit the person she was today. She'd outgrown them. She'd moved on. And besides, she valued her friendship with Portia way more than a flirtation with a man who wasn't even going to stick around. What he did with her friend was none of her business.

She drew in a deep breath as the feeling of guilt that had taken up residence in her mind slipped away, taking with it that other undesirable imposter that had made her feel so uneasy: jealousy.

TWENTY-EIGHT

Joss

Bill Campion was sitting at the table reading the newspaper while Joss served up their evening meal – he'd raided the freezer and pulled out another one of Debbie Welford's casseroles – and the delicious aroma now filled the kitchen. He stole a look at his father. He still hadn't got used to how much older than his Uncle Joe he looked despite being a couple of years younger. But he was pleased to see some colour had returned to his sallow cheeks. He'd gently encouraged his dad to take it easy; he was keen for him to build up his muscles, get a bit of weight back on him before he took on anything strenuous at the farm. It had caused more than a little friction between the pair.

Earlier that day, he'd rushed to his father's aid when he'd found him struggling with a large bag of feed. 'Dad, I'll do that. It's heavy, you shouldn't—'

'Don't tell me what I should and shouldn't be doing, lad!' Bill had yelled at him, his eyes flashing angrily. 'Stop treating me like a bloomin' invalid. I'm perfectly capable.'

Joss had swallowed, his heart racing; it had been a while since he'd been on the receiving end of his dad's fierce temper. 'I'm sorry, I just—'

'Aye, well don't bloomin' "just" anything. I'll tell you when I need help. In the meantime, leave me be.'

His dad had been prickly ever since, saving the few kind words he doled out for Sid, who appeared to think he was fabulous. There was no accounting for taste, Joss thought.

It wasn't the only time his dad had snapped at him. Throughout the day, there had been several occasions when he seemed to slip back into his short-tempered, angry persona, snarling when Joss tried to make conversation, then apparently back-tracking when he realised that's not how things were between them anymore.

'It's good to see the barn doors fixed, lad,' Bill had said after he'd bitten his son's head off for asking something inconsequential about the dairy herd. Joss had struggled not to snap back. He was finding the outbursts from his father draining and was getting fed up of feeling like he had to tread on eggshells around him. He'd gone to walk away, remove himself from the reach of his father's sharp tongue, stopping when he'd recognised the clumsy olive branch.

'Aye, Pete Welford gave me a hand.'

'He's a good bloke is Pete.' Bill had nodded and wandered off.

Joss had sucked in a deep breath, his gaze following his father, thinking his time at Camplin Farm was going to be a long, drawn out affair if things continued in this way.

It was why he was so relieved when the landline had rung earlier. Joss had answered it to hear Jimby's jovial tones on the other end, inviting him to join him and Vi and a few friends for an informal party as his house later that evening. 'Sorry for the late notice, I thought Vi had mentioned it the other night, and she thought I had. Typical, eh? But you're more than welcome to join us. And you'll probably be pleased to know it's a kid-free zone; Pippin's having a sleepover at Vi's parents' place; they live in the village now.'

'Pippin?'

Jimby had given a hearty chuckle. 'Ah, force of habit. Pippin's our little girl. Real name's Elspeth, but she was nicknamed Pippin before she was born on account of Vi's mad craving for apples when she was expecting her. Seems to have stuck. Anyroad, it'd be great if you could get yourself here.'

The thought of getting out of the house had lifted his spirits and Joss found himself very tempted, but he wasn't sure how his father would feel about being left on his own. 'Thanks for the invite, Jimby. I'll get down if I can.'

'Good stuff. Seven-thirty. Rowan Tree Cottage. The new one just up from the Sunne near the green. Can't miss it.'

The brief taste of village life Joss had experienced so far, combined with the warm welcome he'd had from those he'd met, had chased away his earlier unease. Now the need to hide away and keep folk at arm's length no longer seemed necessary.

When he'd broached the subject of the party with his father, he'd been surprised to find it was met with a positive reaction. 'You should get yourself there. I can manage. In fact, it'll be a nice change from having you fussing round me like an old mother hen. Driving me mad, you are. You can leave Sid with me; he's no bother, are you, lad?'

Sid gave a swish of his tail.

Joss made his way steadily down to the village. It was a clear, still night and the frost at the edges of the road glittered in the moonlight while the moors were bathed in a pale, ethereal glow. A tawny owl swooped down in front of him, disappearing with a flap of its wings before a rabbit shot out of the hedgerow, dazzled by the Land Rover's headlights, making his heart stop. He slammed his foot on the brakes, the anti-lock system jumping to action. 'Flippin' 'eck!'

Before long, Joss was in the village, parking up and scanning the road for the newly-built Rowan Tree Cottage. On the green just near the pub stood a huge Christmas tree festooned with hundreds of shining warm-white lights. That was a new addition to the festivities since he used to live here. Christmas tree lights sparkled in the windows of the squat cottages, some even had trees in their gardens. It created a homely, magical effect that gladdened the heart.

Joss arrived outside the solid oak door of Rowan Tree Cottage, which was adorned with a huge festive wreath, its fairy lights twinkling merrily. He sported a bottle of wine in each hand; he'd picked them up in the village shop earlier that day. In a moment, the door was flung open and Jimby's beaming face peered out, music and happy voices spilling out onto the doorstep. 'Now then, Joss! Come in, mate.'

'Now then, Jimby.' Joss stepped into the hallway, welcoming the wave of warmth that swept over him.

'It's great to see you.' Jimby patted him heartily on the back. 'Vi, look who's here.'

'Can I give you these?' Wiping his feet on the mat, Joss handed the bottles to Jimby.

'Ey, there was no need, but it's very kind of you. Just hang your coat up there.' He nodded in the direction where a load of coats and jackets were piled on a row of coat pegs.

Vi appeared, smiling and looking über glamorous in a figure-hugging dress in a rich shade of deep-plum that flattered the glossy waves of her aubergine hair. 'Hiya, Joss, I'm really glad you could make it. Come on through, everyone's here, well, except for Rosie and Robbie, they can't make it; they're visiting Robbie's parents.'

'What can I get you to drink?' asked Jimby.

'Erm, I'll have a shandy, thanks. Sorry to be boring, but I'm driving.'

'Hey, I get it, we've all been there, and you need your wits about you in this weather.'

Joss followed the pair down the hallway, taking in the thick pine garland wrapped around the bannister of the oak staircase, decorated with yet more fairy lights and rich purple baubles.

Soon he arrived in a huge, sleek kitchen. Though it was a contemporary build, the ceiling boasted rows of sturdy-looking light-oak beams. He found the contrast of old and new styles appealing. A track from the nineties was discernible above the convivial babble of chatter, and amongst the throng he spotted Ollie who nodded and came straight over, holding out his hand. 'Good to see you here, Joss.' Ollie gave a friendly smile. 'How's your dad doing?'

'Hi, Ollie, he's better in health than temper, thanks,' he said with a laugh.

'Ah, right. Well, it must be a relief he's out of hospital.'

'Aye, it is.'

Jimby reappeared, thrusting a glass of shandy at Joss. 'There you go, get that down your neck, lad.'

'Cheers.' Joss raised his glass and the other two men mirrored his gesture.

'So, how's things up at the farm?' asked Jimby.

Joss understood the subtext: how are you and your dad getting along? 'A lot better than I expected to be honest. Don't get me wrong, neither of us is finding it easy but we're both trying to make the best of the situation. I'm hoping it'll get better as the days go on.'

'Sounds like you've earnt a night out,' said Jimby, grinning. 'Shame you can't have a few beers, let your hair down.'

'Trust me, I'm just glad to be out.' The prospect of another evening sitting in the living room with his father, watching the television with an awkward silence swirling around them, wasn't at all appealing. He'd never felt more like a stranger since his return than he had last night.

A man with close-cropped dark hair was heading in their direction. 'Joss, allow me to introduce our GP, Dr Zander Gillespie. Zander, this is Joss Campion, Bill's son, he's looking after the farm,' said Jimby.

Zander flashed a friendly smile and held out his hand. 'Pleased to meet you, Joss.'

'Likewise,' said Joss, the warmth of his smile matching Zander's.

'Zan lives along at Dale View Cottage, just out of the village. He's married to Livvie over there; they're expecting their first baby.' Jimby nodded to where Livvie was chatting to Freddie and Lucy from the village shop, smoothing her hand over her huge bump.

'Ah, right. I met Livvie in the shop the other day,' said Joss.

Zander laughed, shaking his head affectionately. 'Buying cleaning products no doubt; she's scrubbed the cottage from top to bottom several times over. Even our Labrador hasn't escaped her cleaning frenzy; poor old Alf's coat's never looked so glossy.' The three men chuckled.

'And how's your father doing?' Zander asked Joss.

'Not too bad, thanks. I'm still trying to get him to take it easy 'til he builds his strength back up. Doesn't like to be told though; I have to choose my words very carefully.' Joss took a glug of his shandy

'Hm.' Zander nodded. 'Well, you know where we are if you need us, but if you'll excuse me, I just need to get a top up of water for Liv. Good to meet you.'

'Aye, you too.'

Joss scanned the room, his heart jumping as his eyes alighted on Ella. She was having an animated conversation with Kitty and Molly. Molly said something and Ella threw her head back, roaring with laughter, while Kitty covered her mouth and giggled. He was struck by the fact that Ella was wearing a dress; he couldn't ever remember seeing her in one; she always favoured trousers even if she was going somewhere smart. He took in her simple black number, its short, fan-sleeves, the soft fabric decorated with a scattering of black, matt sequins, skimming over her curves. She looked stunning. She caught his eye and smiled, sending happiness rushing through him.

Five minutes later, he found himself standing beside her, the sweet, familiar smell of her perfume wafting under his nose. All of his senses stood to attention.

'Hi,' she said, her dark eyes shining as she looked up at him, one hand fiddling with the infinity pendant of her necklace.

'Hi.' He was struck by how achingly beautiful she was. Her hair was out of its usual ponytail and hung in rich waves past her shoulders. He had an overwhelming urge to run his fingers through it. Her cheeks were flushed from the warmth of the room, assisted no doubt by the wine she'd been drinking, and her eyes looked tempting and smoky. His gaze fell to her mouth, sending a pulse of desire through him. He swallowed, quickly meeting her eyes again. 'Had a good day?' was all he could think to ask thanks to the wayward thoughts that suddenly dominated his mind.

'Not bad. You?' She smiled, taking a sip of her wine, peering up at him.

'Erm, let's just say it's been challenging, but nowhere near as much as I was expecting.' He laughed.

'That's got to be a good thing.' She laughed too. 'Rich been in touch?'

'Nope.' He shook his head, giving a small eye roll. 'After what I've heard, I wasn't really expecting it. I sent him a text saying Dad was out of hospital, but he hasn't replied.'

Ella nodded. 'Probably just as well.'

Joss grinned, amusement dancing in his eyes; he was finding it hard to think about Rich when she was standing in front of him looking irresistible. 'I was just trying to remember the last time I saw you in a dress.' Her hand moved from the infinity pendant to tuck her hair behind her ear; he resisted the temptation to mention the necklace, and his surprise that she still wore it.

'Er, that would be never.' She chuckled. 'I think I can count on one hand the number of times it's happened and I'd go so far as to say I was probably aged ten or under.'

'You should wear one more often; you look really pretty.' In fact, he thought she looked good enough to eat.

Ella's face flushed to a deeper shade of pink, and she was just about to reply before a familiar well-spoken voice got there first.

'*There* you are!' They turned to see Portia, a glass of freshly-poured Prosecco in her hand. She was looking effortlessly glamorous in a diaphanous pale-grey silk dress shot with a fine silver thread. It stopped just above the knee and had a dangerously plunging neckline. Her hair was scooped up in a chignon, and tiny diamond studs glittered at her ears, while a pair of impossibly high, strappy, silver sandals adorned her feet. She sidled up to Joss, slipping her arm around his waist. He felt himself tense.

'Hi, Porsh. I was beginning to wonder where you'd got to,' said Ella, smiling.

Joss thought Ella looked genuinely pleased to see her friend. Was she relieved? he wondered. Relieved that he wouldn't be able to continue their conversation?

'Hello, Portia.' He was aware of Ella's eyes on him; it was almost as if she was assessing his reaction to Portia. Was she checking to see if Joss was guilty of leading her friend on?

'Got waylaid helping Mum at the pub,' Portia said, airily. 'But I'm here now, and I'm jolly keen to make up for lost time.' She waggled her glass of fizz, flashing a dazzling smile at Joss. 'So, tell me, what have I missed?'

'I've just got here myself,' said Joss. From the way her hand was roaming up and down his back, she clearly hadn't got the message about wanting to cool things. He felt a prickle of annoyance. He'd been enjoying his conversation with Ella; if he was honest with himself, she was the main reason he was here, not just to escape from his father for a couple of hours.

'Been pretty tame so far, unless you include Jimby giving us a quick demo of his salsa dancing skills.' Ella's smile widened.

'Now that's something I'd like to see,' said Joss, grinning, his memory harking back to the years when he was a local. Jimby was always upbeat, always smiling and always game for a laugh. He'd been a bit of an idol of Joss's when he was a youth.

'He can dance salsa?' asked Portia, impressed, her eyes wide.

'Umm. I wouldn't say that exactly, but what he lacks in talent, he makes up for in enthusiasm, as I dare say you can imagine.' Ella chuckled.

Portia gave a tinkling laugh, tapping her foot in time to the music that had suddenly cranked up. 'Yes, I can.'

The three of them chatted for a while, Joss feeling increasingly uncomfortable with Portia's attentions. He was relieved when Vi called for everyone to help themselves to the food that adorned the large island in the centre of the kitchen. Jimby had warned him there'd be nibbles on, and Joss was glad he'd only had a small plate of food earlier at the farm. There was no way you could call this gargantuan feast "nibbles".

He'd been chatting to Molly and Camm when Portia slipped into the chair beside him at the table, her hand finding its way onto his thigh. His heart sank and he struggled to hold in the irritated sigh her presence had generated. He tried to move his leg out of the way, but she was undeterred.

'So,' Portia said, leaning forward to look at Molly, 'what can you tell me about this naughty boy here and his misspent youth?'

Molly gave a throaty laugh, her dark curls shaking. 'Hah, he was a right little rascal. Full of mischief; in the same vein as our Jimby. Him and Ella were inseparable; you never saw one without the other. Always running around, off on their adventures, wearing the same t-shirt, jeans and wellies. She was a regular tomboy, complete with scuffed knees and a mucky face. Mind, she bossed him about something shocking but he loved it. Isn't that right, Ells?' Molly nodded towards her cousin who was talking to Kitty and Vi.

'What's that?' Ella made her apologies to the two women and went to join the conversation at the table. Joss watched her, curious as to how she'd react.

'I was just telling Portia how you and Bugger-Lugs here were joined at the hip when you were kids, and how you used to be a right little bossy-knickers with him.'

Joss was pleased to see a huge smile spreading over Ella's face as if she was thrilled by the memory. 'Yeah, that's right. Though I wouldn't say I was that bossy.'

'Well, I would,' said Joss, making them all hoot with laughter. 'You were a right little bossy-boots. Remember that time you told me I had to go skinny-dipping in the river with you?' The amused look he shot defied her to deny it.

'Skinny-dipping?' Portia's face fell.

'We were only ten at the time,' Ella said, smiling. 'It was all very innocent. And if I remember rightly, you didn't take much convincing. You were always up for a daft laugh.'

'Well, I don't remember it being much of a laugh. My abiding memory is of how freezing it was. I'd waded in right up to my waist, freezing my nuts off. Then you just stuck your big toe in and declared it too cold; said you'd changed your mind about coming in.'

'Which is a woman's prerogative,' said Molly, chuckling.

Ella covered her mouth with her hand in an attempt to suppress her giggles. 'The funniest part was when two dogs sneaked up and ran off with his clothes. I hadn't noticed 'til they were too far away to chase after them. It was hilarious.'

'Yeah, hilarious is the word,' said Joss, his heart feeling light at the memory. 'I was blue with the cold and had to walk home in my wellies – which the mutts very kindly left behind – and your cardigan wrapped around me, covering my modesty. I felt like a right turkey.'

Ella snorted with laughter. 'I can't deny, you did get a few funny looks on the way back.'

'Can't guess why.' He grinned at her, the happiness in her eyes sending a wave of warmth through him. 'And what about the time we got chased by that bad-tempered bull your dad had? We thought we could calm him down by pretending to be "bull whisperers".' He put finger quotes around the words.

'Jeez, yeah. Unfortunately the bull had other ideas and charged after us. I don't think I've ever run so fast in my life. We were stuck up a tree for hours.'

'Sounds to me like you were a right couple of rascals,' said Camm.

'Oh, that they were,' said Molly. 'Regular little partners in crime. Actually, we always thought they'd end up together, they were that close.'

'Why did you think that?' asked Portia, removing her hand from Joss's thigh, her smile faltering.

Molly was prevented from answering by a flurry of excitement as Gabe Dublin arrived. He popped his head around the door, his dark hair decorated with a handful of snowflakes. 'Hiya, folks. How're you all doing?'

Joss looked on in disbelief. Was he really under the same roof as the chart-topping, multi-award-winning, global artist that was Gabe Dublin? No way! This was completely surreal. Joss had all of his CDs, his songs featured on all of his favourite playlists and he'd been singing along to his latest single only the day before. He watched the singer as he chatted away to Jimby and Vi. From what Joss could gather, he had an easy-going manner, seemed down to earth.

'How d'you fancy a bit of a sing-song after we've all finished eating?' asked Jimby. 'Gabe here's brought his guitar.' His words were greeted with a wave of noisy enthusiasm.

'Gabe Dublin!' Portia's voice came out as more of a gasp, and she pressed her hand to her chest. 'I saw him up at the castle, he's utterly delectable. I must go and say hello, I didn't get a chance before.' With that, she got to her feet and sashayed her way in his direction, Joss apparently forgotten.

Joss breathed a sigh of relief.

'She won't get much joy there, I'm afraid,' said Molly. 'He's only got eyes for Noushka. I reckon he'll be expecting to see her here. Little does he know she's babysitting at Kitty and Ollie's.' She popped a stuffed pepper into her mouth and chomped on it.

'Poor lad, he's really smitten. Has been for the last year,' said Camm, a sympathetic smile on his lips.

'Unrequited love,' said Molly. 'Poor bloke.'

Joss stole a look at Ella. He knew exactly how that felt.

TWENTY-NINE

Ella

Gabe Dublin had been regaling them with his indie-folk-rock songs for the last hour, his voice rich and smoky. That it was infused with a hint of his Southern Irish accent only added to its charm. 'Come on, Jimby, go grab your guitar and get your butt down here along-side me.'

Jimby didn't need asking twice, and in no time he was sitting on a stool beside Gabe, a huge smile plastered across his face. 'Here we go, folks. Don't forget to join in,' said Gabe, strumming out the opening lines of his latest catchy festive song. The voices of the two men filled the room, Jimby's a good match for Gabe's, if not a little rougher around the edges. Everyone was singing along and clapping. Molly took Camm's hand and started dancing with him, his dark eyes smiling down at her indulgently.

'Right, I think it's time to turn the tempo down,' said Gabe. 'Time to grab yourself a partner and get a little smoochy.' He gave a cheeky waggle of his eyebrows.

Livvie dragged a reluctant Zander to the make-shift dance-floor in the middle of the room, the two of them smooching awkwardly thanks to the size of her baby bump.

Before Ella had time to think, Joss was beside her. 'Remember the last time we had a dance?' he asked.

Her heart was pounding hard. 'Country dancing in the village hall when we were nine. You're the reason I can't wear high-heels; your do-si-dos had my feet in tatters. They still haven't properly recovered.' Smiling, she lifted her gaze to see him looking down at her, his eyes soft, sending a buzz of electricity through her.

'Er, some of your moves weren't quite so hot either. That one where you have to join hands at shoulder height then turn; I seem to recall you just about throttled me several times when we attempted it.'

'Yeah, sorry about that,' she giggled. 'Still needs a bit of work, I'm afraid.'

'You still do country dancing?'

'No.' She giggled. 'Just joshing. Though there are sessions every now and then in the village hall. Belly dancing too.'

'Right, maybe I should sign up for them.'

'What? Belly dancing?' Ella giggled at the thought of Joss rocking up to join the room of regulars.

Joss roared with laughter. 'No! I meant country dancing, and I was only joking about that.'

'Oh, right. But I'm quite enjoying the mental image of you wiggling your hips around the village hall alongside Big Mary and her chums.' Ella giggled mischievously.

'Sounds scary. Anyway, don't suppose you're brave enough to risk a dance with me tonight? And I don't mean belly dancing.' Smiling, he held out his hand, his eyebrows raised expectantly.

'I suppose we could give it a try as long as you promise to keep your feet to yourself.' Grinning, she put her hand in his and he led her to the middle of the room where he pulled her close, his hands slipping around her waist.

'I'll do my best.'

She swallowed, feeling the warmth of his body against hers, hoping he couldn't feel how hard her heart was hammering against her ribcage. She resisted putting her arms around his neck, instead resting them on his chest, feeling the solid wall of muscle beneath. The mossy scent of his cologne rose, warm from his shirt. Sensing he was looking at her, she glanced up, her heart doing somersaults as she registered the look in his eyes. He pulled her closer and she reached her arms up and slid them around his neck, resting her head on his chest, succumbing to the feelings that were surging through her body. Being in his arms felt indescribably good. She sighed, closing her eyes. It felt like where she belonged.

All too soon, the song finished, Gabe declaring he was parched and needed a beer. Joss's arms were still wrapped around her when Ella felt a tap on her shoulder. She turned to see Portia glaring at her.

'Well, isn't this cosy?' she said, her nostrils flaring, her mouth pinched.

'Cosy?' asked Ella as she released herself from Joss and took a step back.

'Would've been nice if one of you'd had the courtesy to mention you'd been getting close. Stopped me from making a complete fool of myself.'

'Porsh, it's not what you think, really it's not. We were best mates, that's all. Honest. Like we said before, we go back a long way; we grew up together.' Ella flashed a look Joss's way, noting the uncomfortable expression on his face as he watched things unfurl.

'It looked like you were more than best mates from where I was standing.' Portia pouted and folded her arms. 'And I can't understand why you've never mentioned this friendship to me before now.' She glared at Ella.

Ella was cringing inside, the last thing she wanted was a scene at Vi and Jimby's party. She hadn't mentioned it because it would have been too painful to resurrect those memories, but she could hardly tell Portia that.

'It's my fault.' Joss stepped in. 'I asked Ells if she wanted to dance. We'd been having a laugh about when we were country dancing partners at primary school and I wanted to show her my dancing skills had improved. That's all there is to it,' he said, holding up his hands.

Portia snorted, folding her arms. 'Well, I think she'd agree they have.'

'We haven't seen each other for years, not since I came back the other day.'

'It would seem you're making up for lost time.'

'Porsh, it really isn't like that.' Ella went to touch her friend's arm in a conciliatory gesture but Portia stepped out of her reach.

'I just don't like to be made a fool of, that's all.'

Ella felt her stomach twist. Had she made a fool of her friend? She hoped not. She was relieved when the music came back on; she'd noticed people beginning to look in their direction. 'Porsh, you've got to believe me, Joss and me are just friends, nothing more, isn't that right?' She looked at Joss imploringly, hoping he'd back her up again. She hated seeing her friend so upset.

'Nothing more.' He nodded. The hurt expression in his eyes pierced her heart.

What are you doing? And who do you think you're kidding? What about the way you were feeling when you were in his arms less than two minutes ago? Explain them, why don't you?

'And to be honest, Portia, I'm not sure why you're getting so upset. I mean, I made it perfectly clear right from the offset that I wasn't interested in a relationship. From what you said, I thought you felt the same too,' Joss said, wearily.

Portia huffed, glancing between the two of them. 'I did. I didn't! I do! I mean, I thought things might turn out differently, that's all. Ella knows how I feel, that's why I'm so shocked at the way you two were dancing like you were an item.' She gave a petulant shrug.

'Like we've both said, we're not an item, Porsh. I promise you. I don't want you to think I was trying to deceive you.' Subconsciously playing with her necklace, Ella's eyes flicked over to Joss who was watching her intently. Portia was taking some convincing.

'So, can I ask, were you aware how Joss felt about relationships? Have you two been discussing me?'

Oh, hells bells. Ella felt a moment of panic, she struggled to find the right words. 'I... I—'

'Ella didn't know anything.' Joss came to the rescue once more. 'I thought I'd said enough to you by telling you how I felt.'

Ouch! Ella cringed. Much as she was glad Joss had stepped in with his white lie, she felt uncomfortable for Portia who had locked eyes with Joss, though she was relieved to see her body language had softened.

'Fair enough, I suppose you did,' Portia said, backing down. 'And anyway, there's no way I'm going to play second fiddle to anyone, nor am I so desperate I'm going to chase a man who doesn't want me.' She smoothed an imaginary crease from her dress. 'I apologise for getting it wrong. I hope I haven't spoilt your evening.'

Ella's heart squeezed for her friend. 'Oh, Porsh.'

'No need to apologise, Portia,' said Joss with a quick smile. 'It's forgotten.'

'Right, I'll see you later.' With that she turned on her silver high heels and strode out of the room, Ella and Joss watching her go.

Joss puffed out his cheeks. 'As uncomfortable as that was, at least she's got the message. She was starting to get a bit full-on.'

'Poor Porsh, all she wants is to find someone to love and for them to love her back.' Ella couldn't help but feel sorry for her friend, and she felt sorry for Joss too; after all, he had made his position clear. 'I'm just glad she seems okay about it.' Ella had already made up her mind to speak to Portia the next day when things had cooled down a bit, when moods were less sensitive and prickly. Something in her gut told her Portia's feelings for Joss ran no deeper than an infatuation. She sincerely hoped she was right. Ella didn't like to think her friend was hurting, and she definitely didn't want to lose her friendship over this.

. . .

'Right, I think it's time I was heading home.' Ella stifled a yawn and set her empty wine glass down on the table. Music was still playing in the background, though a little more softly now, and she was beginning to feel just a little too comfy.

Portia had been chatting to Gabe Dublin and Ollie since her outburst. Ella was relieved to see her friend's usual happy and relaxed demeanour had returned, her earlier upset apparently all but forgotten.

Joss pushed up his sleeve and glanced at his watch. 'Yeah, it's just gone half-ten; I've stayed longer than I expected. I've got to be up early.'

The pair heaved themselves up from the squishy sofa where they'd been chatting to Kitty, Molly and Camm and headed down the hallway.

'Are you going to be okay walking home in those? Your feet'll be freezing.' Joss looked down at the pair of black kitten-heel Mary-Janes she was wearing.

'I came in my wellies,' Ella said.

'Ah. Very wise.'

After bidding their farewells – including a friendly one from Portia who smiled and gave a little wave – the pair headed down the path and out onto the trod, Ella with her shoes in a canvas tote bag slung over her shoulder. The temperature had plummeted and the ground glittered with a thick hoar frost, the smell of woodsmoke from the chimneys suspended in the brittle air.

The pair walked along, chatting away, the sharp cold catching at the back of Ella's throat. Her eyes were drawn to the velvety-dark sky, a wisp of a cloud drifting across the moon. It took a couple of seconds for her to focus on the glittering constellations. She sensed Joss follow her gaze. 'Clear night,' he said. He didn't need to tell her his mind had travelled back to their teenage years and the hours they'd spent gazing up at such a sky; hers was there too.

'It is,' she said wistfully.

Reaching the gate of Rose Cottage they stopped. 'I'd invite you in for a cuppa if you didn't have to be up so early,' she said, her teeth chattering.

'I could make an exception, just for tonight,' he said, holding her gaze. 'It's not as if there'll be a warm welcome waiting for me at the farm.' He gave a small laugh, rubbing his hands together.

'If you're sure you won't regret it in the morning when your alarm goes off.' She felt a ripple of anticipation rush through her as she pushed the gate open.

'I won't regret it.'

The warmth hit Ella in a rush along with Tabby-Cat who shot out of the living room, mewing loudly.

'Hi there, Tabs. Ooh, you feel lovely and warm, have you been snuggling up by the stove?' She bent to stroke the cat who was now rubbing up against her leg. 'Joss, meet Tabby-Cat, Tabs, meet Joss.'

'Hi there, puss,' said Joss. 'Another one of your rescues, Ells?'

'Well, I'm sure she thinks she rescued me.' Ella laughed as she unwound her scarf from her neck. 'She just turned up one day and never left.'

Joss hung up his coat on the hook next to Ella's and followed her into the kitchen. 'By, it's nice in here. Seems to have everything even though it's a small space.'

'That's thanks to Ollie's carpentry skills; he's really talented. He made the oak bar in the pub too.' Mention of the pub suddenly made her think of Portia. She hoped she was okay.

'Wow! The bar's an amazing piece of craftsmanship; you're right, he is very talented.'

Ella felt his eyes on her as she filled the kettle and threw teabags into the pot. She placed a brace of mugs on the table and tipped some milk into a jug, setting it beside them. 'Still take half-a-dozen teaspoons of sugar in your tea?' she said with a mischievous grin.

Joss laughed, hooking his thumbs into the loops of his jeans and leaning back against the worktop. 'Not anymore. In fact, you'll probably be surprised to know I don't take any.'

'Wow! A reformed character.'

'I only used to pile it in when I was trying to beef myself up. Don't tell me you've forgotten how puny I was. Dad used to say I was like a string of donkey snot, I was that skinny.'

Ella laughed. 'Ah, yes, I remember that rather charming analogy. My dad used to describe Greg in much the same way.'

'I'd try anything to fatten myself up, not that it ever worked. Aunty Babs used to say I had hollow legs, I ate that much without putting an ounce of weight on.'

'I suppose you were a bit skinny, not that I really noticed at the time.' She stole a look at him, her eyes roving appreciatively over the ripples of his biceps, his strong shoulders. It sent a wave of longing through her. He definitely couldn't be accused of being skinny now.

Joss chuckled. 'How did you think I got the nickname Joss Stick?'

Ella pursed her lips together and frowned as she considered this. 'To be perfectly honest, I never really took any notice. I thought it was just a name you had with some of the lads you were friends with, you all seemed to have daft nicknames I could never understand. I mean, Aaron Keithley was known as Banger. How on earth did he get stuck with that?' She poured the boiling water into the pot and carried it over to the table where she pulled out a chair. Joss followed her, sitting down opposite.

'Would you believe it's from a cricketing term? He earnt it thanks to his bowling prowess and it just sort of stuck.'

'Cricketing?' Ella cocked an eyebrow. 'Well, you learn something new every day.' She looked across to see him smiling at her, his eyes soft and kind. His days of Joss Stick were long since behind him and sitting before her was an incredibly handsome man. She felt a sudden urge to kiss him, making her face burning hot. Instead, she grabbed the teapot and gave it a quick swirl in a bid to chase the impulse away. Clumsily, she poured the tea into the mugs, splashing it everywhere.

'Ey up, bit of a dribbly teapot,' said Joss, jumping up and grabbing a piece of kitchen roll, swiftly dabbing the puddle away.

He sat back down and drew in a deep breath. 'It's been good to see you again, Ells. I'd honestly intended to keep away from the village, was keen to avoid everyone in case I bumped into folk asking questions; I didn't fancy being the subject of gossip again. And I was worried about seeing you, worried how you'd react. But I'm so glad you were at the farm when I got back that day.'

'Me too.' She smiled shyly as she blew across the surface of her tea.

'And you're still wearing the necklace,' he said softly.

Her hand reached for the pendant. 'I've never stopped wearing it.' Their eyes locked, the air around them suddenly charged with unspoken words.

'That situation with Portia...' A frown fleetingly troubled his brow.

'You don't have to explain yourself to me.'

'I'd like to.' He looked down at his mug. 'I got stung pretty bad by Manda, and since the divorce I vowed I'd never let myself get close to a woman again. There's been a couple of meaningless flings, but that's it. Then when Portia showed an interest, I was flattered. Weak, pathetic man that I am. But I honestly didn't consider it to be anything more than a fling; thought she did too, as I keep saying.'

'Honestly, Joss, I understand. My experience with Owen wasn't anything like what you had with your ex but it still left me feeling wary, that I wanted to be on my own. I haven't got the stomach to face all that hurt again, so I know where you're coming from.'

'Yeah.' Joss ran his hand across the back of his neck. 'See, the thing is, I didn't bank on feeling the way I do about you.' He looked at her, his eyes glittering, betraying exactly how he felt.

Ella held his gaze, aware of the increasing gravitational pull towards him. After several glasses of wine, her resolve to be on her own had suddenly lost its appeal. She remembered how good it felt to have his arms around her when they were dancing, him holding her close, the feel of his heart beating against hers. She closed her eyes for a second, sliding into the memory.

Just as he reached across and took her hand, her eyes pinged open and logic kicked in. What was the point of giving into temptation? Getting involved with Joss was bound to end in heartache. He'd made it perfectly clear he had no intention of sticking around; once his father was fully-fit, he'd go straight back to Skeller Rigg Farm and that would be it. No, Ella was going to stick with her vow of keeping her heart firmly out of harm's way.

She sat back, easing her hand out of his. 'So, when do you think you'll be heading back to Skeller Rigg?' She registered the flicker of surprise in his eyes, and felt a twinge of guilt.

'Erm, well, I suppose it'll be as soon as my dad's properly back on his feet.' He frowned, giving his head a quick scratch. 'He could do with a bit of help though. I think I'll advertise for someone to come and give him a hand with the milking, if the farm can afford it. I still need to get to the bottom of what state it's in.'

Ella got to her feet, rinsing her mug out under the tap. Joss was clearly going to leave Lytell Stangdale as soon as he could. She hoped he'd take the hint and leave her before her resolve did a vanishing act and she found herself rushing over and kissing him, which was exactly what she was struggling against at this very minute.

'Right, I'd best be off.' He drained his mug, an expression of regret pulling his smile down.

In the hallway, Joss paused at the door, looking down at her. Ella's heart was racing. It would be so easy to reach her arms around his neck and find her lips on his. She took a deep breath and tore her eyes away from his. She cleared her throat. 'Erm, I assume Mum or Dad mentioned that you and your dad are welcome to join us for Christmas dinner at Tinkel Bottom?' *Nice and neutral, that's the way to stay in control of your wayward emotions.*

'Yeah, your mum did. It's very kind of them.'

'Well, if I don't see you before, I'll see you then.' She added a breezy tone to her voice which, even to her ears sounded fake. She cringed inside, hoping Joss had missed it.

'Yep, see you then.' He bent to kiss her cheek but she ducked out of the way and went to open the door, pretending she hadn't noticed.

With the door closed firmly behind him, Ella leaned against it, her hand pressed against her forehead. 'What is happening to my life?'

The following morning, one matter vied for attention above everything else that was taking up headspace: Portia. Ella desperately needed to see her friend, to talk to her in the cold light of day, make sure they were okay. It was important to know their friendship was still intact.

She picked up her phone and called Portia's number.

'Come over for a coffee, darling. Mum's made some gorgeous breakfast muffins; there's plenty to go round.'

The relief Ella felt at hearing her friend's familiar jolly tones sent her anxiety rushing away. 'Are you sure your parents won't mind me turning up when they're so busy?'

'Of course they won't mind; you're as good as family, they'll be pleased to see you.'

Fifteen minutes later, Ella found herself perched on a bar stool opposite Portia at the peninsular of the stylish kitchen in the pub's living accommodation. Bea had even decorated this space with her customary flair, painting the units a rich, dark blue and finishing them off with a mix of chrome and leather handles.

The mouth-watering aroma of fried bacon and toasted bread hung in the air, the scent of freshly ground coffee beans circling amongst it.

'Here you are, darlings.' Bea set down two plates of muffins topped with creamy scrambled eggs, fried bacon and mashed avocado sprinkled with paprika. She'd added a dollop of home-made tomato chutney to cut through the richness. 'Enjoy. Jonty and I have had ours so we'll leave you to it. There's more freshly-squeezed orange juice in the jug in the fridge if you need it.'

'Thanks, Bea, this looks gorgeous.' Her mouth watering, Ella could hardly wait to tuck in.

'Right, come on, you two. Time for a walk.' Bea clicked her tongue at Nomad and Scruff who'd been watching the preparation of breakfast with great interest.

'Yes, come on you two gluttons. Let's leave the girls to enjoy their food in peace,' said Jonty, and the pair reluctantly followed them out of the room.

Ella waited for the door to click shut. 'Look, Porsh, I just want to make sure we're okay. I mean, I really didn't want you to get the wrong impression about Joss and me.' She looked at her friend earnestly. 'Nothing's happened between us and nothing's going to. We're friends from a long time ago, a very long time ago, and that's all.'

Portia finished her mouthful and took a glug of orange juice. She dabbed her mouth with her white cotton napkin. 'Honestly, Ells, there's no need for you to apologise; I'm the one who owes you and Joss an apology. I hope you didn't think I created a scene last night, it's just I was so shocked to see the two of you smooching away like that.'

Ella cringed. 'I know how it must've looked, and I'm truly sorry about it.'

'Please stop putting yourself through it. You really don't have to explain yourself. Joss was right when he said he'd told me about not wanting a relationship, but I foolishly chose not to hear it.' Portia laughed, rolling her eyes jokingly. 'When will I ever learn?'

Ella smiled, relief rushing through her that their friendship appeared to have survived unscathed. But it still didn't stop her feeling a little guilty about her growing attraction to Joss. 'I'm just glad we're okay.'

'We are, darling. No hard feelings at all.' Portia raised her glass of juice. 'To friendship.'

Ella giggled and clinked her glass against it. 'To friendship.'

'But you can't honestly tell me you haven't noticed the way Joss looks at you.' Portia popped a forkful of scrambled eggs into her mouth, quirking her eyebrows at Ella.

Ella swallowed. 'The way he looks at me? What do you mean?'

Portia's eyebrows switched from a quirk to a waggle. 'Like he's passionately in love with you and wants nothing more than to scoop you up into his arms and carry you off.'

'He does not!' Ella inwardly cursed the blush she could feel flaming her cheeks as she tried to push away the memory of what Joss had said to her the previous evening.

'Oh, but he does. And I'm not the only one who thinks that. Gabe spotted it too. And Jimby and Vi. And Molly and Camm. And Kitty and Ollie. Shall I go on?' Portia grinned mischievously.

'No! Stop!' Ella covered her glowing face with her hands. 'You've all got it wrong, we were just really close friends years ago – nothing more! – and I suppose we've kind of picked up where we left off – as friends. That's all,' she said, struggling to make eye contact with her friend.

'Oh, really?' An amused smile played over Portia's lips.

'Really,' Ella said with more conviction than she felt. 'And anyway, how did you get on with Gabe? You seemed to spend an awful lot of last night with him.'

'Hm. Lovely as he is, he spent the whole time talking about Noushka. Asking what he could do to win her round, to make her agree to going on a date with him. Bless him, he's got it really bad for her.'

Ella's smile fell as she remembered the recent conversation she'd had with Kitty, her cousin saying how worried she and Ollie were about Noushka. The young woman had been going out with a boy called Damon for just over a year and since that time she'd lost her sparkle along with lots of weight. Kitty was concerned Damon was a negative and controlling influence on her step-daughter and wished she'd dump him. 'Well, let's hope Gabe succeeds. Noushka could do with hooking up with someone who adores her,' Ella said thoughtfully.

'So, much as I hate to disappoint you, darling, you're barking up the wrong tree if you think there's any chance of me getting into his boxer shorts – much as I'd love nothing better.' Her eyes gleamed wickedly and she gave a cheeky smile before popping some bacon into her mouth and chewing. 'But I did speak to Saffy last night.'

'Saffy?'

'Mm-hm.' Portia nodded slowly. 'We spent ages talking when I got back here after the party. Turns out she's been missing me. Can't get me out of her mind. Wondered if I fancied giving it another go.'

'Wowzers! And how do you feel about that?' Well, this was a turn up for the books.

'Nothing ventured, as the saying goes. And we were rather good together. *Exciting*,' she said with relish. 'And, if I'm being completely honest, she still has a huge chunk of my heart.'

'Does that mean you're going to see her again?'

'I'm heading back to my flat the day after Boxing Day and we're going out for dinner. Taking it from there.' A huge grin spread across Portia's face.

'You look like the cat that got the cream.' Ella smiled back, thrilled to see her friend looking so happy.

'Oh, and don't I just feel like it.'

The two women finished their breakfast, chatting away, all traces of the previous evening's awkwardness banished. Ella helped Portia stack the dishwasher and wipe the mats on the peninsular.

'So, what are your plans for the rest of the day?' asked Portia, hooking her hair behind her ears.

'Nothing particularly rock 'n' roll. A quick tidy round at the cottage, finish some last-minute pressie wrapping, then head over to the farm and tend to my little menagerie there.' She still hadn't shared her plans for the kennels with Portia, so didn't add that she and her parents were going to chat further about that. 'How about you?'

'I intend to tackle my to-do list for the castle lodges with great gusto. I'll be setting to work on my shopping list, ordering everything from bespoke sofas to lampshades. I can't tell you how much I'm looking forward to that,' she said, rubbing her hands together gleefully.

Ella laughed, zipping up her coat. 'You don't need to, I can see!'

'Before you go, darling, bear in mind what I said about Joss and his feelings for you.' Portia gave a knowing smile.

Ella stuffed her hands in her coat pockets and pulled a face of weary disbelief.

'Oh, it's all very well you looking at me like that, but it just so happens to be true.'

Before she could say anything further, Ella hugged her friend. 'Thanks for breakfast. I'm glad we're okay.' She gave her a quick peck on the cheek, determined to put an end to that conversation. 'See you round the Christmas tree for the carol singing tomorrow evening.'

'You will indeed. And a word to the wise, don't let something wonderful slip through your fingers just because it's the easiest option. The best things are worth fighting for, or not fighting against.'

'Right, that's it, I'm definitely off. You're speaking in riddles and my poor brain can't keep up. See you later.' Ella shook her head, laughing as she headed through the door.

Something wonderful? How could Portia possibly think there could be anything wonderful between her and Joss?

THIRTY

Joss

Once the morning's milking session was over and done with, Joss settled down to some breakfast. His dad was evidently still in bed, and Joss left him to enjoy his sleep. While he ate, he seized the opportunity to look over the information he'd managed to put together of the farm's accounts and was relieved to find things weren't quite as bleak as he'd first imagined. There was the house that Rich had lived in with Dawn and the kids over at Danskelfe. It would seem Ivy Cottage had stood empty since Rich and his family had moved to Middleton-le-Moors six months earlier. And, as it was owned by his father, Bill was perfectly within his rights to rent it out and earn some much-needed cash in the process. Puzzled as to why this hadn't already happened, he made a mental note to tackle his dad about it later that day, albeit very gently. He had a funny feeling it would have something to do with Rich.

Though he was focussing hard on the paperwork, he was conscious of his thoughts drifting to Ella. He took a bite of toast, savouring the buttery flavour. He was sure she'd felt the energy between them, felt the same frisson of attraction he had. What was running through her mind? he wondered. That she didn't want to get involved with him, that's what. Just as well he wasn't going to be sticking around. The sooner he got the farm sorted out and help in place, the better. He huffed out a loud breath, wondering if he really meant that.

Joss had returned home the previous evening relieved to find his dad had gone to bed. His mind had been all over the place since he'd left Ella's and he didn't feel up to one of the awkward, stilted conversations with his dad – they were still negotiating this fledgling relationship between them, and things could get a little bumpy at times. He and Ella had gone from having a laugh together to her practically pushing him out the door. When he'd got back to the farm, he'd been pleased to see his buddy Sid, who was curled up in the large dog bed Joss had dug out from the attic under instruction from his father. He'd lined it with a couple of cushions and a blanket he'd found up there too. After all, Sid was entitled to his creature comforts. After a quick welcome and a thorough sniffing, Sid had left Joss to his thoughts and returned to his bed. Feeling tired but perplexed, Joss had sloped off upstairs, his mind whirling, pushing sleep away. And no matter how hard he tried, he just couldn't get Ella out of his mind.

The following day, Joss bumped his way along the track from the farm, the heating in the tractor cab barely taking the edge off the cold; the old vehicle wasn't a patch on the one at Skeller Rigg Farm. Not that Joss was complaining. With his history, he was the last one who had the right to grumble about the state of the farm's vehicles. It was Christmas Eve and the sky had taken on a wintry hue as he headed from the top field nearest the farm where he'd decided to move the sheep from Thistle Field on the edge of the village. He had a feeling the weather was going to turn and bringing the flock closer would make his dad's life easier. And judging by the clouds that were gathering in a foreboding shade of battleship grey, it looked as though he was going to be proved right.

He'd been mulling over the conversation he'd had with his

father about the Danskelfe cottage at lunchtime, unable to shift the feeling that something just didn't ring true. By all accounts, Rich had told his father that Ivy Cottage wasn't fit to let out. Apparently the electrics were unsafe and some of the plumbing was dodgy. On top of all that, he'd said the heating wasn't working properly. His dad may have fallen for it hook-line-and-sinker, but Joss hadn't. He couldn't see Rich living in such unpalatable conditions, never mind Dawn and their daughter, Amy. No, there was definitely something amiss. Having found the keys to the place, Joss decided he was going to drive over there and take a look for himself. He wouldn't mention anything to his dad; he'd only get worked up about it which would set their delicate truce back. Lord knows, it didn't take much. Just that morning, Bill had bitten his head off for leaving him to sleep for so long.

'But you obviously needed it, Dad. Don't forget you've not been long out of hospital after collapsing,' he'd said. He'd thought better of asking why he hadn't set an alarm for himself; the resultant savaging it would generate just wasn't worth it. Pick your battles, he'd learnt to reminded himself in these early days with his father.

Back at the farm, Joss made his dad a cup of tea, telling him he was heading out for a while. 'But I'll be back well in time for milking,' he said.

Bill looked a little disgruntled and passed some comment about Joss always sloping off. Joss bit his tongue, and chose not to rise to it. Some things would never change and his dad's grumbling was one of them. And, anyway, there were other things on his mind that needed the full focus of his attention right now.

Since he'd returned from fetching the sheep, the snow had started with a vengeance. Joss stood in the yard, large flakes of the stuff swirling around him as he debated the wisdom of heading over to Danskelfe. 'Stuff it! I'm going,' he said aloud. He was on a mission; if he didn't go now, it would bug him like crazy until he saw for himself exactly what the state of play was at the cottage.

And anyway, Danskelfe was only a few miles away; he'd be back before he knew it. Before the weather turned too dangerous.

He climbed into the Land Rover and made his way steadily down the track, the lights of Tinkel Bottom Farm catching his eye. His thoughts, once more, turned to Ella. From what she'd told him, he knew she'd be there right now. He felt himself smiling, wondering if he filled her thoughts the way she did his. *Don't bank on it, buster!*

Joss was relieved to find the road down in the village had only a light covering of snow; the hawthorn hedges and trees that lined it formed a barrier from the wind meaning there were no drifts to contend with. But as he drove on, the road steadily climbing, it soon became a different world. The snow was tumbling relentlessly from the dense sky and the high, exposed moorland meant the wind had free range to howl all around it, which is exactly what it was doing right now, buffeting the Land Rover with all its might. Joss clenched his jaw and upped the speed of the wipers, his eyes narrowing as he focussed hard on the road ahead, the vehicle crunching over the snow. Being such a high spot on the moors, it had clearly been snowing here a good while longer than it had in the village.

'This is bad,' he said to himself, as it became impossible to tell where the road ended and the verges began, hiding deep gullies where a tyre could easily come unstuck. Snow drifted across the road in huge swathes, banking up against the dry stone walls. It wouldn't be long before the road became impassable.

He was contemplating turning round and heading back when through the blizzard he caught sight of a car's headlights. As he peered out, it soon became apparent that there were two vehicles. A figure jumped out, waving their arms frantically. The road must be blocked; they must be stranded. Joss applied the Land Rover brakes delicately. As he came to a stop, the figure rushed over to him, head bowed against the raging weather. He opened the door and jumped down, the bitter cold taking his breath away. The snow was way deeper than he'd expected. 'Ella! What the heck are you doing up here? It's dangerous.'

'It's Livvie,' she said, having to raise her voice to be heard above the shrieking wind. Her face was red with the cold and she was blinking quickly to rid snow from her eyes. And there was no escaping the concern etched across her face.

'What about Livvie?' Joss could feel his heart begin to race.

'She's gone into labour early. She couldn't get hold of Zander or Rhoda so she set off for the hospital herself. Apparently, she started with pains this morning, but thought they were just practise ones. Looks like they were the real thing. She says the baby won't wait.'

'Seriously?' With his hand shielding his face, Joss glanced across to the small snow-covered car which he could now see was at an odd angle. It must have skidded off the road. His stomach clenched. 'Is she okay?'

Ella nodded. 'Yeah, her car left the road but she's not hurt. It's just the labour pains; she says they're really strong and close together. I'm no expert, but I don't think that's a good thing.' She brushed a wet straggle of hair off her face. 'She's still in the car, with the engine on, keeping warm. I asked her how long she'd been there, but she says she can't remember; thinks it's been a while.'

'Right.' Not knowing what to expect and with his stomach clenched, Joss strode over to Livvie's car, his wellies sinking deep into the snow, Ella close behind him. He opened the door carefully, holding on to it with all his might as he battled with the wind. Inside, he saw Livvie laid out on the back seat. One of her hands was gripping tightly onto the driver's headrest, the other holding onto the one on the rear passenger seat. She was taking short, rapid breaths through her mouth. Beads of sweat peppered her brow and her face was distorted by pain. He didn't like to say anything, but he didn't think they stood a hope in hell's chance of getting her to the hospital in Middleton-le-Moors in time, or at all, the state the road was in. His mind started scrambling for how to best deal with the situation. 'Don't worry, Livvie, everything's going to be fine.

Ella and I will make sure of it.' He spoke with more conviction than he felt.

'Joss! Please help. The baby's coming.' She gasped, her eyes pleading as the raging wind rocked the car. 'I'm scared.'

The urgency in her voice sent a spike of panic rushing through him.

'Don't be scared, Liv, we've got this, haven't we, Joss?' said Ella.

'We have. But I think we need to get you across to the Landie where there's more room; I've had the heating on full-blast so it's nice and warm; your little car's going nowhere I'm afraid.'

'I don't think I can walk.' Fear gripped Livvie's face.

'We'll help you, don't worry.' Joss turned to Ella. 'Have you got any blankets or cushions in your car? Anything to make Livvie comfortable?' He noted Ella looked as worried as he felt.

She nodded. 'Yeah. I've got a couple of woolly blankets.'

'Good. You go and get those, I'll get the Landie engine back on. We won't be a minute, Livvie, hang on in there.' He flashed her the best reassuring smile he could muster and backed out of the car.

The wind was raging about them, lifting huge swathes of Alpine-like snow and hurling it across the road, nipping spitefully at their exposed skin. It was bone-numbingly cold. Joss couldn't think of worse conditions for a pregnant woman to find herself in, never mind one who was in the midst of labour.

'I don't think we're going to get her across to Middleton in time,' said Ella.

'We're not. And I don't think we should risk it anyway. The weather's far worse than I expected; I'd forgotten just how quickly it can change up here. We just need to get her into the Land Rover. I'll fold up the bench seats in the back, make more room for her to get comfortable.'

'Do you think we should try driving back to Lytell Stangdale?'

'Do you think she'll last that long?'

Ella wiped snow from her eyes with the back of her gloved hands as they battled against the elements, snow hurling at them, the wind shrieking across the moortop. 'I'm not sure.'

He glanced around. Dusk was already descending. With the weather like this, it wouldn't be long before it got dark. 'If Livvie's so close to giving birth, I think it might be best if we stay put. And once she does, if the road's not too bad back to Lytell Stangdale, maybe we could risk tackling it.'

'Good plan. I can ring for Molly to give us a hand until we track Zander down. She's not a nurse anymore, but she'll know more than us about childbirth, and I dare say Camm will have cleared the road from Withrin Hill to the village.'

Childbirth! The word sent fear surging through him. He sent a silent prayer heavenwards, hoping everything would be okay.

It hadn't been easy getting Livvie out of her car with labour pains gripping at her and the wind howling around them relentlessly. But finally, they'd managed, and with Ella at one side of her and Joss at the other, they'd supported her over the snow and into the back of the Land Rover. In Joss's other hand was the hospital bag Livvie had had ready for the last fortnight.

In the warmth of the Land Rover, Ella and Livvie were safely ensconced in the back while Joss occupied the driver's seat, his mobile phone in his hand. Livvie had given him Zander's number and he was busy tapping it in. The storm raged on outside, but the three of them were too focused on unfolding events to notice.

'Come on, Liv, let's get that wet coat off,' said Ella, helping ease it off Livvie's back which was a bit of a struggle in such cramped conditions. They were almost done when another labour pain struck.

'Arghh! This one's really hurting.' Livvie gasped, scrunching her face up and grabbing Ella's arm. 'Oh, my God! Ow! Ow!' She let out a juddery sigh when it had finally passed. 'I thought first babies were notoriously late, not this flaming early, and I thought first-time mums were supposed to be in labour for hours and hours with them. Trust me to be different,' she said, breathing heavily as Ella wiped beads of sweat from her brow with a tissue.

'Aye, but you can't always go by what the text books say.' A sudden forceful gust rammed at the side of the Land Rover. Joss glanced up at the windscreen to see the view had been obliterated by a thick layer of snow. He flicked the wipers on to clear it, revealing a swathe of white looking back at him.

'Oh, God! No! Here's another one.' Her eyes scrunched up tight, Livvie practised the breathing she'd learnt at the ante-natal classes, her face turning a deep red. 'I need Zander. Joss, have you got hold of Zander yet?' she asked when the wave of pain had passed.

Joss turned to see Ella's panic-stricken face. He showed her his phone screen, mouthing, 'No signal.'

She mouthed back, 'Oh my God!' before turning to Livvie who was panting heavily. 'It's okay, Liv.' She smoothed her friend's damp hair off her clammy brow and gave her a reassuring smile.

'It's not okay!' Livvie's voice came out in a shriek. 'This baby's on its way now! I'm scared! Please help me!' Her eyes were wild with panic as she kicked her legs, trying to push her boots off.

'Here, I'll help.' Ella pulled them off, chucking them over into the passenger footwell where they landed with a thud.

'What can I do to help?' asked Joss, anxiety making his pulse race.

Ella pulled a face and shook her head. 'I'm not sure at the moment.' Joss picked up on the nervous tone in her voice.

'My tights!' Livvie hiked up her skirt and started rolling her tights over her huge bump.

Joss averted his eyes while Ella helped her.

'Ella, I'm scared.' Livvie reached for her hand, squeezing it tightly. 'My baby. Will my baby be okay?'

'Of course it will. We'll make sure of it,' said Ella, but Joss saw fear in her eyes when she glanced up at him.

'There's stuff in my bag. A baby blanket, baby clothes, nappies and stuff. Oh, my God, I can't believe this is happening.' Her face crumpled and she stifled a sob. 'Why didn't I just stay at home?'

'It's fine, Livvie, everything's fine and under control. Don't worry, I'll get the baby stuff ready.' Ella rubbed Livvie's arm reassuringly before flicking the interior light on. She leaned across to the front passenger seat where Joss had placed the holdall. Unzipping it, she scrabbled through the neat piles until she found what she needed, the distinctive soft, powdery scent of freshly-bathed baby rising up from it.

'Here we are, I've got the things you need.' Ella crouched beside Livvie, the young woman grabbing her hand, clenching it in a vice-like grip.

'Zander wanted to be with me when our baby was born.' Tears rolled down Livvie's face. 'Arghh!' She bent her head, gripped by pain again. 'Oh, my... Arghh!'

'Livvie, you're going to have to let go of my hand. I need to check how you're doing,' said Ella.

But Livvie didn't appear to hear her.

'Joss, you're going to have to get yourself round here really quickly. One of us needs to be at the baby end of things and I'm afraid that's going to have to be you.'

Joss thought his heart had stopped. What did that mean? 'Right.' He gulped, taking a moment to absorb the implications.

'Quick, Joss!'

Hearing the urgency in Ella's voice, he leapt out of the vehicle, the arctic conditions taking his breath away. He climbed into the back as quickly as he could, pulling the heavy door shut with a mighty slam before the valuable heat escaped. Seeing Livvie's face, dripping with sweat, sent shockwaves through him. He hurriedly shrugged off his coat, trying to avoid snow falling from it and over Livvie, which wasn't easy in such close confines, and threw it over to the driver's seat. He rolled up the sleeves of his jumper and reached for the bottle of hand sanitiser Ella had brought from her car, giving his hands a thorough dousing while Livvie's pants and gasps filled the air.

'I can't say I've ever delivered a baby before, but between us, Ella and me are going to make sure you and your baby will be absolutely fine.' He injected more reassurance into his smile than he actually felt as he rubbed in the sanitiser liquid.

Livvie was panting rapidly. 'At this precise moment, I don't bloody care if all you've delivered is a calf, a foal or a sodding hamster. All I know is I want you to help me get this baby out.' She grimaced, pushing her chin into her chest. 'Arghh!'

Joss shot Ella a worried look and she returned an equally anxious smile.

'Oh, jeez, bloody Zander! I'm going to kill him when I see him. This is all his bloody fault, taking risks. We wanted to wait before we started a family. I did warn him but he wouldn't listen. Bloody man!' Livvie blew her hair off her clammy face. 'Oh, God... I... need... to... push!' She let rip with a blood-curdling, guttural cry, gripping fiercely onto Ella's hand. 'Waaaarghhh!'

With adrenalin pumping round his veins, Joss braced himself. He stole a look at Ella who flashed him a reassuring smile.

Livvie flopped back, taking ragged breaths. Moments later her cries started up again. Joss ventured a look to see the head and shoulders of a baby. Instinct told him to hold his hands ready and before he knew it, Livvie's baby plopped into his hands.

An exhausted Livvie slumped with relief, gasping. 'My baby, how's my baby?'

'This is so incredible!' Joss laughed in awe, his eyes dancing as he took in the little miracle, euphoria pumping around his body. 'It's just so amazing. Congratulations, Livvie, you've got yourself a beautiful little girl.'

'A little girl. Oh, Zander will be over the moon.' She beamed, tears of happiness spilling down her cheeks.

'You're a mum, Livvie!' Ella said, smiling as she peered over at the little scrap Joss was busying himself with.

With the cord taken care of – Joss was thankful he kept a First Aid kit in the back of the Land Rover – he gingerly handed the slippery bundle, so tiny in his huge, shovel-like hands, to Ella who quickly wiped a towel over the baby before swaddling her in the soft, fleecy blanket. Seconds later the air was filled with the lusty cries of a newborn, making the three of them laugh.

'Congratulations, Livvie. She really is beautiful, and she's got your gorgeous auburn hair.' Ella's voice cracked with emotion as she handed her friend her little daughter.

'Oh, my goodness. Well, hello there, little Holly. What was the rush all about, eh?' Livvie said softly, resting her baby girl in the crook of her arm and kissing her brow, her eyes filled with love. 'You've got your daddy's eyes. And I know he's going to be so happy to see you.'

Joss sat on his haunches, suddenly aware of how crowded it was in the back of the Land Rover; he hadn't really noticed until now thanks to the adrenalin that had been surging around him. Suddenly overcome with emotion, his eyes met Ella's to see tears pouring down her cheeks. She quickly averted her gaze. He knew not to say anything; he remembered from when they were kids how Ella liked to put on a front of being tough, and never admitted to shedding a tear. He knew different of course. He always had.

Joss headed round to the driver's seat while Ella helped Livvie get cleaned up and ready to set off for the village. While the drama had unfolded in the back of the vehicle, winter had raged on, relentlessly dumping snow. Joss didn't like to take the edge off the moment, but the road looked to be level with the wall in places. Even in the Land Rover, it was going to be risky heading back.

Livvie had just finished feeding Holly when they were suddenly aware of a set of bright lights reaching out through the blizzard. They seemed to be heading straight towards them. Joss looked on as the unmistakable sound of a snow plough scraping along the road reached his ears, his hopes lifting inexorably.

'It's Camm,' said Ella, relief in her voice, her eyes lighting up.

The tractor stopped several feet away and sure enough, Camm jumped down from the cab. Joss went to meet him, closing the door as quickly as he could.

'Now then, Joss, it's a bit wild to be out on the moortop.' Camm pulled his woolly hat down further over his dark curls as the savage wind hurled itself at them.

'Tell me about it.' Joss huddled down into the collar of his coat as the cold nipped at his cheeks. 'We've had a bit of a drama.'

'Oh?' Camm's face took on a worried expression. 'That's Livvie's car, isn't it? Is she okay? The other one looks like Ella's.'

Snow flurried around them as Joss quickly explained what had happened.

'Right then, we need to get Livvie to the surgery; you'd best follow me. Hopefully, Zander will be there now. While Liv and the baby are being looked after there, I'll plough the roads up to their cottage.'

'Cheers, Camm,' Joss said gratefully as a wave of relief rose through him.

'No worries. The weather changed that quickly, it took us all by surprise today. I think Ella's best off travelling with you; we can come back and get the cars tomorrow. They're off the road, so they won't come to any harm where they are.'

'Okay.' Joss wasn't going to argue with that.

Soon, Joss was driving steadily behind the tractor as they made their way to Danskelfe, the weather not relenting for a moment. The two women sat quietly beside him. Livvie cradling her tiny bundle, her eyes never moving from baby Holly's little crumpled face. Ella was squashed into the middle seat, her leg pressed against his. It felt somehow reassuring. He stole a sideways glance at her and she met his gaze, the pair exchanging a wide smile that made Joss's heart leap.

Today certainly hadn't turned out at all how he'd expected.

THIRTY-ONE

Ella

With Livvie and Holly safely dropped off at the surgery, Joss brought the Land Rover to a stop outside Rose Cottage. 'Well, here we are,' he said. 'Or would you prefer me to drop you at Tinkel Bottom Farm? Sorry, it's daft of me, I never thought to ask.'

Ella's body was charged with emotions, ranging from euphoria after helping deliver Livvie's baby, to the anxiety of travelling on such treacherous roads. She was still conscious of the adrenalin pulsing through her veins.

'Here's fine, thanks.' She paused for a moment, her hand on the door-release, looking out into the darkness. The snow had finally eased and only a handful of flakes were falling half-heartedly from the sky, picked out by the Victorian-style streetlamps. 'Don't suppose you fancy coming in for a bit, do you?' She glanced across at the dark windows of her home, suddenly not looking forward to being alone. Or, if she was being honest with herself, not wanting to leave Joss just yet. It was as if their experience up on the moors had created a new bond between them and she wanted to bask in the happy glow with him a while longer. Sitting by herself, her euphoria having nowhere to go, just didn't hold much appeal.

'Um.' He checked his watch.

'It's okay, I forgot you'll need to get back for your dad and for milking. And it's best to get home and safe as soon as you can in case we get more snow.' She went to climb out. Asking him in was a bad idea anyway, what was she thinking? 'Thanks for bringing me home and for all you did with Livvie. I dread to think what would've happened if you hadn't turned up.'

'I'm sure you'd have been fine, Ells. You've always been a coper.'

'Hm. I'm not so sure about that. Anyway...' She searched for something to say, reluctant to close the door, hoping he would say something that meant their time together wouldn't have to end.

'Don't know about you, but I could murder a cup of tea.' He gave her a lopsided grin that made her heart jump. 'Maybe with loads of sugar in this time; help with the shock we've just had.'

She grinned back at him, happiness rushing through her. 'Cup of tea it is.'

Once inside, and after an effusive greeting from Tabby-Cat, Ella turned to Joss. 'Phone signal's still down, so I just need to ring my parents on the landline, let them know I'm okay.'

'Of course. I'll stick the kettle on while you do that.' His words sent a shimmer of warmth up her spine; she liked that he felt comfortable enough in her home to do that.

With mugs in their hands and a fresh pot of tea on the table between them, Ella felt herself begin to relax, adrenalin leaching away from her body. Tabby-Cat was purring loudly, rubbing herself against her leg. 'Well, that was some afternoon we've just had.' She raised her eyebrows at Joss. Had they really just helped deliver a baby in the back of a Land Rover?

'You could say.' He shook his head as if sharing her disbelief.

His face turned suddenly serious, making Ella's smile fall. 'Anyway, what were you doing up there? I know you've got a four-wheel drive, but I thought you'd know better than to head out when the weather's like that.'

She felt a prickle of annoyance. Who did he think he was? Her dad? 'I was on my way to Danskelfe surgery to pick up Grandma Cecily's prescription then drop it off for her. The snow wasn't that bad when I set off, then I saw Livvie's car. I had to stop and help; I couldn't just drive past.' She did nothing to hide the note of irritation in her voice.

'I get that.' He nodded. 'It wasn't that bad when I left the farm either.' He paused, looking down into his mug. 'It's just the thought of you being stranded up there, taking a risk like that...' His eyes met hers.

The way he was looking at her set Ella's heart skittering about in her chest. Where was this conversation going? 'I would've been fine; I would've set off walking back home. But Livvie was a different matter; she was hardly in a position to walk anywhere.'

Joss went to say something, but stopped himself, apparently thinking better of it, the words loitering on his lips. Instead he beamed. 'Can you believe what we've just been a part of? We've just helped deliver a baby.'

His smile was infectious and Ella found herself matching it, happiness racing inside her. 'I know! I was absolutely bricking it at the time, but just kept telling myself to stay calm for Livvie's sake, that everything would be okay. I mean, I know you've actually delivered livestock, and I've helped my parents with the process, but a real-life human being giving birth is a whole different level.' She pushed her hair back off her face and laughed. 'Oh, my God, it's going to take a heck of a long time to properly sink in.' She looked across at Joss; from the expression on his face, he was clearly enjoying the same buzz.

'Yeah, them that describe it as a miracle are spot on; after seeing it for myself, I can honestly say, that's exactly what it is.'

Five minutes later, they were still talking about it when the landline rang. Reluctantly, Ella pulled herself away to answer it to hear Zander's voice on the end of the line, thanking her effusively, his voice thick with happy tears. 'I can't thank you and Joss enough; I'm indebted to you both for keeping Livvie and Holly safe. Thank you. Thank you.'

'Hey, it's the least we could do, Zander. Joss is just here actually, we're sharing a pot of tea to wet the baby's head,' she said with a giggle.

Zander laughed and asked if he could speak to Joss, he was keen to thank him personally too.

The call over with, Joss returned the handpiece to Ella. 'Well, he sounds like one happy father.' Joss chuckled.

'He does. Christmas has come early in the Gillespie household.'

Joss checked his watch and pulled a regretful face. 'Well, I suppose I'd better be heading back to the farm.'

'Oh, of course.' Feeling a shard of disappointment, Ella batted it away and smiled up at him. The way he was looking at her triggered a somersault in her stomach.

'What a day, and it's not even over yet.' His eyes twinkled at her as he zipped up his jacket.

'Yep, I'm not sure how Christmas Day's going to top that.'

'I reckon I can think of something,' he said huskily.

Her heart flipped as the expression in his eyes changed, his pupils darkening. He ran his finger down the side of her face and bent to her, his lips brushing against hers, all warm and delicious, sending sparks flying.

Before she had a chance to get her thoughts in some semblance of order, he'd taken a step back. 'Forgive me. I shouldn't have done that.' He dragged his hand down his face. 'When will I ever learn?' She was disappointed to see the look in his eyes had changed to one of regret.

Ella's mind was racing, her chest was heaving and her knees felt as if they could buckle at any minute. Words evaded her. She was yearning for him to kiss her again, and the urge to throw her arms around him and press her lips against his was almost too much to bear. Her mind hurtled back to that summer's day at Arncliffe Crag.

He looked at her beseechingly. 'Please, can we just forget I ever did that? I don't want my stupid, impetuous behaviour to affect our friendship again.'

Ella took a steadying breath. *His stupid behaviour?* It felt anything but stupid to her. Nothing could have felt more right. But it must have been driven by the thrill of what had happened up on the moortop and now he was obviously regretting it. She fixed a smile to her face, and injected a nonchalant air into her voice, hoping she didn't betray her true feelings. 'All forgotten. Don't suppose I'll see you at the carol singing around the Christmas tree this evening?' Her heart was still racing.

'What time does it start?'

She could tell he was trying to sound casual. 'Six. Followed by a buffet in the Sunne. It's always a good night, though I reckon numbers might be down thanks to the weather.' Much as she would love to see him there, Ella wasn't keen on him risking the roads; even if they'd been ploughed, plummeting temperatures could make them treacherous.

'I reckon I won't have finished milking by then, but have a great time if you go.'

His smile couldn't mask the regret in his eyes. Ella felt for him, she knew he was beating himself up inside. She wanted to say something, but words escaped her. Surely the fact that she hadn't pushed him away and run off like last time should tell him she hadn't found his kiss abhorrent. Her gaze was drawn to his mouth, those lips that had only moments ago been on hers. Come to think of it, his kiss had been gentle and tender. It had left her wanting more. Much more if the feelings currently raging around her body were anything to go by.

'Thanks, I'll definitely be there. I mean, news of little Holly's dramatic arrival into the world is bound to have made its way around the village by then. One of us is going to have to be there to share the details,' she said jokingly, hoping to ease his mind. 'Anyway, if I don't see you there, I'll see you and your dad at my parents' for lunch tomorrow.'

'Yep, course.' Pulling his keys from the pocket of his jacket, he headed for the front door, apparently reluctant to make eye contact with her. 'See you,' he said, stepping out into the night.

Ella watched him head down the path, her eyes lingering on his broad shoulders until the wind reminded her just how bitterly cold it was. She closed the door gently, her hand reaching to her mouth that was still tingling from his kiss. She'd never felt so torn. Part of her longed for him, but another part of her knew there was no point; he wasn't sticking around. And, much as she'd like to take things further with Joss, Ella knew she'd never be able to give herself up to a quick, no-strings-fling. It would be best to keep her feelings safely under wraps.

Ella had changed her clothes, adding extra layers for warmth, before heading out for the carol-singing session. After the biting cold of the moortop, she didn't fancy getting chilled to the bone again quite so soon.

As she approached the village green she could see there was already a good turn-out and, despite the bad weather of earlier, groups of people were gathering around the towering Christmas tree. Moorland folk were a hardy lot, and the locals of Lytell Stang-dale were well-known for the keenness to support village events, and the happy sound of their laughter and chatter was proof of that. There were whoops and shouts from the children who were running around, throwing snowballs or helping to build a giant snowman. Ella spotted Kitty and Ollie's three children amongst them, Lily patiently helping her little sister, Lottie, make a smaller version.

The Christmas tree dominated the green, its pine fragrance scenting the air, its warm-white fairy lights peering through its snow-dusted boughs. Thankfully, the weather had remained calm since their return from their moortop adventure and, despite her warnings to herself about not getting too attached, Ella held onto the glimmer of hope that Joss just might pop down and join the festivities.

Seeing her parents in animated conversation with Kitty and Ollie, she headed over to them.

'Ella, lovey. Come here! Your dad and me were just on our way over to you.' Her mum, whose nose was red with the cold, threw her arms around her and squeezed her hard. 'What a day you've had. Who'd have thought you and Joss would end up delivering Livvie's baby in the middle of a snow blizzard?' Debbie stood back, her hands on Ella's shoulders. 'Honestly, your dad and me didn't know whether to be worried sick or as proud as punch.'

'Aye, when Cecily rang saying you hadn't turned up we were past ourselves,' said her dad. 'We weren't half relieved when you rang, I can tell you.'

'I'm sorry you were worried. I think that massive dumping of snow took us all by surprise.'

'Ella, you're a star, coming to Livvie's rescue like that.' Kitty pulled her cousin into a hug once Debbie had released her.

'You are that,' said Ollie, a beam lighting up his gentle face.

'I'm not so sure about that, but I have to say Joss was amazing; he took care of all the tricky stuff, I just held Livvie's hand.' Ella felt suddenly overwhelmed by all the praise being heaped upon her.

'Ella! Oh, my days! We've just heard.' She turned to see Violet heading towards her. Even dressed for snow, Vi managed to look the height of glamour. 'You and Joss are the talk of the village. How are Livvie and her baby?'

Before Ella had a chance to answer Jimby appeared wearing his customary grin. 'Ey up, Ells. I gather you and Joss are the heroes of the day, coming to Livvie Gillespie's rescue up on the moortop.'

'We're so proud of her, aren't we, Pete?' said Debbie, her face wreathed in smiles now she'd seen her daughter was okay.

'Hey, anyone would've done the same in our position.' Ella was keen to play down her role; she wasn't fond of being the centre of attention. 'I'm just so relieved Joss turned up in his Land Rover when he did. I can't imagine how it would've been if Livvie had given birth in her little car.' She gave an involuntary shiver at the thought.

'It'll end up being one of those village stories that's passed down through time; it'll become a Lytell Stangdale legend,' said Kitty, her eyes shining.

'Warghh!' A snowball hit Jimby square in the face, everyone turned to look. 'Lucas! You little horror!'

'Gotcha, Uncle Jimby!' Hooting with laughter, Lucas, Kitty's teenage son, raced off, his feet sliding all over the ground as he went.

'Lucas!' Kitty was struggling not to laugh as her brother spluttered and wiped snow from his eyes.

Jimby bent down and scooped up a handful of the stuff, forming it into a ball as he hurried off in pursuit of his nephew. 'You're going to regret doing that, big time.'

'Who's the biggest kid?' asked Vi, shaking her head as she watched her husband slip and land in a heap on the floor.

Searching the crowd for Portia, Ella spotted her at the other side of the tree, chatting away to Lady Carolyn Hammondely, her husband, Sim, and Gabe Dublin. She caught her friend's eye and waved, happy when she received an equally enthusiastic one in return.

Before long, with song sheets handed out to everyone, the carols started up under Jonty's supervision. The voices of the villagers rising up to the clear night sky, carried off over the dale on the frosty air. Ella was singing along, her mind drifting to Joss, when she felt a nudge on her shoulder. She turned to see Molly smiling at her.

'Hey, well done, missus.'

It took her a moment to realise what her cousin meant. 'Oh, hi, Molly. Thanks.'

'Camm and Livvie filled me in on what had happened. By all accounts you and Joss were amazing.' Molly reached her arm around her cousin, giving her a little squeeze. 'Thank heavens you two found her.'

Ella had tried not to think about what would have happened to Livvie if they hadn't shown up when they did, consoling herself with the fact that at least Camm had been out ploughing the roads so Livvie wouldn't have been stranded up on the bleak moortop on her own for the night. 'Camm was amazing too, we wouldn't have got her to the surgery if it wasn't for him. And we were so relieved to see you were there.'

'Aye, the old nurse training still comes in handy every now and then. Though it's usually for assessing cut fingers and bumped heads. Checking over babies delivered in the back of a Landie on the moortop in the middle of a raging snow blizzard is a first.' Molly chuckled.

Camm peered around his partner. 'Now then, Ella. I was just doing my job, nowt special. It was you and Joss who did the tricky stuff.'

Ella beamed at him. 'Hi, Camm, I honestly can't tell you how glad we were to see you! I could've done a cartwheel,' she said, making them all laugh.

'Anyroad, as you know, it's not the first time Livvie's come a cropper in her car in the snow, she came off the road a couple of years ago. I got her to promise me she wouldn't make it a third time.' Camm shook his head good-naturedly.

'Too right,' said Molly. 'But at least it all turned out okay.'

When Livvie and the baby had arrived at Danskelfe surgery, Molly had been there collecting prescriptions for her dad and Granny Aggie. With the place getting ready to close and the practice nurse having left for home an hour since, there were no medical staff around to help. Zander was still out visiting a patient and it was his partner's day off. Molly's days as the local district nurse kicked into action and she led Livvie, clutching baby Holly, into the midwife's room where she gave them both a thorough checking over.

Not long after, Zander had arrived, his face a picture of disbelief when he saw his wife sitting there looking exhausted but happy, a mewling bundle in her arms. Afterwards, Camm had ploughed the road to Middleton-le-Moors hospital, Zander, Livvie and their newborn following steadily behind them in Zander's sturdy four-wheel drive.

'So where are Livvie and the baby now? Are they at home?' asked Livvie, briskly rubbing her hands together to warm them up.

'Hospital. Just overnight though. Zander's staying there too. It probably still hasn't sunk in for him yet. Camm said he still looked absolutely gobsmacked when they reached the hospital,' Molly said, chuckling.

'I'm not surprised.' It suddenly struck Ella that she hadn't seen Molly's youngest, little Emmie. 'No Em?'

Molly shook her head. 'She's with my mum and dad; he and Em are both full of cold. We didn't want her to overdo it and not enjoy tomorrow so we left the three of them watching a Christmas movie in front of the fire, drinking hot chocolate which they all seemed happy to do.'

'Ah, bless her. I hope she feels better for tomorrow.'

With more carols sung, Ella joined Bea and Jonty, each of them armed with a tray, offering small cups of piping-hot mulled wine to the carollers. The aroma of cloves and citrus swirling under Ella's nose sent a wave of happiness through her; it was so evocative of Christmases with her family.

In no time, the warming beverage was consumed and the carols were once again resumed. Ella was singing heartily when she heard a voice behind her. 'I hear your singing hasn't improved.' She felt a huge grin spread across her face as she turned to see Joss smiling down at her.

'Hey, you! I thought I was doing really well.' She couldn't help but laugh, delivering a playful punch to his arm.

'You really weren't.' He struggled to keep himself from laughing. 'What I heard just then was quite frankly, bloomin' awful. Strangled cat springs to mind.'

'That's so mean.' Ella giggled.

'Mean, but true. Anyway, I think it's kindest for everyone if I keep you talking so it stops you from howling like an injured animal. These poor folk have been tortured enough.' His eyes danced with amusement.

'I'm going to treat that comment with the contempt it deserves and move the conversation on,' she said, laughing. 'Did you come with your dad?'

'Nope, I tried to talk him into it, but he was adamant he didn't fancy it, insisting I should come alone. I told him I wouldn't be long.'

'Fair enough.'

'Any news of Livvie and the baby?'

Ella filled Joss in on the situation. All the while her heart was leaping about in her chest. To say she was thrilled he'd turned up was an understatement. She felt suddenly light-hearted and carefree.

Neither of them noticed their friends looking on with interest, exchanging knowing looks.

THIRTY-TWO

Joss

With the carol singing over, most folk headed to the pub, though Ella's parents had decided to make their way home, saying they'd pop in on Bill on their way back. The bar was stuffed to the gunnels and it was beginning to look like Joss and Ella weren't going to get a seat until he became aware of a voice calling above the throng.

'Joss! Ella!' He followed the direction of the voice. Being taller than most people there, he managed to see over their heads, his gaze landing on Vi. She was sitting at the long table by the inglenook fire, beckoning them across and pointing to the banquette.

He smiled and gave her a thumbs-up. 'This way, Ells.' He reached for her hand and led her through the wall of bodies.

'Ollie grabbed an extra seat and me and Kitts have shuffled right up so you two should be able to fit on the end there,' said Vi, looking festive in a rich, green velvet dress that complemented her dark aubergine hair. 'I haven't a clue where Jimby is, but he can sit on the seat here next to me.'

'Speak of the devil,' said Molly as Jimby appeared looking harassed, his face covered in vivid-red lipstick marks.

'Jimby! Care to explain why your face is covered with kisses?' asked Vi, amused, arching a plum-coloured eyebrow.

'Blame that Maneater woman.' He went to wipe his face with the back of his hand. 'She's bloomin' terrifying!'

'Here, try these.' Molly handed him a handful of paper tissues from her bag.

'Thanks, Moll.' He scrubbed hard at his face, looking at the lipstick-soiled tissues in disgust. 'Honest, fellas, you really want to watch yourselves with her; she's prowling around, armed with a massive sprig of mistletoe and jeez, does she know how to use it. Grabbed me in a headlock before I had a chance to escape and started slobbering all over me. Man, it was gross, like being kissed by an ashtray. I don't even want to think about where her tongue went.' He gave an exaggerated shudder.

'Or where it's been,' said Molly, sniggering.

A chorus of 'Molly!' followed.

Jimby winced. 'Thanks for that, Moll. I'm now scarred for life.'

'Get over yourself, you drama queen,' said Vi, her shoulders shaking with laughter.

'And to make matters worse, I've got a wet backside from when I landed in the snow chasing Lucas.'

'Looks like you could do with a pint, mate.' Ollie handed his friend a glass of amber-coloured beer which he took gratefully.

Joss slipped his jacket off and tucked it under the seat as Ella unwound her woollen scarf, releasing a waft of her fresh perfume. He sat back and took a deep breath, the scent so evocative of their summers together. It triggered a yearning deep inside him. He took a sideways look at her, his heart filling with a rush of emotion. She was listening as Jimby and Ollie recounted a story about a charity calendar shoot they'd done a few years earlier, and how Anita Matheson had tried to get involved. Ella threw her head back and laughed uproariously, her eye catching his.

'You okay?' she asked, smiling.

'I'm good. Glad I came.' He couldn't take his eyes off her. This feeling that had taken hold of him was something else.

'Me too,' she said, almost shyly.

Christmas Eve was never a late session at The Sunne Inne, and before long, numbers had thinned, with parents heading home to get their excited children bathed and tucked up in bed, ready for the big day.

With calls of, "Merry Christmas" and, "Goodnight!" echoing around the village, Joss and Ella made their way along the trod, stopping when they reached his Land Rover. Frost had crept over everything and sparkled in the moonlight, and the shrill screech of a barn owl could be heard from the depths of the dale.

'That was fun,' said Joss, wishing more than anything that he could take Ella into his arms.

'Yeah, carol singing's always a good night. Shame your dad didn't come.'

Joss nodded. 'Too stubborn for his own good, that one. Maybe I'll be able to get him to join in next year.'

Ella smiled, her eyes shining. Evidently his kiss hadn't scared her off or she wouldn't still be standing here talking to him, he thought.

'Right, I'd best head back,' he said reluctantly. She looked so beautiful in the moonlight; he could feel his desire building. It wouldn't take much for him to kiss her again, but he told himself he wasn't ready to push his luck so soon after the last one; he was still uncertain as to what she'd thought of it.

'Yep. Drive carefully. See you tomorrow.' She gave him a small wave and headed off in the direction of her home. Joss watched, the bobble on top of her hat bouncing, until she disappeared around the curve in the road. His heart was thumping in his chest, his mind all over the place. Woah, she'd really turned his world on its axis.

When he arrived back at the farm, he half-expected his dad to have gone to bed. Instead, he followed the sound of the television from the living room where he found him in good spirits, looking comfy on the sofa. He was stroking Sid's ears who was curled up beside him. Sid leapt down as soon as he spotted Joss, his tail wagging happily as he ran over to greet him.

'Hi, Dad.' Joss made his way over to his usual armchair and flopped down into it, his eyes alighting on the two red and white knitted stockings in a Scandinavian design that were hanging either side of the fireplace. He felt a lump form in his throat. His mum had bought them for him and Rich when they were both at primary school and she'd hung them there every Christmas Eve. They'd rush down on Christmas morning to find them stuffed with gifts and treats.

'Now then, son. Had a good night?'

Joss composed himself. 'Yeah, it was great. You should've come with me; you'd have enjoyed it.'

'Ah, well, me and Sid had things to do, didn't we, lad?' After fussing Joss, Sid had climbed back up next to Bill, who was now smoothing his head indulgently.

Joss nodded, his breathing heavy. 'You hung up the stockings.'

'Aye, one's for you, t'other one's for Sid here.'

On hearing his name, Sid's ears pricked up.

Joss wondered what his dad had found to put in the stockings; as far as he was aware, his father hadn't left the farm since his return from hospital.

As if reading his mind, Bill said, 'I asked Pete and Debbie if they'd pick up a few bits from the shops for me, and they very kindly dropped them off tonight while you were out.'

So that's why they headed off so early. Joss noted his dad was looking brighter; he had roses in his cheeks and his eyes had lost the sad, defeated look they'd had when he first saw him in the hospital ward. 'That was kind of them.'

'Aye, they're good folk the Welfords. And their Ella's a grand lass.'

'Can't argue with that. It's very good of them to have us for Christmas dinner.'

'Aye, it is. The last few years, going to Rich and Dawn's has been bloomin' grim, I can tell you. Neither of them wanted me there, they made that plain enough. I was a nuisance they could do without. I'd already made up my mind I wasn't going to trouble them again when...' His words tailed off and he glanced up at Joss. 'Well, you know what happened.'

Joss nodded. 'Yeah, I do.'

This was the most relaxed his dad had been since Joss had returned from Skeller Rigg Farm. Though he was discussing something that had caused him a shedload of grief – and had the potential to continue to do so – Bill spoke without the bitterness that usually laced his speech. And much as Joss could see why his brother and sister-in-law hadn't been exactly thrilled at having his morose father with them on Christmas Day, no doubt casting a cloud of gloom over the celebrations, the thought of his dad feeling unwanted tugged at his heart. He suddenly wondered how Manda would have reacted if he'd suggested his father join them for Christmas Day. Not well, he thought, wincing inwardly.

Though the situation between the two men still couldn't be described as properly comfortable, Joss had to admit, the tension that had stretched between them for so many years was fading away. That was something he'd never thought possible. He'd always believed too much bitterness and hurt loomed large between them, creating a vast, insurmountable barrier, making reconciliation impossible. Just goes to show you never know what's around the corner, he mused. His dad had never been a great talker, but while they'd sat together in the evenings, relaxing – as best they could in the circumstances – they'd shared tentative conversations, from which Joss had gained a valuable insight into his father's thoughts. It was no understatement to say he'd been surprised, and not a little saddened, at what he'd learnt. Such a conversation from the previous evening when his dad had opened up more than Joss had expected had played over in his mind all day.

'I know things changed after your mum... well, after we lost her, and now all these years have passed, I can see now perhaps I didn't handle the situation as well as I could've done,' Bill had said as they'd been sitting in front of the fire in the living room.

'Listen, Dad, there's no need...'

'Let me finish, son.' Bill had kept his eyes fixed to the mug of tea he'd been nursing in his lap. 'I felt like I was in shock, numb for years after. Felt full of hell with the world, blamed everyone. Took it out on you and Rich; I can see that now.' He'd swallowed audibly before taking a gulp of his tea.

Joss had observed his dad, unsure of where the conversation was heading.

'Thing is, I seemed to forget you two lads were grieving too, that you needed the support of your father, but I was too wrapped up in my own sorrow to help you.' Two tears had plopped onto Bill's cheeks, rolling slowly down. Joss had jumped up from his seat but Bill had waved him away. 'Leave me be, I'm all right.' Sid, who'd been curled up beside Bill on the sofa, had looked up with a whimper and rested his paw on Bill's arm.

'We had Aunty Babs and Uncle Maff, they were brilliant,' Joss had said.

'Aye, they're good folk.' Bill had looked thoughtful for a moment. 'Reminds me, I need to speak to them, apologise for how I spoke to Babs; I was a bit harsh; she didn't deserve what I said to her.'

Though Joss had felt he couldn't argue with that, he'd kept his thoughts to himself.

'Anyroad, when you went to our Joe and Hannah's I won't deny, it was a bit of a relief to start with; I'd told myself it was one less daft lad to deal with. But I honestly thought it would be just a temporary arrangement. Never expected you to stay there permanently.' For the first time, he'd looked Joss in the eye, the pain clear to see. It had tugged at Joss's heart.

'I never knew that was how you felt, Dad,' Joss had said, rubbing his fingers across his forehead. 'I thought you'd had enough of me. You were so angry that last night.'

'Aye, I have to admit I was full of hell when I'd seen what had happened to the tractor.' Bill's shoulders had heaved with a sigh. 'I can understand why you'd want to get as far away from here as possible. But, in truth, I was angrier with myself than I was with you, what with the tractor not being insured. That was my fault, and I regret to say, you got the full force of my temper. I'd always expected you to come home when the dust had settled. I might've been angry that night, but this was your home; it is your home. When you showed no interest in coming back, I just assumed you were happier living with Joe and Hannah than being here.'

Joss had felt his heart squeeze as he'd absorbed his dad's words. 'That must've been hard for you.'

'Was like kick in the guts, to be honest, but it was no more than I deserved. Didn't like to dwell on it so I just accepted it. In truth, things have never been right since we lost your mum; even now they aren't.'

Joss's eyes had roamed his dad's face, noticing how his features appeared to cling on to years' worth of sorrow. 'Mum's watching over us, Dad, I'm sure of it. And she'd be chuffed to bits to see us sitting together like this.'

'Aye, I reckon you could be right there.' Bill had given a small smile.

'Well, I don't know about you, but it seems to be a good time to put the past behind us, to move forward and be positive.' He grinned at his dad. 'Fancy giving it a go?'

'Aye, why not.' The grin that Bill had returned had sent a warm glow through Joss. *Progress.*

Joss had spent hours mulling over the conversation. He was no expert, but from what he could see, his dad still appeared to be grieving the loss of his wife, even after all these years. He'd make discreet enquiries with Zander and find out what could be done about it.

In another conversation Joss had touched on how his father had become almost reclusive.

'You know, Dad, it would do you good to get down to the pub more, the atmosphere there's so welcoming.'

'Aye, you're right; the Latimers have done a good job of turning it around, and I had been popping down for the occasional game of dominoes, but with me starting to feel under the weather, I was just too shattered to go after I'd done all that needed doing here.'

'Well, there's no excuse for you not to go now.'

'True, lad; I'll have to try and make an effort.'

And now he was sitting with his father in the living room, his reasons for leaving had sprung up in his mind again. Why hadn't he returned to the farm? Could he honestly say he really believed he'd been banished by his dad? He felt shame prickle over his skin. If he was being completely honest with himself, Joss had relished being part of a family again, with a mum and a dad at the helm. He'd been made to feel welcome, spending his days working on the farm with his Uncle Joe, returning to the warm, cosy farmhouse, filled with love, where he'd enjoyed Aunty Hannah's hearty meals. It had felt like what he'd had before his mum had passed away. And he'd so very desperately wanted to feel that again, be a part of what his aunt and uncle had created. Staying there had meant his life had suddenly become a whole lot easier and he'd been utterly doted on by his aunt and uncle. When Lawry came along, Joss had considered him as much a brother as Rich. And he'd found himself not wanting to leave.

Joss looked across at his dad, the glow from the fire dancing across his face. It would seem neither of them were completely blameless for their estrangement. He felt a sudden rush of pity for his father. He could only imagine how devastating it must have been for him to lose his soulmate at such a young age, and be left with two young sons to bring up on his own. He hadn't been able to see it as a teenager, but as a man, Joss now had a greater under-standing as to why his father's grief had manifested itself in anger, lashing out at those closest to him. It hadn't been personal as such; Bill just hadn't known how to manage his heartbreak and sorrow.

Joss took a deep breath as an image of his mum filled his mind. It was her memory, and the love she'd had for them both, that had brought them back together, got them talking to one another. Feeling suddenly fired up, Joss made himself a promise there and then: he was going to do all he could to get his relationship with his dad properly back on track. He wasn't going to step out of his father's life as quickly as he'd stepped back into it. He scratched his head. Only, he wasn't exactly sure how his dad was going to take this news.

'What are you thinking, lad?' Bill interrupted his son's musings.

Joss met his eyes. The anger in them had gone, and he could see his Uncle Joe's gentle expression reflected back at him. 'I was actually thinking how much I've liked being back here at the farm, the village too.'

'Aye, I can see that.' Bill smiled, all the while stroking Sid's head that was resting in his lap. 'Any news on the doctor and his wife?'

A smile spread across Joss's face. 'They're all doing fine. I'm told they're staying in hospital overnight, just to make sure Livvie and the baby are all right. Should be home tomorrow.'

'You did good there, son.' Bill's eyes went back to Sid as he continued to stroke him. Sid groaned in unabashed delight.

'It was teamwork; Ella and Camm were amazing, and Livvie was so brave. It's still sinking in that she gave birth in my Landie.' He shook his head in disbelief, images of that day playing out in his mind.

A brief silence hung in the air, and for once, it wasn't tinged with its usual hint of awkwardness.

Joss sat back in his seat. 'I haven't told you this, but when I first got here, I'd sworn to myself I was going to keep out of the way of everyone, not venture down to the village, so I could avoid anyone who might remember me.' He gave a small laugh.

'And how did that pan out then?' asked his dad, chuckling.

'Not at all.' Joss caught his dad's eye and the two men laughed together.

'Thought not. Seems to me you've enjoyed becoming a local lad again.'

'Aye, I have.' Joss thought about how he'd been made to feel welcome by everyone, his smile growing wider.

'So does that mean you're thinking about staying on for a bit longer?' His dad's expression became serious, and if he wasn't mistaken, Joss detected a hopeful look in his eye.

Joss switched his gaze to the film that played out on the television, rubbing the arm of the chair distractedly. 'I'm not sure.' He paused. 'How would you feel if I did?'

'Reckon I could put up with you around the place for a bit longer seeing as though you make a decent cup of tea.' Bill sniffed. 'And what about Ella?'

Joss felt his heart leap at the mention of her name. 'What about Ella?'

'Oh, nothing. Only, if I didn't know better, I'd say you seem to mention her a fair bit, and your face lights up whenever you say her name.' Bill's mouth twitched with a smile.

'Uhh. Hadn't noticed. Are you sure you're not mistaken?' Joss asked, feigning nonchalance. *Who exactly are you trying to kid, Joss Campion?*

'Oh, I'm not mistaken. And I reckon if Sid here could speak, he'd agree with me, wouldn't you, lad?'

Sid opened his eyes and looked up at Bill, quickly closing them again. Joss sat speechless.

'I seem to recall you were sweet on her before you left. That's a heck of a long time to be holding a torch for someone without doing anything about it.'

Joss felt his heart rate gather speed. If only his dad knew the half of it. 'Really? Can't remember that far back.'

'Anyroad, it's none of my business. All I'll say on the matter is that I knew better than to let your mum slip through my fingers.'

He gave an exaggerated yawn and pushed himself up from the sofa. 'It's time I was heading to bed if I intend on helping you with milking in the morning.'

'I don't expect you to do that, Dad. Why not wait until you feel properly better? There's no point setting yourself back by doing too much too soon. I can manage.'

'Why don't we just see how I get on, eh? If I don't feel up to it, I can always break off but we'll never know unless I try, will we?'

Joss couldn't argue with that. He wanted to tell his dad not to overdo it and risk spoiling his Christmas dinner at the Welford's but he bit his tongue and, instead, watched him head towards the door. 'Night, Dad.'

'Night, son. Don't forget to put the guard up against the fire before you turn in.'

'I won't.'

Joss listened to the sounds of Bill getting ready for bed upstairs, the water-pipes humming as he ran the tap at the bathroom sink, the squeak of his bedroom door opening, followed not long after by the sound of his bed creaking as he climbed in and settled himself down.

His mind was teeming with thoughts, not least of which was how his father had picked up on his feelings for Ella. He can't have been hiding them as well as he'd thought. And if he wasn't mistaken, he'd almost got the impression that his dad seemed keen for him to stay on a little longer. Joss was surprised to find that rather appealing, especially if it meant he could spend more time with Ella.

Ella. Oh, heck, what was he going to do about her? He rubbed his hands briskly back-and-forth over his face. There was no mistaking his feelings for her and his longing to take things further. But where would that leave them? Helderthorpe wasn't exactly on the doorstep. And from what she'd said about her plans for setting up a boarding kennels, she was clearly keen on staying put in Lytell Stangdale.

There was also the fairly major fact that couldn't be ignored:

Ella was keeping him firmly at arm's length. Did she think he was a player after what had happened between him and Portia? Or did she think he wasn't ready for commitment? He couldn't blame her if she did, after all, he'd told her as much. And she'd confessed after her last relationship she was happy being single and in no rush to change her status.

'Ughh! You'd be better off getting Ella out of your mind!' he said aloud.

He watched the glowing embers of the fire, rubbing Sid's proffered stomach with his foot – once Bill had gone to bed, Sid had loped over to Joss and flumped down at his feet. The conversation he'd had with his dad that evening had left him feeling hopeful. Losing his customary scowl had made his father look like a different man, the resemblance between him and Uncle Joe more noticeable.

When he'd arrived a week ago, greeted by Rich, Joss hadn't expected the farm and the village to work its way under his skin as they had. Adding Ella to the equation, and the loyalty he felt for his aunt and uncle, he was feeling utterly torn.

'Right, Sid, this isn't getting us anywhere. I think it's time for some shut-eye, then we can see what tomorrow's got in store for us.'

THIRTY-THREE

Ella

Christmas morning arrived with a brittle frost and a clear blue sky. Ella's heart felt light; she was looking forward to the day ahead, especially as Joss featured heavily. She'd given the guinea pigs, Dave and Nigel, fresh bedding and topped up their food before adding a couple of chews she'd bought them for Christmas, the sweet smell of sawdust filling the shed. She chatted away to them as she fixed their bottle of fresh water to the cage. 'Merry Christmas, boys. Enjoy your festive chews.'

She'd already given Tabby-Cat the soft toy from the stocking she'd bought her and the cat was currently rolling it between her paws in the living room.

It wasn't long before Ella was wrapped up and heading out into the crisp morning, her arms loaded up with bags of brightly-wrapped presents. She smiled to see the village looking Christmas-card-pretty as she crunched her way along the trod to her car. The thatched roofs of the houses were covered in a thick layer of snow that sparkled in the pale sunlight. The bells rang out from the church tower, proclaiming to the villagers it was Christmas morning.

'Morning, Ella, lovey. Merry Christmas.' She looked up to see Livvie's step-mum Rhoda beaming and waving from her garden; Freda, the old lady who'd been staying with her for the last year was standing beside her, tending the bird feeder.

'Merry Christmas,' said Freda.

'Morning, ladies. Merry Christmas to you both.'

'I must thank you for all you did for Livvie yesterday. I don't know what she'd have done without you. Joss and Camm too,' said Rhoda. 'It was so lucky, the three of you turning up when you did. Talk about a dramatic entrance into the world!' She chuckled.

'It was dramatic all right. And, honestly, there's no thanks necessary. It all happened that fast, we just sort of acted on autopilot. Little Holly arrived before we had too much chance to think about it.' Ella grinned. 'I gather they're coming home today.'

Rhoda's smile lit up her gentle face. 'Yes, they are,' she said, her voice brimming with enthusiasm. 'They were going to join us and Len here for Christmas dinner, but we've had a change of plan and we're decamping to their cottage so they can get little Toots settled into her new surroundings. I'm cooking dinner up there. It'll be better for Liv to be in her own home too; I can't wait to spoil her. But really, thank you again.'

'Well, it definitely made for a Christmas we won't forget in a hurry.'

'You're not wrong there.' Freda chuckled. 'Seems a lot of Christmases round here are unforgettable.'

'Just a bit.' Rhoda laughed.

'Anyway, I'd best be off before my parents start wondering where I've got to. Hope you have a lovely Christmas, and you manage to get loads of cuddles with baby Holly.'

'Ooh, I can't wait,' said Rhoda, her eyes shining brightly. 'My first Christmas being a step-grandma; it's the best present ever.'

It took a good few sprays of anti-freeze before the windscreen of Ella's car was clear enough for her to set off for Tinkel Bottom and it had barely warmed through when she arrived there.

She walked into the kitchen to the smell of roasting turkey and the sound of her mum singing along to her favourite festive crooners CD. 'Good to know where I get my singing skills from.'

'Ella, lovey! Merry Christmas.' Debbie put down the potatoes she was peeling and rushed over to her daughter, wrapping her arms around her and delivering a noisy kiss to her cheek.

'Merry Christmas, Mum.' Ella giggled. 'Where's Dad?'

'He's just out seeing to the sheep but he shouldn't be long. He says to tell you he's mucked out Clive and the goats so you don't need to.'

'That's kind of him, but I wouldn't have minded doing it. I'll just put these under the tree then I'll give you a hand.' Ella raised the bags of gifts to demonstrate.

Back in the kitchen, Ella got stuck in to peeling the vegetables. Soon the smell of the turkey was joined by the scrumptious aroma of Yorkshire puddings, Debbie's homemade roast chestnut stuffing, and sautéed onions for the gravy.

By the time Campion father and son had arrived, Pete was lifting the turkey out of the electric oven – it being too big for the Aga roasting oven – the juices hissing and bubbling. 'Bloomin' 'eck, love, what the heck have you stuffed this bird with? Feels like a ton weight.'

Sid's nose shot up in the air, sniffing enthusiastically.

'Crikey me, Debbie, it's the size of an ostrich! Anyone would think you were feeding the whole village,' Bill said, chuckling heartily.

'It's the same every year, Bill. We're still eating turkey in February.' Ella smiled, noticing he looked so much better than the last time she'd seen him; his eyes were brighter and there was colour in his cheeks. He was smiling too, which seemed to make the world of difference, transforming his usually dour features.

'Aye, it's turkey curry, turkey casserole, turkey omelette, turkey pie, turkey everything. You get the picture? I honestly started to think I'd sprouted a set of wattles I'd eaten that much of the stuff last Christmas.' Grinning, Pete set the vast roasting tin down on a couple of trivets.

'Thanks, love,' said Debbie as she hurried over, covering the bird with a sheet of foil before she started spooning the juices into a jug for the gravy. 'While I do this, can you pour the fizz?'

'S'okay, I'll do it,' said Ella.

'Need a hand?' asked Joss. He looked achingly handsome in his burgundy-coloured shirt, his hair slightly ruffled. Ella's heart gave a little leap.

'Any good at taking corks out of Prosecco?' She handed him the bottle.

'Not bad.' He took it from her, gently easing the cork out and speedily pouring it into the five glass flutes lined up on the work top. 'Woah, nearly wasted a bit there,' he said, as the pale golden liquid rushed up the glass in a mass of frothing bubbles.

Ella handed everyone their drink, her mum wiping her hands down the front of her apron before she took hers. 'Thanks, lovey.' Her smile suddenly slipped from her face. 'Oh, Bill, I've just remembered, are you okay to have this?'

'Aye, I made sure to have my medication. I should be fine as long as I don't go crazy.'

'Phew!' she said, relief pushing her smile back up.

'Merry Christmas, everyone, and thanks for joining us, fellas,' said Pete, raising his glass, clinking it against the others.

A chorus of 'Merry Christmas!' rang around the room.

'Thanks for inviting us, we're chuffed to be here.' Joss caught Ella's eye, making her blush while her stomach performed a quick somersault. She couldn't help but return his smile, wondering as to the reason for the loaded look he was giving her.

'Aye, that we are,' said Bill.

Before long, they were all sitting round the table, tucking into their Christmas dinner to a backdrop of festive music. Conversation flowed, laughter ringing out as the friends reminisced, talking fondly of old times. Ella couldn't remember when she last saw Bill looking so happy and carefree; it knocked years off him. His cheeks were flushed, his eyes shining as he recounted tales of the Young Farmers' rallies he and Sue had attended with Ella's parents, the three of them laughing so hard at the memories, tears were pouring down their cheeks. Joss, who was sitting opposite Ella, caught her eye and smiled, apparently reluctant to break eye contact with her.

'Managed to get over yesterday's drama up on the moortop yet?' he asked, breaking the spell.

She laughed and blew out her cheeks. 'Just about. Seems like longer ago than yesterday though. And I still can't believe it actually happened; that we were involved in delivering Livvie's baby.'

'I know what you mean; seems surreal. And definitely not something I'll forget in a hurry.'

'Too right. I saw Rhoda this morning; she's chuffed to bits to be a step-grandma.'

'Ah, bless her, she'll be a lovely granny,' said Debbie.

'Sounds to me like the perfect time to make another toast. Has everyone got something in their glass?' asked Pete, his face flushed from the warmth of the kitchen, his eyes merry.

When everyone confirmed they had, he lifted his flute aloft once more. 'To new beginnings; seems there's been a lot of those around this Christmas.'

'To new beginnings.' Everyone tapped their glasses against one another's. Ella locked eyes with Joss once more, electricity sizzling between them. Out of nowhere, regret suddenly pierced her bubble of happiness, cruelly reminding her that Joss would soon be gone. She struggled to keep her smile from faltering.

THIRTY-FOUR

Joss

With the Christmas feast devoured and the table cleared, they'd all reconvened to the living room with a large pot of tea, faces ruddy and paper crowns all skew-whiff. The dark, low beams, yellow ochre walls and warmth radiated by the wood-burner made the room cosy and homely.

Joss flopped down on the large sofa beside Ella, his leg resting against hers, a waft of her perfume floating under his nose, triggering a rush of his pulse. He'd always enjoyed Christmas Day with his aunt and uncle, though not so much when he was married to Manda who hated having to join them for Christmas dinner; the build-up to the day was always something he dreaded, with her moaning and refusing to go. She'd turn up at the last minute with a face like thunder, tainting the festivities with an undercurrent of discomfort. But today had been wonderful for lots of reasons, the main one being he was spending it with Ella. Though he'd only been back in Lytell Stangdale a week, in those few short days, he'd come to realise being in her company was where he felt happiest, felt most at ease. She imbued him with a feeling of contentment he hadn't had since his mum had been alive. And it had made him think long and hard about his future. About where he truly belonged.

From the corner of his eye, he picked up the knowing smiles that passed between her parents who took the armchairs opposite. They'd evidently sensed the vibes passing between him and their daughter.

Bill eased himself down beside him on the sofa, Sid flumping on the floor between them with a contented groan. 'That was a truly delicious meal, thank you, Debbie.' He rubbed his hand over his stomach.

'It was,' said Joss. 'I'm not too hopeless in the kitchen, but I dread to think what I'd have rustled up for us.'

'Aye, me too.' Bill chortled.

'It was a joint effort; Pete and Ella chipped in too, but you're very welcome all the same.' Debbie smiled at them over her mug.

'Aye, I can peel a pretty mean sprout when I put my mind to it,' said Pete, grinning as he mimed doing just that.

Before anyone could add anything, a melody of beeps and buzzes rang out as their respective mobile phones suddenly pinged to life.

'Ey up, looks like signal's been restored,' said Joss.

'Thank goodness for that,' said Debbie. 'I was hoping to send a text to our Greg, see how him and Bronny are getting on with my mum. Fingers crossed she's behaving herself.' What had happened with Livvie the previous day had been a stark reminder of how dramatically the weather could change on the moortop and they'd all agreed that rather than Grandma Cecily spending Christmas dinner at Tinkel Bottom, as she usually did, she should stay close to her home and spend it with Greg and his family in Arkleby. Everyone declared themselves content with that decision.

'I think she was secretly quite excited to be spending the day with Riley and Tamsin while they're still young enough to be excited about Christmas.' Ella turned to Joss. 'Riley's six and Tammy's five, so they still believe in Santa.'

'Ah,' he said, nodding. Not for the first time he felt a wave of relief that he and Manda hadn't started a family. After the way she'd carried on throughout the divorce, the thought of how difficult she'd have made things if kids had been involved didn't bear thinking about.

'And how's things over at Skeller Rigg this morning?' asked Pete.

'Good. I rang them first thing, everyone was in very high spirits. Lawry's chuffed to bits; he got a car for Christmas.' Joss smiled as he remembered his young cousin's words. "Honest, Joss, it's dead mint. I had a quick drive round the farm, it's like shit off a stick! Wait 'til you see it." Joss hadn't let on that he hadn't just seen it, he'd had a hand in helping his aunt and uncle choose it for him. 'Aye, well, promise me there'll be no boy-racer stuff, Lawry. The idea was to give you a bit of independence, not for you to end up in hospital,' he'd said, a serious note threading through his words.

He was jolted from his thoughts when Ella's arm brushed past his as she reached for her phone on the coffee table, sending a ripple of longing through him; it felt indescribably good having her this close. He reached in his back pocket for his phone as, mobile in hand, she sat back and started scrolling through her messages. 'Ahh! I've got a text from Livvie and she's added a photo of her holding baby Holly.' She chuckled. 'You should see the size of Zander's smile. See.' She went to pass her phone to Joss.

But he was too transfixed, unable to tear his eyes away from the screen of his own phone. Amongst a slew of messages, there was a text from Rich, wishing him a merry Christmas in a passive-aggressive tone that surprised him. Frowning, Joss moved on to the next. It was a number he didn't recognise and he tapped on it hesitantly, his stomach twisting, his face morphing from shock to disbelief as he read, then re-read the contents. The chatter in the background faded to a mumbling noise, he was vaguely aware of Ella heading over to her parents, sharing something on her phone with them. He could sense concerned glances being cast his way, no doubt wondering what it was that had gripped his attention so. He picked up the odd word of the conversation going on around him, his mind running over what he'd just learnt. *Could it be true?* If it was, it changed everything. He found himself being slowly pulled back into the room.

'Ah, look how wide Zander's smile is; he looks proud as punch, and young Livvie looks absolutely radiant,' said Debbie, her hand touching her chest. 'See what I mean, Pete.' She passed the phone to her husband who took it, chuckling.

'He looks ready to burst, he's that happy. Good work, you two.' Pete glanced across at Joss, a frown replacing his smile. 'You okay, lad?'

'Aye, I was just about to ask that myself, your eyes have been glued to that screen ever since you picked it up,' said Bill. 'What's up?'

With his heart already racing, Joss said, 'Er, it's nothing... s'just a text.'

'Doesn't look like nothing. Who's it from?' asked Bill, turning to his son.

Joss blinked, confusion writ large across his face. He'd been in two minds about opening the message and now he wished he hadn't bothered. Now wasn't the right time to share what he'd learnt. But everyone could see he'd received a text that had knocked his equilibrium for six.

Ella made her way back over to the sofa, sitting down gently beside him. 'Are you okay?' she asked, resting her hand on his arm, the simple gesture touching his heart.

'I don't know how to say this...' He paused summoning the right words.

THIRTY-FIVE

Ella

Ella's heart was thumping hard in her chest and her mouth felt suddenly dry. Her first thought was that the text was from Manda, hinting that she and Joss get back together. He'd confided in her even after the divorce was finalised, his ex-wife would occasionally get in touch, usually late at night, after she'd downed a few glasses of wine, telling him how she'd consider giving him a second chance if he complied with her propositions. Though Joss had told Ella it was never going to happen, it still didn't stop doubts tumbling into her mind. Afterall, he'd also said despite it being right that he and Manda were no longer together, he regretted being divorced; how he'd never thought it would happen to him. 'We were never going to work. Being married to a farmer wasn't the life she wanted, unfortunately. I can see that now,' he'd said.

Please make it not be her. Please make it not be her. That would surely hasten his return to Skeller Rigg. Anxiety squirmed in her stomach. Why was she feeling this way? Joss was always going to head back before too long. But now she was potentially faced with that prospect, it affected her more keenly than she'd expected.

Sensing her mum watching her, she forced a smile, trawling her mind for something light-hearted to say but finding nothing.

Beside her, Joss paused. She watched his eyes run over the text once more before drawing in a deep breath. She could feel her pulse drumming in her ears, bracing herself to hear the worst

'I've had a text from Dawn.'

'What? Rich's wife Dawn?' asked Debbie.

Relief flooded through Ella as Joss nodded. *It's not Manda!*

'What's she texting you for?' asked Bill, his face incredulous. 'Have you heard owt from Rich?' He shuffled in his seat, peering over at his son's phone.

'She's kicked him out. He's still been seeing that woman from Arkleby; apparently she found some uncompromising photos on his phone.'

'What? After all he said about it being finished! The bloomin' idiot! Will he ever learn?' Bill spoke through pinched lips, his expression clouding over. Pete and Debbie looked on, wearing matching looks of concern.

'When did that happen?' asked Ella, feeling a rush of sympathy for their eight-year-old daughter Amy; Christmas was going to be ruined for the little girl now. What a shame they didn't wait until after today, but then again, kids picked up on things, no matter how hard you tried to disguise your feelings.

'I don't know.' Joss pushed his fingers through his hair, making his fringe stand up on end. 'But it's not the only thing she said.'

THIRTY-SIX

JOSS

'Are you okay?' Ella asked softly.

Joss lifted his gaze to her to see the happiness that had only moments earlier been shining in her eyes had been replaced by concern. He felt bad that he'd been responsible for that. But there was no going back now. 'The tractor... the accident... it wasn't me... wasn't my fault.' He spoke as if he couldn't quite believe the words that were coming out of his mouth.

'What do you mean?' Her eyes searched his as if he wasn't making sense, puzzlement drawing her thick brows together.

'It was Rich...' His voice came out shaky and he took a moment to regroup. Puffing out his cheeks, he clasped his hand to his forehead, his mind hurtling back to that day. He heard his father gasp beside him, felt his body clench rigid with tension. 'I've always felt absolutely certain I'd put the tractor in park mode; couldn't work out why I had such a vivid memory of doing it. Turns out Rich was the last one to use it, not me. When I was in the house, he'd gone out, climbed into the cab... set the engine away but then had a call from Dawn and jumped out, leaving the yard to get a better signal so he could speak to her. It was his fault the tractor ended up trashed and your quad bike wrecked, not mine. As Dawn puts it, he's lied by omission for all this time.' He felt Ella's fingers clutch tightly onto his arm, her other hand fiddling with the pendant around her neck.

'Oh, my God!' she said softly.

'Bloody hell,' said Pete, his mouth falling open.

'How does she know this?' asked Debbie, looking equally stunned.

'She says he confessed to her when he was drunk one night years ago; swore her to secrecy.' Joss glanced around at them in disbelief.

'And this is her way of getting her revenge.' Ella flopped back in the sofa. 'Wow.'

'So it would seem,' said Joss

'Well I never.' Pete rubbed his hand slowly over his chin.

'And he's let you take the blame for all these years.' Debbie tutted and shook her head gravely.

All eyes turned to Bill who had been sitting quietly. The colour in his cheeks had drained away and the pallid hue of less than a week ago had returned.

'You okay, Dad?' The change in him startled Joss.

'It was Rich?' Bill's hand started shaking, tea spilling from his mug, sloshing onto his jumper. Debbie jumped up and took the mug gently from him, setting it down on the coffee table. Bill turned to look at his son, tears shining in his eyes. 'What sort of person keeps a secret like that for all these years?' His voice was no more than a croak. 'I just can't get my head around it. Like Debbie says, he sat back and let you take the blame when all along it was him.' He shook his head in disbelief. 'I'm ashamed of him and I'm ashamed at myself for not believing you. I'm so sorry, lad.' A tear trickled its way slowly down his cheek.

Joss sat back, dragging his hand down his face, suppressing the surge of anger the revelation had triggered. Dawn had certainly picked her moment. But it was Christmas Day, they were enjoying the Welford's hospitality; showing how furious he was with his brother, venting his feelings, wasn't appropriate. It was only right he should save it for later. He coughed, clearing the lump of anxiety that had lodged in his throat. 'Rich is the one who should apologise, Dad. And anyway, I'd like to think you and me have moved on from that; it's not right to dwell on it today. It's already spoilt too many years between us and I really don't think we should let it ruin any more.' He took a moment to steady his breathing. 'It's Christmas Day. And in all honesty, yes, I can't deny I'm annoyed with Rich, 'cos I am, but our best friends have very kindly invited us to spend the day with them and we'd been having a great time 'til that text came through. I think we should try as best we can to put it out of our minds and get on with enjoying ourselves.'

'Wise words, lad. Joss is absolutely right, we have been having a great time, and you shouldn't let Rich, or Dawn for that matter, spoil it, Bill,' said Debbie. 'Park what you've just learnt for now, there's plenty of time to deal with it later. You've had a hell of a year, you deserve to relax and enjoy yourself. And besides, it's just about time for the Queen's Christmas message, which we *never* miss.' She straightened her paper crown then clapped her hands on her thighs before jumping up and retrieving the television remote, skilfully dissipating the serious mood of the room as the television blinked into life.

Joss watched the screen, his mind too busy unpicking the other thing Dawn had revealed in her text to take in what was being said. But after dropping the tractor bombshell, he didn't have the heart to tell his dad what she'd said about the cottage at Danskelfe. That it was unfit to rent out had been another one of Rich's lies. He wondered what else his brother had been keeping from them.

THIRTY-SEVEN

Ella

Joss stretched out his arm, resting it on the back of the sofa in the living room at Tinkel Bottom Farm, disturbing the warm, woody notes of his cologne. Ella inhaled deeply, savouring the scent that was unequivocally Joss. She allowed herself to follow the urge to lean into him; for once there were no voices telling her to keep her distance, and she nestled under his arm, savouring the warmth of his body. A wave of contentment washed over her as his arm slid from the sofa and wrapped around her. After the earlier revelations she figured he needed a bit of comfort. Needed to know she was there for him if he wanted to talk.

Her mind drifted back to the banter around the table as they'd tucked into the Christmas dinner. The decades of friendship between the two families had resurfaced and the atmosphere had been jovial. Ella had laughed until her cheeks ached over a story Bill and her dad had taken it in turns to tell of when they were young boys and the pranks they'd played on Mr Roberts, a particularly ill-tempered schoolteacher they'd had at the local primary school, slipping under his desk undetected and tying his shoelaces together being one of them. Understandably, Mr Roberts hadn't taken it well when he'd leapt to his feet with the intention of yelling in the face of another pupil, and ended up falling dramatically onto the floor, taking his chair with him.

But what had captured her thoughts was when they'd pulled the silver, sparkly Christmas crackers and read the little notes inside.

'Mine says, "Don't put off to tomorrow what you can do today",' Pete had said. 'Fat chance of that with Deb keeping me on my toes.'

'It's just as well I do.' Debbie had given him a playful nudge with her elbow, making him jump. They'd all fallen about laughing.

'What does yours say, Bill?' Pete had asked.

Bill had squinted before slipping his reading glasses on. 'Erm, let's have a look. It says, "Don't take everything at face value. Sometimes, things aren't what they seem". By 'eck, that's deep,' he'd said, chuckling.

'Bloomin' 'eck, Deb, where did you get these from? I thought Christmas crackers were supposed to have jokes in them. You know, be a bit light-hearted, not full of codswallop like that.' Pete had laughed.

'Hey, they weren't cheap, I'll have you know. I got them from that fancy new shop in Middleton-le-Moors.' Debbie had given her husband another nudge. 'Here, let's see what mine says.' She'd held her note between the finger and thumb of both hands, her arms extended as far as they'd go. 'Erm, let's see; the writing's a bit small, I could really do with my reading glasses.' She'd read slowly, squinting. "Guide those you love with a gentle hand". Oh, I do my best. Some more gently than others.' She'd giggled.

Pete rolled his eyes, grinning. 'Aye, sounds about right. And how about yours, you two young 'uns? What little pearls of wisdom have you got?' He glanced between Joss and Ella.

Ella had felt her cheeks glow as a blush spread up her face. 'Oh, mine's as daft as yours. Says something about not letting love slip through your fingers.' Waving her hand, she'd feigned a dismissive air, hoping no one would latch on to the words and make more of them than necessary. She'd been vaguely aware of her memory snagging on something Portia had said along those very lines.

'Ooh. I wonder what that could mean?' Debbie had cast a knowing look around the table. 'And what does yours say, Joss?'

Ella had sensed him squirm and hadn't been able to look him in the eye. 'Erm, it says the same as Ella's.'

'Well, fancy that! Seems the universe is talking to you two.' Pete had met Debbie's gaze, the pair of them hitching up their eyebrows.

'I said pretty much the same thing to m'laddo here last night.' Bill had sniffed.

Ella had stuffed her note firmly into the pocket of her jeans, telling herself it was nothing more than a silly coincidence that their notes issued identical advice. But it hadn't stopped her thoughts from going back to it.

With the Queen's Christmas broadcast finished, Ella felt herself getting a little too comfy in the warmth of the room. And, much as she was savouring her close proximity to Joss, her eyes were feeling heavy and she was in danger of falling asleep. Her snoring and drooling was definitely not something she wanted Joss to witness.

'Right, I'm going to grab a breath of fresh air before I nod off.' She eased herself up, Joss's arm falling away.

'Can't we tempt you to a game of charades?' asked Debbie. 'That's usually pretty lively especially when it's your dad's turn.'

'Not just now, Mum. I'm going to go and check on Clive and the goats.'

'Mind if I join you?' asked Joss. 'I was beginning to feel sleep beckoning too.'

With everything he'd learnt that afternoon, Ella very much doubted that. 'Not at all, I'd be glad of the company.' *Especially yours.*

Seeing Joss get to his feet, Sid jumped up, suddenly alert. His ears were cocked as he looked intently at his dad, waiting for the word.

'Come on, fella, you can come too.' Sid scampered to the door.

The fresh air hit Ella like a slap in the face, such was the contrast to indoors. 'Wowzers, it's nippy!' she said, pushing her hands into her woollen gloves.

'Woah, just a bit.' Joss laughed, his breath billowing out in a huge puff of condensation. 'And looking at that sky, I reckon there's more snow on the way.'

Ella followed his gaze to see a huddle of dark clouds, heavy with trouble, encroaching on the sky.

'So, how are you feeling?' she asked as they made their way over to the sandstone stable block, daylight already slipping away. Sid raced around in his usual upbeat way, his nose to the ground.

Joss blew out a noisy breath. 'Shocked, relieved, angry, confused. All of that.'

'It's understandable.' Ella slid the bolt to the top half of the Clive's stable door, opening it wide and releasing the familiar scent of hay and manure. Clive plodded over to them, his head peering out as she offered him a carrot, the palm of her hand flat as he took it. 'There you go, lad, get that down you.'

'Now then, Clive.' Joss patted the donkey's solid neck. 'By, he's a grand lad.'

Ella nodded. 'He is, I've had him a while now. He's lovely, aren't you, Clivey Boy?' she said, scratching between the donkey's ears.

With Clive and the goats checked, Ella was still reluctant to head back indoors, enjoying the time on her own with Joss too much. Instead, she wandered out of the yard, making her way over to the fence of the top field overlooking the dale. The white landscape was punctuated with little dots of glowing yellow lights from the farmsteads, while a thick line of snow-dappled trees edged the river that threaded its way across the land. Ella and Joss had spent many a happy hour down there as children, fishing for tadpoles and sticklebacks.

He stopped beside her and sighed. 'I didn't share everything Dawn said in her text. Didn't seem the right time.'

'Oh?' Puzzled, Ella looked up at him.

'The cottage at Danskelfe where Rich used to live belongs to the farm. Only thing is, Rich told Dad it wasn't fit to live in. That it was standing empty while he waited for it to be put right; said he was dealing with it apparently.'

'And he's not?'

'No. Dawn said there's nothing wrong with it. It's another of Rich's lies.' He gave a sardonic laugh. 'The funny thing is, I had a gut-feeling something wasn't right, and I was on my way over there to take a look yesterday when I saw you and Livvie. Anyway, according to Dawn, the cottage is being lived in, with the rent going straight into Rich's bank account.'

'What? You're joking? Surely that can't be right?' Stunned, Ella hastily searched her mind for any knowledge she had of who was living at the cottage, but nothing came up. 'Is Dawn certain about that?'

'She seemed pretty sure. Said he'd told her the rent from it would go some way to making up for the years of what he described as the "crappy wages" Dad had paid him. Apparently, he'd referred to it as "payback time", so it's unlikely she's making it up just to spite him.'

'Payback time?' Ella's top lip curled in disgust. Rich was abhorrent. She'd always had a bad feeling about him, always felt uneasy in his company, but hadn't been able to put her finger on why. This proved her gut instinct right. 'That's dreadful and, I should imagine, illegal. I can totally understand why you didn't want to tell your dad about it today; he'd have been even more upset.'

'Yeah and, much as I'm dreading it, I'm going to have to tackle Rich about it at some point. He's left me a right mess to sort out.' He turned to face her, pressing his lips together in a small smile. 'Seems I'm going to be staying here for a bit longer than I'd expected.'

The thought of Joss being around for longer sent a thrill

rushing through Ella, followed by a quick prickle of guilt, wishing it was in better circumstances.

She pushed her hands into the pockets of her jacket as a sudden gust of icy air rushed up the dale, blowing a wave of dry snow across the land. 'I know it's a daft thing to say, but I hope Rich hasn't put too much of a dampener on your day.' She looked up into those clear green-blue eyes of his, feeling a tug in her heart.

He held her gaze for a moment. 'How could he when I've spent the day with you?' he said softly, brushing a strand of hair off her face. Before she knew it, his lips were on hers, warm and soft, a groan escaping between them. Just as she felt herself melting into him, he jumped back, his eyes full of regret. 'Blast! I've done it again!' He hit his forehead with the heel of his hand. 'When will I ever stop behaving like a total idiot with you?'

'Joss, I—'

'One day I'll get the message you don't see me that way, I promise. I'm so sorry. Please just ignore that, pretend it didn't happen.'

She wished he'd stop talking and give her a chance to speak. Wished he'd listen to her before he steamed on, so eager to smooth things over when it wasn't necessary.

'Joss, it's—'

'Honestly, there's no need to... ughh! It's probably a good idea if I head back home; it's almost milking time anyway.' He grabbed the top of her arms, looking at her intently. 'I'm truly sorry. I don't want my stupidity to affect our friendship. Please, please forget I did that.'

'Friendship?' Ella said to herself as she watched him stride back to the farmhouse, Sid trotting behind him. She heaved a sigh. Stuff this business of "Don't let love slip through your fingers", it was a load of old codswallop! Maybe friends were all they were destined to be.

THIRTY-EIGHT

Joss

Joss lay in his bed that night, his mind in utter turmoil. With so many worries vying for his attention, he didn't know which to tackle first. An image of Rich conveniently pushed itself forward, his chin jutting arrogantly as it did when he was confronted. Joss had always known his brother was a little on the sly side, but his recent behaviour had reached a whole new level. To put it in its most basic form, Rich had been stealing from the farm. From their father. He was no better than a common thief. He should count himself lucky their dad hadn't contacted the police. As if that wasn't enough there were his lies about the cottage at Danskelfe and syphoning off the rent money to contend with. What a lowdown scumbag.

And then there was the other matter. The one that had caused the rift between Joss and their father that had lasted years. What sort of man could live with that knowledge? The sort of man who thought nothing of lying, cheating and stealing.

The last thoughts that floated through Joss's mind before he drifted off to sleep were of Ella. Of the look on her face as he was apologising for kissing her again. She'd looked stunned. He groaned, regret squeezing his insides. He'd only got himself to blame if she ended up avoiding him, but he hoped with all his heart she wouldn't. It was unfortunate he was going to have to stick around longer than he'd planned. Seeing the back of him was no doubt what she wished for most.

The following morning, after he and Bill had enjoyed a post-milking cooked breakfast, Joss headed up to his bedroom to call Rich. He wanted to get this over and done with as soon as possible. After only two rings Joss was surprised hear his brother's voice. 'Rich!'

'Ah, Joss, to what do I owe this pleasure?' There was an arrogance in Rich's voice that set Joss's hackles rising straight away.

'You mean you don't know?'

'I suppose I've got an idea.'

'I got a text from Dawn.'

Silence travelled down the line.

'Dawn?' Rich swallowed audibly. 'Why would she get in touch with you? I didn't even know she had your number. Are you sure it wasn't someone else with a wrong number?' There was an unmistakable note of panic in his voice.

Joss felt his anger rising. 'It was definitely Dawn, and the message was definitely intended for me. I have no idea how she got my number, not that it matters.'

'You'll know we've separated then?'

'I do.' Joss walked over to his window, casting his eyes down to Tinkel Bottom Farm. A small car was weaving its way along the track. Ella's car. He felt a swirl in his stomach and turned away. He couldn't deal with thoughts of her and what he'd done right now. 'I also know about the cottage at Danskelfe, how you've been having the money paid into your bank account.' He paused. 'And I know the truth about the tractor.'

He heard a sharp intake of breath from Rich. 'She's lying! She's a spiteful cow! Can you honestly see me letting you take the blame for that for all these years? We're brothers, for Chrissake. And the payment for the Danskelfe cottage is a mistake. I gave the tenants the wrong bank details. I've given them the right ones but they haven't changed them yet. It's their fault, I can't be blamed for that. Dawn's just said all that to get back at me for my relationship with Julie. She's been so bloody controlling, watching my every move. It got that I couldn't breathe for her and her flaming dad wanting to know where I was going, what I was doing and who I was doing it with. I felt like a naughty school boy; it was bloody stifling. And I can't believe you'd take her word over mine.'

'Actually, I can believe you'd stitch me up; I think that's exactly what you did.' Joss jumped in, hoping to bring Rich's defensive gabbling to an end. 'And I can also believe what you did about the cottage. The more I think about the things you've done over the years, the excuses you've made, almost encouraging me to keep away from here, the more I think Dawn deserves a medal for putting up with you.'

'What? You haven't got a clue what you're talking about.'

Joss flopped down on his bed. 'I think you'll find that I do. I've had a good think about things, seen what's been going on with the farm finances, listened to what Dawn had to say. You ought to be ashamed of yourself, Rich. You had everything and you've thrown it all away through your own greed and selfishness. Nothing was ever good enough, was it? Not here, not Dawn. You always wanted more.'

'You cheeky little bast—'

'You can say what you like about me. But you knew Dad was ill and you did nothing to help him. I don't even want to think about your reasons for that.' Though he was shaking with anger, Joss kept his voice eerily calm. 'But let me tell you this, I don't believe what you say about giving the tenant at the Danskelfe cottage the wrong details by accident. I believe it was deliberate. And unless you change those details immediately I won't hesitate in going to the police and telling them everything you've done.'

'You wouldn't! You can't! You've got no proof. Don't think I'm going to stand here and let you get away with blackmailing me like this!'

'From where I'm standing, you don't have much choice. And it's not blackmail, it's an ultimatum.' He could hear his brother's breathing coming in shallow bursts down the phone line as he contemplated his options.

'I've got nothing, Joss. Nothing.' His voice cracked. 'Dawn's kicked me out, I'm sleeping on a mate's sofa. Rod's taken my car and threatened to break my legs. My daughter doesn't want to know me. Neither does Julie. Great Christmas I'm having, eh?'

His brother's self-pity only served to stoke Joss's anger. 'And whose fault is that, Rich? It's not Dawn's, it's not Dad's, it's not Rod's, it's not Julie's, or whatever she's called, and it's not mine. That only leaves you.'

'That's a bit harsh, but I might've known you wouldn't understand. You've had it easy all these years over at Skeller Rigg, treated like a little prince. And now you've found yourself having to dig the farm out of the crap like I've had to do, you can't stomach it. I'll do what you ask, but don't come running to me when you want to go back to your precious Uncle Joe and expect me to take the reins again. I'm afraid you'll be disappointed.'

Joss was barely keeping the lid on his anger, and was struggling to stop himself from yelling down the phone line. He counted to ten in his head before he spoke, digging his nails into the palm of his free hand. 'Asking you to come back to the farm is the last thing I'd ever do.'

There was a moment before Rich replied. He sighed heavily down the phone. When he spoke again, his voice had taken on a softer tone. 'Look, Joss, it was hard for us all after Mum died; it felt like we were all in some kind of limbo; didn't help that Dad retreated into himself, leaving us two to muddle our way through. To be honest, I don't think I could've got through those first few years if you hadn't been going through it with me. I mean, I know we didn't always see eye-to-eye, but having somebody else in the same boat made it somehow easier to bear, if that makes sense.'

Joss felt his throat thicken. 'Yeah, I get that,' he said, doing his best to keep his voice steady.

'And then when you went to Uncle Joe's, you have no idea what the house felt like after you'd gone; it was empty, quiet, even more miserable. And as for Dad's moods... well, he just got more and more morose. And then I start hearing reports from Aunty Babs and Uncle Maff of how well you'd settled in at Skeller Rigg, of how you were like a son to Uncle Joe and Aunty Hannah, of how they thought the sun shone out of your backside. And all the while, I'm left at Camplin Farm, working my guts out without a word of thanks from that miserable old grouch who calls himself our father. As the years went by, it just started to eat away at me.'

Joss felt a mix of guilt and pity swirl in his stomach. 'But it wasn't my fault; I had no choice but to go to Skeller Rigg. It was your fault, Rich. If you'd come clean about the tractor, you'd have been the one to live with Uncle Joe and Aunty Hannah; you'd have been the one who was like a son to them. Not me.'

Rich snorted. 'Well, it's a waste of time going over old ground. I stand by what I said, I won't be around when you're sick of life with Dad and you want to head back to your precious sanctuary at Skeller Rigg – and if reports are right, you even got your swanky barn conversion for next to nowt.' It hadn't taken long for Rich's temper to rear its head again.

Joss bit down on his anger. 'For your information, that's not true, it's a tied cottage and belongs to the farm. I pay them rent.'

'Yeah, right,' Rich said with an irritating snigger.

Now that the conversation had taken another unpleasant turn, Joss was keen to end it; it would only serve to add to the hostility between the pair of them if they continued. 'Just make sure those bank details are sorted out. Speak later,' he said, ending the call.

He threw his phone on the bed and dragged his hands down his face, adrenalin surging through his veins. What a week it had been. When he'd set off from Skeller Rigg, he hadn't expected any of this. He'd known it wasn't going to be easy, but he'd envisaged the problems would be relating to his father and him not getting along, not Rich and his deceit. It would seem he'd opened a can of worms, and by all accounts, he'd done it just in time to stop the farm from going under.

A light tap at his door, followed by his father's voice, made his heart leap once more. 'Joss, lad, are you okay in there?'

'Yeah, I'm fine, Dad.'

Bill opened the door a crack, and peered round. 'You sure? Only, I thought I heard voices.'

'Honest, I'm all right. I was just catching up with a mate from Helderthorpe. He's having a house party and wondered if I was going to be back in time for it.' He smiled up at his father, hoping to alleviate his concerns. It wasn't a complete fib; his friend, Adam, had sent him a text asking if he was free the following night and inviting him to a party.

Bill's face fell. 'Oh, and you can't get back in time? That's my fault, I'm sorry, lad.'

'Hey, no worries. I don't fancy it anyway; I'd rather be here.'

Bill's smile lit up his face. 'Oh, right. You sure about that?'

He returned his dad's smile. 'Course I'm sure,' he said, meaning it.

THIRTY-NINE

Ella

'What have them spuds ever done to you?' asked Debbie, her hands on her hips. She was in the kitchen of Tinkel Bottom Farm, watching Ella whose shoulders were hunched and her teeth gritted as she vigorously mashed a bowl of potatoes, ready to mix it up with the other ingredients for bubble and squeak.

'Uhh?' Ella looked up, a frown creasing her brow.

'Well, the way you're going at it, seems you're bashing the living daylights out of the poor little blighters. I'm scared to let you loose on this turnip for fear of what you'll do to it.'

Ella let her shoulders drop. 'Sorry, Mum, I was miles away.' She took the proffered bowl of turnip, threw it in with the potatoes and resumed her mashing, though with less vigour this time.

'Aye, I could tell. Dare I ask who was in your mind as you were giving those potatoes what fettle?'

Ella shrugged. 'No one in particular. Just... things.'

'Ah, *things*.' Debbie nodded. 'And would I be right if I said a certain young man by the name of Joss Campion featured in those *things*?'

Ella nodded, feeling her eyes swim with tears. 'Yeah,' she said, her bottom lip wobbling.

'Oh, lovey, come here.' Her mum rushed across the room, taking the masher from Ella's hands and wrapping her arms around her. 'For what it's worth, that lad thinks the world of you, you can see it in his eyes, the way he looks at you.' She rubbed soothing swirls across Ella's back. 'And you can tell me to keep my beak out, but I reckon you feel the same about him too.'

It was pointless denying it; her mum could read her like a book. Ella nodded into her mum's neck, tears pouring down her cheeks. 'Yeah. Yeah, I do.'

Debbie stood back, resting her hands on her daughter's shoulders, smiling. 'Don't you think it was funny the way you both got the same note in your crackers telling you not to let love slip through your fingers? I think that was more than any old coincidence, don't you?' Ella gave a watery smile back. 'In all seriousness, chick, I think you and Joss need a proper heart-to-heart. You need to set your cards on the table and see where you go from there. I reckon you'll find what he learnt yesterday has changed a few things.'

Ella was wiping her tears when her dad bowled through the door. 'What's up, Ells?' His smile fell as he kicked off his wellies.

'It's nothing, I'm fine.' She mustered up a smile as if to prove it.

'I don't believe that for a minute. Nowt much makes you cry; you're as tough as old boots as a rule, lass. Is it owt to do with Joss?'

From the corner of her eye Ella saw her mum give a brief nod.

'Ah. Well, if you want my two-penn'orth, you two are meant to be together.' He headed over to the sink to wash his hands, looking at her over his shoulder as he spoke. 'That lad is totally smitten and if you feel the same you'd be daft to let him go.'

'See, that's exactly what I said, isn't it?' Debbie said to her, her eyes soft with affection as she rubbed Ella's arm.

'You know what? You're absolutely right.' Ella swiped her tears away with her fingers and rushed over to where her coat was hanging on the peg. She shrugged it on, pulled her woolly hat down over her ears and pushed her feet into her wellies. 'Thanks for your advice. Won't be long,' she said, her parents watching her as she headed out of the door.

Outside, she could hear a dull thud, thud, thud sound echoing along the dale. It appeared to be coming from the direction of Camplin Farm. She hurried across the yard, crunching over the fresh snow that had fallen overnight, the cold air catching at the back of her throat. Once round the back of the house, she could see a figure in the top field at Camplin Farm. Joss! Before she could stop herself, she'd jumped over the fence and was heading towards him. Three fields separated them; two relatively flat ones belonging to Tinkel Bottom and one steep one belonging to Camplin Farm. She used to run across them when she was younger, never giving the distance a second thought. So why should she now? she mused as she ploughed on.

Thanks to the drifting, the snow was deep in parts, coming almost to the tops of her wellies, making progress slow. But she was undeterred and found herself quite enjoying the exercise, especially after the last couple of lazy days, doing nothing much more than sitting and eating.

From afar, the fields looked as smooth as the surface of a wedding cake, but walking across them, Ella could see they were peppered with a variety of animal tracks. She spotted deer, rabbit, badger and fox amongst them, as well as the distinctive claw marks left by pheasants.

Soon, the cold that gripped her body was replaced by a growing warmth, and by the time she'd reached the field Joss was working in, she was sweltering, beads of sweat shimmering on her brow. She knew she looked about as far removed from glamorous as was physically possible, but she didn't care. She just had to see Joss. Had to tell him how she felt. And she knew he wouldn't bat an eyelid at her scarecrow appearance.

She was drawing closer, her arms swinging as she went, her heart hammering as much from exertion as it was from anticipation. Joss looked up, the hammer falling to his side as he watched her approach.

She stopped before him, his face a picture of confusion. 'Ella, is everything okay?' His gaze went to her tracks across the field. 'Have you walked all the way?'

She nodded, her chest heaving. 'Yeah.' A sliver of doubt crept in. What must she look like? What if he told her he didn't feel the same? *If that was the case, why did he kiss you? Duh!*

He frowned. 'Right.'

'I just wanted to say...' Her mind went suddenly blank and before she knew it, she was standing on her tiptoes, reaching up, taking his face in her hands, and kissing him hard.

His eyes widened before he took her in his arms, returning her kiss with eighteen years' worth of pent-up passion.

The feel of his lips on hers unleashed a flurry of butterflies in her stomach as she allowed herself to fall into the kiss. She never wanted this moment to end.

'Wow! I wasn't expecting that,' he said, laughing, his eyes shining with happiness when they finally pulled apart.

Ella was gasping, her mouth throbbing from the impact of their kiss. 'I just want you to know, for what it's worth, that I love you, Joss Campion.' She gasped some more. 'I had to tell you before... well, I don't know if it makes a difference to anything, but I just had to let you know. I love you.' God, it felt good to say that.

Joss was beaming down at her; he looked fit to burst. 'And I love you, Ella Welford! I always have.' He scooped her up and spun her round, sending her hat flying. 'Woohoo!' He set her down again, the pair of them laughing hard. 'Someone pinch me, I must be dreaming! I can't tell you how much I've wanted to hear you say that. I honestly thought I'd blown it yesterday; thought I'd scared you off.'

'Well, if you'd given me a chance to speak, you would've found out then, but you didn't come up for air,' she said giggling.

'He put his hands on his hips and roared with laughter. 'Fair point. But now, I feel so happy, I want the world to know.' He cupped his hands around his mouth and shouted across the dale, 'I'm in love with Ella Welford!'

Ella's cheeks glowed with happiness as she fell into a fit of the giggles. 'And I'm in love with Joss Campion!'

'About bloomin' time!' Her dad's voice wafted up from Tinkel Bottom.

It was quickly followed by a loud, 'Woohoo!' from her mum.

Before Ella knew what was happening, Joss had scooped her up in his arms and was kissing her hard again. She reached her arms up around his neck, feeling his firm body pressed against hers, his warmth seeping into her.

They were both so engulfed by their moment, neither of them heard Bill appear around the corner, asking what all the shouting was about. Nor did they notice Sid race up to them before he started rolling excitedly in the snow, his legs kicking everywhere, making Bill chuckle. 'Come on, lad, let's leave 'em to it,' he said, and Sid scampered behind him back to the house.

FORTY

Joss

Joss gazed down at Ella, his eyes dark with passion. He bent and kissed her once more, oblivious to the cruel wind nipping at his face. The feel of her soft, plump lips against his sent his emotions into overdrive. What he'd like more than anything right now was to take her straight to bed. But with his dad sitting in the living room, it might look a bit obvious if he sloped off upstairs with her. There was also the possibility she might not be ready to do that just yet.

Reluctantly, he pulled his lips from hers and smiled. His eyes drank in her fresh face, devoid of even a scrap of make-up. 'I don't think I've ever told you how beautiful you are.'

'Don't be daft,' she said, shyly, her face flushing. 'I bet I look a right fright. I just set off here on the spur of the moment.'

'I'm not being daft. I've always thought that. When other lasses were clarting their faces up with make-up, I was always glad that you didn't.'

'Yep, that's me, ever the tomboy,' she said with a giggle.

'That's not what I meant; you didn't need it; you're a natural beauty.' Seeing she was embarrassed by his words, he kissed her again, which only served to set his hormones raging once more.

'Well, since my mum and dad know how we feel about each other, do you think we should go and tell your dad?'

'You're probably right, though I reckon, knowing how fast word travels round here, he probably already knows.' He threw his arm around her and they crunched their way through the snow to the old farmhouse, Joss beaming broadly, unable to take his eyes off her.

Inside, Bill greeted them with a wide smile as he filled the teapot. Three mugs were set beside it. 'By, that was good timing.'

Sid shot over to them, the squeaky toy he got for Christmas – now minus its squeak – clenched between his teeth, his whole body wiggling in his joy at seeing them.

'Hi, Bill. Hiya, lad.' Ella giggled and bent to fuss Sid whose coat was still wet from his earlier escapades.

'Now then, Dad. From the way you're smiling I'm guessing you've already heard,' said Joss, pulling off his woolly hat and hanging up his jacket. Ella followed suit.

Bill chuckled. 'I heard voices shouting and came out to make sure you were okay. I saw Ella had paid us a visit and I didn't want to disturb you so I came back in.'

'Ah.' Joss grinned, catching Ella's eye. She beamed back at him.

'Anyroad, I reckon the two of you'll have a bit of talking to do, so I'm going to make myself scarce while I read up on these dairy parlours.' He waved a farming magazine at them.

'Dairy parlours, eh?' Joss said when Bill had left the room. 'Well, that's a turn up.' During a recent conversation, his dad had asked about the more up to date herringbone milking system that had recently been installed at Skeller Rigg. Joss knew he needed to tread carefully. 'The herringbone system here's perfectly adequate, just a bit tired, like the one that was in over at Skeller Rigg. But we were surprised at how much more efficient the newer one was and how much time it saved us each day,' he'd said.

His dad had listened quietly, his face impassive, but he'd obviously been mulling over what Joss had said.

'Mm,' said Ella. 'He must be feeling much better if he's bothering with the farm again.'

'Well, that's the thing,' said Joss, pulling out a chair and sitting opposite Ella. 'We had a big chat this morning. Talked about everything: Mum, Rich, his diabetes diagnosis – that shocked me more than anything; up to now he's done everything he can to avoid discussing it! We talked about the farm and its future too.'

'Sounds deep.'

'It was.' Joss nodded, lowering his voice. 'I couldn't bring myself to mention anything about the cottage at Danskelfe just yet. I'm hoping Rich gets the bank situation sorted quickly or I'll have to go and speak to the tenant direct, which isn't ideal. Reminds me, I don't know if there's a tenancy agreement in place. If there is, I don't know if Rich has named himself as landlord or the trust the farm's in.' He smoothed his fingers over his forehead. 'Ughh! What a headache! Anyway,' his expression suddenly brightened as a smile swept over his face, 'let's forget about that for now, we should be celebrating!' He reached across the table for her hand, squeezing it. 'This is taking a bit of sinking in, you and me. I think I'm still in shock.'

The smile Ella returned made his heart dance. 'Me too. The only thing is...' her face turned serious, the happiness in her eyes dimming, '...what happens when you go back to Skeller Rigg? I mean, what do we do? It's kind of what made me hold back from telling you how I felt.'

'Oh, right.'

She averted her eyes, her cheeks flushing. 'Since you got back I'd kind of been aware that my feelings for you had grown. If I'm totally honest, I think the right word is "reappeared".'

'Reappeared? Sorry, I sound like an echo.' He laughed, sensing the atmosphere around them had changed.

A smile flickered over her mouth. 'When you kissed me on Arncliffe Crag all those years ago when we were sixteen, it sent me into a real tailspin.' She switched her gaze to him.

'I'd noticed.'

'I don't think you realised the feelings it had triggered. Jeez! I honestly didn't know what to do with them. The thing is, I'd felt our friendship changing. What I'm trying to say but making a hash of it is, I'd gradually become aware that I'd stopped thinking of you as a friend. I was attracted to you... actually, I really fancied you, and that scared me. All I could think about was if things went wrong, then I'd end up losing my best mate, which I did anyway.' She shrugged.

'Wow! I had no idea. I thought I'd repulsed you; I hated myself for it.' He pushed his fingers into his hair and scratched his head vigorously.

'Quite the opposite.' She gave him a rueful smile. 'But before I could get my head around what had happened, you'd gone and that was the end of it.'

He sat quiet for a moment, absorbing her words. 'Until now.' He flashed her a beaming smile.

'Until now.' She grinned back at him. 'Which brings us right back to where we started this conversation. What happens when you go back to Skeller Rigg?'

He could see concern hovering at the back of her eyes. 'Well, that's something we really need to discuss. How about we—' He was cut off by the sound of his mobile phone ringing. 'Blast! Who's that?' He pulled his phone from his jeans pocket, his face clouding over when he saw Rich's number illuminating the screen. He groaned. 'It's Rich. I should speak to him.'

Ella held up her palms, splaying her fingers. 'Of course, yes, it's important you do. I'll head off.' She got to her feet and headed over to where her coat was hanging.

'Let me give you a lift. I can call him straight back.'

'No, you speak to Rich. You can pop down to my cottage tonight if you're free. Any time after seven's good for me. Say goodbye to your dad from me.'

Before he had time to argue, she was out the door.

FORTY-ONE

Ella

After treating herself to a languorous soak in the bath, the soothing scent of the bath salts lingering in the steam, Ella set about making the cottage look cosy and welcoming. With the curtains closed against the frosty evening, she flicked on the table lights and made sure there were plenty of logs stacked on the hearth to keep the wood-burner going for the night ahead. Adding to the effect created by the festive fairy lights, she dotted scented candles in mercuried glass votives around the rooms. Soon, the air was infused with the exotic aroma of frankincense.

The light knock at the door, heralding Joss's arrival, sent Ella's heart racing. After a final glance in the mirror to make sure her hair wasn't looking too wild – she'd set it free from her usual ponytail – she hurried to the door, opening it wide, light spilling onto the path, catching the snow that lingered in the corners. Her stomach flipped when she saw him there, his broad frame filling the doorway, a heart-melting smile on his face.

'Hi,' he said.

'Hi.' She beamed at him. 'Come in.'

He stomped the snow off his boots and stepped inside. 'You

look beautiful.' Before she could answer, he cupped her face in his hands and kissed her. She wrapped her arms around his neck, pulling him close, desire pulsing through her. She closed her eyes, losing herself in the moment.

'Ey up, what's going on there then?'

Ella would know that voice anywhere: Jimby Fairfax.

A chorus of whistles and cheers followed, accompanied by a round of applause.

'What the...?' said Joss as they pulled away from one another, turning to see Jimby, Vi, Ollie, Kitty, Molly and Camm, standing on the trod opposite, wrapped up well in their winter gear, wearing huge smiles.

'Finally got there, did you, Campion?' said Jimby, chuckling. 'I reckon you've beaten Ollie's record, and it took him ages to get it together with our Kitts.'

Ollie rolled his eyes, smiling.

'Hey, I'm a happy man now.' Joss squeezed Ella closer to him.

'You look great together,' said Vi.

'At least you finally got there.' Molly gave Ella a knowing wink.

'Stop embarrassing them, you lot,' said Kitty, trying to bustle them away.

'Have a great night.' Jimby waggled his eyebrows at them. 'We're just heading to the pub to start badgering Moll and Camm here about setting a date and making it official.'

'You can clear right off if that's what you're thinking.' Molly gave him a forceful nudge.

Camm shook his head, laughing. 'Hey, it's not for the want of trying, but she won't have me.'

'It's not that I won't have you, I just think if it ain't broke, don't fix it.'

'Ah, the voice of true romance,' said Vi, her words sending a ripple of laughter running around them.

'Anyway, we'll leave you to it. Have a great night,' said Ollie.

'We will.' Ella giggled.

'You too,' said Joss, closing the door with his foot. 'Now, where were we?' He bent and kissed Ella once more, making her heart sing with happiness.

In the warmth of the living room, the pair sat side-by-side on the sofa, glasses of white wine in hand. Music played softly in the background and flames danced in the wood-burner, Tabby-Cat stretched out in front of it, purring. Ella, her legs curled on the sofa beside her, rested her head on Joss's shoulder while he wound a lock of her hair around his finger, smoothing it with his thumb. She couldn't ever remember feeling this content.

There was just one thing tainting her happiness, gnawing away at the back of her mind, eager to be heard. How long did they have together before Joss headed back to Skeller Rigg Farm? Admitting her feelings to him had been a huge leap of faith, and now they were out there, how was she going to feel when it was time for him to leave? Feeling the squirm of discomfort in her stomach, she scrunched up her eyes tightly, pushing the niggle away; she didn't want think about that now; she just wanted to enjoy tonight.

'So,' he said, interrupting her thoughts. 'The reason I'm here tonight is to talk about where we go from here, punctuated by lots of kisses, of course.' Placing his finger under her chin, he tipped her face up to his and kissed her deeply, sending her heart all of a flutter, her worries scurrying away.

'Mmm, that was nice.'

'Well, I'm very pleased to say they're on tap, right here.' He puckered his lips and pointed his finger at them.

'On tap?'

'Yep, whenever you fancy a kiss, just help yourself. Totally free of charge.'

'You're a nutter.' She giggled and prodded him gently in the stomach. 'Anyway, you're right, we do need to talk about what happens next.' She sat up straight and turned to face him. Maybe it was time to bite the bullet after all. 'It's the thing that's bothered me the most about us getting together.'

'Well, as I mentioned earlier, Dad and me had a good chat, a really good chat. We got everything out there about how we were feeling. It was no mean feat, I can tell you, he's been tight as a clam since I got back, but anyway, he was different this morning; seemed keen to get stuff off his chest.'

'Right.' Ella felt a frisson of nerves rush over her as she anticipated what Joss had to say. It would be too cruel if he was only here for a short time when they'd finally got to this point and put their feelings out there. And much as she felt deep inside her they were meant to be together, she really couldn't see a long-distance romance amounting to anything; it would just be a waiting game to see who got fed up first, and that was just too horrible to contemplate. *If you want something really badly, you make it work,* said a little voice, but she wasn't convinced.

Ella sat quietly, listening as Joss explained how Bill had been feeling disillusioned with farming for some time, which was why he'd let Rich take the reins, something he'd seemed happy to do at the time. What his father hadn't realised was that diabetes had been creeping up on him, and that, along with the arthritis which had been slowly getting more painful, had been making it difficult for him to continue working at his usual capacity. He'd been struggling on, feeling lethargic and generally run down.

'Some days it felt like I was trudging around in a pair of lead boots, like I wasn't firing on all cylinders,' Bill had said to him.

Rich leaving had been the catalyst to big changes at the farm. It had dumped the pressure of everything squarely back on Bill's shoulders, not to mention the added stress it had caused when the state of the farm's accounts came to light.

'Which is why I'm definitely not going to mention the Danskelfe cottage to him just yet,' Joss said to Ella.

'I think that's wise.' She nodded.

Joss went on to say how he'd had several lengthy talks with his Uncle Joe and Aunty Hannah. He'd explained all that had been going on at Camplin Farm and, in turn, they'd told him that Lawry had come up trumps, helping on the farm and taking up Joss's jobs.

Joss had also told them of his feelings for Ella which had tugged at their heartstrings; his aunt and uncle were well aware of the shared history between them.

Ella's heart started racing as Joss paused. This was it, this was the moment she was going to find out if they had a future together. She held her breath, bracing herself.

'So, between the four of us, we've come to the decision that I should move back here with a view to it being permanent. I'm going to take over the running of Camplin Farm, which means Dad can take more of a backseat, which he's keen to do, and Lawry's going to take over my role at Skeller Rigg, keeping his one day a week at agricultural college.'

'You're going to stay?' Elation flooded Ella's body. Wild horses couldn't stop the smile that was spreading across her face.

'I'll have you know, I'm taking the advice of the note in the Christmas cracker very seriously; I'm not letting love slip through my fingers.'

Ella sat a moment, soaking up what he'd just told her, making sure she'd understood him properly.

'So how do you feel about it? Think you can put up with having me around as a permanent fixture in Lytell Stangdale again?' He was watching her closely.

Ella swung herself round, straddling his lap. She placed her finger on her chin, casting her eyes upwards, as if giving his question deep consideration. 'Hmm, let me think about it a moment. Erm, yes, I dare say I might be able to.' She giggled as he put his hands on her hips and pulled her towards him.

'Do you really think I'd risk losing you again?' he asked, his eyes suddenly serious. 'I'm going to do everything I can to make this work, Ella. Everything.'

'Me too.' Her expression matched his.

'I never thought this day would come,' he said huskily, kissing her once more.

When they finally came up for air, Ella said, 'I think this calls for a celebration. I've got some fizz in the fridge, let me go and get it.' She eased herself off his lap.

'Much as I hate to be a party pooper, I'm driving and I've already had my quota, I don't want to risk anymore. But I'm quite happy to celebrate with a lemonade or something similar if you've got one. Maybe dress it up for the occasion with a slice of lemon,' he said with a chuckle.

Ella paused, her thoughts guiding her in one direction. 'You don't have to drive.' Her heart took off as the words left her mouth.

'I don't have to drive?' he asked, looking puzzled.

'Well, I'm not suggesting you should walk back if that's what you're thinking.' She laughed. 'You could leave here early in the morning and get back to the farm in plenty of time for milking. It's only a few minutes away.' She watched his expression change.

'Ella Welford, I do believe you're asking me to stay the night,' he said, grinning.

'I am.' She couldn't help but giggle.

He got to his feet, towering over her. 'Well, in that case, I think the fizz would benefit from chilling a little longer. Any suggestions of how we could fill that time?' He ran his finger down her cheek.

'Now you come to mention it, I think I have.' She stood on her tiptoes and whispered in his ear, his eyebrows shooting up to his hairline.

When she'd finished, he gave a low whistle. 'Well, it's a long time since I've heard it put in such vivid terms, but I'm always up for a challenge. I just hope I don't disappoint.'

'If those kisses are anything to go by, you won't.' She took his hand, threading her fingers through his.

'Promise you'll be gentle with me.' He gave her a lopsided smile as they headed upstairs.

FORTY-TWO

SIX MONTHS LATER

Joss

Bouncing over the field on the quad bike, the sun blazing down on his back, Joss could see Ella feeding the rescue hens they'd taken delivery of the previous week. It was mid-morning, the second week in June, and summer had arrived in a blast of golden sunshine. Joss had just finished moving the sheep to another field, assisted by Sid who'd been tearing about, helping gather them up just as he'd done at Skeller Rigg Farm. Though he had a playful temperament, Sid had proved highly trainable and an asset on the farm.

Reaching Ella, Joss stilled the bike and climbed off. The sound of the hens' clucking filled the air. A woodpecker drumming for insects joined the cacophony as Ella made her way over to him.

'Hi,' she said, squinting and shielding her eyes with her hand. 'Time for a cuppa?'

'You bet.' He bent to her, placing his hand at the back of her head and kissing her full on the mouth. She looked good, he thought, in her yellow t-shirt trimmed with daisies, and denim shorts, showing off her tanned legs. 'Girls doing okay?' He glanced over to where the hens were scratting about in the grass.

Ella beamed. 'They've settled in really well. Beryl over there is definitely the matriarch. She's a right old bossy boots.'

Joss laughed. 'Ah, she's the one who gave Sid an angry flap of her wing when he got too close, isn't she?' He turned to Sid who'd sought shade under a gnarled apple tree, eyeing Beryl warily, his tongue lolling from the side of his mouth as he panted. 'Keeping well away now, aren't you, fella? Very wise,' he said as he and Ella ambled over to the farmhouse, his arm flung over her shoulder.

Cup of tea in hand, Joss and Ella wandered back outside, stopping at the fence of the field that overlooked Tinkel Bottom Farm, taking in a wide sweep of Great Stangdale that was bathed in golden sunlight. The landscape was a mix of verdant shades of green, the fields teeming with animals – farmstock and wildlife alike. A huge heron took off from the pond below, its grey silhouette against the blue sky almost pterodactyl-like. A flimsy breeze skimmed over their sun-warmed skin, carrying with it the bleating of sheep, the higher pitched cries of the lambs still easy to distinguish from the deeper tones of their mothers.

Joss sighed contentedly, slipping his arm around Ella's waist and kissing the top of her head, inhaling her warm, flowery scent. She leaned into him, pushing her hand into the back pocket of his jeans. Sid flopped down beside them, still panting, his whiskers dripping from lapping at his water bowl.

Joss still found it hard to believe how things had changed from six months ago, when he'd reluctantly arrived at the village with the intention of hanging around for as short a time as possible, avoiding the locals at all costs. He hadn't banked on one thing: Ella Welford and his feelings for her. And now here he was, living in his childhood home with his childhood best friend who just so happened to be his first love. How had that happened? There were still moments when he woke in the night, disorientated, blinking into the dark, thinking it was all a dream. And then he'd hear Ella's gentle breathing, feel the reassuring warmth of her body as she lay in his arms.

As he glanced around the dale, absorbing the view that had

changed so very little from when he was a boy, he thought how funny it was that time moved on, events moulding them, influencing their decisions, yet here it seemed to stand still. He found it unexpectedly comforting.

'I got a text from Portia earlier,' Ella said, pulling him back to the moment.

'Right.' Joss nodded. 'How's she doing?'

'Good. Seems things are going really well with her and Saffy; they're off on holiday together in a couple of weeks. Sorrento.'

'I'm glad to hear things have worked out for her.' Joss was relieved Portia hadn't reacted badly when Ella had told her they were an item. The last thing he'd wanted was to cause a rift in their friendship. He was sure Saffy's reappearance on the scene helped smooth things over.

'And your dad rang. Said he'd tried your mobile but it just went to voicemail. Anyway, he didn't want to leave a message, but he wants you to know he's enjoying himself at your Uncle Joe's and Aunty Hannah's.'

Joss gave an easy smile, glad that bridges had been built between the two brothers. 'That's great news; I thought he would; Uncle Joe and Aunty Hannah are very welcoming.' Over the last six months, he'd watched his dad recover and regain his strength, the sunken look to his eyes gradually disappearing. There was still a way to go with their relationship – Bill's reluctance to talk wasn't an easy habit for him to break, but Joss could see he'd been trying, doing his best to keep a lid on his temper. Letting his anger take over rather than addressing unpalatable subjects had been his default mode for over twenty years and Joss appreciated changing such an ingrained habit wouldn't be easy for his dad. But it didn't stop Joss from feeling frustrated from time-to-time, having to leave the room before he said something he'd regret and set them back.

During these chats, it had been a huge relief to learn that the farm's financial situation wasn't as bad as Joss had initially feared. Bill, not fully trusting Rich, had kept a separate account where the bulk of the farm's funds were invested, which gave them some much-needed breathing space. Joss had made a mental note to make an appointment with the manager of the suppliers who'd become reluctant to deliver to them owing to Rich's non-payment of their invoices. It had taken some persuasion on his part, but eventually the suppliers had agreed to set up new accounts. Joss made sure their bills were settled quickly, and, hopefully, their good faith restored. It was one less thing to worry about.

Though things were moving fast for Joss and Ella, their burgeoning relationship felt intrinsically right to both of them. From day one, she spent the bulk of her free time at Camplin Farm, with more and more of her clothes hanging next to Joss's in his wardrobe. It was during a chat over the dinner table with Bill that the suggestion that Ella should move in was first aired. Bill had confessed he felt it was time for him to move out of the farmhouse, said he had a yearning to settle in a smaller cottage, preferably in the village.

'I hope me spending so much time up here hasn't made you feel that way, Bill.' Ella had looked between father and son, alarmed.

'Not at all, lass,' Bill had said, shaking his head. 'Here hasn't felt properly like home for me since I lost Sue. I like the idea of living somewhere small and just coming here to work with Joss. It'll be like having a proper fresh start. And besides, this is a family home. You and our Joss might as well start making it your own, decorating it how you want it before you make a start on having a family.'

'Oh, right.' Ella had blushed furiously; she and Joss hadn't had *that* discussion just yet.

'Steady on there, Dad, that's a way off,' Joss had said, laughing, sensing Ella's embarrassment. 'There's no rush for you to leave.' Though he'd made light of it, Joss had regularly found himself daydreaming about his future with Ella, of their own children running around the fields just as they'd done when they were younger.

'Aye, well, maybe so, but it's your time here now, lad. Camplin

Farm's ready for some fresh blood at its helm with new ideas to safeguard its future.' His voice had wavered.

Joss had felt his throat constrict and swallowed down the lump of emotion. 'But where will you go? It doesn't seem right to turf the tenant out of the Danskelfe cottage.' Joss had finally confessed to his dad about the situation there, putting it as gently as he could, relieved when the news had been taken better than he'd expected.

'Ah, well, I've been giving that some thought too. I was going to ask Ollie and Kitty about renting Rose Cottage when Ella moves out.' He'd beamed at them, pleased with his idea.

'You clearly have been giving this some thought, Dad.'

'Just a bit, son.' Bill had followed up with a wink.

And so, on a sunny Saturday in May, in a bubble of excitement, Ella swapped homes with Bill. Though Bill had shed a secret tear at leaving the farmhouse that had been his home for the bulk of his life, he'd admitted to the young couple he was relieved to be starting afresh.

They hadn't seen hide nor hair of Rich since Christmas. And though Joss had doubted his brother would fix the rent situation with the tenant at the Danskelfe cottage, he was relieved when the rent payments had landed in the farm's accounts. It saved him having to tackle his brother about it again, which was something he'd been dreading. And much as he was still furious with Rich he didn't want to lose contact with him the way he'd done with his father. Those times were over as far as Joss was concerned. But despite having texted Rich several times, each message had remained unanswered. 'Well, if that's the way he wants it, that's fine with me,' he'd said to Ella when they'd been discussing it, curled up on the sofa one evening. 'I'll be here, ready to talk whenever he decides to get in touch. If he ever does.'

She'd patted his chest reassuringly. 'I'm sure it'll all work out. Just give him some time. It'll still be a bit raw for him; he'll be feeling pretty embarrassed, I should imagine.'

'Hmm.' Joss hadn't been so sure.

FORTY-THREE

Ella

Moving in with Joss at Camplin Farm had been one of the easiest decisions Ella had ever made. Maybe they hadn't been together long, but something deep inside her told her unequivocally he was "The One". That this was it; they'd be together forever. And he'd made no secret he felt the same. Everything seemed to slot together so seamlessly, as if it was meant to be. So much so, she still had to pinch herself.

Handing her notice in at school hadn't been easy, Mrs Prudom hadn't been able to hide her disappointment. 'I'll be very sorry to lose you, Ella, I had high hopes for you here, you're a real asset to the school, and you'll be greatly missed,' she'd said, tears glistening in her eyes. 'I don't suppose there's a chance you'd consider staying on 'til the end of the academic year, would you? That way it'd give us time to find a suitable replacement.'

Ella had agreed to the request without question; it had always been her plan to give plenty of notice, timing it so that her new venture would be ready to go by the time she'd finished at the school.

And, much as she had, for a fleeting moment, wondered if she was doing the right thing, she knew that setting up the boarding kennels was what she really wanted to do. She'd thought long and hard about it, the only problem being where to site it at her parents' farm. Nowhere seemed to be quite right, access being the main issue, but she was determined to get things up-and-running before the summer holidays started. Since word of her plans had got out, she'd been inundated with locals from Lytell Stangdale and the surrounding villages showing an interest and keen to book their pets in just as soon as the business was ready. Her excitement was building; she was raring to go.

'You could always set it up at Camplin Farm. I reckon yon side of the old stable block would be ideal,' Joss had said one night. They'd been tucked away in a cosy corner at the Sunne, discussing it over a couple of drinks. 'We'd just need to extend the track along there so cars wouldn't have to come into the yard. That way we'd retain our privacy.'

'Are you sure you'd be okay with that? And how about your dad? Do you think he'd mind?'

'I'm sure he wouldn't; he's keen for the farm to diversify. And, I mean, it's not as if you're going to be taking hundreds of dogs, is it?'

'No,' she'd said, shaking her head. 'Eight per night, tops, that'll give me time to get some jobs done on the farm too.'

'Well then, by the stables should be perfect.'

'Oh.' The logistics of his suggestion had set Ella's mind whirling. She'd searched his face, rolling the idea round her mind, gradually warming to it. 'Now you mention it, I can see how it would work well.'

'Me too.'

'I'd pay rent for it.'

'Don't be daft, course you wouldn't! We're a couple. Camplin Farm's your home now.' He'd looked offended. 'Would you charge me rent if it was the other way round?'

'No.'

'Well then.'

'It's a brilliant idea! Thank you!' She'd flung her arms around him, kissing him noisily on the cheek, making him spill his beer. 'Oops, sorry.' She'd giggled.

Once he'd dried himself off, she'd snuggled into him, savouring the steady rhythm of his breathing. Though they hadn't been an item for long, their reconnection had been so strong, so seamless, it truly felt that the years they'd lost had been wiped away in one huge sweep. 'It's been a whirlwind six months,' she'd said, peering up at him.

Filled with affection, his eyes had met hers. 'You could say. All this doesn't feel too soon for you, does it?'

Her hand had instinctively gone to the infinity pendant round her neck. 'Doesn't feel too soon at all; it feels just right.'

He'd squeezed her tight, beaming. 'Feels just right to me too. We've wasted too much time already. And now I'm looking forward to what the next six months have in store for us.'

'Same here.'

'Love you, Ella Welford.' He'd gone to kiss her but paused. 'I still can't get over how good it feels to say that.'

'Love you too, Joss Campion – and again, same here.' She'd giggled as his lips met hers.

Not wanting to be left out, Sid had pushed his head between the two of them on the banquette, his tail drumming against the table leg. He'd looked up at them blinking, food crumbs on his whiskers, making the pair burst out laughing. 'And we love you too, fella.' Joss had ruffled his head affectionately.

'We certainly do.' Ella had sighed happily. She couldn't imagine feeling any more content.

'Here's to the three of us.' Joss had raised his glass in a toast.

'The three of us.' Ella had clinked her wine glass against it.

'Now if you'll excuse us, Sidney, we have some unfinished business that needs our urgent attention.' Joss had placed his glass on the table and taken Ella's face in his hands and kissed her softly.

Her stomach had looped-the-loop as she'd fallen deeper into his kiss.

'Mmm. I'd say that's very urgent business,' she'd said when they'd pulled apart, her forehead resting on his.

A LETTER FROM THE AUTHOR

Huge thanks for choosing to pick up *A Cosy Countryside Christmas*. I hope you were hooked on this instalment in the Life on the Moors series and getting to know Ella and Joss – and all their moorland friends. If you'd like to join other readers in hearing all about my new releases and bonus content, you can sign up for my newsletter!

www.stormpublishing.co/eliza-j-scott

We won't share your email address, and you can unsubscribe any time.

If you enjoyed this book and could spare a few moments to leave a review, that would be hugely appreciated. It doesn't have to be long, just a few words would do, but for us authors it can make all the difference in encouraging a reader to discover our books for the first time. Thank you so much.

As ever, I enjoyed popping back to Lytell Stangdale to see what the folk there have been up to and to have an imaginary wander down the main street lined with quaint thatched cottages. I'm sure you'll agree when I say a trip there wouldn't be complete without joining Kitty, Molly, Vi and Co. at their usual table by the fire at The Sunne Inne, enjoying a glass of wine and a good old giggle. And I thoroughly enjoyed exploring Ella and Joss's story. I'm so thrilled they finally got together!

I never tire of revisiting Lytell Stangdale and the surrounding villages, especially at Christmastime, when I can indulge in cosy, festive descriptions of bushy Christmas trees, twinkling fairy lights and brightly coloured baubles against the snowy backdrop of the beautiful North Yorkshire Moors. To my mind, there really is nowhere better.

www.elizajscott.com

facebook.com/elizajscottauthor

x.com/ElizaJScott1

instagram.com/elizajscott

bookbub.com/authors/eliza-j-scott

bsky.app/profile/elizajscott.bsky.social

ACKNOWLEDGMENTS

So, we've arrived at the point in the book where I get the chance to say thank you to everyone who's helped get this book ready for publication day. As ever, first up is my wonderful editor at Storm, Kate Smith, whose support, encouragement and enthusiasm I appreciate enormously! She's also incredibly kind. Thank you for being so fab, Kate, and for suggesting Storm take on the Life on the Moors series!

Next up is the man at the top, managing director Oliver Rhodes. Thank you for setting up Storm, Oliver, and for gathering such a wonderful team together. Chris Lucraft needs a mention, too. He's Storm's digital operations director and I'm in complete awe of his techy wizardry skills. Thank you for all you do for my books, Chris! Storm's editorial operations director Alexandra Begley also deserves a huge thank you for all she does in getting my book shipshape for publication day. This leads rather nicely onto a thank you for newly promoted assistant editor Naomi Knox in her role, offering production support and file formatting – amongst her many other skills. Thanks are also owed to Elke Desanghere, who is Storm's head of digital marketing. Big thanks for all your hard work on the marketing side of things and for creating such beautiful social media graphics, Elke. And thanks also to publicity manager Anna McKerrow for her fab social media posts. Rose Cooper needs a mention, too, for the beautiful new cover she designed for *A Cosy Countryside Christmas*.

I must also send out a huge thank you to three fabulous people for their input in getting this book ready for when I self-published it earlier. They are: editor Alison Williams – thank you so much,

Alison; I learnt a huge amount from you. Berni Stevens for the book's beautiful first cover, and Rachel Gilbey of Rachel's Random Resources for organising a fab blog tour. Thank you so much, all of you!

As ever, massive thanks to my lovely author buddies Jessica Redland and Sharon Booth, for all of their kindness and words of support when the dreaded imposter syndrome strikes. Thank you for being so awesome, the pair of you!

I'd also like to send out an enormous thank you to the amazing book community. Your kindness and support over social media is heartwarming and humbling.

Next up, I'm sending a huge thank you to my fabulous family. Thank you for believing in me and encouraging me to follow my dreams – fuelled by copious supplies of Yorkshire tea and ginger biscuits.

My final thanks goes to you, the reader, for choosing my book and taking the trouble to read it. Thank you so much for being a part of this exciting journey with me; I really am most grateful. I do hope you'll stay in touch and follow the further adventures of the friends in the Life on the Moors series.

Wishing you all a very merry Christmas and a peaceful and happy new year.

Much love,

Eliza xxx

Printed in Dunstable, United Kingdom